EENY MEENY MINY MOLE

By 9 am the Square was fully operational. Rumour after rumour dashing from car to car, requests for information overloading Matron's switchboard, press insiders wanting to know more details about Berlin and whether it was true the Stationmaster had disappeared. That fact at least, though hotly denied, was true. There was no trace of him in London or anywhere.

The Relatives were as confused over the Berlin situation as anyone else, unable to make a move or statement until Washington got to work. The President had given orders that he should get a good night's sleep, nothing short of war was to wake him up. "Well," as Hallam had observed to Mitchel only an hour before, "that is all we are short of."

EENY
MEENY
MINY
MOLE

Marcel d'Agneau

ARROW BOOKS

Arrow Books Limited
3 Fitzroy Square, London W1P 6JD

An imprint of the Hutchinson Publishing Group

London Melbourne Sydney Auckland
Wellington Johannesburg and agencies
throughout the world

First published by Arlington Books 1980
Arrow edition 1981
© Marcel D'Agneau 1980

Made and printed in Great Britain
by The Anchor Press Ltd
Tiptree, Essex

ISBN 0 09 926300 9

CAST OF CHARACTERS

THE SQUARE
Hugh Grimly   Retired Chief
Steven ***   The Stationmaster
David Gallant   Grimly's Swordbearer, Headhunter
Peter Hallam   No. 2
Philip Oosty   First Secretary to Stationmaster
Simon Caw   Head of Lipsnatchers
John Welland   The Butcher's Boy
Calon   Cabinet Office
Sir Charles Edgeware   Foreign Office
Bill Jukes   Lipsnatchers
Sandy Bleak   Courier
Sussie Sutzman   China Crystal Ball
Doc Sludgeon   Russian Crystal Ball
Will Strawson   Deceased Former No. 2
Bloater and Nolan   Matron In-House functions
Croc   Outfielder
Willy   Ex-outfielder

THE RELATIVES
Mitchel   Chief at Grosvenor Square
Sol Guss   No. 2

MOSCOW CEPHAL
Tinkabelle/Larianov   Head of Moscow Intelligence
Stephan and Misha Kostavitz   Field agents
Zavrel/Captain Hook   Assassin
Cosmo   Assassin

And introducing Sylvia Kostavitz as Wendy Hallam

Contents

ONE

A Rumour Does The Rounds

Perhaps it was in El Vino's, that house of debauchery in Fleet Street, or some other murky, favoured gathering-place of London's invisible people – the Intelligence mob. But whoever, or wherever it was first said, it was said again and repeated in every corner, even as far as the Colonies – little more than a day later, coming back to the ears of the Stationmaster at the Square, like the bitter taste of his heart pills.

Never mind heart pills, he'd often considered taking standard issue termination pills since the dark days of Will Strawson's demise, and the fourth, fifth, sixth and all the way up to eleventh man had been unmasked by the Square master sleuth, Hugh Grimly. Ah, but the boys had been clever. Their friends had fixed that. The schoolboys had fixed everything.

"They're our boys, Stationmaster, one of us. Cads, bounders, rotters for working for the Russians all this time, almost running the Secret Service, but never mind that. We've let them have Strawson, good riddance, let them have him. As for the rest, well we've smacked their naughty hands and they've given their word; from now on they work for us or not at all, as long as we honour their pension. No, don't question it. They have given their word as gentlemen. My God man, of course their word is good, as old Etonians then, will that do? And come off it, old chap, not so much traitor; it was ideals, more sneak than traitor, don't you think? Come on, no-one has been compromised, it is all in the past now. Look, it's over, no use carping over dead meat. Time to look forward, build anew. It will blow over, it always blows over."

But then, Philip Oosty, Section Officer on the fourth floor at the Square heard the word in El Vino's.

It was Croc he heard it from. Croc, the survivor of countless newspaper mergers, old colonial himself, seen time in India before the collapse, Northern Rhodesia, then Fiji, even Hong Kong. He never could get used to living in London at a desk – his bones needed the heat.

Croc was holding court, as he always did once the midday gun had been fired – no-one had ever had the gall to point out that there was no midday gun. But there was a lot of respect for good old Croc. The old wisdom tooth, flag waving remnant of an Empire long lost and not missed.

"Philip, my old son, you can see the way it goes, you're in there, one of the boys now. No use in denying it. I know you sit there on the fourth floor polishing your desk, pretending it all matters, that the Square still has a function in this blighted world. But tell me this, is there one man, is there one man in the whole British Secret Service who doesn't work for the Russians?"

Croc cast an earnest gaze into Philip's dumbfounded eyes and then knocked back the rest of his gin. "Because if there is, old son, I want to be the first to shake his hand."

*   *   *

Philip had gone running to his master like a loyal dog, agonising over whether to report this idle piece of gossip. The Stationmaster wouldn't be amused. He hadn't survived the scandals, the hatred, the years of IDC (interdepartmental chaos) for nothing. There was jealousy. Even before Strawson's cover had been blown by Grimly. Being Grimly's protégé was considered bad form, they had demoted poor old David Gallant fast enough. But Grimly had been too old, even then. Everyone knew that. They had wheeled him in from out of retirement, the only man they could trust. Good old Grimly. Made him acting Stationmaster. He was urged to:

"Clean it up, Hugh, get the moles out." And Grimly had trusted only Gallant and Steven, his Number Five back then, promising him the throne if all went well, saying: "It's a big step, Steven, but who else? Who else?"

The Stationmaster had known for a long time that there was no-one else. There were few left who had done time in the last war. He himself had been in the RAF. Joined at eighteen, ended up in '44 as Squadron Leader in Alabama, teaching Yanks to fly at night. God, they couldn't fly in the damn broad daylight let alone at night. Tuscaloosa was a hole, a hole. But luckily they'd needed someone in Washington, someone who could speak fluent Russian and who could fly, better still an old Etonian. The Foreign Office had insisted upon it. At twenty-two you don't know what you're doing, you just follow orders. You fly into Latvia; fly people out. You don't ask what American and British officers are doing so far behind enemy lines, you accept their right to be there. The war transcends questions.

And after the war it was, "Stay on, Steven, help us out at the Square. You're young, complete your studies, we will help you out at Cambridge, this is a lifetime service, good pay, none of the war-time pennies. Official cars now, it will help you keep in the swim of events and climb. The Square will grow, you'll see, there's cold war coming."

Only the climb was much slower than he'd planned on. There were people ahead of him. And of that original fourteen, only three were left, only three who weren't working for the Russians. He often had to ask himself, where did he fail? What was it that he hadn't said or done that they had seen fit to leave him out? He spoke Russian, didn't he? He'd been to Eton, hadn't he? Why no secret Swiss bank account for him, or sunshine cruises on the Black Sea? His smiling picture in Pravda's *Sunday Magazine* with some glamorous blonde. It was all so unfair.

So Grimly had cleaned them up and gone back to his house in the country. He couldn't have carried on, not Grimly. He was already too old when they brought him out of mothballs in '65, let alone for his last sojourn in 78–79. Seventy-five, or more. They should let sleeping legends lie.

Not that Stationmaster was a youngster, fifty-nine didn't seem so very old though, not to him. Still some spring in his left foot, although the right one was getting lazy. His doctor had said, "Don't cross your legs, kills the circulation."

What do doctors know, had they never heard of comfort?

And young Philip Oosty had come running in to tell him what Croc had said. Well, Stationmaster could see Philip was upset. The boy was too emotional, far too emotional. He sought to calm him.

"We've cleaned it up, Philip. There's no more, not now. The Relatives have given us a clean bill of health, they are sharing again. They wouldn't do that if we were still a risk, would they?"

Philip tried to control himself, fight back the tears.

"I'm sorry, sir. It's just that malicious gossip gets my goat, sir. This is the best organisation in the country. People don't know that we are all that stands between them and the collapse."

A flicker of a smile passed over the Stationmaster's chalky face. Oosty's loyalty sometimes amused him, possibly the boy's only endearing quality, other than his shock of red hair.

"Perhaps we should advertise, Philip. Perhaps you could run an ad in *The Times* Announcements column. 'We wonderful lads at the Square would like you people out there to know we have saved your neck more times than you've had hot dinners.' In code, of course."

It wasn't what Philip had in mind, quite frankly he was surprised to hear the Stationmaster suggest it. It wasn't on. Not even in code. Philip supposed it was a joke and laughed the permissible four seconds.

"That will be all, Oosty, Oh," the Stationmaster remembered something, "Get me A through to DQ files, won't you."

14

"Yes, sir."

Philip departed, backwards, for he accorded the Stationmaster an almost royal respect and he'd never quite got over his training session at Gib, which held one must always watch your behind. No need to mention that there was always someone watching Philip's behind.

The Stationmaster was worried. That old fool Croc gossiping in El Vino's, it wasn't on. The British Intelligence Service was clean now. God, there were so few secrets to betray, so few men in the field. It was all satellites now, but a satellite couldn't tell you about the rumours, it wasn't an ear on the ground. Now they had to rely on scraps tossed from the Americans' table, it was demeaning. Little would get through anyway if young Oosty wasn't having a steamy affair with Mitchel's secretary, Leon. Never thought there would be a day when the Square's existence would rely on pillowtalk. Even then, all they got was Dolphins off Anguilla, food riots in Jamaica, Cubans stirring up trouble again. Didn't need a satellite to tell him that. Just pick up a phone and dial Jamaica. You could hear the rioting, nothing secret about it. The Stationmaster sat and stared at his green phone for almost an hour, the last spread of daylight disappearing from Soho Square.

The sun had already set in his eyes. There were sometimes moments when he wished things could be as busy as the old days. God, he would have been glad of a secret to betray, just one, but the cupboard was bare. The truth was DBB had set in at Soho Square. Death by boredom. No secrets to betray. The fieldmen were sending in gossip, hardly worth the trouble of decoding. The Israelis, they had secrets, even the Danes, but no-one trusted the British anymore, and once the Moscow Cephal had no-one inside to send their lies to and direct agents' activities, the Soviet information had stopped dead. At least with them pissing inside the tent you knew something.

He sighed. It was lonely being the Chief Indian of an almost extinct tribe.

Philip returned with the files, carefully dusting them before placing them on the Stationmaster's desk.

"Call Matron, Philip. I want to speak to both Bloater and Nolan, the Northern Irish sector have been making far too much use of our Matron's services. If they want false documents so badly, the least they could do is ask politely. We have other enemies more important than hooligans in Belfast."

"Matron is stocktaking today, sir. Full twenty-four hour stand-down. Nolan did say that Lipsnatchers would cover."

Stationmaster nodded, his eyes misting over a moment. Grimly had set up the Lipsnatchers. If it hadn't been for them, Will Strawson would still be in operation on the fifth floor.

"Who is there now?" he asked, looking directly into Philip's grey eyes.

"Simon Caw, sir. Heads up the division, it's mostly computers now. He talks to them," he added, hoping for a reaction from his chief, "like plants. He talks to his computers."

"Well, when they answer back, Oosty, I'll be too old for this job." He opened up a file. "Tell him to call me, won't you?"

Philip affirmed he would and silently left the wood panelled office, his feet echoing across the marble inter-office section. Somthing was up. The files out, it meant something, he could feel it. The signal was up.

Stationmaster was worried. Croc wasn't one to spread rumours without foundation. Of course it was preposterous that . . . The phone jangled into action. The blue phone, his direct link to the Relatives in Grosvenor Square.

"Mitchel," the mid-Western nasal excuse for a voice declared on the other end. "Bad news, Stationmaster. Very bad news."

Mitchel sounded guarded, angry even. He was not one given over to drama usually. Stationmaster suddenly cheered up. Bad news meant something had happened, he was always grateful for that.

"I'm sending Sol Guss over to break it to you gently, Steven. You aren't going to like it."

"Can't we discuss this over the phone. It's a safe line."

"There are no safe lines anymore. Tinkabelle is awake! Sol will be there in nine minutes."

Mitchel disconnected. Stationmaster was furious. In the old days there would have been politeness, the deference. Nine minutes – nine whole minutes. He buzzed the rear lobby, Dancer's Lobby.

"Sol Guss, Dancer. Straight up you hear. Straight up. Don't let the first floor delay him. Eight minutes."

"Got you, sir. Got you, straight up."

Dancer was of the old school. If the Stationmaster wanted the Americans in the backway and up the private elevator, it was all right by him. Against the rules, but all right by him.

* * *

"Tinkabelle is awake," Croc said, later that night. He turned to his longstanding friend, Lancaster, and tapped the cage. The dismal parrot fluttered a grey wing and attempted to nip Croc's finger, but Croc was too fast for him. "Yes, you old bugger. Tinkabelle is awake. No use pretending he isn't, 'cause everytime anyone says Tinkabelle doesn't exist another agent dies. Old Grimly knows. Grimly caught himself the big one, they'd been trading blows for years, since the Spanish Civil War and Grimly won. But long live the King, Lancaster. Tinkabelle is back and he's got a fistful of aces."

Lancaster scratched at his perch, he'd heard all this before. Croc slipped off his shoes and sat back on his narrow single bed, staring at the towering mound of *Daily Telegraphs* stacked in the corner of the room, contaminating everything with their decomposition. Croc never liked to throw a newspaper away, one never knew when it might be needed. He'd been collecting for years, no matter where he was, whichever country, even in Fiji. The *Telegraph* would arrive looking for Croc. He had a soft spot for the rag. All the more puzzling then that he wrote for that Paris piece of tissue paper, the *Tribune*. But Croc liked to think he was international, that the one or two pieces they carried a week gave him the edge over the Page Three crowd. He didn't want any part of a rag that ran nudes first, news second. Didn't they know there's a war on? No time for naked flesh on a *news*paper. It wasn't proper, legal or decent.

"Mark my words, old son, Stationmaster's going to have a fit when he hears the news I've heard. There will be questions in the House and the streets will run with blood." He laughed, the sound of it vibrating across the gas heated room, whilst he peeled off his well-used socks, black tipped toes greeting him. "But that's running ahead of things, Lancaster. There's other trouble to come first. Tinkabelle is going to land like thunder, mark my words."

It was then the front door bell signalled attack.

Croc cast an eye at his electric clock, present from the boys in the Hong Kong Press Club. 'We won't miss you' inscribed on its side. Funny lot the Hong Kong boys, not a true loyal Brit amongst them. All they were interested in was the pox and graft.

It was 11.55 pm.

"Not a friend, Lancaster. Not a friend. Not at this time of night." The bell jangled again, someone persistent out there. Lancaster let out a shriek and turned his head 180 degrees. He'd given his opinion.

"All right, I'll go. I'll go. Should put my shoes on, but . . ."

Croc went barefoot. Muttering to himself, wishing he'd got around to laying carpet on the lino. You don't need carpet on the lino in the tropics, bugs would eat it away.

"Who is it?"

"Steven," the empty voice returned.

Croc undid the chain and opened the door, not particularly surpised.

Stationmaster walked in, two large overstuffed briefcases hanging at the end of his straining arms. The man looked pale, much older than Croc remembered.

"Tinkabelle got you in a panic then?" Croc said with a half welcoming smile, relocking the door and pulling down the blind, a war relic, much abused by moths.

"You still have that spare room?" Stationmaster asked, putting his heavy burden down on the lino.

Croc nodded, indicating for his old friend to go through to the only warm room in the house.

Stationmaster removed his coat, inhaling the inevitable odour of newspapers and bacon. Croc hadn't changed in a thousand years.

*   *   *

At 4 am, or nearer 4.15 am, no-one was able to pinpoint a precise moment afterwards, Henrietta, the woman on Listening duty at the Square, put down her Mills & Boon novel and loosened her tie. She had only just returned to night duty, she wasn't adjusted yet, her body felt like cement, her head slow. She couldn't sleep in the day, her mind too active. She knew she should tell Oosty that the doctor had said no definitely not fit enough to return to work, but she couldn't live on half-pay. Who could? Half-pay was nothing. So she had come back to work a month early. Reluctantly, but she had no choice. Henrietta stretched, then reached forward for her flask. Another cup of coffee would help. Help what? No calls coming through tonight. None expected. Of course, the Stationmaster was upstairs. The old bastard practically lived there, always deciding to make an appearance just when you're away in the loo, or your eyes have grown too heavy and you're practically unconscious anyway. For all that, she liked him. She liked the old school, better than the youngsters entering the Service now.

She drank the coffee. Hot, black, no sugar. It was awful. She'd begged the doctor to let her use honey instead of sugar, but he'd refused, said it was just as bad.

She knocked her pen onto the floor. She leant over, creaked the old body down. Getting too old for night duty, she thought. Fifty is no age to be a woman doing night duty. They should get someone younger. Her plump hand grasped the pen, but it seemed ridiculously heavy. She pulled at it, but it stayed there. Now her head was between her knees, both hands on the recalcitrant pen. She had to have the pen, no question about it. She pulled with all her strength, but all that achieved was her head even closer to the ground. Her chest was giving her sharp stabs of pain, her eyes bulging with an excess of blood behind them. She wasn't surprised, all that coffee and her bending down so suddenly. But, nevertheless, the pen was a real mystery, so heavy, like a magnet had attached itself. But it was a plastic pen! She pulled in one last effort and then, as her mind was overwhelmed by a sudden pain, soundlessly, Henrietta fell to the floor. If anyone had passed the Listening Room two or three minutes later, they would have heard her sigh one long last sigh. Night duty was over.

It was then the call came.

And because it wasn't answered, the automatic override on the tape cut in and took the call, in the process triggering a red light in the Stationmaster's office and ringing the home of Number Two, Peter Hallam.

A heavy, hairy arm reached over young shoulders to answer the incessant warble by the bed.

"Hallam." A 4 am gravel voice, eyes still closed.

"Listening Post alert. Square unmanned."

"Who is this?" Hallam asked, then realised that he was listening to a tape.

"Station machine 106–emergency intervention procedure 9b."

"All right. Call Wandsworth Duty Officer," Hallam said, again realising that the machine would do just that.

"Stationmaster not answering call," the tape told him, which could mean either the old man was asleep, in the can or anything. What the hell could a machine know?

Hallam slammed his phone down. Bloody machine had ruined his first good night's sleep in weeks.

The figure beside him stirred when he switched on the

bedside light. She reached out an arm, resting her hand on the thigh nearest her.

"Hallam?" she asked, blinking, burying her face back into the pillow, and pulling the sheet over her head.

"Got to go, Wendy. I've got to go. Spot of bother at the Square."

"No, don't go," she wailed, flinging the sheet back, looking for the clock, shading her eyes from the light.

Hallam looked down at the slim child and attempted a smile.

"You'll be all right, you'll go back to sleep in no time."

"You'll come back?" A well-practised, imploring look. She could play his emotional strings like a harp.

"Not before you go to school," he answered, heading for the bathroom.

Wendy was cross. He'd promised to spend the whole night with her, he'd promised. She didn't like to wake up alone.

"But you promised, Peter," her English wavering with her tiredness, the pout her second line of attack.

"Then tomorrow night, my little one. There's always tomorrow and we can play those 'games' again." Hallam's pacifying voice.

"A new game," she insisted, sitting up in the bed and studying her breasts for any sign of new growth.

Hallam stared across the room at her as he began to dress, aware that his own passions were rising again. He wondered what it would have been like if he'd been playing 'games' like this when he had been fourteen. The child was beautiful, of course, completely natural, a menace, needed his attention all the time and was practically a zombie when he wasn't around, but he couldn't think of a word to say against her. And she learnt the 'games' so well. Quite simply he loved her. Wendy was staring at his legs, she always stared at his legs.

"I want to lie on top of you next time. I want to squash you," she said quietly. Then, looking down at her breasts, she sighed. "You promised to stay."

21

Her crooked smile crept back onto her face as he looked up into her eyes and approached the bed. He knelt in front of her and cupped her head in his hands. Her head rested heavily on them, content and safe with him like some mellow pussycat. That was the way Hallam wanted it, he could never achieve a lasting relationship with an older woman. He was always reminded of his mother. He was in love with Wendy as a father to a child and a bit more. And why not? This was a long relationship. She'd been in his care for over three years. The 'games' had only just begun, a month no more. Though it was true she had been sneaking into his bed since the night she arrived. She had said she'd always slept with her brother, so why not him? Hallam, whose sexual record was laughable, and who had reached the age of forty-five practically a virgin, despite a fracas in Hamburg and a brief liaison in Rome with a former member of the Square. None of those encounters mattered a jot compared to the devotion he felt to Wendy. Peter and Wendy, he thought of themselves as a couple. He kept himself fit. Squash twice a week and sometimes he pretended it would always be like this, that Wendy wouldn't grow up, that she wouldn't wake up one day and discover he was an old man already. That she would stay and play 'games' for ever.

"Go to sleep, Wendy. I'll see you in the afternoon. Get yourself a present." He laid down a five pound note.

She was sleepy again and, anyway, his legs had disappeared into his trousers. Hallam switched out the light and gave her a quick kiss on the nose, breathing in that uncontaminated scent that belongs only to a child.

"Your chin," she complained, as his overnight stubble tickled her. Then, as he pulled away, she leapt up and planted a sloppy kiss on his cheek. "Bye, Peter," she whispered, dropping back on the pillow.

Hallam left for the Square in a contented mood.

*   *   *

The distress call, picked up in the Listening Room and stored until the summoned Square personel could arrive, was fast becoming irrelevant. Events were moving rapidly worldwide, silent, stealthy as a panther, rapid, all of it a surprise.

The first Berlin Square HQ knew of it, was when the giant iron ball of the wrecking crew shuddered to a halt on their outside wall and, before any of them had fully comprehended or awakened even, the exterior wall, unused to the force of one ton of iron thrown against it, fell in a heap onto the road below. Slowly, but inevitably, the rest of the building followed suit, giving the bewildered agent in the Listening Room, only thirty-five seconds to send a distress call, based no more than on what he could plainly see out of the gap where his wall had only just been.

It was obvious to anyone at once. The Soviets, or at least their puppets the East Germans, were dismantling the wall. Now, the hotly debated sense of moving Berlin Square HQ into the last remaining house in the British sector situated up against the wall, had proved disasterously wrong.

The crowd watched in growing horror and amazement as giant machinery and scores of blue overalled workers attacked the wall, demolishing it with a simple ease that hadn't seemed likely only hours before. Machinery and ball-breakers were lined up against the entire British sector. Lights concentrated on the battleground of human liberty. But was it a trick, had the British negotiated something in secret, was Berlin to be divided no more? Slowly, but steadily, the news of the miracle marched around the city, bells began to ring in the cathedral. Moscow has developed a heart, some said; Moscow has seen the folly of their ways and allowed compassion to enter politics. Just the British sector, others asked? How can it be just the British sector and not the American? How will they stop people from entering the American sector? What will happen if all the East Germans start to flood in and steal our jobs, contaminate our society with their communist ideals?

After the euphoria came the creeping fear. No-one asked about the house that had disappeared on Horsch Street, that

23

funny house with all the aerials lying on the road now, soldiers with dogs and torches picking up scraps.

The café at the top end of Horsch Street began to put up shutters, long in store, not used since the war. Others began to remember bitter, past days and hurried back home to dig up hidden pistols, find that pile of timber to cover the windows, fill the bath with water, stocktake. Children listened wide-eyed as elders told them scarey stories of men from the East who boiled children alive. Others heard the sound of the tanks, though none had been sighted. "They are there," they said, "they never really went away."

And the wall fell, as spectacular as Jericho. The British soldiers were roused from their beds, but even after an hour, no word came from London. They could only watch in dismay and make tea as the brick dust gathered in thickness, spreading like a fog in that part of town.

*   *   *

There was something like a fog, too, going on in David Gallant's mind as he drove to Soho Square. He had returned from Subs section in Barrow-in-Furness only hours before, and had been disgusted to find his name on the emergency alert roster. He'd been hoping for a lie in. The Triumph hadn't much enjoyed starting up at 4.30 am either. Not that it enjoyed starting up anytime.

Gallant arrived at 4.55 am, only a minute after Peter Hallam. Both stood unshaven and weary-eyed on the first floor lobby, waiting for the computer to clear their ID cards.

"Gallant," Hallam acknowledged, rubbing his ears.

"Hallam," Gallant returned, wondering what all the fuss was about. The Square wasn't on special call-up. "Nothing spectacular happening, is there?" he asked.

"All quiet on the Eastern front last time I looked."

"Any ideas?" Gallant asked.

Hallam shook his head. "We are just the suckers of call-up

roster. Perhaps Matron is lonely. It's bound to be a false alarm."

Gallant thought so too. He was also aware that Hallam was Number Two at the Square. If anyone should know what was happening, he should.

"You're with the Finsbury Group now, aren't you, Gallant?"

Gallant took his card back from the computer, shaking his head. "Wandsworth. Monitors and Headhunters."

"Ah yes. With Grimly gone, I suppose you lost your mentor. You were his swordbearer, weren't you?"

It was true, but Gallant didn't like it spoken as so. "The clean up," he replied, "the clean up washed up a lot of bodies. I'm still in with a foot in the door."

Hallam took his own card, pocketing it. "Lucky I was in Washington when it all blew up."

Gallant knew that, too. Hallam had all those friends in Washington, they gave him a clean bill of health. One had to have the Relatives' approval to get ahead in the Square these days. They were running the show really.

Both men cleared and advanced towards the elevator, conveniently ready to transport them to the third floor Listening Rooms.

"We were at the Crêche together, weren't we?" Hallam asked, observing Gallant had lost none of his Adonis stature. Graceful sod. Envy stirred in Hallam's heart, it was always there.

"Aden?" Gallant asked.

"No, Gib," Hallam countered. It was the Aden crowd who had let the side down. No-one admitted to being trained in Aden. Will Strawson's crowd. His little scholars. Damn nest of spies, all of them.

"Gib wasn't much fun," Gallant remarked as the elevator began to climb.

"Never understand how they got it to rain inside," Hallam remarked, rubbing the sleep from his eyes.

25

Matron was already in attendance.

"What's up, Bloater?" Hallam asked, noting the woman laid out on the iron bunk in the Listening Room.

"It's either DBB, sir, or Henrietta has had a heart attack. She's been ill a long time, sir, Doctor says that . . ."

Hallam held up his hand for silence. He wasn't interested in a dead woman. He detested staff details.

"Any calls in?" he asked.

"A stream, sir, hasn't stopped. They are in the Transcription Room now."

"Get onto that, will you, Gallant," Hallam instructed. Gallant left immediately. Hallam turned to Bloater. The man had been with the Service since Grimly joined, he could handle all the staff problems. "The Stationmaster been told?"

"I've called his room, sir, put in a call to his home, too, but no word."

Hallam pursed his lips. It wasn't unusual. The Stationmaster didn't like to be disturbed, at anytime. An aloof man.

"I'll go up to the fifth floor. We'd better let him know. Henrietta was one of the girls, was she?"

Bloater said "yes" with his eyes. Everyone in the Square was the Stationmaster's little Indians, everyone a loyal and trusted soul, if only because they all conformed to the regulation standard of incompetence. Grimly and the Stationmaster were agreed on that point. Appoint the ones who would be the most surprised and grateful to get in. Loyalty was more desirable than bright bastards with honours degrees in sleight of hand. That was Strawson's crowd. Too bright, too easily seduced by ideology. Would they have been so easily, so willingly fooled if there had been a welfare state during the depression, if the stability of England was so entrenched as now?

Hallam believed that the 'Philby Generation' had finished with Strawson and Blunt. It was all in the past now. Finished with, a black mark in Intelligence history. The moles had all been smoked out of their holes by Grimly and the mundane had papered over the cracks. The Square was safe again.

Afghanistan had swept the doubt from those still swaying in the breeze, wiped the mist from their eyes. The Soviets were easily recognised as the wicked Uncles now, the West the ailing Princess in the Tower. You don't even find that sort of weak-kneed liberal in the corridors of Peterhouse any longer. England was aroused in its indifference, content to allow *Soap* to tickle its intellectual appetites, or International PEN to forage in foreign jails for undernourished, ignored activists in need of an audience for injustice. The Square was glad to let them carry on, theirs alone was the heart of British Intelligence. Concentrate on the heart and all else will follow, true blue.

Hallam walked up the wooden stairs to the fifth floor. The building was a disgrace. Time they redecorated. It may have been fine for Bevan's boys, but the latrine green had been overdone in his opinion. Flakes of paint, some of it an inch thick, littered the stairway. Too much like school. Far too much like school. He passed Strawson's old office, then abruptly remembered it was his own now. The ghost of Strawson the traitor lived on, him with his fine taste, Savile Row suits and hand-stitched shoes. Where did he get the money for all that? His boyfriends, he supposed. Boyfriends were very useful in that way. Which reminded him of Wendy. He'd promised to take her to see that Disney film in St Martins Lane. God, he hated Disney films. At least Julie Andrews wasn't in it. Julie Andrews was the absolute limit. Too much of her and he wouldn't wonder if half the nation defected to Moscow.

The Stationmaster's log was in its rightful place.

Last entry made by Philip Oosty. Now there was an oddball. Just what did the Stationmaster do in his room all the time? There wasn't much going on. No operations. Why sit in there and brood? It wasn't healthy. Far better to get out along the river and get some fresh air into his lungs.

Hallam opened the door, observing the crack of dawn had beaten him to it. A shaft of grey light hung on the wall like some masterwork at the Tate. All the same, he switched on the light. And that was when he received the second surprise of the morning.

"Gallant! Gallant, call out the dogs!" he was yelling down the phone. "The Stationmaster's gone. The office has been stripped bare. It's been cleaned out, Gallant. The Stationmaster's gone."

All the papers in his drawers gone, his favourite ashtray, all the notepads, even the portrait of Tinkabelle with the holes in it, which Strawson had used for a darts game.

Gallant arrived, stepping into the room unannounced.

"My God, it's true." His first reaction. It looked as if Pickford Removals had moved in and stripped it bare, leaving only the desk, metal filing cabinet and chair, and those only because they were screwed down to the floor.

"It's impossible," Gallant said. "Matron would have noticed. There are trip alarms in all the filing cabinets. The Lipsnatchers would have reported activity."

"The question is," Hallam asked, staring out of the window across the Square, "did he go voluntarily? Has he moved out or taken a lot of work home with him? Is it abduction, treachery or a defensive move?"

Gallant studied the back of Hallam's dyed head, a creepy feeling of horror had come over him. Hallam was calm, far too calm. The Stationmaster gone, that made Hallam Number One, and was it on for the Square to be run by a paedophiliac? What tit-bits did he whisper in little Wendy's ear at night?

Hallam turned to meet Gallant's gaze. "Do we call out the dogs, or do we play it by the book, Gallant? Track down all the Stationmaster's little haunts before we admit he has flit the coup? And did he go because he knew something we don't? What was on the tape?"

Gallant ignored the question, he himself had not quite come to terms with either the message on the tape or the Stationmaster's vanishing act.

"Philip Oosty signed the book, he was the last in this office."

"I know, call him in, Gallant. Look, even that ridiculous

motto of Steven's is missing, 'It's all public money'. Well I'm glad that's gone. What was the gist of the tape messages, Gallant?"

Gallant went over to the filing cabinets. All were incredibly empty, he pulled out every drawer, slamming each shut with increasing anger. "I'll call Oosty now. I want an explanation for this, and quickly. Classified files out of the building, it's unheard of!"

Gallant, obviously angry, dialled Oosty's home from a number he had listed in his Square Mandarin list. The nine below the Stationmaster in descending order. He listened to the bell ringing on Oosty's end and handed over a typed brief on the situation in Germany.

Hallam took it, read it, then read it again, falling back into the Stationmaster's seat, the blood instantly drained from his astonished face.

"They can't have Berlin, it's ours," he said in a still, small voice, his legs suddenly beginning to shake. He looked at the note again. It was a full scale alert. The wall was down, the Square HQ had been demolished. Thousands of East German troops were being concentrated on the East German side of the town. Berlin in a state of tension. All with no warning. What were the implications? Would it mean war, and with what? The British tank was in for repairs.

"Oosty," Gallant was saying, "you took your time."

"Sorry, took some pills, trouble with sleeping these days. Who is this?"

"Gallant at the Square. Two questions. When was the last time you saw the Stationmaster?"

Oosty shook the sleep from his eyes, looking across the bed at Leon, spread out, his graceful form comatose.

"Gallant, we don't talk on the phone."

"Today we do. It is in National Interest, now tell me."

National Interest? Now Oosty was interested. "What happened? Is the Stationmaster ill?"

Gallant grew impatient and, besides, Hallam was indicating he wanted to call the Minister. Gallant had little time for that whining whimp Oosty. He'd been a whimp at school, too.

"Oosty, answer me. What time?"

"Just after 5 pm. He wanted A through DQ files."

Gallant knew he hadn't heard correctly. "Five pm and the A through DQ files?"

"Correct. Placed them on his desk. I signed them out with Bloater, ask him."

Hallam picked up the other phone.

"That was your second question, Oosty. Report to your office at once. Hallam wants a word." "But . . ." Oosty began, trying to point out he was due at the House every Friday morning.

"Now, now. This is a Blue Alert." Gallant disconnected.

Oosty replaced his receiver and looked down at sleeping Leon. Just another five minutes. Leon was so beautiful . . . just another ten minutes . . .

Hallam was still reeling about Berlin. He'd woken the Minister. The Minister had hit the roof, then his mistress had come on the phone to say that he'd had a stroke and was she entitled to half his pension? Gallant had disconnected her, worried about the A through DQ files.

"Those files, Hallam, the Stationmaster's gone away with our entire personnel records."

"What's that?" Hallam asked, his voice cracking under the sudden strain, thinking he should be doing something about the situation, but he didn't know what. The Cabinet would need logistic information, trouble was how to provide it with Berlin HQ a heap of rubble?

"I said the Stationmaster has all our active personnel records with him," Gallant repeated, preferring to ignore Berlin. He'd never liked Liza Minnelli anyway, the city had no special place in his heart.

Hallam frowned. A good alternative to the expressionless external he normally displayed in office hours.

"Call the Relatives. Call an extraordinary meeting for 11 am. Everyone, the Cabinet and Foreign Office, everyone who normally comes to the first of the month briefings. Then find out as much as you can, Gallant. We have to cover our arses on this one. We shall have to look backwards, see what the signals were and how we missed them."

Gallant began calling round. Hallam sank into a depression that even the thought of little Wendy's legs wrapped around his chest in the morning, couldn't help. Someone had lit a short fuse on the future. Berlin without a wall, it was monstrous, there was no provision for it. The Stationmaster choosing this moment to go missing, all before breakfast, it was intolerable. What was the country coming to?

*   *   *

They came at the normal time. The black Granada stood outside the house in Ladbroke Grove, as it always did at 8.30 am every school morning. Wendy, late as she always was, grabbed her coat, satchel and, with socks dribbling down her legs yelled "Bye, Maddy," to the housekeeper and flew out of the front door and down the granite steps into the waiting car.

The car was already turning into Holland Park Avenue when she realised that it wasn't the regular driver. She asked, as yet unconcerned, "No George today?"

The driver didn't answer at first, undertaking to pass a bus dominating too much of the road.

"Where's George?" Wendy repeated.

"You won't be seeing George again, Sylvia," was her answer.

Wendy's jaw dropped in horror. Instantly she understood what had happened. She had been kidnapped. "No, No," she screamed, rushing to open the rear door. But it was locked and there was no way to undo it. This wasn't the normal Granada, not in the least like it. Fear raced through her, her voice emitted a strangled cry of terror.

"No use in panic, Sylvia," the driver explained, using his and her native tongue.

Wendy tried banging on the window, but realising the futility of this she lunged forward to grab the driver's head

31

from behind. Even as she moved, however, he accelerated, sending her spinning back into the wall behind the seats as a metal mesh screen snapped into place between them. She hadn't noticed it hanging from a hinge on the roof.

"I'm not Sylvia!" she yelled, though she knew it was a lie. She turned, wildly trying to attract the car behind, an empty gesture as the glass was smoked black and the car was a Diplomat registered vehicle.

The Granada continued up towards Notting Hill Gate, with Wendy crying, still trying to beat at the fixed windows with her satchel. The driver turned into Kensington Palace Gardens, straightaway turning right into the Czech Embassy, driving into their underground carpark.

"Welcome home, Sylvia," the driver said, attempting a smile. "Your father will be very pleased to see you."

This was worse. She stopped crying. She almost stopped breathing. "My father is dead," she shouted in English. "My father is dead." Wendy felt hysteria rising within her, all the old pains that Peter had made go away. Where was Peter now?

But when she climbed out of the car and was marched to a wide metal door, it was her father who turned to greet her with a broad smile and a shout of, "My child."

Wendy stood stock still, her eyes wide open in shock.

"Sylvia, Sylvia," her father was saying. The same father they had said was dead, killed by a car bomb along with her mother in Paris. The same bushy eyebrowed father and sad face, the broken front tooth.

Wendy, who had only been Wendy for three years, still couldn't make a move, despite urging by all around her. Her father was not as tall as she remembered, but he did really look like him, sound like him, she dared not believe it was him. She had been to Paris for the funeral, with Peter. Peter and her father had been friends, why else had she been made ward of court to him? And *she* chose Wendy, she wanted to be English.

"Sylvia," her father repeated, "it is I, your father." He extended his right hand. She saw again the rugged hand with the third finger missing. No-one could pretend a thing like that.

"Papa?" she said, hesitantly, a well of long forgotten tears springing in her eyes, her heart beginning to race.

Her father knelt down and showed her the scar on the back of his head. The same scar she had always been so fascinated with. The one he had received from the British in the war, an accident, he'd always said.

"Sylvia, it really is me. Come give your Papa a kiss."

But her Papa was dead. Wendy's mind stalled on this one problem and, abruptly, without warning, her eyes turned upwards and she fell into a dead faint.

Her father rushed forward, just catching the last part of her fall. He turned to the driver now discarding his jacket and hat. "Better not tell her that her mother is alive as well, just yet. One surprise at a time, I think."

"Yes, a little at a time," the driver replied. He looked down at the young girl's pale face. "She looks quite well, Comrade, she looks quite well."

*   *   *

By 9 am the Square was fully operational. Rumour after rumour dashing from ear to ear, requests for information overloading Matron's switchboard, Press insiders wanting to know more details about Berlin and whether it was true the Stationmaster had disappeared. That fact at least, though hotly denied, was true. There was no trace of him in London or anywhere.

The Relatives were as confused over the Berlin situation as anyone else, unable to make a move or statement until Washington got to work. The President had given orders that he should get a good night's sleep, nothing short of war to wake him up. "Well," as Hallam had observed to Mitchel only an hour before, "that is all we are short of."

The Press, particularly the radio, had made a big fuss, the

33

newspapers being too late to cover such an unprecedented event. Early editions of the *Standard* had found themselves out on the street, however. BERLIN INVADED ran the none too accurate headline. The fact was, just the wall had gone, no-man's–land was still there with its minefields and watchtowers. It was a puzzle. No word from the East Germans either.

Gallant had overdone his interrogation of Philip Oosty. Matron had had to tear them both apart, administer hot tea to a shaking Oosty. It would be talked about in the Club. Bobby Richardson was a friend of Oosty's. One didn't bully Oosty and get away with it. Oosty had been Richardson's fag at school, always would be. Gallant hadn't been liked then. The fellow was an upstart. Didn't belong in the Square anyway. Family had nothing, were nothing. Only because he had been with Grimly that he had any position at all. The real men, the quality crowd, had sunk with Will Strawson. Intolerable that so many good men had been thrown to the wind whilst a person like Gallant was still there to throw his weight about.

At 9.08 am Hallam began to think everything was coming under control once more. He hadn't actually solved anything, but at least his head was clear and he had managed to get a few biscuits to go with his coffee. Everything was falling into place, until Simon Caw came on the line from Lipsnatchers. It was a full green phone scramble. For his ears only. The computer played a little tune and they were locked into each other; anyone listening in would only get a snatch of Angela Rippon's laugh repeated *ad nauseam*. Hallam pressed his speak button and Angela's squawk came out of the earpiece loud and clear. If only, he thought to himself, we had had a weapon like that to throw back at Lord Haw-Haw, we'd have won the war. At last he found the right combination.

"Caw?"

"Mr Hallam, sir."

"Damn machine – foxes me every time. What is it, Caw, any word on Berlin?"

"All lines of communication down. We are trying to contact via satellite. British Embassy still doesn't answer. Sent one of

34

the Canadians around to have a look and he says that it doesn't look as though anyone is up yet."

"Still in bed? On a morning like this?"

"Could have been a party last night, Mr Hallam."

"Quite," Hallam conceded, "could have been a party. Well, keep me posted, Caw. It's a sensitive spot. Looks like we lost a few good men."

"I have other news, sir." A long, pregnant pause followed. Hallam's reviving good humour began to sink.

"Go on," he ordered.

"Hamish Baumann, our South African fieldman has disturbing news to report. It came in last night on our line."

"Don't tell me there's trouble there as well, Caw. My gold shares won't stand it and we are stretched to our limit here as it is."

"Israel-South African Atomic Energy Pact. Baumann is positive they are going for an underground test in South-West, sir."

"Israel and SA together!" Hallam felt the blow below the belt. It was always to his bitter shame that South Africa had been driven out from under the British umbrella. 'The running dogs of capitalist shame,' Stationmaster had called them.

"That's the FOs bag, Caw. Though it is something to offer the Relatives, they won't be happy. Israel is a thorn in their side as it is. Thank you, Caw. On balance that's a plus. How sure are we that the Relatives don't have this already?"

"Hamish Baumann is pretty reliable. His report came in well scrambled. I doubt if Grosvenor Square is monitoring Lipsnatchers yet, I've still got a few tricks to keep off the bloodsuckers. Baumann has just returned from Oranjemund. Lot of Israelis drinking in the local hotel bar for past week. High ranking technical staff."

Hallam was pleased. "Send him a bone, Caw. Tell him we love him, usual stuff."

"Yes, sir, I'll stay in touch, sir."

"Oh wait. The Stationmaster's offices. Who monitors the bugs there?"

"No Lipsnatching in Stationmaster's office, Mr Hallam. He has a sweep once a month. He won't allow it."

"And mine?"

"Leo monitors your office, sir, all your offices. Leo is a third generation IBM."

"I want everything said in the last thirty hours transcribed and in my office by 10 0'clock this morning."

Caw whistled. "Trouble?" he asked.

"Can you do it?"

"It's done. Your secretary will be receiving Leo's instructions through the desk monitor. It's all on disc."

"Thank you, Caw."

Electronics constantly amazed him. Thirty hours of transcript in three seconds. It was an amazing world. He unfolded his body from the steel desk and wandered into Hazel Dowson's cubby hole. Joint personal secretaries didn't get much in the way of elbow room in the Service.

Hazel was staring at her VDU on the desk beside her, astonished to see that the screen was displaying the most shocking profanities she had ever witnessed on a TV screen. She hadn't realised they had Lipsnatchers in the loo as well. She blushed. Marlene and herself had been proper caught out.

"Who said this disgusting filth? What *did* Marlene do with the vibrator?" Hallam wanted to know, peering in amazement at the screen, noticing the deep purple hue advertising his secretary's shame. "Call Matron, Hazel. I want this read. Every filthy word. There has to be some clue as to where the Stationmaster went."

Hazel dialled Matron's section. Gallant picked up the phone. "Mr Hallam looking for Matron, Mr Gallant."

"Tell him Bloater is off-duty, Nolan is gathering dossiers for me, Carter is on leave and Brown is in Passports. I'll come up. What does he want?"

Hazel looked up at Hallam. "Mr Gallant says he'll do it."

Hallam nodded. Gallant was an outsider, best to have an outsider, a Wandsworth man reading the minutes, than an in-house man who might find himself compromised.

"Soonest," he ordered, returning to his office.

*   *   *

John Welland, the Butcher's Boy, looked down from his bedroom balcony overlooking Malta's deep water harbour, and watched in amazement as two Soviet missile-carrying destroyers steamed into the harbour.

The boys on the third floor had sent him to Malta. Welland was the Butcher's Boy, the commoner. Unwritten rules, handed down since Palmerston's day, had decreed that only first class citizens could represent the British abroad. Everyone in the Square, especially that effete snob, Will Strawson, had condemned the recruitment of Welland. It was Strawson who had said, 'The service is going to the dogs if we let in Grammar schoolboys, sons of butchers and spotwelders. The popular classes have no inherent loyalties, they have been weakened by social security, no moral fibre, no backbone when it comes to the crunch. They will squeal at the first sign of interrogation. No butchers' boys in the Service, blackball the bastard who lets them in.'

But Grimly had let Welland in. Grammar schoolboy. Scholarship to Cambridge, recruited there by Grimly in person, though only narrowly escaped falling under charms bestowed from the archives of the Courtauld Institute. Grimly had steered him round, explained a few facts of life. Grimly needed allies, and who better than an agent who had been allowed to cross the tracks, enter a reserved occupation. Strawson had been livid, and for once there was someone at the Square who did not find him charming, someone who survived his reign.

It had happened like magic. Overnight, fourteen Soviet vessels had come to rest in Malta. No warning. The Government hadn't said a word, but the implication was clear. The Third World, of which Welland counted Malta a part, was lining up loyalties. Right across the world countries were deciding their fate. Either support the West and get bombed out of existence; or go passive, allow facilities to Soviet ships, give yourselves basic protection.

And Malta had made that decision – apparently between 9 am and dawn. This was a serious problem. To lose Malta without having reported anything, without giving any warning to the Square would be unforgivable. He'd sat on the information, slowly extracted from the mouths of children attending the school for Soviet children. He had courted their teacher, Nina, for four months. Only in the last month had she felt comfortable enough in his bed, to talk freely of her life and the conversations she had had with her class.

Out of the mouths of babes had come startling information. He had pieced together the snatches and snippets, turned garbled stories into sense and had quickly realised that the Soviet attachés on Malta knew more about the Square and the Relatives than was healthy, that something was about to happen that would fundamentally alter the status quo in Europe. This action on Malta was one such move, and the panic on the radio about Berlin was another.

Welland dressed with frantic speed and cursed the eternally slow elevator as he descended to street level. He sprinted down the slippery cobbled streets, the day unusually cold, heading for the Associated Press Office, already full with other correspondents stunned by the suddenness of the day's arrivals. Fighting each other for phones and swapping horror stories, all secretly glad to be filing something of importance for a change. MALTA INVADED; MALTA COURTED BY THE BEAR; MALTA SWALLOWED UP BY THE REDS. Each man with his own style. MALTA LIBERATED filed the correspondent of the *Morning Star*. For the first time in living memory, he bought the beers that morning; Geeson, the wag from an Australian rag, called up the *Guinness Book of Records*.

*   *   *

On that same morning, for it was a mother of a morning,

38

Sandy Bleak, courier for the Square, arrived in Paris. It was a matter of routine for him. Letters from the Stationmaster to the Paris Stationhouse. It used to be a whole house, but economy measures had forced the Service to cut back. They had rented out the first floor to an audio visual company. Stationmaster had been distressed at first, but then realised that, as cover, Slide Show Manufacturers was not only good cover, but also very useful when it came to borrowing equipment late at night, at no extra cost, always a concern for the budget fellows.

Sandy Bleak enjoyed being a courier. It was a way of not being behind a desk and getting paid good money to do what you liked most. Travel, get a sun tan. He'd enjoyed the training in Gib too. Considered himself lucky to have gained entry into the Service – his second-class public school had been against him, that and his father being a director of only two companies. However, his aunt was Sir Charles' wife and Sir Charles was the Foreign Office. They had waived the fact that he had had to leave King's College in disgrace. He would not forget it easily. Nor would his bedder, Mrs Hargreaves, who had caught him with the explosives and made him throw them away. She'd been most persuasive, which was a pity, for instead of the purpose being the removal, by force, of an offensive gift by Henry Moore to the College, the result was the total disintegration of the town's brand new Seddon refuse truck. It was fortunate that no-one had been killed.

Luckily the Dean had appreciated that one could feel passionately for or against Henry Moore, that Bleak had been recklessly interfered with by his bedder and, with his father donating a new refuse truck to the town, he had been sent down without too much fuss. Thus he was most grateful when Sir Charles had intimated that there were far more constructive ways he could serve his country than by sabotaging Henry Moore. So Sandy Bleak was in Paris delivering classified documents.

Paris, itself, was electric this rainy morning. Bleak was

ahead of schedule and wondered if he had time for a cup of coffee and croissant in the Rue St. Denis, prior to visiting the Stationhouse. He decided that there was time.

The café was typical. The Parisians had invented the institution. Perfect coffee, too strong, cold croissants, indifferent service and flat-capped old men poking their foul-smelling Gaulloises into their peasant faces. Bleak had little time for peasants, glad they weren't prone to invading British coffee bars. He was of the opinion that the coffee bar was for the use of gentlemen only. Not peasants.

He unravelled his morning paper, the *Daily Telegraph*, bought at the stand outside the Metro exit. Bleak could read French, and would normally have bought *Le Monde*, but he had spotted the London paper and preferred what he was most comfortable with. Bleak could, in fact, speak French like a native, having learnt it from his mother, a petite exile from Cannes, forever bemoaning the fact that she had married an Englishman who lived in London. His knowledge of languages enabled him to travel; Bleak was forever grateful to his Mama for that.

However, this morning he could not concentrate. The couple of flat caps in the corner were conferring together in a most conspiratorial manner. He could plainly see them out of the corner of his eye, their low monotone voices distracting him from the paper. More intriguingly, their manner was most un-Parisian in Bleak's opinion. Peasants usually didn't care who listened in on their conversations, but these two birds were most secretive. He concentrated on their voices, whilst staring up at the ceiling fan, moving around with all the effectiveness of a feather.

"... Opening up Marseilles to the Russians. Marchais to be coopted into the Government ... umbrella of the Eastern Alliance. Safeguard oil supplies to Lyons."

Single, indistinct, preposterous statements. France to ally with the Soviets? Marchais in the Government? Impossible. An Eastern Alliance? What of the Common Market? Oil supplies?

Training in Gib taught one, 'Idle gossip is stock in trade.'

The peasants looked across the smoke-filled café at the crazy Englishman staring at the ceiling fan. They had known he was English by the way he had entered the café and ordered "Coffee and sticky buns." Things like that easily gave one away. The young man was obviously an idiot. "The English," remarked one of the peasants, "they always back the wrong horse."

But Bleak didn't detect much bitterness. He drank his coffee, thinking about the horse the British had backed.

"There will be no war, not now France has chosen sides," the same peasant added. "England will pay for not sharing her North Sea oil."

But it sounded to Sandy Bleak as if that was as good as any reason for war. He picked up his paper and briefcase and deposited twenty francs on the table, before leaving the café. The Stationhouse would be waiting, they would be interested in what he had just heard.

"The English won't be so smug soon," was the peasant's parting shot. They all laughed, a cackle of conspirators in a café on the sideway of life. Was this then the *vox populi* or something more sinister?

Sandy Bleak formulated a short, concise report in his head. Any truth in the rumour, etc. He was glad he had something to say, anything at all.

*   *   *

The gathered assembly hardly had time to reach the Square, let alone sit down in the Games Room, the high raftered, poorly heated excuse for a conference room. It was 11.05 am, still Friday, and no-one was glad to be there. Calon, from Cabinet Office, had ignored requests for the session and had gone down to Devon for the weekend as planned. Instead, Sir Charles Edgeware, Foreign Office, former Ambassador to Greece and India was there. A valuable man, highly protective of the Square, had a noted dislike for that commoner, Hugh

Grimly, but respected the fact that there would not be an Intelligence Service at all, if it had not been for his efforts. Then there was Dr Sludgeon, or Sludge, as he was known by the fifth floor. Head of the warren, research, intelligence records and the Russian Crystal Ball. Joined by Sussie Sutzman, the eccentric, but indispensable China Crystal Ball. She was a living museum of Chinese Intelligence, political and social history. She knew all the names.

Of course, Philip Oosty, David Gallant, Peter Hallam and Hazel represented the Square, whereas Mitchel and Sol Guss had reluctantly wandered over from Grosvenor Square to make up the balance. Only the Stationmaster was missing.

Gallant was trying to arrange his report in order of priorities, difficult to decide which was the least important.

Sir Charles had to have his say first. He was the most senior, and that mattered in Sir Charles' opinion.

"I know you're going to squawk over Berlin," he growled, "but we know very little about what is going on there. Gallant tells me he has some news, but I have none. Except to say, it is quite obvious that Malta has made a radical left turn with the arrival of the Soviet fleet. We do have a few piddling boats there bobbing about, but it's laughable. With Berlin, I'm convinced it's to deflect world opinion, for they haven't as far as I know made any attempt to enter the British sector. But all this is inexcusable, Hallam. Not a damn word, not a bleep from your department, nor you, Mitchel."

Mitchel looked nonplussed, as usual. "It was as big a surprise to us as Afghanistan," he said, itching his thin hands.

"That's the trouble," Sir Charles protested. "You didn't see it coming in Iran, you didn't see it coming in Afghanistan, and now Malta. What are your boys doing, looking the wrong way? Do we have Intelligence, or do we not? That is the question, gentlemen. Where does our public money go?"

It is possible that Hallam might have answered there, but Simon Caw was on the green phone again. Hallam avoided Angela Rippon this time, excused himself as Doc Sludgeon weighed in with his opinion that Malta hadn't offered the

Soviets exclusive rights to their port, it was just a small country playing survival politics. They would welcome our own fleet, if we had one.

Sol Guss disagreed. He saw it as a major, strategic calamity, a realignment, a defeat for the West. Berlin was a catastrophe, a collapse of will. A signal to the rest of the world of the West's weaknesses. No wonder Malta had realised that to go East was to stay intact.

Hallam replaced his phone and jotted down a note to himself on his electronic notepad (a toy he had bought for Wendy, but kept for himself).

Mitchel wanted to discuss Berlin. "It is obvious that they are going to cause trouble in your sector and, with due respect, your sector was chosen because it is the weak one. The pressure is on Sir Charles. They want Berlin. They want reunification and Strauss has been playing right into their hands."

Gallant threw in a tit-bit. "I know why the wall is down," he said. All eyes turned to him. "According to one of our agents in the field, not in Germany, I might add, the removal of the wall is a giant public relations exercise to prove to the Third World that the Bear is Mr Nice Guy after all. The whole world will see this as a symbol of peace. Peace offered by the strong to the weak, us. What they aren't telling the Third World, and it won't appear in their papers either, is that they are installing, even as we speak, power complexes at 300-yard intervals. In short, Laser beams which will frazzle any would-be defector. A short automated death. It's a cosmetic move, made to make them look good and, unless we get out this information to the press immediately, they will be claiming that we in the West would prefer a wall after all, that our carping about their inhumanity was hogwash."

"Laser beams?" Sussie Sutzman whispered. She was thinking of the power they would consume in a city already short of energy.

"Then we release a joint statement on this issue this morning," Sir Charles said. "Make sure it gets to the BBC World Service. We might as well let the Third World know the worst, let them know the Russians aren't angels after all."

Hallam, pleased that Gallant had come up with that one, signalled to Oosty to bring his report forward.

"We have word that your friends, the Israelis, are linking up with the South Africans, Mitchel."

Mitchel looked across the table at Oosty, wondering where Leon was, the two were inseparable, then remembered it was Leon's morning at the hairdresser. "Israel isn't my country or my friend," he said. "Now what have those two peace-loving havens of humanity been up to?"

Oosty was enjoying the suspense. "Not much, but we have an almost definite confirmation that they are planning a joint nuclear test in South West Africa very soon. Imminent, I would say."

Mitchel sat staring at Oosty with his mouth sagging open. As it sank in, he saw the problem quite clearly. They couldn't complain about the Soviets' expansion and at the same time claim innocence if Israel, their ally, exploded weapons, especially nuke weapons. It was a disaster. He turned to Sol. Sol knew what to do.

"Got to make a call," Sol said, reaching for his radio phone, on hand in his jacket.

Mitchel obviously had to save face. The British had scored twice this morning. It was a rare occasion, but unnerving.

"Tinkabelle is awake," he said, as if he was announcing lunch. Gallant looked at Hallam, then across to Sir Charles, who lit up a cigar and asked, "Which Tinkabelle? Ours or theirs?"

"The Moscow Cephal's Tinkabelle. Ours is called Lipsnatchers, Sir Charles, it is just the press who call it Tinkerbell. That's all right by us, we like a bit of confusion as far as the press is concerned. Talking of the press," Oosty said, "I had better go and draft that statement on the wall, time is short."

"Good thinking," Hallam told him, glad to see the boy go. He didn't like him, even if the Americans did.

Mitchel was smiling, he was back at pole position. "We

made contact. Washington is persuaded Moscow Cephal has Tinkabelle back in control. He was seen."

"Seen?" Sussie Sutzman exploded. It was unheard of. No-one had seen Tinkabelle in years. Even Grimly, who'd seen him once during the Spanish Civil War, and, it was rumoured, in Cairo a few days before Suez.

"Grimly said he was dead," Hallam declared.

"The same could be said for Grimly," Sir Charles muttered.

Doctor Sludgeon laughed, but really it was no laughing matter. Hallam considered it very bad news. Stationmaster would be alarmed. Hallam rejoined the conversation.

"Hugh only surmised he was dead. It was something we accepted when Rocov took over Moscow Cephal in '78. But Rocov is in disgrace following Afghanistan. They have obviously brought Tinkabelle out of retirement."

"We should have made sure he was dead," Dr Sludgeon declared, lighting up an old cigar.

"He must be seventy, at least," Gallant said.

"Age no deterrent in Moscow, experience is all that matters. The revolutionaries don't give up easily," Mitchel pointed out.

Hallam looked at his electric notepad again. It was a shocker. He would have revealed Simon Caw's message right then, but Gallant, annoyed the Americans had evened up, threw in his rock to make a big splash.

"I have bad news for all of you. The Stationmaster has disappeared."

Gallant surveyed their faces. All registered suprise, excepting Hallam, who expressed annoyance, because he wasn't aware that they were going to let on about that just yet.

"He disappeared late yesterday afternoon, took all the files, all Square personnel files relating to current operations, and his daybook. And before the Relatives, who look most surprised at the end of the table there, say the Square has messed up again, that we have another Will Strawson on our hands, I have been through the day to day minutes, Mitchel. The last person to speak with Stationmaster was Sol Guss, when they took the private elevator down to street level. I have a photo of Sol and Stationmaster standing in Dancer's lobby. Dancer is our security man."

Mitchel realised that they had him in a corner again.

Sol placed his radio phone on the table and took a sip of conference table water. "First things first," he said, his fish-like eyes watching Hallam and no-one else. "Washington confirms Israel presence in South West Africa. They have them under observation. They cannot confirm nuclear inter-est, suggest that Oranjemund is a diamond centre and Israelis are not strangers to diamonds. However, the matter is getting high priority attention."

Gallant muttered, "Good," pleased the Yanks were doing something.

"As for your Stationmaster, yes, I saw him yesterday. Under terms of exchange of information, negotiated in Washington by your Ambassador, we are obliged to release information to the Square which we feel is in your National Interest, even if this information is not entirely savoury."

"For God's sake, man, spit it out," Sir Charles insisted. He didn't like Americans, never had, not since he'd seen what quantity of rations it had taken to get an American soldier to go to war, as opposed to a British one.

"We informed the Stationmaster that Tinkabelle was alive and that we have every reason to believe that there's a Second Eleven – here, at the Square and in the Foreign Office."

"A Second Eleven?" Sir Charles blurted out. "Good God, man, this is no time to discuss cricket. We don't even have a First Eleven. The House has a cricket team, but the Square? Not under this Government, I can tell you."

"The FO has a First Eleven," Dr Sludgeon pointed out. "Played the Civil Service at Wickers last August."

"Yes, but not the Square," Sir Charles insisted.

Sol Guss was bewildered. He'd just dropped a bombshell and here were these English discussing cricket.

"What precisely do you mean by Second Eleven?" Hallam

asked, hoping it wasn't going to be the answer he thought it was going to be.

Sol was grateful for the sanity offered. "Strawson, Melchette, the third, fourth, fifth, sixth and up till eleven, Hallam. The First Eleven. Forget them. That is all water under the bridge. They are all old men put out to grass in the golden fields of Moscow. The First Eleven played a long game, good and hard, they suckered you, and although they didn't sucker us, we knew in '51, they drained the Square. We all know every last damn detail about them. I'm telling you now, just as I told the Stationmaster, Hallam, seeds were sown, caps were handed down and you have now gotten yourselves a new Second Eleven out on the holy ground. Better still, you don't have a damn clue as to who they are."

Sir Charles threw his pen clear across the room. "I just can't believe it. Russia is ideologically bankrupt, there's no attraction anymore. Burgess and Maclean weren't heroes, no-one would be fool enough to fall for that Marxist claptrap now."

"You aren't alone, Sir Charles," Mitchel soothed. "We have our Philip Agees, but at least we know who they are."

"A Second Eleven," Gallant muttered. It was inconceivable.

"Stationmaster has all the details," Sol reminded them.

"But he's disappeared," Sussie Sutzman squeaked, for she was terribly fond of the Chief, as she called him.

"And no wonder," Doc Sludgeon stated with disgust.

"He's taken A through DQ files, did you say, Gallant?" Hallam asked.

Gallant nodded.

"Then he hasn't run away. He's gone into hiding. He's opted out of the Square's parameter. It isn't safe here. He's gone looking for the blighters," Sussie uttered in a spirited voice. "Oh, if only I knew where he was, I'd help him. A Second Eleven, who would have thought it?"

Hallam couldn't agree more, it was incredible. "Then I have one other piece of business," he said. The others fell silent once more, impatient to be off to spread all the bad news. "I'll accept, for the moment, that Stationmaster's gone to ground following your revelations. The pattern fits. I have now received word, via our Paris Stationhouse and corroborated by our agent in Moscow. If it is true, then we are all in deep trouble." Hallam eyed them all, making sure he had their complete attention. Finally he got it out. "Simply put, a Paris Moscow mutual defence pact."

There was stunned silence around the table.

"A defence treaty that allows the Soviets use of their ports in time of war, or aggression, Marchais in the Cabinet. All this in exchange for a guaranteed supply of Gulf oil. I must stress these are unconfirmed reports, hearsay – no more – but in the light of today's events, worth investigating."

Mitchel couldn't believe it. Didn't even want to think about it. Even if it was only half true. The Brits had trounced him again.

"And Second Eleven, or no," Sir Charles said, "I think that was 3–2, game to us, what?"

British laughter rumbled around the room. Oosty came back for a statement to be signed by Sir Charles and read by Mitchel. Both sides agreed to adjourn and digest, if it was digestible.

Hallam approached Mitchel, took him by the elbow to the tall, misty windows.

Even as Hallam was about to speak, he noticed that Hazel was trying to attract his attention towards the black outside phone beside him. Michel stopped complaining about the French inherent and historical lack of loyalty and waited for Hallam to answer the buzzing phone.

Hallam snatched it up impatiently. "Hallam."

"If you want Wendy to stay alive, walk across the green at 1.05 pm. Come alone. Tell no-one. You will be contacted."

Hallam was holding a dead phone in his hands. Mitchel saw the blood drain out of his face, as Hallam replaced the handpiece and looked for a chair to steady himself with.

*　　*　　*

But even with this earth shattering news of the Second Eleven, events far more significant than either France turning left, or South Africa exploding bombs, more significant even than Wendy's abduction, were already taking place.

Matron heard it first. Matron in charge of household budgets would naturally be the recipient of such a memo. It entered in the usual way. Calon's office sent a letter in an ordinary buff envelope, with perfectly innocent Ministry paper inside it. Signed by Calon and the entire Cabinet.

Matron, in the guise of Nolan, took it straightaway to Philip Oosty, who already had a headache, and had just released the Berlin and Malta statements to the press. An informed, reliable source, or as Sussie Sutzman had put it, an inflamed source; either way, the press were hungry for details and swallowed the 'leak' whole.

As far as Oosty was concerned, there was too much going on all at once, and he missed the Stationmaster. The day before – nothing. Now it was like a D-Day movie.

"What is it, Nolan?"

"Memo from Calon's office, Mr Oosty. I think you should see it."

Oosty didn't really have time to read any of Nolan's petty memo litter. The installation of computer terminals hadn't reduced the plethora of paper at all. Far from it, now the terminals issued memos. It was ridiculous.

"Read it, Mr Oosty," Nolan insisted, holding it under his nose.

Oosty tried to concentrate on it.

'It has been decided, in line with general economic guidelines, issued by Cabinet Office (series 6E) that a reduction of 31% in the overall annual budget of the institution, known as the Square, will take effect from April 1st. The vehicle and petrol allowance will be reduced accordingly, as will staff cuts (these being achieved by natural wastage). Operating costs will be seen to be adequate, running at no less than 80% of the previous calendar year.

Also, in view of high rental and heating costs of location of said

Square, it has been decided that it would be desirable to relocate the Service to a more suitable Government-owned building in South-West London.

Signed Calon, Cabinet Office.

It was the end of the world. South-West London. Of all places, South-West London. This wasn't a budget cutback, it was a firing squad. They wanted the Square to curl up and die. Ever since they had reached power, they'd decided the Square was undesirable. Since Strawson, nothing had been right for them. It was an attack. Just because of a little failure, that was all. But this Square was producing. South Africa and Paris today, that was proof. That had set the cat amongst the pigeons.

"Do they mean it?" Nolan asked, hoping the memo lied.

Oosty gave him a withering smile. "We can only hope that it's a warning, Matron, but if it is real, in case it is, requisition everything you are short of at once."

"Done," Nolan returned with a cheeky smile. "And as for 31% of the vehicles, at least 40% don't work and they never did. We should never have let them deliver us Hunters – junk that's all they are. We could do with a few Mini Metros."

Oosty shuddered. "It isn't becoming for Chiefs of Staff to ride in Mini Metros, Nolan."

"Black ones," he said, trying to mollify. "I meant black ones."

Oosty decided to speak to Hazel, Hallam's secretary. He didn't feel sufficiently strong or brave enough to face Number Two with the budget cuts himself. No wonder Calon hadn't turned up at the emergency meeting.

"Not a good day for Henrietta to die," Nolan said sadly, leaving the way he came.

Oosty had forgotten about Henrietta. He wondered if her body had left the Listening Room yet. That would be one case for natural wastage if ever there was one.

He left clutching the memo, looking for Hazel.

*   *   *

Sir Charles had already made his decision. He mentioned it to the PM at lunch at Number Ten. The Square was in need of help. Things were serious, it was quite obviously falling apart. Only one man could fix it. Root out the Second Eleven, sort out Berlin, turn Malta around, put a cork in Israel's bomb, charm Paris and fight this Tinkabelle character. The PM was reluctant, but agreed. Grimly was the one. With Stationmaster presumed missing, Hugh Grimly was the *only* one.

*   *   *

Simon Caw leapt out of the van. His thin, permanently breathless body seemed to dangle in the wind as he crossed the road onto the green. His dark face betrayed a mixed ancestry, rooted somewhere in the confused and most often depraved Eurasian past of the English Raj. Simon Caw was not one of those attractive mixtures. He had not been blessed with a beautiful mother, the second line was not a pretty one. But even without breeding, he had progressed. Even though not part of the Square, he had risen in stature and importance as each new capacity came on line. Lipsnatchers was growing so big, it was beginning to swallow all the little fish, as machinery and electronics replaced people.

As Head of Department at Lipsnatchers, he liked to stay ahead of the game. He had worked himself up through the morass of bureaucracy, recruited by Grimly when still a young twenty-six. Now a wiry, but old thirty-eight and a family man, he was an acknowledged electronic genius. Without him, freedom of speech would be a foregone conclusion in the UK and who knew what would be the outcome of that. As it was, Lipsnatchers – or Tinkerbell, as the angry hard-kneed *New Statesman* had decreed his department – could monitor up to 5000 separate calls in London alone. More sophisticated equipment was on its way. By 1984, Simon Caw's urgent deadline, he hoped to be able to listen in, via the phone, whether in use or not, to nearly one million separate numbers. Then, area by area, take random samples of all the twenty-six million subscribers. It wan't a fixation, no thought to the rise of Central control and State interference, it was just that it was possible and it was the only way to combat the IRA or any other left wing plotters. "Forewarned is forearmed," his personal motto.

He was standing in the centre of Soho Square. It was 1 am precisely. So far it had been a worrying day. The development in Berlin and Paris looked ominous. The KGB was active in so many places now, their so-called 'technical staff' invaded so many organisations. It worried him that the Square should have so many problems on the same day the Stationmaster should choose to disappear. The long arm of coincidence stretched back to Moscow, he was sure of it.

This Second Eleven, it was a big shock. He'd been lulled into thinking that, with Strawson gone, the last of the 'Philby Generation' had been rooted out; that it had been an unique, never to be seen again phenomenon, directly related to the political outgrowth of the industrial society and its abuses, resulting in the depression – the now discredited Marxist solution. So a Second Eleven would have had to have been recruited some other way, perhaps unaware of just what they were doing. Moscow Cephal penetrating organisations, ensnaring unwitting agents. Left wing ecology groups, the 'no more nukes' crowd, using the freedom granted under open government, to destroy the system within. He and Grimly had watched in bewilderment as Soviet ciphers exploited the US Freedom of Information act. Simon was set firm in the belief that the opening up of that act and the subsequent, brilliantly engineered destruction of the CIA, had all been masterminded by Moscow Cephal.

A worried Simon Caw then, stalked Peter Hallam as the man entered the small green park occupying the Square. Hallam looked agitated, excusable given the news of the day. He'd been warned of the arrangements by the monitor, Leo, who listened to all the conversations in the Square, looking for key words, like 'come alone'. Certainly Caw knew Hallam would go to the rendezvous. What man wouldn't worry about the safety of his young ward and under-aged lover? Hallam's Lolita, as she was known, was a concern to many at the department, not least to those who were supposed to be protecting her and him. Caw had called the school and confirmed that the girl had not arrived. That the regular driver, George, had not reported for work.

Simon Caw approved Hallam's motives for adopting the orphaned girl, but not his behaviour. But then the girl was a little stunner, he'd noticed at the Christmas party. A ripe little stunner and man hungry. Hard to resist something like that.

Hallam was approached by a short, plainly dressed woman, a headscarf covering her hair, lines of someone prematurely old covered her face. She appeared to be asking the time, but Caw, who was tuned into the directional mike operating from the Ford van he had left in good hands the other side of the Square, listened with interest.

"Walk, Mr. Hallam," the woman insisted. A foreigner with an East European accent. "Walk normally. You told no-one of the meeting?"

"No-one," he anwered. "Wendy? Where is my Wendy?"

"She's safe. Being well looked after, Mr Hallam. I can ensure that no harm is contemplated against Wendy, as long as you cooperate."

"Who are you? Who do you work for?" Hallam asked, his voice strained, his throat constricted, dry, hands shaking. He didn't like the idea of losing Wendy at all.

"You know better than to ask that, Mr Hallam. Walk, we are friends, walk, admire the flowers."

"There are no flowers, it's winter. What are you? Where is Wendy?" Panic showing in Hallam's voice.

"Calm down. Listen, Mr Hallam. This is a message from Captain Crewk. Wendy will be returned to you unharmed, if you cooperate."

"Cooperate?" He had never liked that word.

"Just two items, Mr Hallam. Simple items. You'll know what we mean. We want the whereabouts of the Butcher's Boy. That's one." She looked around the park. Simon Caw

53

began to walk, waving to some invisible person a little to the left of him.

"I don't know any butcher's boy, or what you mean," Hallam exclaimed. "How can I tell you something I don't know?"

"The second, Mr Hallam, is much easier." She smiled, taking his arm, turning him around so that they walked back into the park. "You are to declare Amsterdam Stationhouse unsafe. Close it down. You're Number One now, Mr Hallam. Yes, we know the Stationmaster has disappeared. He was old, you're the Chief now. Captain Crewk told me to tell you that he doesn't want to hurt Wendy. She is a pretty girl, so sad to see someone so young go blind." The woman dropped a brooch on the ground.

"You wouldn't," Hallam shouted, tearing his arm away from the woman. She simply turned with that same smile on her face saying, "I'll be visiting you in a week, Mr Hallam." Then she was walking away. "Who knows, perhaps Wendy will be with me. Do try to get something done."

And she was gone. Hallam stood stunned, staring with accumulated horror at Wendy's glass brooch lying on the tarmac. Not only was what the woman asked impossible, but he had only a week in which to do it and no guarantee that Wendy would be safe. He couldn't move, the brooch seemed to stare back at him, his legs felt they might give way at any moment.

Simon Caw had three men detailed to follow the woman. He took himself off to a waiting Vauxhall and ordered his driver to take him back to Putney. It had been a very interesting lunchbreak. A kidnapped child, information the ransom. So open, too, they must be very confident. Captain Crewk, something about that Russian name that rang a *je ne sais* whatever it was. The thing is, do they wait for Hallam to come to them, or do they watch and wait? Certainly it would be worth tracking down the Butcher's Boy, whoever he was. He sounded worth knowing.

As Simon Caw's car circled the Square, he saw Hallam

stoop and pick something up off the ground, quickly bring it to his mouth and kiss it. The man was a piteous sight. Being blackmailed was no picnic, not with a kid involved, and there was no doubt that Hallam loved the child. It was practically all the man's life outside the Square, everyone knew that. But there was no need to assume he would automatically walk over to the other side, not yet, give him time.

TWO

The Cabbage Run

The road to Petworth was particularly dicey that evening.
David Gallant, already tired from his short-lived night of rest,
wrestled with the wheel as black ice and thick fog lurked
strategically at every blind corner and hill top, conspiring to
have him in a ditch, eating away at the short fuse, always a
style of his driving. The Triumph sounded rough and long
overdue for a service, the soft top whistled where it failed to
seal properly. It was possible that Gallant drove the TR7
convertible to conceal his advancing years, preserve his youth
and ensure the heads of young girls were turned in the Fulham
Road. It was possible, too, that it had not occurred to him that
the very fact he could afford the car and the insurance, set him
at an age way above those females he so earnestly sought. Still,
it worked well enough. The passenger seat was more often
than not filled with a Debbie Harry look alike. He collected
look alikes. The year before it had been Brooke Shields, and
Headhunters was an ideal career for him, collecting people.
He'd been doing it all his life.

The road was murder, Petworth still another twenty miles.
It annoyed him that the old boy couldn't have retired closer to
London. This wasn't the first time he'd had to go racing down
there either. Why no phone? Was he afraid the Square would
be onto him night and day? Didn't he know Stationmaster and
Hallam had too much pride to do that? If they didn't know, or
couldn't do, they would much rather muddle through. It was
time honoured. The Easton College actually preferred it.
Once a member had retired from Intelligence – leave him be.

56

His memory is suspect, he may have an axe to grind. Rely on the archives, respect the written facts, that is what they are for.

Only the archives hadn't revealed Will Strawson's treachery. How could they? Had he not systematically destroyed any incriminating documents, so cowed the Archive Director, Sally Dancer, niece of Dancer the security man, that she was destroying vital, sensitive documents herself, protecting Strawson from a communist plot. It never dawned on her that the only plot had been hatched by Strawson. His charm and flattery had bewildered and bewitched her. Even now the archives were suspect. Fifteen years under Strawson's supervision, they were a testimony to the perfect mole. The one who leaves such a hole under the foundations that the slightest disturbance would send the whole deck of cards crashing to the ground. For fifteen years that hole had drained the Square and bled the Intelligence Service white. Sally Dancer had slashed her wrists. They had found her, of course. She didn't die, but spent every day of her life without her pension, wishing she had.

A truck blocked the road ahead, deliberately slowing down to hold Gallant back. It was probably because of the fog, but Gallant saw something sinister in every action impeding his right of way. The road was too narrow and visibility too poor to overtake with safety. Thirty miles per hour all the way to Petworth, it was enough to make his blood boil.

*   *   *

It wasn't foggy in Petworth itself, but it was excessively dark. Mr Hugh Grimly was not especially fond of walking on frosted pavements in the dark. Nor on such a narrow and undulating pathway that graced the side of North Street. He had been visiting, under duress, the Darlings at North House and had sat politely whilst Mr John Darling had complained, non-stop, for more than an hour, about Lady Bettina Grimly. The scandal she had caused, the embarrassment to all the little Darlings in North Street.

Grimly had sat by their meagre, one lump coal fire, and stared forlornly at the dusty tapestry on the wall and an ageing grand piano crammed up against the door, played, no doubt, by their favourite son, John Junior, the subject presently under discussion. No-one ever discussed their other son, Michael: he was a taboo subject, despite the fact that at the age of forty, he still wandered around the town talking to an enormous stuffed teddy bear. It was an acute embarrassment to all the town, not least because the bear was always doing most of the talking. Michael was not so dumb he couldn't throw his voice and mitigate his lunacy with a warped character transference to the bear. The bear would cause most trouble in church, where he would creep in and heckle the vicar and howl during Mr Walker's hymns. Mr Walker, the organist, had been seen threatening the bear on more than one occasion after morning service had ended.

But it was John Junior that concerned Mr Darling. The first born and spry fifty year-old managing director of a local insurance agency.

Grimly was not in the habit of listening to gossip, far from it. His days were fully occupied with reading or writing: he fancied a reconstruction of the Spanish Civil War, from his point of view; and talking with a few of his friends, like Milne, the poet: their lost dreams and foolishness before the fire curtain had gone up on the Second World War.

However, it was difficult to live in dignity, even at his age of seventy-five with such a mother as Lady Bettina Grimly prowling the town bars in search of some grist for her mill. One such grist had been John Darling Junior. Quite how this perfectly normal and, from all accounts, good looking man of fifty had found Bettina, a coquettish, yet evergreen ninety-three year-old, sexually attractive, Mr Darling Senior couldn't fathom and Grimly couldn't entertain it. It was to his constant shame and utter bewilderment that his mother still took lovers at her age, when most women would have been polite about it and ignored the urge.

But not Bettina. She had found a new lease of life at eighty, helped in no small part by her yearly sojurn to Cape Town and the Mount Nelson Hotel, for a tan and vigorous swimming in the cold Atlantic off Camps Bay. For Hugh Grimly it was a repeated nightmare to venture into the local pub or grocery shop and be greeted with, "How's your mother, Hugh?" Complete strangers, usually male, leered at him, and it was rumoured that Bettina had slept with half of Sussex and wouldn't give in until she hit her century.

Mr John Darling Junior, her latest conquest, was, even as Mr Darling Senior spoke, driving Bettina to Brighton for dinner and dancing. The shame cut both ways in Grimly's opinion; it was the wives who got hurt the most, but at fifty or sixty to be trumped by an Isadora Duncan of ninety-three it came as a shock. Petworth was a town of shame, not a man over fifty was safe.

Grimly stopped at the kerb. A plump man, but not as plump as he used to be. Unaccustomed exercise in the garden had removed his pasty, desk-bound look. He was short, he'd always been short and wore a hat to deceive himself only. Invisible, because he had the sort of face one could never remember, only his expensive and slightly Edwardian clothes distinguished him from the local population. He wearily continued up North Street, crossing over the road by the church to where he'd left his car. He always bought British. It had been instilled in him from his earliest memories, thus it was confusing that this Leyland car had all the appearance of being a Honda. Patriotism was a difficult commodity to buy in the eighties and Rovers were far too large these days.

"Damn the Darlings," he raged. "How dare they whimper about my mother, when their youngest thinks he's a bear. Who do they think they are? My mother is entitled to company. Is old age a sin?"

But as he started up the engine and drove out into the Pulborough Road, he had to admit to himself, it was a sin in Petworth. The town was too small for his mother and himself. He should return to London perhaps, back to the Kensington apartment. As it was, people knew that Bettina wouldn't let him into the Manor House, family home for more than six generations. That he, Mr Hugh Grimly, retired acting Stationmaster OBE etc (though to be fair the townsfolk thought he was something in postage stamps), was forced to live in the cottage, adjoining the neighbouring farm.

It was all very well for Elgar to come to Fittleworth and live in this remote place on the edge of the Sussex Downs, but he had not been forced to because his mother wanted to wander naked from room to room and chase her lovers from floor to floor whilst both consumed vast quantities of Champagne and (though she denied it) snorted cocaine. It was a scandal, but what could one do? She had all the money, the three deceased husbands, all millionaires who'd catered to her slightest whim. No wonder she had turned out so badly.

Grimly had tried to encourage her to stay in Cape Town the whole year, but then the hotel had written to say that their male staff needed a rest. It was an impossible situation for him. Thank God he had Brinkwells to hide in. Hardly anyone knew it was there, the gate and the long hawthorn bush drive, like any other farm lane, bordered with cows and an excess of country air. One had to know exactly where it was, an Elgar lover, or personal friend to find this flint and thatch cottage, lovingly rebuilt by the aforementioned Walkers, some years before.

So, as Grimly clung to the bastard Leyland and wound his way up the single lane road encrusted with glittering frost towards his hideaway, he was neither too tired, nor too long removed from the Square to notice a car's tracks preceding him. Even more interesting, was the way they suddenly slurred to a stop outside his gate before moving on. Grimly deduced that a skid mark was most likely due to a rabbit leaping across the road, or some such animal. It was that sort of road. He checked the gate padlock. Still locked and frozen to the gate, so he was assured that no-one had progressed before him. Still, there was always the possibility, that uneasy feeling. The days at the Square were not so long ago that he wasn't aware that enemies made during a lifetime in the Service, might still seek him out with vengeance on their mind.

His eyes were better than they used to be. He'd taken to using, for reasons of vanity and the fact that he constantly lost his glasses, contact lenses. Almost the only modern thing he was prepared to accept. Of course, his friends said he looked naked without his glasses, but he didn't have those headaches either, nor any need to hide behind dark rimmed frames. No need to exercise any firm authority, except over the weeds in his garden and the cows who constantly strayed into the cabbage patch. His domain had shrunk from the world to a cabbage patch, invaded by a recalcitrant Jersey called Moomin.

As he drove down to the cottage, he felt that tiredness come over him again. When it came, it came suddenly. His doctor warned him that senility was not necessarily a gradual affair. He'd known it come overnight on very able and fit patients, some in their sixties. The first sign was this sudden tiredness, so sudden you could be sitting in the loo and find yourself still there hours later, your legs cramped and chilled; or be out in the cabbage patch, where an attack had once come on so sudden Grimly was unable to cry out, not that anyone would hear. It was fortunate Bettina had popped over to enforce his attendance at Lord Nana's cocktail party. He might otherwise have frozen to death.

That was when the drugs had begun.

It was humiliating that Bettina should be so active at her age, but she'd confessed her secret, and now both of them were on 'Dr Mowbray's Battery Charger', as she called it. Grimly didn't even want to know what was in it. All he knew was that if he didn't have his daily injection, he would sleep the big sleep and one day he'd be at the wheel of his car, or crossing the road. An injection was nothing if it gave him dignity in his old age.

Nevertheless, he was tired. The Darlings had annoyed him with their pathetic moaning. Why complain to him? If their son didn't know how to behave at fifty, when would he know?

He parked the car, glared at the fence glistening in the dark, no sign of the bovine vandals for a change.

It was by the door that he paused. Signals. The knocker. He always left the knocker leaning left. That way anyone entering through the door couldn't help but disturb it. It was now hanging straight down. But then it could have slipped. The paper chips were still in place, an old Square trick. The door-step free of any foot imprint in the frost, as far as one could tell on a particularly obscure moonlit night. All indications were that it was safe, the house was empty. He couldn't help this ritual. He'd always been obsessive about security, insisting that Nolan or Bloater taste his tea, a man full-time at the camera obscura on top of the Square building before the video camera had come of age. Caution the mother of survival.

Nevertheless, inside, the lights on, his slippers already on the end of his feet instead of the hard brogues, it was a full five minutes before he noticed the smell.

"Lucky Strikes." He'd know that brand of cigarettes any-where. Only one person he knew who smoked them and rightly incurred the wrath of all who had to inhale his fumes.

"Gallant?" he asked, turning around, walking into the only other room on ground level. "Gallant," he repeated, sure that it was him. The coincidence of another intruder who smoked 'Luckies' was too remote.

"I'm up here," Gallant replied from the bathroom. "Have you got any asprin?"

Grimly climbed the perilously narrow wooden stairs, grip-ping the handrail with infirm hands and, panting, walked halfway into the bathroom. Gallant was dabbing cotton wool and Dettol onto his scratched face. Blood dribbled from his hands. A cigarette lay burning on the ceramic bath rim.

"Lucky for me you left the backdoor open, Chief. Cold out there tonight."

Grimly felt that one in the heart. To forget the back door. What could he have been thinking of? He was a fool, an old, bumbling fool.

62

"Gallant, why are you bleeding?"

"Approaching your cottage with caution, as is my manner and advised in the Easton manual, when I was attacked by a large vicious cow. It knocked me into some brambles and I have a bloody headache."

"Moomin," Grimly muttered, "it's always Moomin."

Gallant pulled the plug in the basin and dried off his hands.

"Don't get comfortable, Hugh. We have to chase the hounds."

Grimly saw Gallant's bloodied face for the first time in six or seven months. It was the first time, too, that he'd noticed wrinkles around his eyes. It comes to all of us, he thought.

"London, Hugh," Gallant added, studying his hands for more thorns. "You'll need a toothbrush."

Ten minutes later, swaddled in his quilted overcoat with the monk's hood up to keep his ears warm (never mind the indignity, he didn't like his ears being cold), Grimly was squatting in the tartan seats of the silver Triumph. A far cry from Debbie Harry and probably as pleased as she would be to be trapped in a draughty sports car sliding over the icy roads in Sussex. Their destination was Richmond, famous for its view and access to the Park and, incidentally, the town house home of Mr Paul Calon from Cabinet Office, entrenched adviser and seal of influence on a nest of surviving Quangos and liaison between Intelligence and the heads of state. A vital organ, or as Gallant would have it 'Medusa'. Grimly had never thought of Calon as Medusa, but then he himself had rolled a few heads in his time.

"How's Bettina?" Gallant asked, dipping his headlights, changing up to third and pulling out, passing an antique Morris Minor, almost an indigenous creature in Sussex.

"Fine, just fine," Grimly answered, turning the heater full on.

"London must miss her," Gallant said, pushing the car up to eighty miles an hour and slipping into fifth, sweeping through a waist-high bank of fog.

63

"I wouldn't say that," Grimly replied, pointing to the speedometer. "Perhaps Calon would prefer it if we arrived alive, David."

"Sorry," he muttered, easing his foot off the floor, "just want to get back, tired y'know. It's been a long day."

"Of course." Grimly knew all about long days.

THREE

Over the Rainbow

It was later than Slighty thought. Outside he'd observed things as being pretty normal, considering the shock of the night before. It wasn't every night that history was made. The wall coming down like that had sent a tremor through every adult in Berlin. It was difficult, very difficult to conceive of the two sides being accessible. Of course, the BBC had let everyone know very smartly about the laser beams. If the Russians were going to crow, they'd left it too late. A full hour before the official Moscow announcement had been made, the World Service and local afternoon papers had screamed their heads off about the brutal, inhuman, invisible rays, set to fry those foolish enough not to believe it was there.

There was no doubt in Slighty's mind, the people in Berlin were in shock and they were looking to the British and the Americans to sort it out. And not much in the way of concrete advice had come from Her Majesty's Government as yet, that was the worrying part. Typical of the Reds to start all this on a weekend, just typical.

Which brought him around to thinking about his other 'problem': the loss of the Stationhouse and all the men presumed dead. The army was still searching the rubble for bodies. Only one so far. But it had been sudden; logic pointed to them all dying pretty quickly, no suspicion of bodies dragged off into the night. It wasn't that sort of operation. You didn't knock down the whole Berlin wall to get at four men in a run-down listening post. Of course, it would have helped if the British Military Government had been aware of all this happening before hearing it on the news, with their breakfasts in front of them. Not a good image to put out, loss of face all round on that one. Slighty was sensitive to that sort of criticism, him being Chancery Registra, the ugly side, as he called it, political archives. Ultimately, it wasn't his decision, or his place to make judgements. Nevertheless, at 4 am at the beginning of this interminable day, the HQ had been all but empty. There had been no warning and, although Lady Miller had put a good face on it, the fact of the matter was that her husband, the British General Officer of Command, Sir Harold Miller, was not at home. Then, or now. Though the sentries outside had him listed as 'in.'

Julian Nibs, Head of Chancery, had put out a statement, several, in fact. The usual: 'Keep calm, the British MPs and army garrison are on full alert. Please, no panic buying, live life as normal, nothing has really changed.'

What else could he say? And to some extent that was what people were doing, adopting a wait-and-see attitude, but you could sense the suppressed panic and fear in their eyes, almost reach out and touch the sweating walls of a city come down with a fever.

At Checkpoint Charlie, thought to be redundant in the first flush of rubble, security was tightened up and rumours travelled on false documents in both directions.

Slighty, filling in for Blake, the Information Officer who was on leave in Bonn (of all places to go on leave), was answering a worried telegram from a British TV crew, on location at Colditz Castle, concerned that war might break out and they would be the first in the queue of inmates, accidents of a long re-run of history. 'Keep calm,' telegrams had flown in all directions, all day long. It was just a manoeuvre, a game plan in a complex no-win game.

Slighty, a long, steamrollered figure, with little hair to stop the impression he was just a stick of celery, played with a bent spoon in his tea mug. He and Nibs were going to give it until 9 am before raising the alarm. Give Sir Harold time. It was the least they could do. He wouldn't appreciate it if they pushed the panic button. Lady Miller was taking it well. The children were too excited to notice and, with the fuss and excitement outside and on TV, no-one was speculating. Observers and press alike were chasing each other's tails, uncovering resistance movements, already pledged to keep the East Berliners at bay. No-one wanted to share the wealth. A neurotic city or not, they wanted it for themselves.

Just like Sir Harold Miller had wanted Regina Schmidt. A simple love story. The General Officer of Command meets cultural representative and city tour guide Regina Schmidt. She is a curly blonde in a cute way, but wears no make-up, nor needs to, for her Audrey Hepburn looks are enough. She speaks impeccable English, especially for a German girl of twenty-one. She has an amusing laugh and is an immediate centre of attraction wherever she appears. And 'appears' was the key word, for Regina was an East Berliner, a privileged and rare bird, who could live on the East side and laugh on the West. Then what could be more natural than that the GOC Miller, the fourth in a long line of Army Millers, emanating from the soft hills of Hexham-on-Tyne, should fall in love with this girl he'd casually met at the British Trade Exhibition six months before. Even more natural to get this same Regina pregnant, almost immediately after their relationship had begun and, as Slighty noted, recommenced buying lavish gifts for his dear wife, now sadly neglected.

Slighty and Nibs had discussed the matter and had allowed the affair to blossom. After all, it only continued when Regina came over to the British side; and a convert was a convert, if she *was* a convert. Her permit allowed for her to study business methods at the Berlin School of Business Studies. Few ever got this permit and it had since been established that Regina's father, a man with the Electricity Department, would have been in a position to enable such a remarkable permit to exist. Nibs had noticed that the permit was only issued the day after Regina had met the GOC, but then, it was true, her studies had also begun that day and they would hardly issue a study permit to give her a holiday in the contaminated West. True, too, she was most happy to return home each night, seemingly unaffected by the gift of freedom the East Berlin authorities had bestowed upon her. However, she was a good Communist, weren't they all? Sir Harold assured them that politics was never part of their conversation. It was love, love and sex, hardly any talk at all. And Nibs, performing a bit of extra curricular lipsnatching had confirmed this: 'billing and cooing' was all he had on tape.

Slighty believed that it was possible for a British GOC of forty-six to be in love with a twenty-one year-old foreigner. He himself had married a woman eight years *older* than him. A mistake, of course, but she'd left him for another all the same. The affair between Sir Harold and Regina Schmidt was consummated at a little Gasthof in Junger Strasse and, duty bound, either Slighty or Smee, the security man from Camden Town, would stand guard in the reception room drinking coffee and reading *Stern* or *Welt*, or with luck *Oui*, whilst Sir Harold caressed his little beauty upstairs.

All had been well until a week ago. Complications with the pregnancy. She'd been told to rest. The family, her family, were said to be ashamed and hurt. But Regina had insisted upon having the baby and Sir Harold was making plans for Regina and child to live in the West. But now, sick and confined to home, though she wasn't big, hardly noticeable really, not big like most people were at six months, there was a silence.

Sir Harold had decided in his mind to adopt the child. Regina had not been so sure. However, being a career girl, she hadn't discouraged this notion and by all accounts her family thought it a good idea. Until a week ago when her permit had been rescinded.

Sir Harold had written, he'd telephoned regularly but he had not been able to get through to his 'heart of hearts.'

It was he himself who had decided to go in. Go under a pseudonym. Ronald Dorset, air conditioning salesman. He couldn't go as the GOC – GOCs didn't go visiting stray pregnant East German girls. He didn't want this to be picked up and exploited by the East Germans, or, for that matter, the West German press. They had enough scandal to be going on with. Better he just "popped across and sorted things out, take her a bit of money, help her along. Who knows, if there's trouble, smuggle her out in the Diplomatic bag, eh?"

Not much thought there for his wife, who suspected but raised no alarm. Little thought either for the propriety of an air conditioning salesman visiting air conditionless East Berlin in February with temperatures well below zero.

Nibs had helped naturally. Tried to insist Smee should go with him, but Sir Harold had declined. Besides, they only had one false set of documents with Sir Harold's Ronald Dorset picture on it. An emergency possession for use in time of war.

"No need, Nibs, old chap. No problem, quick in and out. Feel a bit of a heel about this, she mustn't think I'd ever let her down. I'm an honourable man, besides I'm in love and there's precious little going on here right now."

And he'd driven over in a hired car, all by himself, the night before. Not a damn word since. Nibs was worried, to say the least. Not just because trouble might have arisen the other side, particularly with that false passport, issued by the Square two years before and questionably still valid, but because only an hour after Sir Harold had donned his business suit and shaved off his moustache, leaving by the side windows, a compact and concise brief landed on their doorstep from the Relatives. Nibs had decoded it immediately, if only to keep his nerves steady and his mind occupied. It read: '*Alert. Tinkabelle possible new activity. Believe problem to be young blonde female, age 21-22, working under name Schmidt. Connection Junger Strasse. End.*'

Unusually tactful for the Relatives and, as usual, too late to be of any use. Nibs was glad it had come to him. If the Stationhouse had got this, the siren would be blaring all the way back to London. The Relatives were trying to let them get out of this one without embarrassment, or some Yank fancied Regina and wanted Sir Harold to drop his hot potato. But then, who would want a six-month pregnant girl?

Both Nibs and Slighty were agreed. It looked as though they were in it up to their necks and Regina was not the convert they were hoping for, far from it. If Tinkabelle was involved, then the worst had already happened.

"But give it until nine," Nibs had said, a confessed optimist, "He'll be back by nine."

* * *

Out in the field, literally out in the field, wedged into the back of a grey anonymous Renault 4 van, Robert Thorn, new recruit to the ways of the Square and recent graduate of Easton and Gib, sat and nervously smoked a 'Gitanes' *filtre*. Hated the things, but the manual said local colour, blend in. His bloody French didn't blend in, never had, that's what comes of going to a second class public school. *HMS Worcester* had been so second class it had gone bankrupt and been towed away for scrap to Belgium. Follow that with three wasted years on the Ellerman Line and you're ready for scrap yourself. He'd hated naval college, still couldn't spit and polish, and was positively allergic to Ajax and Brasso. Second class bloody life. If he hadn't got into gun running to the Provos he'd never have got out of the rut. And he'd been so good at dodging the police pirates on the Irish Sea, the Square had decided he was raw material.

At least Gallant had. A career with prospects and good money, within the law. Just trade in the Irish yobos who are getting the guns. A show of patriotism (after you've taken the money) and second class public school or not, you can sign up for life. Join the first class.

For some reason, perhaps because all he did meet were gangsters and yobos, the offer had seemed attractive. It wasn't often you had a job that could use his ticket. Training him for the Merchant Navy had never made much sense, but the older generation couldn't see the Empire, didn't need British deck officers any more. Might as well have dragged the whole cadet force to scrap in Belgium while they were at it. Training kids

70

to a redundant career had become a special feature of British life. Lucky the Headhunter had turned up when it did, so easy to run to seed and make a mistake on the Irish Sea run. Unreliable, spiteful lot, the Irish. At least the ones so keen to murder kids for a living. Knew about their guns though, knew how to use them with maximum impact. Someone was training them well, somewhere.

Robert cursed the mattress under him. Sitting in the back of a Renault is a hazardous and difficult problem. It is neither long enough, nor wide enough. Nor is it quiet enough. The aircraft passed overhead, so close and at such a steep angle, he was sure that it was possible the noise could flatten steel.

It was damn cold, too. Bitter cold. This despite his arctic underwear and padded jacket. He stubbed his cigarette out on the roof, listening for footsteps. He'd been waiting for these damn footsteps for an hour already, although the man had said 9 pm, not before. He would have liked to have listened to his radio, but a passer-by might hear – if there could be such a creature in a remote scrap heap at the end of a runway of a military air base.

He didn't think much about the man he'd come to see. Gaston Tulle. There was nothing to think. The man needed the 50,000 francs. Who didn't need that kind of money? Besides, it was chicken feed compared to the information he was supposed to receive. There was an element of risk. He, Robert, wouldn't know, or couldn't hope to know what was on the computer printouts and circuit diagrams the man was supposed to be bringing with him. But Gaston had played the game before, given them the details on the Mirage VI engine problems. Useful knowledge when it came to selling the Tornado or Jaguar to those countries who could afford them. Always best to be armed with the real dirt on the opposition, and Gaston Tulle was a real expert on dirt. He was Mr Fix-it at this airbase. It was lucky he had a sick son, someone who needed caring for. Fifty thousand francs now and, if the material was useful, that ear operation for the child done free in London. A good deal, operation like that could ruin a man.

And now the latest Migs were landing in droves at the airbase, only 45 km from Paris. The Russians had flown in two squadrons, on a friendly visit, the very latest designs according to the boys back in London. It wasn't the plane Robert was interested in though, if they wanted that kind of information they could look it up in Jane's. It was the guidance system, the new electronic hardware inside the cockpit. They had to know and soon, for it was obvious something was up. France could even be a no go area, at least to the Square. He couldn't see them turning away the tourists, they liked their prosperity too much to give that up. But if this rumoured Mutual Defence pact wasn't true, as all French Government sources were denying, then why were Migs flying in and Russian battle cruisers moored in Le Havre?

Caught everyone with their pants down that had. Germany and Italy had gone into shock, the mark and lira into a spiral, and the first burst of a refugee problem evident in the airport lounges. But was France really going to relinquish her independence? What did the French people make of this?

He heard the footsteps. The crunch of feet making contact with stray debris and grass frozen to a crisp. A snatch of Beethoven's Fifth whistled twice. All clear.

Robert pushed open the van doors, grabbing the 50,000 francs, glad the man was on time. As his feet reached the ground, the searchlights snapped on, 5000 watts flooded the van. Silently, ten French soldiers aimed their guns at his head. Gaston Tulle stepped out front and spat on the ground, saying, "That's him."

*　　*　　*

The A3 motorway was a blessing. Even though there still was this fog, at least the road was wide and smooth and Grimly could relax a little. Gallant's driving made him very nervous, anyone's driving made him nervous. He hadn't reached seventy-five to die on a foggy night on the A3. Traffic was slow, bumbling along in doubt, drivers in constant fear of each

72

other, confirmed by the hazy silver streak of Gallant's Triumph as he weaved in and out of the wary sheep.

Grimly had been dozing; he awoke with a start, resting his eyes on Gallant's dimly illuminated face. Just a schoolboy really, was he forty yet? Probably not, he still dressed as if he were twenty-five.

"You're awake then," Gallant noticed. "You'll have a few questions, Hugh."

Grimly pursed his lips. Yes, he had a hundred questions, but it wasn't his nature to wheedle. Gallant would have to tell him what this was about soon enough. Instead he tried the personal track. "You're still in work, David. I should have thought you would have been transferred."

"I was. The day you retired, all the Grimly fans were disbursed. The new Stationmaster wanted a clean sweep, his own loyal pall-bearers."

"Steven has never been a trusting soul. That's why I chose him. A man who trusts, well, he'd be fine in the Ministry of Arts, but not at the Square."

"I was sent to Easton first. Spent my first month cementing the swimming pool. Resting me, Stationmaster called it. Eventually we got a batch of graduates in from Bristol and some northern universities. Hopeless bunch. I don't know who recruits these days. Jerry Rattle, I suppose, but my God, he can't tell a fizz from a wet one. Hardly a spark amongst them."

"It was always that way, even at Aden. If I remember, Rattle was far from being a fizz, very quiet and withdrawn. Came from a broken home. Sussex University, I believe."

"Red brick," Gallant said with scorn. "Knew there was something second class and flaky about him. Red brick would fit."

"Easton a success then?" Grimly enquired. "I mean, since Will Strawson's influence has been negated."

"Sixty-five graduated and left for Gib three weeks ago. One abandoned ship for Boots Training College at the other end of the village, some girl he met in Winchester. Eighteen failed,

73

for ideological reasons. Too right wing. It's an odd thing, Hugh. All my life and certainly through yours, universities have spawned the lifeblood of communist loyalists. We all toyed with the pink for a while, even you, Hugh, I'm sure. Now they read Nietzche and Superman comics. The kids want a materialist society, urbanised, marriage, a house, a job. All the things we rejected and they demand them as a right. It's a jungle of hybrid left and right wing theory coming out somewhere on the side of the social security cheque. How do you recruit from people who have Philip Agee for a hero and demand that it's the right of every British citizen to own a foreign car?"

"Come now, David, it isn't all like that. Sixty-five graduates is a good number. I've known years when we've had less, far less."

"I just wish I could believe they were doing it for their country and not the high salary, and hopes of two years of graft at Little Sai Wan in Hong Kong.

Grimly pulled his coat closer to him. When he'd started at the Square there was virtually no salary at all. Expenses yes, but loyalty and patriotism were quite enough for the Mandarins then.

"What are you now, David?" He was pleased to see a sign announcing Richmond only five miles distant.

"Headhunters - Wandsworth."

Grimly nodded thoughtfully. Nasty lot, Headhunters. Loners thrown together, linked by a common ally, the gun or knife. They were the cloak and dagger boys, who finished off work too difficult and messy for the cocktail circuit. Intelligence work with the subtlety of a jackhammer. But it was necessary sometimes to fight fire with fire. Gallant was a good choice. The defectors and opportunistic ballet dancers would fall readily into Gallant's hands. Someone who was as strong as the people they were used to. There had been a time, in the feckless sixties when it was considered polite to send along a wishy washy liberal, when the punters were told that they

74

should think it over, consider their family and friends. This resulted only in the defectors perceiving the weakness and indifference of the West and discouraged many; killed more than a few, caught between a hollow salvation and a blocked return. Will Strawson again. 'Caution policy – let them stew for a while.' Stew whilst he made sure Moscow Cephal was in the know and nobbled the pleading dissident. Of course, Will Strawson had hated ballet dancers, he had been jilted more than once in the back alleys of Covent Garden.

"What would Plateau policy mean to you?" Gallant asked, taking the Richmond turn off.

"Nothing, should it?"

"It's the Square currency now. We used to sit at the cross-roads and send out signals four ways. Your policy. Now we sit on a Plateau and overview."

"That is our policy?"

"It began when Stationmaster took over. He wanted more in-house control, less autonomy in the field. Less captains, more soldiers. He cut down the Stationhouses by almost half and improved our telecommunications by linking up with Lipsnatchers full-time."

"Ah, Simon Caw, a good man."

"So Lipsnatchers have sunk their teeth into the Square. We now have this satellite link with all the Stationhouses – the Plateau."

"So the outfield stations are merely post boxes and exhange?"

"The power is back in London. Stationmaster wanted to give ourselves more strength against the Relatives."

"The Relatives are our enemy now? Things *have* changed."

"No, but the rivalry is back, or was until today."

"Ah yes, today. I heard about Berlin. It did cross my mind that you might contact me."

Richmond Hill, twisting through the wooded vale at its base. The fog had lifted here, just the frost remained, fastened to the ground in mysterious white streaks. A half moon made an appearance in the star-filled sky. Grimly liked a clear night. There had been precious few when he'd been a boy. London was altogether a better, cleaner city now.

Gallant remembered his important news. "The Stationmaster has disappeared. Completely vanished, taken A through DQ files with him."

Grimly didn't say anything as Gallant filled in the rest of the details. He knew why he'd been sent for and he could see he'd need more than a toothbrush.

They were ushered in by Calon's plain wife, Maggie. She seemed harassed and didn't offer them much of a smile, nor offer any hospitality.

"They had to return from Devon. Calon had taken the weekend off," Gallant whispered, mitigating the hostility.

"Oh," Grimly nodded, taking off his coat and hanging a dour expression on his face. They hadn't thought of his weekend, only Calon's.

The house was a mess. Bought for something over £100,000, a bargain for Richmond Gate and a rambling four-storey affair, filled with accumulated junk of long gone teenage children.

Grimly and Gallant were ushered into the study, Grimly's head filled with disbelief at all the information Gallant had just poured in. Tinkabelle alive, he couldn't believe it. The study was the same as always, the usual Oxford, St Anthony rugby boot nailed to the wall, inscribed with dents and bruises delivered by the Welsh thugs Calon had befriended there. Not an item had changed in this room since the early fifties. A sign that Calon was getting old too. His youngest child must be all of twenty-five already, the eldest thirty-six at least. An imitation gas log fire burnt in the grate, the metal logs spurning the blue yellow flames.

Calon stumbled in, cross, no civility on his face, or welcoming smile. He wasn't going to forgive the loss of his Devon trip easily, nor let East Berlin or the Stationmaster forget it.

"Hello, Hugh," he snapped, "this is a cock-up, what? Bet

you've been glad to be out of this business, eh? Times I wish I was."

Calon was an owlish figure of a man. No longer as bulky as in his youth. His eyes were too far apart and his fierce eyebrows constantly moved about his face as he talked. His strong jaw line reflected his father's Presbyterian background, and his mother's line, something obscure in midland textiles, provided the wealth for his two fair-skinned daughters early and disasterous marriages.

He occasionally made the society page in *Harpers*, but more often than not the hate list in the *Times* letters column or veiled daggers in *Private Eye*. Calon just enjoyed the intolerance of Government and played the game close to the wind.

"The country is less tolerable at this time of year," Grimly offered, to soothe the way.

Calon was not to be dug out of his sulk. "But Jenny is getting married," he explained.

"I thought Jenny was married already?" Gallant protested, adjusting the cushions of his ricketty chair.

"Her second marriage. I promised to go. Would be there now if the police hadn't had a manhunt going to track us down. We'd got as far as Salisbury."

"A pity then," Grimly said, sitting back in his chair, in desperate need of refreshment, but too polite to ask.

"And your mother, Hugh? How is Bettina? Still taking Sussex by storm?"

Grimly resented this continued interest in his mother. "Better than could be expected," he replied, which he realised could mean anything. But Calon was watching the door, not listening to anyone. It was obvious a fourth man was expected.

"Berlin a mess. Hard to believe it really," Calon said at last. "Gallant fill you in on that?"

"A little, luckily I listen to the World Service. The wall coming down is certainly a propaganda coup for Moscow, whatever the alleged laser beams might do. I hear we are paralysed?"

"I'll say we are paralysed. Only it's not the wall, Hugh. It's Sir Harold Miller. He's defected. Our General Officer of Command has defected to East Berlin. Our Ambassador that side hasn't heard a word and he's worried for their own safety."

This was certainly as big a surprise to Gallant as Grimly.

"It's hard to believe. We were at the same school," Calon complained. "He was after me, of course, but a Harrow man changing sides – quite a shock. The clubs will be ablaze with talk tonight. They say your friend Tinkabelle is behind it."

"My friend?" Grimly asked.

"Well, you met him once, Hugh. You're the only one who has, and you have been enemies forever, haven't you? Of course, you did say he was dead."

Grimly had indeed declared him dead, though there were never any witnesses. Damn Will Strawson. His irrefutable evidence – Tinkabelle's mother in mourning, the rise of Rocov. Certainly, the style of the 'walk' had changed, a certain ham fisted approach had developed, not so devious as before. A new hand was directing Moscow Cephal and Tinkabelle had gone to ground. It seemed right at the time to pronounce him dead.

"You have proof Tinkabelle is alive?" Grimly demanded to know.

Gallant crossed his legs. "The Relatives would have us believe it's so."

Grimly nodded, staring down at his winter shoes, a forlorn expression on his face. "So that's the reason I'm remembered. You think the Stationmaster has taken to the hills."

"Well partly, Hugh. We just hope the hills he's taken to are our hills. We are waiting for another visitor, however. Perhaps he might shed some light on this for us," Calon sighed, then, "I suppose you want coffee?"

"Not if it's your chicory blend," Grimly said plainly.

"Now, Hugh, don't get uppity. Economy cuts have to be made somewhere. You can always have tea, or would you prefer Scotch?"

78

Grimly was not a drinking man. Not like Gallant or Calon. But really he could not endure Maggie's tea or coffee. He was tempted to do without everything, but it had been a long drive and if Tinkabelle was alive, then he needed something stronger. If only to exhume his own ghost still back at Brinkwells digging the garden.

"A whisky and soda I think, no ice. Thank you," he said at length.

Calon was pleased to be doing something he liked for a change. Drinking whisky was a simple pleasure, but an honourable one in his book. However, nothing would compensate for Devon. Nothing.

The sound of Bruckner's Fifth filtered through the study walls. No doubt Maggie's way of displaying her annoyance of a second marriage missed. As a childless, wifeless man, Grimly had no understandings of these emotions. He cared more for the worries of a Europe long past or T.S. Eliot. The past couldn't annoy or disturb you. It was there, fixed, immovable and a constant wonder to him. Children a mere whim on the breath of time.

The drinks had hardly reached their lips when two pairs of footsteps were heard clattering on the maple wood hallway floor. Grimly noted one pair of shoes had a metal wedge heel – not a man who lived by stealth then. The door opened and both men walked in. A tall, slightly stooped, thin man preceded the stocky, almost skinhead Nolan. Matron delivering the baby.

Nolan nodded at everyone, particularly at Grimly with whom he allowed himself the briefest tic of a smile. "Mr Grimly, sir."

"Lock the door, Nolan. Help yourself to a coffee or something, but watch the corridor," Calon instructed. He didn't need to, of course. Nolan knew his job. Security was his life. "And ask my wife to play Bruckner with a little less vigour."

"Sir," Nolan responded, closing the door after him.

"You all know Welland?" Calon asked, once the door was locked.

The new arrival took the only seat available, centre stage. "I know Mr Grimly well enough," he said in a familiar tone. His voice was gentle, the base was Suffolk with Cambridge laid thinly over the top. "Welland, sir. John Welland, the Butcher's Boy."

The gas fire flared momentarily, glinting in the new arrival's tinted glasses. His spectre-like pallor and toothbrush moustache, with that thick mop of grey-streaked hair falling in a fringe on his brow, made him look like a masquerading schoolboy. The creased light blue suit and curled up collar of his off-white shirt, suggested a long, uncomfortable journey, to anyone that is who didn't know that the Butcher's Boy always looked like that. He had the air of a bachelor, but it was a reluctant status, his wife had ploughed other fields a long time ago.

"Mr Grimly was my champion, weren't you, sir? If it hadn't been for him, I'd be at the Ministry of Defence pushing piles of paper around, or at the Courtauld discussing the merits of Ruskin Spear against David Hockney. Always had an eye for the Gallery life, still do."

Welland put out his hand to Grimly. They shook with surprising warmth, but then it was true, Grimly had sponsored Welland into the Square. And now he knew that there must be something worse than the GOC going over to the other side, far worse.

For wherever Welland went, trouble was guaranteed. Even when they sent him to Guernsey to bring back a gift from a Pole, riots had broken out all across the island over property rights. He was a positive magnet for trouble. They had asked him to leave New York. He was too good, too efficient, caused too much trouble with other members in the Square not as effective as Welland. He'd turned a Hungarian once. Had him working for the Square, a high ranking politician, well liked in Moscow. Proved invaluable in defence matters, until Will Strawson had found out. Slight and unloved the Butcher's Boy may be, but he had an eight-year track record of success, despite Will Strawson, and that made his voice, his opinion, valuable.

The telephone buzzed twice. Calon angrily snatched it up. He listened a moment, then shrugging, snapped a "No" down the line and an "If I see him", before banging the handset down.

"Simon bloody Caw. Looking for the Butcher's Boy. You're in strong demand, Welland. Now, tell us what is on your mind and tell it quickly, before the last restaurant closes in this God-forsaken town."

"You'll have read my report on Malta. The Russians coming in there was quite a surprise. Well, not a surprise, just unexpected so early on in the game."

"The game?" Grimly asked, sipping at his whisky, trying to make it last.

"The Berlin–Paris–Madrid axis. The grand sweep."

Grimly thought this a joke and attempted a weak smile.

Calon noticed, so did Gallant who explained, "It's true, Hugh. First we heard about the Malta problem. Later, in quick succession, Berlin, the Paris–Moscow Pact, then this afternoon, rumours began on a pact with Madrid too. They caught us on the hop, nothing official as yet, but it looks real enough to us."

"The PM and the US President are understandably in quite a tizz," Calon added. "There's talk of enforced resignations, mine as well as Sir Charles."

"But it's all so much at once," Grimly complained, holding a hand to his head. "Stationmaster, the GOC, a sweep across Europe . . ."

"Not to mention the Israeli–South African nuclear test," Gallant reminded him.

"Tell me this is a jest, Calon," Grimly implored him.

Calon shook his head and Gallant leant forward to say, " 'Fraid not, Chief. I haven't told you the bad news yet."

"The bad news?" Grimly felt the tiredness coming on, yet he wasn't due his injection for hours yet.

"I think John can explain better than we can," Calon said, offering Welland a drink, and receiving a negative answer. Instead he lit up a Rothman's and blew two self-indulgent rings into the stifled air. He began with his eyes closed.

"The Soviets aren't expecting any trouble this end."

"No?" Grimly queried. If he'd been a betting man, he'd have staked the family money on the sabre's being rattled at least.

"This whole move has been planned quite carefully and it's all above board. Mutual defence pacts are not unusual. Nor is a trade pact. After all, we do sell butter and shoes to the Soviets. The Italians design their cars. It isn't as if we just ignored the East, Olympics or no. They've played a smart game and one of the causes originated here. The Stationmaster issued a brief, almost a year ago, in the event of a Republican win in the '80 elections. That brief had been read by everyone in Moscow Cephal before it left the fifth floor here in London."

"You are saying something there," Grimly interrupted.

"Wait, Hugh," Calon advised.

"Anyway," Welland went on. "Stationmaster had decided, and quite rightly in my opinion, that there was going to be a radical shift in alignment in the early 1980's, with the Hawks in power – America in a state of panic about inflation at 24% and building up its war machine, the nearer we are going to come to war. Tanks and bombs are built to be used after all, they aren't toys, though sometimes certain generals think they are. Quite naturally, Western Europe would be involved, not only involved, but most likely the theatre of war. That's the official Gib view anyway.

"Only the British government, with respect to you, Calon, wants that to happen. Only our puppets in Whitehall jump when the US says jump. After all, they are our Relatives. So I was in Malta. Was ours once, remember, Mr Grimly? You used to holiday there, didn't you?"

Grimly remembered. Indeed it was 'ours' at one time. Dom Mintoff remembered that too, but less fondly.

"I'd been ordered there by Stationmaster. He doesn't like

me. Still calls me the Butcher's Boy, but I don't mind. Malta is a nicer hole than most and I speak a good mix of Spanish and Maltese. Of course, Stationmaster was just trying to bury me in the least significant place he could think of. Anquilla was already full of pensioned off agents. But you know Welland, a nose for it, you know that, Mr Grimly. I've always had a nose for trouble."

Grimly didn't say anything.

"It was Nina who tripped the wire for me. I met her at the disco."

Calon snorted his disgust, but Welland ignored him.

"One has to do something. It isn't exactly a hive of cultural activity there. Nina is a schoolteacher. At the school for foreign residents. It used to be an English prep school, the one on Lumely's Hill, cramped white building, well I suppose all the buildings are white. Anyway, she's a hot little number, and I'm paid to look for disaffected Soviet citizens. Mr Gallant knows that, of course we are supposed to look for generals or visiting trade delegates, but a genuine twenty-four year-old, brown-eyed beauty from Georgia is much more fun than generals and this one had no prejudices against the English. (She is a fan of the Police, it's a rock group.) She seemed happy to accept that I was a part-time journalist and full-time artist. It was the other way around, but the journalist cover stinks. As an abstract modernist, no-one can tell you if it's good or bad, and if I may say so, my series on 'Malta at night' is considered to be at the forefront of Maltese avant-garde. My articles in *Now!* magazine are considered plausible, but there hasn't been much to say about Malta recently.

"To the point, John," Calon instructed wearily.

"At Nina's school she's got the Ambassador's son, the Chargé d'Affaire's daughter and various cultural stroke KGB officers' kids. Neat little outfit, a small school, some Czech children there too. Fifty in all. Nina gets quite a lot of freedom considering; at weekends it's not unusual for her to spend the nights at my place overlooking the docks."

"Unusual freedom?" Gallant remarked.

"Not for Malta. She can't leave the island. She's a nobody, a schoolteacher. Not vital, not Embassy, has an apartment she shares with another Soviet girl. She has a local boyfriend. He's learning Russian, so that's all right. Good girls, reliable girls who love their Motherland. Miss it sometimes, too.

"It was only after a month and a bit that I managed to get her to speak to me about the school and the kids. After a little while I was so keen on the place as a source of information that I was becoming involved on an active level. My reports from November last will confirm that."

Gallant made a note to check on that report.

"I picked up most of what I know from the kids, via Nina, it's all in the report, the new one. They knew about the coming changes, no doubt about it. Anyway, we were on familiar terms, OK? Then one night, the other night, she suddenly arrived unexpectedly. She was upset, crying and scared. She wanted me to hold her tight, she was definitely scared. I'd been writing up the report on how I thought the movement of Soviet personnel was running too high. That kids were telling my Nina that they were moving to places like Rouen, Madrid, Barcelona, strange addresses, for it's OK if one Ambassador moves on, but all these children had been telling Nina that within a week they were leaving Malta. Destinations spread right across France and Spain. Nina had talked to me about it, she couldn't understand it. New children were expected, but only five, hardly enough to keep the school going, or Nina in employment. She was afraid they would send her home."

"You said she missed her home," Calon said.

"She is in love with me," Welland pointed out, then more modestly, "at least I like to think she is. She cares about me. It's best that way, it makes everything more convincing. The Embassy knows about it, but then they should. Comrade Berdenikov bought two of my paintings. My cover is good. They flatter me. I'm a residue of the old colonial oppressors, they can play with me as they wish."

"They never ran a check on you?" Gallant asked.

"Of course, but as Mr Grimly knows, my paintings have

appeared in New York and Johannesburg. If they checked out Henry Betand, my workname, they would find I'd exhibited my work for the last ten years. One day I might even become famous and you'll all wish you had bought my paintings whilst they were still cheap."

"His cover is good," Calon remarked. "Even Strawson didn't know he was the Butcher's Boy. Go on, John."

"Well, I was compiling this report, which didn't leave for London until the Soviet ships arrived in Malta I'm afraid. I was caught off guard. It was marked for Stationmaster's eyes only. Went by courier. This was the morning after Nina had come to me in tears."

Calon made a note to check that the report had arrived.

"Nina was beside herself. She, er . . . " He looked up, bashful all of a sudden, his nicotine-stained fingers straying through his hair. "She wanted to make love, immediately. She wanted to talk too. We went to my bed and she was acting like this was the last time. I've been through this sort of thing before. They tell you they are going to get married to the boy next door, or in her case fly back to Moscow.

"But it wasn't like that, she was upset, not because she was leaving, she wasn't. I was!" Welland paused for effect. Then since no one commented, he drew on his cigarette a moment.

"All the English diplomats and press, plus the Germans, Dutch or Belgians, were to be given twenty-four hours notice to leave. I didn't believe her. Well, it seemed unlikely. She was annoyed I didn't believe her and then, in tears again, she told me that she'd been a liar, but she loved me and would I still love her if I found her to be a liar? Well, the upshot is, I said I did love her and I'm sure if she lied, it was to protect herself. I insisted I loved her. At which point she cried again and hid herself under the bedclothes until she'd stopped. Then she told me, flat out, that she was the daughter of General Vladimir Zybira and that he'd placed her in this teacher's job because he wanted her safe, away from home, before the trouble began. She begged me never to tell anyone any of the things she was going to tell me. But it was only because she loved me and

85

trusted me that she had to tell me this. I was to promise that I wouldn't forget her and to meet her again in four months when everything would be over. She would write to all my addresses to tell me when it was safe to meet again. I promised and intend to keep the promise."

"But what did she tell you?" Calon asked, aware that Zybira was a known name in his memory.

Grimly had registered a granite-like expression. It must have been the sudden mention of the name Zybira that had him fixed in his chair, the heavy lids narrowed to almost a slit, his eyes firmly directed onto the bowed figure of Welland, who was slumped in his seat, trying hard to remember the precise details of this night with Nina.

Gallant studied his former chief and experienced a momentary concern, wondering if it was fair to bring back Grimly, press-gang him back into the Service at his age. But after all, was not Winston Churchill practically senile when he lead the last Tory Government into office? And Grimly had never displayed any signs of senility, never had any moment of memory loss, all the more remarkable. Gallant returned his attention to Welland.

"Zybira, I have since learnt was based here in London in '62, as 'technical staff'. Then in '66, after two years in Moscow, he was in Washington, unofficially as a GRU, their Military Intelligence, officially as 'technical adviser' on a joint communications programme until '69. According to Archives, he was then demoted and sent home to his native Georgia. There is no record of him having ever been with Moscow Cephal, no record of him at all since '69, which is strange. I'll have to speak to Doc Sludge about that. Incidentally, Nina was with him on all these trips. Her mother was classified as Interpreter. Altogether an unusual arrangement, but points to their reliability as Soviet citizens that they were allowed to travel intact.

"Nina was very keen to tell me what was going to happen, not only because she wanted me to be safe, but also because she had an idea that I could write an article for my magazine

86

stating that there would be no war, and people mustn't be fooled into thinking there might be. Russia doesn't want war, just peace."

"But that's what they always say. 'We want peace, even if we have to kill everyone to get it.' Now, don't you think this is an odd thing for a schoolteacher to plead. How would she know what only the Politburo can decide, even if her father is a general?" Calon queried, pouring himself another drink, but not offering.

"Nina is sincere. I mean very serious, very. She can laugh with her children, but in reality, she is straightforward and honest. She told me that her father had written to her that morning and told her to stay on the island. They have a code language between them, to guarantee that his mail isn't understood when read by Moscow combers."

"Combers?" Calon asked.

"Mail scanners. They read all outgoing mail looking for key words and insidious material. His code apparently is one they worked out when Nina was a child. Things like, 'I have been sailing,' means 'Come home, all is well.' That's the message she's been waiting for. Anyway, she was told to offer her services to the local Malta High School as a Political Science teacher within twenty-four hours of receiving the letter. She would be accepted and he would contact her again when time permitted. I thought it a strange thing to do, but in the light of subsequent events, it was a good ploy on behalf of her father. By doing this, she would prove her worth to the people back in Moscow, earn herself a little red star. Very smart of her to realise that with Malta becoming, to all intents and purposes, an occupied zone, there would be a need for indoctrination teachers to smooth the way with the local populace.

"But it's the background to all this that is so fascinating. Her father is very active in the south in the Georgian states and, as you know, the rioting there this winter has been very fierce. American satellites picked up amazing pictures of towns on fire and extensive troop movements. Moscow denies it, and insists those photos were of Afghanistan and Pakistan where rioting *is* going on. Her father, Zybira, is apparently Head of Intelligence operating out of Kutaisi City. According to him, and I'm not going to argue at this point, the South is very close to breaking away from the Soviet Union to form an independent socialist republic, on the lines of Jugoslavia. The feeling is that it has to come very soon, because when it does, civil war will break out and the army in the South-East, based in the main with a very high local content, both Slavic and Asian and with a reluctance to accept the direction from Moscow, a European city in their eyes. Couple this discontent and a prolonged and almost deliberate programme of disinvestment in the area, keeping it poor and reliant upon farming and supplying soldiers to the army as its main income, and Moscow has created its own problem. With the dominance of Moscow much in mind, it has come to light that the South now feels the struggle to be worth it. Not only for racial reasons, but also because they had recently discovered large oil deposits in the South-Western area. An economic incentive to rebel. Asians outnumber blue eyes by ten to one, or more. A classic oppressed majority, i.e. a case for struggle against Imperialist forces, a revolution."

"So," Calon said sharply, "you portray a Russia on the verge of civil war. Yet what we see is a strong united country linking up with our former allies to form a wall right along the whole length of the Mediterranean, pincering Germany and Italy between them, making the defence of Europe by NATO a non-starter. The American and British military presence is redundant. If war broke out they would be surrounded and obliterated in minutes, not hours."

"That's just it, Calon. The revolt in Georgia is directly related to this move West. Moscow has to move now, forge working partners and checkmate the US and ourselves, because it *is* going into a civil war. When that happens and if they hadn't made this pre-emptive move, they would be perceived as being weak, vulnerable. Their satellite countries could be encouraged by the US to rebel. Jugoslavia and Hungary, Czechoslovakia, even Poland, would and could see the internal revolt as a heaven sent opportunity to break free. Especially as Soviet-occupying armies would be diverted to the South. Moscow is petrified that this new US hawk Presidency would exploit this weakness and, accordingly, she moved West and took us all by surprise. It's an incredible and fantastic plan. The wall coming down was part of the French President's deal. He wanted to see some demonstrable fact of Moscow's willingness to soften its line, prove it can live at peace. The wall was the icing on the cake.

"Moscow has been talking to France and Spain and, of course, Malta, telling them that it is not the USSR who is the enemy, it is just that they are made to look like bad bears because America wants them to look like bad bears. The burden of maintaining such large armies, the cause of much sacrifice for the glorious Russian people, is directly related to US aggression as demonstrated in Tabas in April 1980. Better still, they can point to the new President's conscription law, proof that America is on a war footing."

"Well, let's hope he can put up a better performance than the last crowd. Iran is a positive embarrassment. We should have let them have the SAS on a lend lease scheme," said Calon.

"I wouldn't suggest it, sir," Gallant said. "Pretty sensitive area."

Welland continued. "So Russia says to its new friends: Tell you what, we guarantee to cut our front line armies in half. Half. If you France, you Spain and Malta join us in a Trade Pact stroke invisible ink defence pact. Not to make war, but to disarm! Disarm? Can we be hearing right, you say. Yes, incredibly, yes. But what about France's thriving war industry? Russia says fine, export it to the Third World, they need protection from the American Imperialists as much as you do. So that's one hurdle over. A Moscow–France–Madrid link up actually prevents the US and UK from using Europe as a threatre of war. The Germans have also been approached, but they are under strong American dominance and they are just as happy to see France, always the loner, always the loser, take the bite of Moscow's apple. Either way, peace is **guaranteed,**

89

the front line is now the UK and we can't count on the Low Countries and Sweden is neutral. The sweetener for Germany is the wall coming down and, when the Americans have been removed, reunification of the Germanies. It is a genuine possibility."

"All this because of rioting in Georgia?" Gallant protested. "It's ridiculous. Our policy doesn't read that way, it's not in the Easton manual."

"Nor is the notion of a Second Eleven, but I'm telling you that the Square and the FO have been infiltrated, that General Philby's little seedlings have sprouted forth and multiplied. Those parties are even now advising appeasement with Moscow and a pull out of Berlin and the Rhine. And what is more, their ideas are falling on receptive ears. After all, economy cuts are the norm, are they not? Calon knows, I hear he's put a cat amongst the pigeons."

Calon blushed. He hadn't realised that his economy cuts would have been announced yet. But that was a different battle and he wouldn't be sidetracked. "Don't you tell me I'm a Second Elevener, Welland. Economy cuts are absolutely necessary. Waste in government has to stop. If you want to find a double *agent*, look for the man who is expanding his departments, there's a sure way to unbalancing our economy. And as for NATO, Welland, never, never, ever, will the Prime Minister give up on that. The Cabinet as a whole are committed to maintaining a role, a leading role, I might add."

"What use a role, Calon, if the play has finished and the curtains down?"

"Welland, I must seriously disagree with you. I think your brain has been curdled by that Russian girl. Hugh," he turned to Grimly, "Hugh, what do you make of all this?"

All eyes turned to Grimly. Calon shook his head in despair.

"Oh wake him up, Gallant. Hugh, Hugh!" he shouted, "Oh really," he added, irritated. "Fill him in on all the details, Gallant, and then let's go and get something to eat. I suppose whilst we've been talking the Russians haven't taken over all the restaurants in Richmond. I care very little for fish and rice, or any other of their indigestible food." Calon shook his head, tossing off the remainder of his drink.

"Really, Welland. I can't accept your theory. The girl was telling you stories. She is twenty-four, they like to sound dramatic at twenty-four. It's quite preposterous, and as for the Second Eleven theory, neither myself, nor Sir Charles subscribe to it. I cannot accept there is a man left in the Service who reads anything stronger than the *New Statesman*. We are sound." He cast another glance at Grimly. "Wake up, Hugh, it's din-dins. Give him another drop of whisky, Gallant. I'm going to wash my hands. Open the door, Nolan."

As Calon left the room, Gallant nudged Grimly awake. Welland poured two glasses of the Dewars, handing one to Gallant for Grimly, then suddenly remembering, "I forgot to mention the split in the Kremlin."

As Grimly blinked his eyes and slowly came alive, Gallant turned to Welland and sarcastically asked, "I don't suppose you have a list of names with you, Welland? It would make it so much easier for the Russians to have given you a list of names, such as the Foreign Minister, or Chancellor of the Exchequer, people they want out of the way, so they can strike a deal for 'Peace in our time'."

"No, no list," Welland replied quietly, aware of the sarcasm, "But I suppose we could start with Sir Harold Miller."

Grimly swallowed his whisky and let it burn its way through to his subconcious before opening his eyes. The first thing he noticed was that Calon was not in the room. He wondered how that could happen, he'd only just blinked his eyes for a second.

"What did Nina say?" he asked wearily.

"Dinner, Hugh," Gallant informed him. "Our friend, the Butcher's Boy has been dallying with a daughter of a friend of yours. General Zybira."

"Vladimir," Grimly bounced back. "An ambitious man. A very ambitious man. GRU earlier on, but Tinkabelle had him in tow. He was always destined for high rank, but he fell out of favour in '69. I hadn't expected to hear his name again."

"Welland says that he is the cause of all our troubles. Personally I think your Nina has been slipping him a few indoctrination tapes in his sleep. You wouldn't have your card on you, would you, Welland?"

"My card?"

"Your Party card."

Grimly stood up, uncertainly wobbling on his feet, noticing the unpleasant tone of Gallant's voice. "John can be trusted. He'll report what he hears. Tell me more about the Second Eleven, John. What did Nina say about them?"

Welland started up a new cigarette.

"It was a child. One of Nina's troublemakers. I came to the school to show paintings and help with the art class. Every Friday. It was the school head who asked me. I speak no Russian, the children no English, they are safe from contamination. I encourage them to draw pictures of soldiers and tanks, the kids are very patriotic and from their drawings I extract information. I ask every child to draw their fathers, making a drawing of their Daddies' office, or other seemingly mundane things. One child, the naughty one, Karl, was good. We seemed to understand each other, he's twelve or so. He told Nina that the English were all stupid, that his Daddy had an English friend. He'd met him at the yacht club. (The bourgeois Russians sail dinghies now.) Karl used to make little jokes about cricket. Not his jokes, his father's friends' jokes. The Second Eleven touring Norway in winter, odd little things like that. He'd mimic too, trying to say it in English. I thought nothing of it, except to think it odd a British cricket team would tour Norway at all, winter or summer. Then a week ago, I met Kevin Currie, our Relative from Atlanta. We were both at the yacht club, Nina with me, and suddenly Nina was waving. It was young Karl out sailing with an older man with white hair. 'Is that his father?' I asked. Kevin chips in straight away with, 'That's Colin Fielding, one of yours.' "

Grimly started. "Colin – the rat – Fielding?"

Welland nodded. "Foreign Office Med. Affairs. Apparently he has an apartment in Malta."

"Works with Sir Charles," Gallant pointed out.

"And he went to Oslo for a Security Conference in January."

Grimly felt a familiar chill course through his body. He left the room to collect his coat.

Welland pursued. "It was Keven Currie who mentioned cricket. He joked about it. Said that Fielding had never been run out."

"An American who knows his cricket?" Gallant asked, shutting the study door after him.

"We still play cricket on the island, there's so little else to do. Kevin plays soccer, too."

"It's pizza," Calon announced from the far side of the house. "It's all that's left open, I'm afraid."

"Where's Colin Fielding now?" Grimly asked in a curious tone.

Blank faces drew all round.

"Beats me," Calon said, joining them with his wife in tow. "Why, who wants him?"

"We should find out," Grimly muttered, asking, "Anyone know why he is called the rat?"

No-one did.

"If there is a war, Calon, do your family textile business a bit of good, won't it? Nothing like a few army uniforms to boost the midlands economy," Welland ribbed with a smile.

"I still don't accept what you say, Welland. I thought France was trying to bury the left. They aren't in any position of power, why encourage them at this moment?"

"Cutting from under, a masterstroke. A real De Gaulle move," Gallant offered. "In one move the Gaullists have taken control of the left, swallowed it whole. The opposition will disappear. Moscow never liked them anyway."

"Correct," Welland agreed. "Moscow has guaranteed the wily French President life-presidency. Who would dare oppose him and Moscow?"

"If it's a smart move, it's a damn dangerous one," Calon stated.

"And if that is so, how do we change his mind?" Grimly asked, "especially with a Second Eleven anticipating our every move."

"That's up to you, Hugh. You've no choice, y'know, you have to come back to the Square. No choice at all," Calon insisted.

FOUR

The Invisible Man

He'd lain in his bed – his empty bed – for most of the night. But unlike the other fifty-five million souls at rest in the United Kingdom, sleep formed no part of his night of agony. Peter Hallam had twisted and fretted, smashed his favourite 17th century porcelain figure of a shepherdess, in a fit of rage, and a familiar knot of pain had developed in his abdomen, a pain forgotten in the last three years. He had tried to write, to occupy his mind. He had drunk a full bottle of French wine and not cared whether it was indifferent or optimistically labelled; for a man who normally cared a great deal for the excellence of wine, he cared for nothing without his Wendy. He had spent such a night of remorse and torture, he was sure it more than equalled anything young Wendy had been through.

How he missed that child. And who was this Captain Crewk? Wendy, Wendy. His life had gone, they had taken her and his life.

He'd risen at seven and, as he wandered from room to room, Wendy's presence seemed to be everywhere. Her records, her posters of rock groups plastered all over the walls. Downstairs her clothes, cleaned and ironed by the housekeeper, lay in a neat pile for Wendy to take to her room. There was a note to him on the calendar: 'Dentist. Wed 4th March. You 11 am me 11.30 am'; and another: '11th March. My birthday. DON'T FORGET THIS YEAR.'

This year he wouldn't forget. He'd never forget a single day of her life with him. She was an imp, she was his angel.

Everyone adored her. Next door were always having her over to tea. Their idiot son had a crush on her. Him fifteen and in love with the girl next door and she despising 'boys'. She didn't like boys. Boys couldn't spoil her, couldn't buy her presents, take her to fancy restaurants or on trips to Hong Kong. Hallam knew her love was bought and paid for, he knew the day would come when the price would be too high, when 'boys' would suddenly mean a lot more to her. Unwillingly, he knew that.

If she was to live. It was in his woeful and distressing realm of knowledge that one in three kidnaps resulted in death for the victim. But he did not want to think about that. Captain Crewk, just what was it about that name? What sort of name was Crewk anyway? Welsh? Czech? He made a note to ask Dr Sludgeon at the Square.

Hallam had made enquiries, discreet probes. He'd checked with the school. "No, no strangers lurking about recently. Yes, they hadn't seen George the driver and yes, he wasn't at home." Neither his neighbours nor housekeeper had noticed anything unusual. A car had collected her as usual, nothing amiss. "Is Wendy sick?" they asked, "is that why she isn't down?"

It was all so completely out of the blue. He suspected the Czechs, but then he always suspected them. But why would they want her back? Not after three years. Not when Wendy's parents had been so tragically killed. She has suffered enough, let the child be.

He thought back to the early years, when he found himself drawn to Sylvia, as she was known then. The Kostavitzs had been in London when she was born, and even then events in Prague were pulling them together, so that by the time Sylvia was three, she knew Hallam well. It seemed strange to outsiders and certainly more than once was brought up in Square inner circles at that time. Fate or deliberate policy, events and slow promotion on either side, meant that whether in London, or Prague, or Washington, as long as Hallam dealt with Czech affairs, he would be dealing with Stephen Kostavitz and, throughout young Sylvia's life, she came into contact with him. It wasn't entirely accepted that Hallam should like the Kostavitzs, and it would have been probable that he would not have been so friendly with them had there been no Sylvia. He had no liking for her younger brother. It was in Washington that their friendship had blossomed into a full, genuine affair, even though it was now known the Kostavitzs were Moscow Cephal runners. The Square back in London didn't object. Will Strawson liked the idea of an open field of contact and he knew, as no-one else knew, that Hallam was not a mole, or the source of leaks, except the ones they wanted to leak.

Hallam would spring embarrassments on the Czechs, and they in return would send him a barbed tennis ball. It was a game they both played well, their social life outside the cock-tail circuit was their own. Unusual, but useful, and therefore encouraged by both London and Moscow. 'Bridges,' said the Easton manual, 'must be kept open at all times.'

But when Sylvia had fallen ill, so sick they thought she would die and orders had been given to fly her back to Prague, even though they knew it would kill her to do so, that was when Uncle Peter, already Sylvia's favourite and almost a godfather, came forward with the herbalist, Dr Paynter. Washington doctors had said it was impossible, there was nothing they could do. Blood disease, complicated and rare, made worse by respiratory troubles and a lung infection. No idea how she came to develop the problems, but adamant that she was incurable. The Kostavitzs were frantic and willing to try anything. Uncle Peter had performed his rescue mission. He drove all the way to New York with Sylvia swaddled in the back seat alone, for the Kostavitzs had to attend a conference on Czech–US trade, and compassion had always been second to trade. Peter Hallam was glad to help. Not merely to demon-strate the West's willingness to break down the East–West barriers, nor to impress the Kostavitzs or Moscow Cephal, but for Wendy. Even at eight, going on nine, she was the light of his life.

Hallam covered his passion for Wendy by veiled hints that

he considered the Kostavitzs prime double-agent material, giving him the excuse to be with them. But no-one was fooled. It caused amusement in some circles that the Kostavitzs and Hallam were such strong friends, sharing cultural delights at Wolftrap in the summer, the children always with Hallam, pestering him for ice-creams and such. For Hallam, it was just the sheer joy of the child, perhaps a way of holding onto his own distant youth. He liked the inventiveness of children. Wendy had learnt much of her Englishness from him and her adopted name, Wendy. He'd offered her Rose or Wendy, she'd chosen Wendy, for Wendy could fly and, above all, Sylvia wished to fly to London again and stay with her Uncle Peter in his big white house over there. It was as if she had been born to the Kostavitzs by mistake and by rights, by all the justice of the heart, she should have been born English and sired by Hallam. The Kostavitzs seemed to live with it, content to let their child be a model of incorrect socialist behaviour. The child had dreams of grandeur, of belonging to that dimmed Empire resting on rusting North Sea metal stilts. They put up with it and, for all outward appearances, the Kostavitz-Hallam quintet was an accepted phenonemon.

It was all the more a wonder for some people on the periphery of power in London, that Hallam was always on the rise in the Square (promoted twice by Will Strawson), but to be fair, by Grimly and the Stationmaster as well. The direct channel to the Czechs had been useful, but his rise to Number Two had had to wait until the Kostavitzs were dead. The Stationmaster trusted dead agents more than any other.

Before that, Sylvia's illness. She'd shrunk, practically shrivelled away. Hallam had himself sought out specialist after specialist to attend to her; money wasted, for she continued to decline. Then he had read in an alternative lifestyle magazine about Dr Paynter, the herbalist. She was as close to a genuine witch as he had ever seen: long flowing red hair, the eccentric dress of a Woodstock flower child who refused to believe the concert was over, committed to alternatives to the FDA and natural cures for natural sores. She was almost famous, a recluse, her waiting-room always filled with the world's poor and the occasional rich whose money had failed the final test. No-one was laughing at mediaeval herbal remedies any longer.

She had been the last ditch. Stephen Kostavitz had sanctioned Hallam's help, and he'd driven overnight to New York, arriving at Dr Paynter's home in Atlantic Avenue, Brooklyn, a revitalised community near the docks.

She hadn't enjoyed being woken at 4 pm, but soon relented when she had seen the 60 lb wreck in the back seat of his Jaguar. She'd told him immediately that he'd left it too late. Best to leave it to prayer, but he'd insisted, proffered money, but it wasn't money she needed. Hallam had pleaded with her to try, and possibly out of the challenge she had accepted Sylvia, ordering Hallam back to Washington, for there were no overnight cures.

He'd gone home. Even prayed, something he hadn't done for many years, and a week later Sylvia was still alive, already an impossibility according to 'specialists'.

Meanwhile, Washington had noticed the deterioration in Hallam and ordered a return to London on a permanent basis. Hallam was sensible enough to realise this was for his own good and took the change as a welcome respite. He knew Sylvia didn't stand much chance and it was affecting his judgment. But, sadly, he lost touch with the Kostavitzs, a change had been forced on them too. Sylvia was left in New York. He heard later that the reason for the Kostavitzs silence was the young son's death, almost immediately after he had left Washington. Too sudden to take him to Dr Paynter, and naturally Sylvia had always slept with him, she didn't like to sleep alone.

Three months later he received a letter, postmarked Paris: *Dear Uncle Peter, I love you forever and ever. Please, please come and see me. I'm still not well enough to fly to you. Love and kisses, Wendy XX*

The visits to Paris grew to two or three a month. Wendy began to grow into her body frame once more. Slowly, week by week, the miracle of life resumed the natural mantle of beauty it had invested in her. By the summer of '77 Wendy was ten and a half years-old and, in Hallam's opinion, the most beautiful little girl in the world. He imbued her with almost magical properties.

And on August 9, a black day in California's history, it became a black day for Paris. The bomb had ignited the moment the Kostavitzs had started up the engine of their car.

Hallam had left for Paris as soon as the Reuter's telegram had reached the Square, not knowing if Wendy was in the car or not; he was in shock, anticipating she had been. His relief that she was in the Clinic for muscle therapy was only equalled by the amazement he experienced when the Czech authorities had summoned him to the Embassy and, with great solemnity, had literally given over Sylvia to his charge. It was either a great miracle of Eastern compassion, or a mistake. No mention of grandparents, or of sending the child to a grim Czech orphanage, nothing but, 'It was Kostavitz's wish'.

They did have a full and complete dossier on Hallam and the Kostavitzs. It was on record that Hallam's intervention had saved the girl's life and they had known each other since her birth. She was given to him, and under other circumstances it might have been considered highly suspicious, but Hallam was not going to fight it. Nor indeed was Sylvia, whose grief had soon evaporated to joy, as only a child's can. The funeral over, a saddened, yet elated Hallam flew his ward home. Wendy and Peter together, just like the stories he'd told her. He kept the implausibility of this arrangement buried deep in his subconcious. He wanted to believe it was his just reward.

And now Capitan Crewk had stolen her, stolen his inheritance. Nothing mattered now. For Hallam knew, if he didn't get Wendy back, he would resign. As well placed as he was now, without Wendy, there was no point, no life at all, a vacuum that could never be replaced. Death, it would be a living death.

So, at 11 am, Hallam was walking along the Earls Court Road; calm, sure of his purpose, deliberately stalking one result. He was firm in his mind that whatever it cost, whatever the losses, he would give Captain Crewk anything he wanted to get back Wendy and his life.

He strolled past W.H.Smiths, pausing to allow traffic to enter Penywern road, crossing and mingling with the assorted internationals that jostled each other for dominance in this stretch of London. Hallam was dressed conservatively, but casual enough for a Saturday morning. He looked like a local resident lost on a stroll from the rich quarter, Kensington, come slumming; or forced into the neighbourhood from need for a pack of cigarettes, or worse, to cruise the soliciting postcards jammed together at the newsagents. Perhaps he did look like a man who'd be looking for a number to while away the afternoon, with Hilda (leather specialist) in a grubby bed-sit, or Francine and John 'Together we will entertain you.'

But Hallam wasn't in the mood, nor had he the need for that kind of diversion. He had forced his unwilling memory down unwelcome paths and come up with a name. It was a long shot, he knew that, but he couldn't risk going to Archives, not yet, not until he was desperate. If he could find the name by other, less obvious channels, then all the better. Already he knew Calon was in a panic, probably planning some drastic action to prevent loss of prestige for the Foreign Office, desperately trying to make the best of the situation, brief the PM and hope that somehow an advantage could be perceived from the mess.

They would be wanting results from the Square, Moscow's intentions relayed to the Cabinet. They would be wanting the Stationmaster back with the missing files. He'd seen the tele-gram marked 'flash' to the Stationmaster, announcing Sir Harold Miller's defection. He wondered if this was the first of many, or an over-reaction, over-simplification. Quite frankly, he found it hard to believe the GOC would defect. He had cabled back asking for more information from Chancery. What the hell was Berlin Chancery doing letting the GOC over the wall anyway? Worse, when would the Soviets use that information to ridicule the West? And the Second Eleven? This was the most worrying aspect. GCHQ had been circulating this sort of thing for a long while now. Suspicions had never actually concentrated on the interior of the Service, but focussed with an unhealthy paranoia on the left-wing press. It was no use telling Simon Caw and his Putney SAVAK team that Lipsnatching left-wing journalists and certain MPs only revealed half the story. The more they smeared, the more filth that stuck to Lipsnatchers itself. The more they spied inside, the more dangerous the philosophy of self-protection became. That was what was so insidious about the rise and rise of Simon Caw. His friendship with Frank Binns-Robson, Deputy Secretary in Cabinet Office and second to Calon in CSI (Coordinators of Security and Intelligence), was a dangerous one. The Square was definitely being squeezed. Lipsnatchers wanted it all. People were saying the Square and its agents weren't effective anymore, that Lipsnatchers with it's £200 million per annum budget was enough. Certainly exports from the Joint Services Research Labs had proved lucrative and the proving case for continued investment in Lipsnatchers expansion programme.

But it was the man from the past Hallam was searching for in Earls Court. His landlady had said he always had his breakfast at 11 am, regular as clockwork. Hallam came to a halt outside Dino's and peered in through the glass door. It was half empty, but even if he hadn't seen Willy for four years or more, he recognised the ears. The long Clark Gable ears either side of a large balding, oiled head, bent over a cup of tea, his back to the door. Four years on and now he sits with his back to the door? Easton would howl. Had he forgotten the most basic rules then? And if he had forgotten them, had he forgotten everything else? Easton kindergarten used Willy as a textbook case, the perfect agent. They let him go when Petty France division was demolished. Just let him go, denied him a pension because there was no record of him. Of course there was no record. Willy was the classic sleeper, the most invisible agent there had ever been. Irritating, his absurdities with details, worries about car parks and security. He took his role as a Defence Department Messenger very seriously indeed.

To anyone outside the Square he was a bumbling fool, a slow witted, gross, red-faced man, always willing to please. Excessively willing to please. Never a cross word or lowly mutter if you overloaded him with work. The classic menial, yet essential cog in Ministry business. Also mysterious, his home in Worthing which no-one ever visited, except a house-keeper who wouldn't even let him down there because of the mess he'd make. Invisible Willy, who made unnoticed visits to the Square and Orchard Street, or Borough High Street, carrying letters, classified documents. No-one would have credited this simple, loyal worker to be capable of delivering lectures on the perfect security agent to students at Easton or Cheltenham Training Establishments. New recruits marvelled at Willy's ability to deliver these informal talks without seeming to draw breath, and the long meanders about Sir Thomas Beecham at the Royal Philharmonic Orchestra, or Lords, momentous moments in cricket, or worse, nights to remember at the Proms, would suddenly turn into the steamy night life of Earl's Court where the strange collection of Poles, South Africans, exiles from every walk of life would gather to exchange views, hopes, secrets and, more likely, fears.

They would listen in fascination as he would tell them about Mike, whose daughter Ethel, whose friend Jo, whose aunt Jane, whose plumber turned out to be a Czech agent sent by Moscow Cephal, and how he would have put all these insignificant people into a patchwork of connections that brought him to a travel office in the Fulham Road specialising in holidays behind the Iron Curtain. It was old Willy, old bumbling Willy who broke the Moscow Cephal retrieval system, where defectors were forcibly returned to their homelands, drugged, chained, by any means at all. He was the only man who still remained invisible and cruised the homing places of London's aliens, befriending the saddest cases, being abused by the stronger ones and humoured by the lonely, who would sit and suffer whilst he remembered a match at Lords in '54 with far greater detail than even the most patient stone could endure. It was this 'character' who blew the Polish exiles recruiting under a false flag for Moscow. It was he who blocked up escape routes for agents wanting out who couldn't claim diplomatic help. The sleepers. Finally, it was Willy who Will Strawson had begun to use as his mailman, thinking his simple way was a guarantee of safety. That innocent Willy wouldn't notice that the green and blue Restricted Highly Secret files and memos, were not cleared by the Square; and some Archive shelves were empty when they should have been full. But Willy, ever curious, had noticed how everything was beginning to by-pass Grimly and Hallam, that green files were being read by the wrong people and how Will Strawson was building an empire outside the citadel walls.

Willy had approached Hallam first. If only because he was one of the few at the Square who knew who he was. Number Seventeen, been there since the war. Only Stationmaster, Grimly and Shepherd in accounts knew him. Others who might have were either retired or had just forgotten the out-fielder still operating in the middle of their territory.

And then Hallam had listened and acted with Grimly. Will Strawson had been wrapped up in a week. Willy wasn't to know they'd been investigating for more than six months. It was entirely their own fault that they had forgotten Willy.

Calon made the unnecessary cruel decision. "Pay him off. He's coming up to his pension. We'd forgotten him. He's blown himself and now we can't use him. Pay him a year's salary and write him off. You would have found Will Strawson anyway."

So Willy, philosophical as ever, had taken his £7,630 with London weighting, less tax, and gone on as before, but unpaid. How to stop a life you've led for forty years? How do you retire from your real life? He had kept on his tiny room in Earl's Court. It didn't matter that the exile Poles didn't trust him with their petty secrets anymore, they told him anyway. Who else would listen? "You'll see. Now Afghanistan is over, it will be West Germany. There's six infantry divisions and two artillery waiting on the Czech border. They could march across Germany in three hours." They could tell Willy everything now, just because they knew no-one was listening to him anymore.

"Listen to what General Grigorenko is saying in Washington, Willy. Why don't your friends at the Square believe him?"

Had Willy anyone to tell, he could have told the Square about the Moscow–Paris pact six months ago. But they didn't ask.

Hallam walked into the restaurant along a crazy marble-paved floor, surrounded by lurid red walls and pale yellow table tops. The Gaggia coffee machine was crackling loudly, and attempting to drown conversations with the roar of hot milk. Neither noise was of any benefit to mankind. He walked on past the tables coming directly to Willy's patch, rear centre of the long room. He was alone, tea and a plate of ravioli in front of him. His *Daily Mail* was tightly wrapped with an elastic band, a letter much creased and read was to one side, occupying his attention, his eyes giving each word careful scrutiny.

Hallam saw that the grey moustache was still in place. Only his National Health spectacles were new. Otherwise, it was the same grey, double-knit suit, the same shirt and blue County Cricket Society tie, as if he had been in store for four years, just put on display now for this Saturday morning. His cardigan was colourless, though it could have been red at one time, like the pen in his breast pocket. In Hallam's opinion, Willy had never been a cover disguise, he lived like this naturally. If he hadn't have been an agent, he would have lived this way, eccentric and secretive, anyway. He had been born to the Service. It was cruel and heartless for it to abandon him at this stage of his life. That's what happens when your illustrious family of explorers, royal designers and one, briefly, Prime Minister, all die before your childhood is over and you are cut off from the seat of influence forever. An exile from his own inheritance, institutionalised and used up by Her Majesty's Government.

Hallam sat down and coughed to attract his attention. Willy started and, although the face didn't betray any surprise, he immediately went into 'role' and began with his apologetic and welcoming routine.

"Mr Hallam. Well, good morning, Mr Hallam, sir. Good morning, even if it isn't a good morning. Will you have a cup of coffee? Do a good cup here, sir. Keep a good score, they do." He turned to a pretty waitress hovering by the food service counter. "Paula, my dear, my little puss, a cup of coffee for Mr Hallam here. Mr Hallam is an old friend. He wants a good cup of coffee."

Conniving, familiar, making even the getting of coffee an event. Each moment, when there was company, was one of mock conspiracy and one became party to it, drawn in. One minute his voice would proclaim loudly to the world; the next it would be hushed, and Willy would place a pink hand on your arm to confide: "It's all hush-hush, the manager is leaving. The restaurant is changing hands."

Hallam knew that unless he asserted himself very quickly and kept Willy calm, it would become increasingly difficult to break through his barrage of banter.

"Have something to eat, Mr Hallam? Some cake, or toast and jam? They do a good bacon sandwich here, you can get brown bread now. Perhaps a toasted bun? Don't see many of the old crowd now. Don't come to Dino's so much anymore. Some still go to the King's Head. Too crowded for me, too full of smoke. My health's been bad, my arm. You know about that, of course, my nervous complaint. Didn't get it until that business with the big Chief. My daughter, she says that I should join her in Sydney . . ."

Hallam, already desperately bored, suddenly found a way in. "Didn't know you had a daughter, Willy. Thought we knew everything about you. When were you married?"

"In the war," he launched off again. "Seem to remember it was in the war. Funny business marriage. Not natural, slave and wage slave. Shouldn't be allowed. Of course, the daughter did all right. Clever move going to Australia. She was always upset with me and when her first husband died, well she was cheesed off, proper cheesed off I can tell you."

Hallam wasn't breaking in at all. The man had been miscast. He should have been in interrogation. People would cough up their secrets soon enough if they knew they had a few days of listening to Willy.

"Never liked Australia myself, too many of them here in Dino's pawing Paula. Paula's a puss, don't you think? Single girl, Mr Hallam, good cook. I like the Portuguese. None of this political nonsense. Don't catch them de-stabilising ordinary folk. No intrigues in the Palace there. I'm afraid the lads in Mount Row wouldn't find much to do in Portugal. You can't wheel the dead hand in a place like that, Mr Hallam. Poland, yes. Our boys at the Square wouldn't find much to do in Portugal. I should think they'd be bored stiff there, know what I mean?"

Hallam watched his coffee arrive in the care of Paula's multi-ringed fingers. Grey coffee with a Fairy Liquid sheen on the milk bubbles covering the surface. He attempted an uncomfortable smile at the girl, bored, uncomprehending Paula from Figueira da Foz. Was Earl's Court better than Portugal? Or had she come just for Willy's company? Hallam sighed, pouring a spoon of sugar in his cup, allowing Willy's nonsense to flow over him. No wonder his cover had been almost perfect for thirty-five years. Calon thought him stupid, expendable. Calon never looked further than his nose. Willy had put on a disguise and grown into it. It would require a surgeon to remove it now, even if it was possible.

"Listen," Hallam hissed eventually, as Willy moved onto the subject of his dead friend who'd been with the Diversified Service Corporation in SW1. "Willy, stop. Stop, Willy! It's me, Mr Hallam. I'm ordering you to stop."

"How's little Wendy then?" Willy asked, not easily ordered to do anything.

Hallam frowned a moment. Not because Willy had reminded him of Wendy and, coincidently, hit the exact reason for his visit, but because he didn't understand how Willy even knew Wendy existed.

"Pretty girl. Lucky to have her, I say. Godolphin and

Latymer a good school, is it? Hammersmith a nice place? She a good student? Bright girl, she should be."

Hallam must have shown his surprise. "How . . .?" he began.

"George says she is a wonder. George Goizaliskas says she is the brightest girl he's ever met. His favourite. I think she's a bit of a devil myself. Strong-willed, don't get me wrong, I like her, but she's got that foreign temperament. George brought her in here," he stuck his tongue into his cheek to dislodge a piece of meat, "yes, she came in here about twice. He's always here mind. Lives just across the road, over the Courtfield, the pub, you can see it from here."

Hallam was stunned, but he realised that there was logic to it. Dino's was the exiles' canteen. Natural that Willy should know George Goizaliskas. A driver, an exile who takes Diplomats' children to school. Willy would know, Willy knew everything, but did he know where this George was now? Or Captain Crewk?

"Where's George now, Willy?" he asked, his eyes levelling with Willy's, a difficult and uncomfortable task when faced with a man who could outstare Mount Rushmore.

"George went to Grimsby, or Cleethorpes. There's a ferry. He had to meet a ferry."

"A ferry in Grimsby?" It didn't seem likely.

"Perhaps it was Immingham?" Willy suggested. "Though there is a bridge there now, isn't there? A Humber Bridge? You wouldn't need a ferry if there was a bridge."

Hallam was barely able to contain his temper. "Why did he go, wherever he went? Why, Willy?"

"Meet a ferry, he said. Hush-hush. Private business for the Square. You should know, Mr Hallam."

Hallam wanted to lunge forward and shake it out of him, but he knew you couldn't rush the man. No way to rush him at all. Always at his own tortoise-like pace.

"And Wendy?" Hallam asked, "did he take her?"

"No, Mr Hallam. Wendy would have to go to school. He swopped duties with Milos, the Czech. Milos met her. He lives in Bramham Gardens, no. 11, two up from me. I haven't seen him for a week. No, more, more than a week. He'd collect Wendy. Everyone knows Wendy, well in there they do."

It was incredible. Everyone knew everything about his Wendy. Matron would have a lot to answer for. Nolan and Bloater arranged the driver scheme. He should have checked himself, but Matron was to blame, completely. Hallam took out his black book and laid it down on the table before him, noting down George and Milos' addresses.

"Wendy in trouble?" Willy asked at last, rubbing his hand, stiff and sore from the ague. Hallam didn't think he had to answer that.

"I want information on two names, Willy. I'm going to pay £100 towards your pension fund."

Willy turned his head away, temporarily embarrassed. "No need, Mr Hallam. I'm not a supply man. I don't take money for my memory."

"You'll take this, Willy. Pension. Inflation's bad. You need it."

"I live well enough. Your Wendy gone? That pretty girl run away?"

Hallam slowly shook his head, withdrawing the £100 from his jacket pocket, and placing it under the blue aerogram letter.

"Take it, Willy. Someone has kidnapped her. Your friend Milos helped him do it."

Willy didn't say anything. He looked down at his cold tea and stared at his plate of cold food.

"Milos wouldn't do that," he said at last. "Milos wouldn't do that, Mr Hallam. He hasn't got his papers yet, he isn't a Brit yet. Too much at stake to do that. Everyone liked your Wendy. No-one would harm a kid."

"The world has changed, Willy. Kids can be killed the same as everyone else. Captain Crewk? Know that name? Crewk, I think I'm pronouncing it right."

"No," Willy replied after a few minutes thought. "No. Never a Captain Crewk. Sounds Czech, means something, doesn't it? You've sent down a googly there."

"A what?"

Willy shrugged. "It's a bit of a bumper this."

"And the Butcher's Boy?" he asked, the real question, for he was sure Captain Crewk wouldn't be known. He'd run the name through Archives computer already; nothing at all.

Suddenly Willy was smiling. "Now there's a good boy. I haven't thought much about him in a long time. I remember the Butcher's Boy. Mr Grimly found him. Sent me around to chat him up a few times. He was painting then. Quite an artist. He was a good wicket-keeper if you get me, good wicket-keeper."

Willy smiled again. "Not in my head," he said, "at home. I wrote it down, oh must have been twelve years ago now. Mr Grimly told me to forget his name."

"And you did?" Hallam asked disbelieving.

"An order is an order, Mr Hallam. Mr Grimly wanted to protect the Butcher's Boy, just like he protected me. A tricky business, very tricky."

A sleeper, thought Hallam. That's why they don't know. He's a sleeper. Not in the Archives. Grimly's a clever one. How many sleepers had that man planted in his lifetime? How many like Willy for God's sake?

"Old Grimly must be batting on now, about ready to be shutting up, I'd say." Willy felt he was being ignored. "I said, Grimly would be drawing stumps soon."

"Quite, quite," Hallam answered, noticing a statue of a woman with a pig in her hands on the wall. There was something quite strange about this restaurant.

"I need some help, Willy. The Butcher's Boy. I need to find him. You're the only one who can tell me his name."

"Mr Grimly knows," he protested.

"Grimly is retired. He drew stumps more than a year ago."

"Good player in his time," Willy said slowly as he felt the slim pile of £10 notes under his letter. He sighed. "The Butcher's Boy then?"

"Yes, Willy. I have to know. If I know his cover name then I'll be able to find him. He's not listed. He's like you, an

110

outsider. Reports only to the Stationmaster and he is away on extended leave."

"You think he has your Wendy?" Willy asked. "One of our boys?"

Hallam's eyes drifted back to the pig on the wall, noticing its lacquered ears. "Yes, I suspect he's turned maverick."

"Not the Butcher's Boy," Willy said with some force. "Not one of Mr. Grimly's boys. I remember him. From Suffolk. His father was a market gardener, not wealthy, not wealthy at all, poor really. Father not much of a businessman. But he was a bright boy, ambitious. I remember he got a scholarship to Cambridge. Peterhouse it was. A good boy. Will Strawson, he's the one who called him the Butcher's Boy. Never met him mind. Grimly made sure of that, but 'X', as he was called, 'X' 's background, the grammar school, it wasn't on. Will Strawson knew he was a commoner. I don't know how he knew, but he guessed I suppose. Mr Strawson had a nose for it. ' "X",' he said, 'our man "X" is a prole, Hugh. You're infiltrating the proles into the Service. I know it.' He knew that anyone who needed a scholarship wasn't one of his crowd. Couldn't afford to buy his way in, like the rest of them. Not a son of a father, no tradition of higher education in the family. Strawson was a bit of a snob, between you and me. Wouldn't look outside Eton or Harrow, not even at Charterhouse. 'This Service is for gentlemen,' he always said."

"And gentlemen traitors," Hallam added. "Willy, I want to know his name. Now, Willy," he insisted. "If you met him so many times, why don't you remember his name? You can remember what Sir Thomas Beecham had for dinner on 11 June 1947, why can't you remember the Butcher's Boy's name?"

"I wrote it down, Mr Hallam. No need to remember what you write down."

"Then let's go," Hallam urged. "For my Wendy, let's go."

Willy, who would not be rushed – not even for £100 or pretty Wendy (even though she was a handful) – quietly folded the airmail letter from his much missed daughter and, with

111

leaden hands hovering momentarily over the money, stared at Mr Hallam, saying, "Milos is a nice fellow, Mr Hallam. He wouldn't take your Wendy. He could have taken her anytime. She wasn't what you call protected."

"If she wasn't at school, there'd be George, or myself, Willy. She was never alone."

Willy finally picked up the money and pocketed it. Not for himself mind, but for his daughter, a present for his daughter.

"She used to go to Holland Park alone, Mr Hallam. George used to take her to Holland Park, leave her to watch the birds. She liked the pelicans, or was it the flamingoes? She liked the birds."

Hallam looked across the table with disbelief. "No, George was under strict orders. He would never leave her alone."

"George has a girlfriend, Patricia. Lives beside the Odeon, Kensington. Your Wendy watches the birds whilst George gets an innings. George likes to get his way, Mr Hallam, and Patricia's husband doesn't come home till the evening."

"Don't tell me anymore." Hallam felt ill. Had he known his Wendy was wide open and unprotected . . . Jesus. She wasn't just any thirteen year-old, not Wendy. She was his, Hallam of the Square. The bastard George had left the door wide open.

"The Butcher's Boy, Willy. Let's go to your flat and look for the name."

Willy didn't say anymore. He went to look for his trench-coat. He had eleven trenchcoats. All identical, all multi-purpose, waterproofed, London Transport Bus Inspector approved, British made, full length trenchcoats. There was something about a trenchcoat that attracted him. Wrapped in it, only inches off the ground and belted up, extended fully, for he was not an insubstantial man, one might have mistaken him for a Hichcocknian idea of a Scotland Yard Inspector. Willy of the Yard. In his own secret way, Willy wouldn't dissuade that assumption. Winter or summer, he felt safe – protected by the shield of his disguise.

"I'm ready," Willy said, "must pay the bill."

"I've paid," Hallam told him. "Now no more tactical delays. I need that name this morning."

Hallam had forced him along Earl's Court Road at a pace Willy had not achieved since boyhood, and his boyhood, at sixty-four, was a long time ago.

"Should have worn my running shoes," Willy said, pausing for breath beside Bramham Gardens railings. "You'll have to wait, Mr Hallam. My breath is still crossing the road outside Smiths."

Hallam clenched his teeth and counted to fifty before nudging Willy along again. "Not far now, Willy. You can rest when we get there."

"I'll have to think," Willy said ominously, "where I put it."

Hallam would have gladly struck the man, but he reigned himself in. Wendy, he had to think of poor Wendy in the hands of this Captain Crewk. Willy was helping. He had been the right man to see. An outsider who knew the inside like his own hand. Someone, no-one would think to ask, or remember. A forgotten man, the original unsung hero, that was Willy. Hallam reflected that he didn't even know Willy's real name. He wondered if anyone ever had.

"Is this the place?" Hallam asked, pushing on an iron gate.

"My steps," Willy answered. "A modest quarter, but a home away from home." His breathing wasn't very good. Gone too fast for him altogether. In Willy's opinion running was something that should be confined to children. He was against all forms of rapid movement. Bad for the heart.

"The basement?" Hallam asked, fearing the worst.

"A rat's hold for a wily rat," Willy announced, fishing for his keys in a fathom deep pocket. "£18 a week, it was only five when I moved in. They want me out, they want me to turn my room into a storeroom. But I won't let them. It's my room. I'm too old to move again."

"But I thought you had a place in Worthing?"

"Worthing. I go there still. Home's a shrine to family heirlooms, Mr Hallam. No room for me. No room at all."

Hallam waited as Willy, sure footed like a goat, negotiated the steps down to the basement. The windows were barred, more security outside his windows than Wormwood Scrubs.

"You'll have to be patient, Mr Hallam. I'm an old man and old men can't play your young games anymore."

Hallam remained silent, following Willy down the stone steps once he had managed to open the door. They walked along a short corridor, coming to another door: notes to laundry men and other inhabitants of this warren were pinned all over it. Beside it was the 1950 Design Award phone.

Willy's breathing was definitely not good, the massive frame uncomfortable to say the least. "My memory isn't what it used to be, Mr Hallam. This trouble with my arm, my nerves. Doctor doesn't know what it is. They never do. Go to them with anything more than a cold and they think you're ready for the morgue. Doctors today aren't what they were, Mr Hallam. They aren't interested in curing you. Curing you isn't number one on their list."

They finally entered his room. The unpleasant odour of an elderly single man filled Hallam's nostrils. Old books, damp carpets, decaying suits hanging on a hook behind the door. Piles of books and pictures torn from old calendars. Calendar girls from 1958 with young, inviting smiles, now old women themselves. A room filled with abandoned memories and half-used dreams. The inevitable signed portrait of Sir Thomas Beecham and a tower of well-thumbed cricket books, lay five feet into the air beside a narrow, single bed.

"I know you're in a hurry," Willy said, slowly, deliberately slowly it seemed to Hallam, taking off his precious trenchcoat. "It's in the cupboard," Willy said. "It'll be in the cupboard."

Hallam opened the cupboard door, a deep six by three recess in the wall. He switched on the dim forty watt light and looked with astonishment at a man's history stacked into eighteen cubic feet, hardly a space left for Willy to penetrate. It was as if they had already converted his room into a storeroom, whilst he was at breakfast: twenty pairs of army boots, ten pairs of comfortable old black shoes, a pile of unused trenchcoats, and pile after musty pile, reaching all the way to the ceiling, of paper bags.

"You never know when a paper bag might be useful," Willy muttered behind him. "You never know." He hung up his trenchcoat.

Hallam estimated five or six thousand bags or more all different. It was a junk museum.

Willy went past him into his cupboard. "Jackson's of Piccadilly bags, Mr Hallam. You won't see their like again. I hear it's a café now. Never thought that day would come. The old bags have all gone now."

Hallam didn't want to believe it. The man treasured paper bags as if they were *objet d'art*; there was probably a catalogue, with them listed bag by bag.

"Perhaps we could look for the book, Willy. It's for Wendy. Every moment we delay she could be slipping further away."

"I work better at night," he answered. "My nocturnal labours are more reliable. Early mornings are never good for me. I've never liked to bat first."

Hallam had gathered that. He stared at the washbasin, the sad array of half-filled liquor bottles for entertaining and rarely used, for all were covered in dust.

"Be there in a minute, Mr Hallam, be there in a minute." He stepped further into the cupboard and ran his hands along the overladen shelves. "It was a diary. One of my MCC diaries. I put them all in a shoe box, won't be long at all now." He bent down to inspect a few loose carrier bags. Hallam watched with horror as the man's jacket caught on a peg protruding from a shelf. And, although nothing seemed to happen at first, as Willy stood up again, the top few thousand bags began to sway.

"Look out!" Hallam yelled.

The other thousands joined in and all came crashing down on Willy, throwing him to the ground under a hundredweight of paper. He completely disappeared. A last brown Oakshots bag fluttered down and settled on the pile.

It seemed like a long time before Willy began to rise and

shake off the debris. He was angry. Very angry. Twenty years of cataloguing gone for a burton. If he'd been the emotional sort, he'd have cried. But not today, not in front of Hallam. Instead, he gradually straightened up and peered at the shelves, long ago forced into a perfect curve by the weight of history.

"The paper shortage still a long way off, I suppose," he said, sulking. It was going to take a week to re-sort this collection. The only thing left on the shelves was a shoebox. Willy peered into it and withdrew a black diary with the faded gold leaf of the MCC on it. Hallam watched with relief. Old Willy was coming through with the name.

Willy opened up the diary. The pages crumbled in his hands. "Mice," he said, looking up into Hallam's incredulous eyes. "Mice," he repeated. "Bloody mice."

Hallam rocked on his heels a moment, unsure whether the anger he felt was going to make him lunge forward and shout obscenities at Willy, or burst a few blood vessels of his own. Instead, with supreme effort of will, he turned and left without a word, along that depressing corridor, slamming the door after him, climbing the stone steps, walking in a blind rage down towards the Earl's Court Road looking for a taxi, the cool white heat of anger misting his eyes. Mice. Wendy abducted and mice held her prisoner.

Willy dipped into the shoebox again. Two baby mice lay blind and still, stunned with fright.

"I've remembered, Mr Hallam," Willy said, suddenly. "I know the Butcher's Boy's name."

But Hallam was already in his taxi, heading back to the Square, cursing Willy, cursing George, cursing himself for being so careless. Captain Crewk was a monster, but it hadn't taken much to be clever, not much at all. Surveillance and Headhunters would be heading to Earl's Court within minutes to hunt down this Milos character. He couldn't risk going himself, not the way he felt and not unarmed.

The telephone beside Willy's door jarred into action. Willy stepped out of the pool of paper bags and managed to reach it before the caller rang off.

116

"Willy, Bramham Gardens," he boomed down the line.

"I've a job for you, Willy," the voice said, "just us old boys in this one. You up to a job, Willy?"

Willy felt the unearned £100 in his jacket pocket, thinking that his stars in the *Standard* had been right for once. "I'm always ready to bat, Croc. Always need a few bright pennies."

"Then you'll be at Brook Green at half past three, Willy?"

Willy frowned. He didn't like to leave all his paper bags on the floor like that and 3.30 pm wasn't so far off.

"Willy?" Croc asked, "you still there?"

"I'm still here, Croc. You said 3.30 pm. Brook Green. Big job is it? Wendy, I suppose."

"Wendy?" Croc asked, wondering if Willy was as past it as all of them had considered he was, all except the Stationmaster.

"Wendy, Mr Hallam's girl. He says the Butcher's Boy has taken her away. Pretty bowled over I'd say, Croc, on a sticky wicket there."

"At 3.30 pm, Willy. You talk to no-one meanwhile, understand?"

"Mum's the word, Croc, Mum's the word."

He disconnected the phone and, still frowning, went back to the battleground in the cupboard. One day someone would care about a Marshall and Snelgrove carrier bag, or a Gamages wrapper. Someday people would be grateful his little cupboard contained such honest treasures of London's history. An odd time for Croc, 3.30 pm. Why the 'safe' house? Why not Dino's? That was where they usually met, never in Brook Green. In all forty-five years he'd known Croc, from their early days in the Essex regiment out in Italy, they'd kept in contact. Even when Croc rose up in the world. But then, Croc had ambition. Been to University. Could put a few good words on paper, could Croc. Not too bad at the after dinner conversation either. Still, he was surprised the Brook Green 'safe' house was still going. He wondered who would be the visiting team. Croc never went anywhere alone.

"Funny day," Willy muttered to himself, shutting his door.

He hadn't expected a rematch. Not after all this time. And Wendy was a tricky one. He didn't like to think of Wendy in trouble at all. Nor the distress of Mr Hallam. Thoughtfully, he studied his stock of shoes and heaved a heartfelt sigh. The past was always there to snatch you back. Funny to pull him in though, funny to come to old Willy with proposals and money like he was some kissing girl in a leap year frenzy. Come to think of it, when had he last kissed a girl? When last had a girl kissed him?

* * *

The office was luxurious, a relic of former glory in the last Gladstone administration, boasting an ornate ceramic commode, lurid Japanese sexual technique displayed on the walls, always a talking point after a visit to Calon's empire.

But the visitor to this seat of power in the early part of the day was not expecting to see Mr Paul Calon; in actual fact, he knew that Calon was at Number Ten, at the latest crisis meeting over the threatened Soviet grab for Persian Gulf oil.

"Good morning, sir," Staunton, Calon's loyal and most favoured Secretary muttered with a barely concealed surprise.

"Staunton," the visitor acknowledged. "Just passing by."

"Ah," Staunton said with an air of wisdom. He knew that no-one ever just passed by, not to Calon's office. Not just because the office was at the very end of the block, but because it was served by a separate and steep marble staircase, with no elevator to get one up to the fifth floor. It was the space and the view, 2000 square feet of oak panelling and the grand vista of the Thames – worth the climb in Calon's view, he enjoyed the exercise. However, Staunton wasn't impressed either way, more concerned with his arthritic condition.

So Staunton was particularly aware of the incongruity of anyone stating that they were just passing by, especially this visitor. Dennis had never been one to pay casual visits anywhere. Any man who had the ear of the PM as Dennis had, any man who had access to all parts of Whitehall, completely without restriction, was not a man to pass by anywhere. It was not for Staunton to speculate on the hidden power of a man who had an almost ombudsman, universal aunt position in the corridors of Whitehall. No doubt the Inner Cabinet felt it was necessary to employ a policeman, someone to fight corruption, sift through the maze of Whitehall and make some sense, reporting to the PM on a daily basis all that he'd heard. The PM had thought up the job. Not just something for Dennis to do, something the PM thought essential. Personal contact by proxy, the *eminence grise* whose easy-going affability was barely skin deep. A man with whom friendship was essential hence his legions of supporters, yet who had all the charm of Brutus cloaked in Savile Row suits and Brook Bros. shirts.

No-one knew much about Dennis' background, just that he had made his money in manufacturing, a businessman, coopted into the Government for hard nosed, no nonsense, clear headed thinking, as if they were in need of more clichés. Dragged into the grey world of nether ministries, in a comparatively short time he had carved out a career for himself that would have impressed even Robespierre. Felling trees, great oaks, long thought sacred cows, untouchable. When one got a visit from Dennis, they said, one should look after one's neck.

It was always, 'The PM thinks there's room for manoeuvre . . . a cut back here, a little surgery there.' In Staunton's opinion cut backs were all very well, but cutting off a healthy man's leg to make him more productive was not something that found favour in his book. So had Dennis come to wield his hatchet in Calon's office? What more could the PM want? One couldn't squeeze the Square anymore than 31%. Or was it to be both legs now and get your own wheelchair?

"It's about this Malta business, Staunton. The PM is very concerned about information coming out of there, doesn't want it to get into the wrong hands. I believe Calon received a visit from the Square man out there, call him the Butcher's Boy, I think."

Staunton bristled. So that was Dennis' game. Not content

with destroying the power of Whitehall, he wanted to wheedle his way into the Square as well. If Mr Calon had indeed had a visit from the Butcher's Boy (which to be honest Staunton had no idea about, considering it unlikely if he hadn't heard about it), then he saw no reason why the PM couldn't ask in person. After all, Calon was there at Number Ten, the PM could invite him into the study and demand to know.

"Mr Calon would know if he had met this Butcher's Boy. I have no knowledge of any meeting."

"Oh, the meeting took place all right, Staunton. It is just that the PM is concerned that the Butcher's Boy could be at risk. A Square member from Malta, given the current situation, could be very vulnerable to Soviet action. He might know something about the situation that they don't want known."

"I'm sure that now Mr Grimly has come into the picture, sir, that the Butcher's Boy, whoever he is, will be protected.

"Nevertheless, I'd like to be sure."

"You could ask Mr Calon, sir. He is at Number Ten."

"I know where he is. I was rather hoping to hear from you. You know everything that's going on, Staunton, it hasn't escaped our notice. Where would Calon be without your organisational ability? Nowhere, that's where. Look, Staunton," Dennis walked to the window and began to clean his glasses, "I'm only worried because the Square seems to be in such a mess. How can we guarantee the safety of the boy from Malta, or anywhere? Things are changing fast. We don't have the organisation to cope with the problems arising in Europe and the Middle East."

No, Staunton was thinking, not after your hatchet jobs.

"Look, Dennis, I don't know. Even if you were to threaten my job, get your thugs in and throw me about the room, I'm not in a position to tell you what only Calon himself can tell you – and I don't know. All I do know is that he missed his daughter's second wedding because the Stationmaster went missing."

Dennis turned to face him, his anger barely concealed. He

wasn't used to such insubordination. Staunton was a marked man now. One step wrong and he would be joining the dole queue. It was essential he had complete cooperation. How could he guarantee to the PM that everything was going smoothly, that the men and women of the crown were safe, when people like Staunton were obsessed with secrecy, holding onto their precious slices of privacy, their jobs, at the expense of those exposed, the ones outside the shelter of Whitehall. It was very serious. Even Lipsnatchers didn't know who or where the Butcher's Boy was. Staunton had to be lying.

"Well, I'm sorry you don't feel like cooperating, Staunton. If the Butcher's Boy comes to any harm, I hope you will remember this conversation. I'm here to make sure things go right. Too long all these separate departments have been divided, working against each other. I'll get the right attitude in the corridors yet, people like you will learn to place the safety of people ahead of petty secrets. Someone has to tell you that we all live and work in the same country. We all belong."

Staunton ignored him. His insults flew past without scoring a hit. Dennis wasn't going to get his thick fingers in this office pie. PM's favourite or not, he could go to hell.

"I'll make enquiries," Staunton said at last.

"That's better." Dennis replaced his spectacles and strolled over to the door. "I'll be calling you later, Staunton. Remember it's the safety of our fieldman I'm worried about. The PM cares about him, make sure you do."

"Oh I care," Staunton lied, wishing it was tea-time. "If only every Government could care for its Butchers' Boys as much as we do, eh?"

Ignoring the insult, Dennis wandered out of the office, time to get out on the beat again.

Staunton sat back in his leather chair and sighed. He'd weathered that storm, but once Dennis had his teeth into a problem there was little chance he'd let go. Did the PM really know how Dennis carried out his responsibilities? Was that what Number Ten wanted – a bully boy prefect lining up his victims outside their office doors, making them do arm circles and press-ups until their hearts gave in? Was Government really more effective with a sadist wandering the corridors like some whipping-boy from Nero's parlour?

No matter that it was half an hour too soon, he had to have a cup of tea, steady his nerves; another victim of the Dennis effect – and Saturday overtime.

* * *

Another troubled brow was that of young Philip Oosty. He'd found himself on unwelcome weekend duty at the Square. Orders had come from above. Stand by. Hold Matron, but clear the building of non-essential staff. Out with the Warren and day to day first floor admin. people.

Nolan and Bloater had read bad signs into this, fearing the cuts were starting already. These economy measures were a tragedy for all of them. Nothing like it in the history of the Square. Oosty was getting up a petition and he meant it to reach the Cabinet table by the next week. The Prime Minister would be forced to reconsider the proposal, a 31% cut was untenable. The petition called for action. The Cabinet wouldn't be able to get away with it.

And as for the move to South–West London, the staff were unanimous. No. A big no. It was bad enough for those operating out of Ebury Road or for Mr Gallant's Headhunters in Wandsworth, but East Putney . . . Nolan had had to look it up on the map and Bloater had bought a new bottle of Valium. It was a shocker all right, but Bloater, an old hand at Ministry ways, had thought of a solution. Unless all cuts were restored, excepting the vehicle cuts (one had to give in somewhere), then from March 2nd, the first Monday in the month, the Square would begin to work to rule and all affiliates, including Lipsnatchers, would be encouraged likewise. It was a radical step, but big chiefs in Cabinet Office had to be taught a lesson, that some things were sacrosanct. The Square, the World Service and *The Times* were the untouchables.

122

Had Grimly or Calon any idea of the strength of passions circulating amongst the downstairs staff, then it may have been possible that events would have been played with more sensitivity, but the truth was, with events moving in tandems of chaos, as they were, little attention was given to the fermenting troubles in their own house.

The problem for Oosty was, he didn't know exactly what he was supposed to be doing. He'd been notified that Mr Grimly was to return and welcomed that. Berlin was still a hot one and they were expecting trouble at any moment. It was puzzling that East Berlin hadn't begun to crow about Sir Harold's defection. But wall down, or no, the wall of silence surrounding all of the Soviets' latest moves was more disturbing, more sinister than their usual belligerence.

He sat at the 'incoming desk', staring at his own reflection in the blank VDU screen. Damn face giving him trouble, he'd forgotten to take his Oxytetracycline tablets. It wasn't fair, acne should go away after thirty; it wasn't fair or decent and thank God for Max Factor. He sighed, trying to keep his hands away from his face. This Moscow–Paris–Madrid axis rumour hadn't hardened any further, but all the same, he wouldn't have liked to be in the package tour industry if it turned out to be true. The Spanish wouldn't take kindly to Russian tourists either. Tipping and bottom pinching would become a lost art, and it was difficult to imagine peasants from the Urals coping with a Madrid disco.

In Oosty's opinion the inclusion of Marchais into the French Cabinet was not a foregone conclusion. The man's past still haunted him, his role in the war. The reports were too sketchy and unreliable. Hallam had already requested clarification from Paris Stationhouse. Not merely a delaying tactic, but until more precise details came to light, British Cabinet ministers were going to look pretty foolish if they began to comment on rumours and half-truths. Best to say nothing at all, especially with the Lincoln by-election coming up. The people of Lincoln would like to believe that the men and women of Government knew what was happening, and rumours of war or advancing Russian tanks, as announced by one of the Daily rags – completely untrue – were hard to deny when their readers seemed to want to believe it.

But whatever Oosty thought, or planned, he wasn't to know that Grimly had already placed the Square into a deep-freeze; that even as Oosty thought of plugging in the TV Chess game to the VDU to relieve his boredom, Grimly was inspecting premises beside East Putney tube station.

* * *

"I've never held with high-rise tit-tat," Grimly said, sombrely staring out of the tenth floor window, looking out across Putney towards the river. He had to admit it was a lovely view, and with opaque curtains the operations centre would remain unpenetrable to other office high-rises across the road.

"How often does the train pass?" he asked, peering at the station, a few passengers awaiting the train from Wimbledon.

"You can't feel it, or hear it," Jukes told him.

Grimly looked at Bill Jukes carefully. "You with Lip-snatchers, Jukes?"

"Five years now, sir. Mr Caw plucked me out of college and steered me here. Product development mainly. I'm the J in JRLM."

"JRLM?"

"Jukes Ranger Laser Microphone. Point your microphone out of the window, say on the fifteenth floor of that office in the distance," and he pointed to the International Computers building, south side of the river, beside Putney Bridge. "I can focus on an object in that room over there and we could hear everything as good as if we were there. We could also send sound down too, bit of your low register inaudibles, nothing like that for giving them a splitting headache. We use it on the TUC a lot, helps disrupt meetings, and it's always useful to know what villainy they are up to next."

"But that building is half a mile away, or more," Grimly pointed out.

"I've done further. There's a limit, of course, but we can penetrate almost anywhere these days. You don't need clumsy fools going in and fixing bugs on the phones anymore. Our new equipment can make a phone active in your room twenty-four hours a day. Looks disconnected to you, but there it would be listening all the time."

"But East Putney, Jukes. Can the Square move to East Putney?"

Jukes looked doubtful. "Well, you'd be close to us and Mr Caw is very keen on that. Close to Sainsburys, too. It's not distinguished, it doesn't have the same history, Mr Grimly, but there's a good squash club downstairs and there's always Richmond and Wimbledon Common. Not as thick with spies as St James' Park, but give it time, Mr Grimly, give it time."

Grimly found himself wearing a half-hearted smile. He didn't approve. The building was so flimsy and so open. If they could penetrate with laser beams, why couldn't anyone else?

"We'd have to put up mirror bafflers at the windows, Mr Grimly. Can't have people spying on the spies."

"I'm running late, Jukes," Grimly said abruptly, feeling uncomfortable in the young man's presence. "Calon will have my decision by Monday. I won't be hurried into this. Practical and logical moves maybe, in accordance with his current economy drive, but I have to think about the reputation of the Square. Where would we put Archives? The sheer pain of the move, not to mention the expense."

"Cheaper than you think, Mr Grimly. You could put all your paper records on microfilm. I believe they have started. Then Archives could go on the next floor. The Government owns the whole building. Mr Calon said you wouldn't need more than three floors, but there are five, room for a cafeteria. You'll need that. There's nothing around here. Can't pretend there is. East Putney isn't a fancy place, not like the Square."

Grimly walked slowly towards the elevator. He wasn't at all pleased with the idea. Moving to Putney, it was too public. Far too modern, far too modern.

Simon Caw joined them in the elevator at the eighth floor. "Looking over the place, Mr Grimly? Nice to see you again, sir. How's your mother? She well, is she? Still the life of the party?"

"Very well, Mr Caw," Grimly assured him wearily. "I'd like a word with you, if I may, outside."

Simon Caw nodded. Bill Jukes got out at the fifth floor. "See you again, sir. Remember, it's convenient for transportation."

Mercifully, the doors closed on any further enthusiasm for this governmental Mecca – East Putney.

"Twisting your arm, is he?" Simon Caw asked, amused.

"Someone has to. I'm not enthusiastic, Simon. East Putney isn't my idea of a perfect location. It's too flimsy. What do they build these things with?"

"Lipsnatchers grew up here, Hugh. You get to like the place eventually."

Caw lead Grimly outside to the waiting Triumph. Gallant was nowhere to be seen. Nevertheless, cold and tired, Grimly climbed into the car and wound the window down. Caw squatted down beside the car.

"What of the Rat, Simon?" Grimly asked. "What of Colin Fielding?"

Simon Caw licked his lips, he'd been expecting this. He dug into his jacket and brought out a packet of Marlboros, quickly lighting up. If only to warm his hands. "Are we operating on a mutual co-operation basis?"

"Equal partners. You are not under suspicion, Simon."

"How can I be sure?" he asked, the smoke escaping from his lips and snatched immediately by the wind.

Grimly didn't want to be cruel, but all he could say was, "You didn't go to Eton or Harrow. Newcastle University is not noted for its left wing politics, you were never really socially important enough, nor showed the potential for recruitment, Simon. You are part of the new breed. No background, technical skills your playground. I've looked into

126

you, Simon. Even if you were a mole, I couldn't topple you. You have made a bid for power and you're in the ascendant. If you are a mole, then we might as well let out the Square as a roller-disco. Am I wrong?"

Simon Caw smiled, his face betraying nothing. "Colin Fielding will be at the Square at 2 pm, Mr Grimly. He's been asked to pay a visit, drop in a report on the Malta situation. He's keen to tell us what he knows. He thinks the call was from the Stationmaster."

Grimly acknowledged that he understood. "It's best that way. Oosty should be there to receive him. Hallam, too, I hope."

Caw looked at Grimly's tired, sagging face. "The Butcher's Boy, Hugh, he's in London. He's in trouble, or soon will be. Have you seen him?"

Suddenly Grimly felt a chill course through his body. The Butcher's Boy was supposed to be a secret. No-one had authorised Lipsnatchers to know he even existed.

"If you know where he is, Hugh, keep him hidden. Keep him out of the way. I don't want to say anything yet. But I believe his life to be in danger."

Grimly felt a familiar twitch in his neck and he sighed, staring at the Upper Richmond Road. He was far too tired for this game, far too tired. "Why? Tell me more, Simon."

"Don't want to commit myself, but keep him out of sight and below stairs. He knows about the Second Eleven."

"I know. He gave us Colin Fielding."

"He knows more, Hugh. Whatever he has told you, he knows more, and the reason I say that is because someone is very keen to make sure he does not tell."

Grimly frowned. He didn't want to admit that he had not, in fact, heard most of what the Butcher's Boy had said, but Gallant had said that he had covered all the bases. There was no more.

"What would he gain by withholding, Simon? He's our boy. He's one of my boys."

Simon Caw shrugged. "Perhaps he isn't sure. He was the Stationmaster's boy too. Perhaps he thinks the Stationmaster is the one he should speak to."

Grimly didn't want that to be the cause. Caw reasoned further. "Perhaps he has a special source. Something he wants to hold back to negotiate with. You know what these outfielders are. Perhaps he does know who the Second Eleven are, but can't tell you because it is one of your boys, Hugh. Right at the top. Fifth floor-fourth floor, perhaps one of Mr Gallant's tribe. After all, they do get out and travel a great deal."

Grimly found himself growing angry.

"Listen, Simon. We don't know if there *is* a Second Eleven."

"We are in Intelligence, after all, let's be intelligent. This might be a very clever move to put us in chaos, just when Europe has become a madhouse. We may find ourselves in the role of 'Witchfinder General' and drowning innocents, burning honest, loyal, useful men at the stake. We must remember they will try their best to disrupt us. Rumour can lose a war before battle commences."

Simon Caw nodded his head, but maintained his silence.

Suddenly from out of nowhere, Gallant was the other side of the car, opening his door.

"God it's freezing, must be 3°F or less."

"Thank you, Simon," Grimly said, with a final glance in the Lipsnatcher's face. "I'll bear your concern in mind."

"I'll be listening," Caw said in farewell, a disconcerting remark. He stood up and stiffly walked back to his cement and glass home.

"It's ideal for him. See-through walls, endless glass," Grimly complained to Gallant. "Bad cover, can't they let the ground floor? It looks so bare and exposed."

Gallant looked across Grimly to the East Putney high-rise, focusing on a '9,000 SQUARE FEET TO LET' sign. He, too, thought it was exposed and bare. Grimly wound up his window.

Gallant announced, "The Prime Minister has just said things will get worse before they will get better again."

"At least they keep their campaign promises," Grimly said, with a dry smile.

"I've got you a toasted minute steak and a hamburger for myself. I had to queue up for hours to get that. At least thirty minutes."

Grimly was tempted to say that he shouldn't have bothered, but scenting the steam from a broiled piece of beef, his stomach had signalled an acceptance, even if his code of honour wouldn't countenance take-aways.

"It's the Square then?" Gallant asked.

"Yes, Oosty and Hallam are manning the fifth floor. Did you call in Sussie Sutzman and Doc Sludgeon?"

"Yes, and there is a bit more bad news I'm afraid."

"Oh yes?" It was beginning to resemble a cliffhanger, all this bad news and them hanging on with a rotting rope.

"You'll have to wait. They didn't tell me what it was on the phone."

"How many field operators do we have in France, David?"

"Not as many as we should," he answered, starting up the car and quickly moving off in the direction of Wandsworth.

"How many? How many from Headhunters?"

"Sixteen. Perhaps twenty-five in all, covering North to South. We also employ locals and, of course, Paris Station-house has a right to recruit part-timers. We pay out a lot in subs for part-timers."

Grimly put his mind to work whilst Gallant tried to inch his way in and out of the Saturday traffic in an attempt to get back to the other side of the river. Battersea was jammed solid and every escape route had become one way, the wrong way. The journey was a long one and the take-aways, therefore, all the more tolerable.

"Call out all our French fielders, David. As soon as we get to the Square, call them in, filter some into Germany and the rest back to London. But I want our men out of France. It is going to be awkward and we don't want any embarrassments at this juncture."

"You think it is that serious?"

"If we do have moles, then we must assume that Tinkabelle knows who is in France. If we don't have a Second Eleven, then we have twenty-five men in hostile territory who need rebriefing. I want them out and back to Easton. Re-education. Remember Détente is supposed to be the peaceful expansion of Soviet dominance, and peaceful means anything short of a declaration of war. We are witnessing a new surge, David. Our boys are at risk. Get them out, before we have to send black-edged cards to their families."

"Yes, Chief. Anything you want brought back? Still a good discount on the ferries."

But Grimly felt tired again. Tired of thinking, tired of this car with its hard seats. Not at all sure he was capable of a battle with Tinkabelle, and wishful thinking had him hoping that all the rumours were wrong.

*　　*　　*

The Square was in a state of panic. Even with the first, second and third floors trimmed to bare necessity, the fourth and fifth were having a cadenza. Registry was in chaos as caller after caller appeared to ask what was going on. Philip Oosty, still smarting about the economy cuts, was half tempted to use this occasion to start his work to rule, but with history being made, even he found it hard to be petty.

Hallam, fully extended with his own burdens, was doing his best to keep Sir Charles and Calon informed. Both men were at Number Ten for a hastily convened full Cabinet meeting.

When Grimly walked into the Square and Gallant announced that the old Chief was once more back in the saddle, Oosty practically fell on his neck, as if he were Baden-Powell relieving Mafeking.

"It's chaos, Mr Grimly. Asbolute chaos. The Russians have us over a barrel. Absolutely over a barrel."

But Oosty failed to mention which barrel or what was in it, as Grimly passed by and took the narrow stairs to his familiar temple grounds. Oosty followed behind like some sleighted puppy, still yapping on about the crisis and barrels.

Upstairs in Hallam's office, the three men found seats and explanations were declared in order.

Dancer, the security man, was on duty downstairs, with orders to allow only senior staff on the premises and to round up the Head of Archives, Mrs Lily Tigre. The Square couldn't function at all if Archives weren't on board twenty-four hours.

Hallam took the lead in the discussion.

"It's another catalogue of disasters, Hugh. If we ever thought we could play the game on this expansion move, we lost the ashes at noon." He looked at Gallant, taking up a pencil and guiding it towards a list he had in front of him. "I received a call from France. It's Robert Thorn, Gallant. One of your boys. He was found in the back of his Renault van with a bullet hole in the base of his neck. Political killing by the looks of it. Pictures on the way. There was a note pinned onto his chest. 'L'agneau est mort'. "

"The lamb is dead," Grimly translated, looking at Gallant for his opinion.

"It was his first run for us," Gallant explained. "We always call each new boy's first time, the lamb run. It's a joke. The French won't eat British lamb. We tell them that to give them courage. Thorn was my own recruit. It's quite a blow. He was onto this Soviet Mig 'invasion' problem. We reactivated a salesman." Gallant was obviously upset to hear the news.

Grimly grew thoughtful once again, thinking of his warning to Gallant only half an hour earlier. He regretted to see his warning come true so quickly. Gallant could do nothing for Thorn, but at least he had made the call to France when they arrived. Perhaps others would be saved.

"The trouble is," Hallam was saying. "The bullet, I can understand, but the note? They knew he was a lamb, Gallant, a first timer. How did they know? Perhaps your salesman had a change of heart?"

Gallant shrugged, one could speculate many things.

Grimly nudged Oosty's arm. "Any chance of coffee?" he asked.

Oosty, who knew Matron had cleaned them out of coffee and biscuits as part of the first attack on Calon's cuts, replied with a smart, "Economy cuts, Mr Grimly. No refreshments at all. Perhaps a glass of water."

"Nonsense, Oosty," Hallam objected, "there's coffee, there's always coffee."

"Not since Calon's cuts, Mr Hallam. There'll be precious few other perks as well. We'll have to buy our own pencils soon."

Hallam made a furious note on his pad. "We'll have to see about this. We can't run an Intelligence Service without coffee, biscuits and pens. What is Calon up to? You see what happens in your absence, Hugh. They treat us like children. This government has no respect for tradition, none at all."

"I rather think Calon wants us to go to East Putney," Grimly said quietly, an after lunch drowsiness coming on.

"East Putney?" Hallam exploded. "Oosty, do you know about this?"

Oosty affirmed that he did. "Economy cuts have become the vogue, Mr Hallam. They have issued thermal underwear to DHSS staff members and done away with central heating altogether."

"It's the dark ages," Hallam protested. "These barbarians are driving us back to the dark ages."

Gallant lit himself a Lucky and ignored this endless and fruitless discussion on economics. He knew Headhunters would be next. Having lost France, he'd have to fight just to keep one man in Paris. The Cabinet seemed to be looking for any excuse to finish off the Intelligence Corps.

"I think we are missing the point at issue," Grimly said with a degree of schoolmasterly censure.

"There might be some tea," Oosty suggested, feeling thirsty himself by this time.

They all agreed on tea and coerced Oosty to go out and

make it. As he rather reluctantly left, Grimly turned to Hallam and asked, "Now perhaps you could tell us your bad news, Peter. I am expecting a visitor at 2 pm, not far off now I should think."

Hallam had a reason for delaying the announcement. "I'm waiting for confirmation from the Relatives, Hugh. It is merely speculation at the moment, but if it is true then we should be prepared for it, since we were warned more than twenty-four hours ago."

"What precisely?" Gallant asked, blowing smoke over Hallam's desk.

"That Israeli–South African bomb. The nuclear test. They exploded it in Namibia, South West. Right on the border between Angola and Namibia."

"Surface?" Gallant asked, extremely surprised that it had taken place at all.

"Underground, but there has been immediate earth fault problems, and reports coming in – our fellow Baumann for instance – suggest that it was a very dirty weapon indeed. But Baumann's information is coming from the French and isn't reliable."

"Dirty? How dirty?"

"Fifty to one hundred kilotons, but that is a sensitive area. SWAPO run that section."

"A genuine no-man's-land. A half-life border patrol," Grimly muttered to himself. "Good idea from their point of view. No-one is going to try and infiltrate a radioactive border. Even ten kilotons would contaminate a large area. I'm not sure this report is credible at all."

"I thought the idea of an underground test was to minimise surface contamination," Gallant said, stubbing out his cigarette.

"Earth's crust could have moved, I suppose. I wonder where that tea is?" Hallam queried.

They all looked at the door, but Oosty didn't appear with the tea. "You look worried, Hugh, what is it?" Hallam asked.

"As a political act, it will have the same effect as if they had

133

exploded it here. It has been rumoured they had the bomb, jointly or separately, for a long time. As long as they didn't use it, we all had happy smiles. But this coming in the wake of a major political realignment in Europe and an active détente probe by Moscow . . . Israel and South Africa have made a grave mistake, a great misjudgement of timing. This is a bad day. The Arabs will gallop into Moscow's arms and demand either their own deterrent, or to be under Moscow's umbrella. The front line states in Africa will take the same line. In neither case will we, or the US be able to countermove. The US is pro-Israel and we are still heavily invested in South Africa."

"But it isn't confirmed," Hallam pointed out.

"Do the press have it?" Gallant asked.

Hallam shrugged. "It's possible. Namib is a desert, but it's not without the press. We must assume the press will have it and will scream from the highest trees with it. The nuclear club is pregnant and when will Pakistan explode hers?"

Oosty came in with the tea. "It's powdered milk. It's Saturday. No deliveries on Saturday around here."

There were moans of disgust. No-one liked powdered milk.

"There's a Mr Colin Fielding waiting in the Games Room, Mr Grimly. He's come to see the Stationmaster."

Grimly was glad of the respite. He didn't want to think of nuclear problems. They weren't his cup of tea.

"I'm going to see him. Will you bring us some tea to the Games Room, Oosty? Also make sure Lipsnatchers are turned on in that room."

"Always on, sir. Voice activated. Lipsnatchers never sleep."

"And, Peter, France is a problem, but Spain? See if you can find someone to run up a profile on Hispanic trade with us and South America. We will need to brief Cabinet Office with something. Our trade will suffer. There's the EEC problem too. Will France stay in, or will she join Comecon? Get someone working on that."

"Yes, Chief." He picked up his brief case and left the room.

Hallam dialled the Relatives again. He needed to keep himself occupied. Milos had definitely not been home for three days. He had some people going through the man's apartment, so far no report. He had to keep himself busy, any gaps and he found himself thinking of Wendy. The pain was just beneath the surface all the time. Grimly was at the door.

"Call Lady Grimly, Oosty. Tell her that some of Dr Mowbray's is needed in London. She'll understand."

"Yes, sir."

Grimly turned and with a heavy heart went to look for Colin Fielding, still wondering how he got the nickname 'the Rat.' He read through the hastily assembled notes on Fielding that Simon Caw had sent via the VDU and which Gallant had printed out for him on arrival. Interesting, he hoped useful. He pocketed them before entering the room.

Colin Fielding sat on a plain tubular chair, the canvas still bearing a faint echo of the Crown imprint. There were several of them in the room and the room itself was long and harshly lit with neon tubes set into an asbestos ceiling. At the end of the room was a portrait of Her Majesty the Queen and she, in turn, stared at an old *Daily Telegraph* map of the world. No doubt disappointed that so little of the surface reflected her glory anymore. She was just lucky that all the pink places had great beaches. An empire of great beaches was something to be proud of, it vaguely made up for the oil-drenched rocks at Brighton.

Colin spotted Grimly slowly making his way towards him. He was eager to impress, eager to be noticed and noted that *he* was on time and that the Stationmaster quite obviously was not.

Grimly was feeling dizzy. This was the first day in almost six months that he had failed to obtain the services of Dr Mowbray, and already the deterioration was quite marked. His face sagged, his eyes felt heavy and even his teeth, still mostly his own, hurt. Fortunately, his mind was still sound and, though swamped by all the trouble that had come the Square's way, it wasn't sinking. In his mind, they were still feeling their way, trying to gauge the extent of the problem.

Something was coming to mind, something that the Station-master had said once. He had a feeling that he had only to look under a quiet corner of his mind and he would remember what it was exactly.

"Colin," Grimly said, staggering to a chair.

"Mr Grimly, sir, nice to see you. Thought you had retired. Come back for a visit have you?"

Fool, thought Grimly. Did he think the Square was like school? One didn't visit the Square like some old boys' re-union.

"You could say that, Colin," he answered. "The Station-master won't be coming. I'm deputising. You can check with Hallam if you like. He is in his office."

Fielding shook his head. "If you say you're in charge, Mr Grimly, then I'm happy. Sir Charles always talks of you. Doesn't think England is safe without you. This place isn't the same anymore. Everytime I climb the steps outside, I think of the old days, the old team."

"You mean Will Strawson?" Grimly slipped in, deliber-ately.

"Yes," Fielding answered, "he may have been a bad boy, Mr Grimly, and you know that more than anyone, but he added some colour to our lives. Will was a man of colour, know what I mean?"

"Mostly red, I think. But like you, he started out light blue."

"Oh steady on , Mr Grimly. Don't put me in the same boat, old chap."

"Will was a very colourful man. People are always upset when a popular man turns out to be a traitor."

"Oh I say, Mr Grimly. An idealist, he did it for his ideals. Never to feather his own nest."

"Nesting isn't one of their known habits. It's easier to be a high liver, big spender, it you're receiving the same amount the other side, building up in a bank account over the years. His nest was well feathered for him."

Fielding affected a boredom with the subject. "There is another matter, Mr Grimly, before I get onto Malta."

"Oh yes?"

Fielding crossed his legs and leant forward towards Grimly. "A confidential matter," he confided, his voice a whisper.

Grimly could see his lips moving, but at seventy-five, he had still not mastered lip-reading. He bent forward, until there was barely a foot between them, but nothing reached his ears.

"I'm sorry, Colin. I can't hear you."

Fielding expressed a momentary annoyance, then repeated his secret. "Oland Shipping, Mr Grimly. They are Finnish. Offices in London, Harwich and Southampton. Word is that a shipping line with only one ship hardly needs three large offices. The ship always seems to be passing through when NATO naval exercises are going on. Just a tip from the wise, Mr Grimly."

Grimly thought about it. He knew, for instance, that there wasn't a shipping company in the whole of the UK that didn't warrant the close attention of the Lipsnatchers, all, that is, except Oland Line. And Oland Line was exempt because it was run by Her Majesty's Government as a cover organisation for electronic surveillance monitoring of Soviet naval forces. What Fielding was trying to say was that Oland's cover had been blown, which suddenly reminded Grimly of why they called Fielding 'the Rat'. Every organisation has a confidential source, a well controlled leak. Fielding was neither well controlled nor confidential. A rat who obtained a flimsy dross from telling tales out of court to – and that was the crunch – to whom?

Had Tinkabelle planted this one about Oland? Or had Fielding come across it in Club-land gossip. One could never tell. Club talk was a netherland of distortions, traded by minnows to elevate themselves into the mainstream that none would ever attain without being swept away.

Grimly began a litany. "There's 300–350 identifiable Soviet Intelligence Officers functioning in this city, Colin. Some legal, most tenuously so. They are involved in the ordinary affairs of legitimate trade. Aeroflot, Tass, Radio Moscow and, of course, the Dips and Consular staffs. Each one running a second stringer, one of our loyal subjects. The point I'm making, Colin, is, are you playing with, or against, the visiting team?"

Colin Fielding blinked with surprise. He hadn't expected this. Not an outright question.

"Colin, I could waffle on. I could listen to your version of Malta, and also to your explanations as to why you maintain a covert friendship with a certain Soviet diplomat there. Your activities in Norway honestly justified in your best Foreign Office innocence, but I'm tired, Colin, I'm not a young man anymore. In other words, Colin, tell me, in confidence for the moment, exactly where your loyalties lie. And if you're thinking of bluffing and running out of here, David Gallant, the Headhunter, is at the end of the corridor. You remember Gallant don't you? He collects rats, Colin."

Fielding showed his alarm. He wasn't used to such blunt talk. His usual bonhomie visibly shrivelled. His crop of greying hair began to sweat.

"I say, Mr Grimly, you can't, you're not serious. Not me?"

"You are the liaison between NSA in Washington and Cabinet Office as well, aren't you, Colin? The Med and Washington. Important aren't you? Who was it you saw in Norway? What did Tinkabelle have to say to you there, or in Malta? What are your orders?"

"Look, I don't have to take this, Grimly," Fielding protested, running his hands through his hair, his nicotine stained teeth visible now as his lips stretched with nervous stress. "I've been with the Foreign Office for fifteen years. I'm highly respected. It is my career you are fooling with, Grimly. My life."

"Colin," Grimly soothed, "don't get excited. I just want the truth. What do you know about Sir Harold Miller for instance?"

Suddenly Colin Fielding grew quite still, his hands clenched together on his lap. Grimly noticed the man's eyes focus on something in the distance behind him, as if he were contemplating bolting from him. As if he knew Gallant wasn't at the end of that corridor.

"I want Sir Charles here. If you are going to accuse me of anything, Grimly, I want Sir Charles here."

But instead of Sir Charles, Philip Oosty arrived, all apologetic, bearing a tray with two cups of tea, the tops of the cups covered with saucers. "Sorry, Mr Grimly, sir. I had to reboil the kettle. Mr Hallam drank the pot. He's one for the tea is Mr Hallam."

Grimly welcomed the interruption. It would soothe Fielding and slake his own thirst, which was becoming quite unbearable. The result of that take-away steak, or withdrawal symptoms.

"Miss Sutzman and Doctor Sludgeon are in Archives, Mr Grimly. Lily Tigre has got them busy on policy. Mr Hallam thought we'd better be prepared to issue something in the way of a summary to the past few days' events."

"Good idea. Any luck with Lady Grimly?"

"I called her, sir. She said she understood and would call the doctor."

Grimly nodded, watching Oosty go, closing the door after him.

"And how is your mother, Mr Grimly? Such a charming woman. Quite missed at the Palace garden parties."

"She has only missed one this century," Grimly told him, sipping his Earl Grey and closing his eyes with relief. For a brief moment he felt the hot liquid recharge and restore him. "Now, Colin, I checked the records," Grimly began again in a friendly, grandfatherly voice, his tone hinting that this was a family confession, just between the two of them. It would go no further. "You were at school with Sir Harold Miller. Sir Harold spent a week in Malta last October. He was with a young girl, an East German girl. I believe he stayed in your apartment?"

"I rent my apartment out to friends. No rules against a bit of business, Mr Grimly. I can't get there as often as I did."

"Bit . . . of . . . business? Is that what you call it, Colin? Sir Harold met the Soviet Ambassador there, did you know that? An East German girlfriend and the Berlin British General Officer of Command. And that was in October."

Fielding was silent, staring at his tea.

"Your boat. Your apartment. This meeting in October and not a word filed, Colin. But you were seen. Seen in October and again last week, sailing with the Soviet Chargé d'Affaires and his son, Karl. As Foreign Office Mediterranean Affairs Secretary you would be expected to be concerned with Malta. I'm not disputing your presence in Malta, nor indeed Norway, Colin, I understand it was a NATO conference. I *am* questioning your silence and your friends. Your friends, our enemy. I'd accept your friends, Colin, I really would, cover is cover and we all need to be on good terms with the enemy to understand him. But not a word, Colin. Not a word passed back to us. Nothing to Sir Charles, nothing to our Ambassador on the island. You were good pals with Sir Harold, weren't you? What did Sir Harold know, eh? What did he have to offer the East Germans? Clever to get a military man to defect, was it? How long was it planned? Did you set up the meetings, played the friendship game, gave him the shoe-in? Something, not just the girl surely, made him jump? Jump on the night the Berlin wall came down. What exactly was the benefit to East Berlin? They get the exact fall back plan for Allied Command? Is that it? Top drawer secrets so they can walk into Berlin and take over with the minimum of fuss. What would they want Sir Harold for?"

"I've done nothing wrong. I must insist on that, Mr Grimly. Many people use my apartment. Sir Charles, for one. After all, we all went to the same school, didn't we?"

Unfortunately that was true.

"You're suspended from duties, Colin. You will be held here for further questioning. Meanwhile, I want the names of all the people who have used your apartment and the names of all the Soviet contacts you've made in the last year, including

Norway. I'll be sending along someone to talk to you, Colin. I hope you haven't made plans for the weekend."

Fielding didn't answer.

Grimly slowly raised his body off the chair, intending to leave.

"You should have said something in October, Colin. Sir Harold wrote a letter thanking you. It's in Archives. He didn't say what he was thanking you for. That omission will hang you."

"How could I know?" Fielding retorted sharply. "I wasn't there."

"No, you were in Italy with Sir Charles. Except for the weekend, Colin. The weekend when you caught a plane at Milan Airport. It's all in the files. I wonder where you flew to?"

"You are just trying to make a frame fit, Mr Grimly. I'm not one of your red cards. Don't play me like you did Will Strawson. This time you're wrong. You're not as strong as before, you're not as young. They won't tolerate your cowboy tactics. You ruined a good many careers last time. You're not going to ruin mine."

Silently, Grimly opened the door and left the room, locking the door behind him and hanging the key up on the wall. He sighed and shook his head, starting the long walk back to Hallam's office, thinking that he should take a look at the Stationmaster's room. His head was splitting with a newly arrived headache. Hallam's news didn't make it any easier.

"All hell's broken loose, Hugh. The papers have it. The Sundays will blast it across their front pages."

Grimly collapsed into a chair with a questioning look.

"The nuclear test, Hugh. One report lists thousands contaminated."

Grimly forced himself to think. "Have you got any asprin, or better, Peter?"

Hallam understood. "Me too. Here, here's a glass of water and two Panadols, they are on standby for the next crisis."

141

Grimly took both of them quickly, swallowing the full glass of water. His head was pounding, nothing like it for years. "I've been thinking, Peter, there aren't thousands in the Namib desert. Very few people at all come to think of it."

"Dying like flies and the South Africans won't touch them."

"Whose report?" Grimly asked, straining to see the telegrams piled on Hallam's desk.

"French," Hallam answered, catching Grimly's disbelief.

"Have the Relatives confirmed it?"

Gallant suddenly arrived at the office door, obviously excited and out of breath. "TASS is saying radioactive winds are drifting towards East German forward positions in Angola. They've got 15,000 men stationed there. Incredible tension down there. Everyone on full alert. South Africa is still denying everything and calling up her reserves. It's incredible. How could they explode a fifty kilotons within contamination distance of a civilian or military presence?"

"Fetch me a map and call – an open call, Hallam – Herman Steyn at Johannesburg Stationhouse," Grimly ordered. He wanted to settle this. He had had enough of speculation.

But before Hallam could call, an incoming alert beeped on the VDU screen. It flashed Blue Code. Extreme Sensitivity – meaning fifth floor only. Hallam lumped Gallant in, there was little point in keeping things from him whilst he was Grimly's swordbearer.

Gallant dug out a map of South Africa and pointed out the area where French reports indicated the test had taken place, running his finger along the supposed line of drift.

Hallam unscrambled the incoming call and turned to Grimly, his voice leaden, a defeated tone to it. "The Paris–Moscow mutual defence pact is confirmed. The French President will be broadcasting to the nation Sunday night."

"With luck Jean-Paul Belmondo will be on a rival channel," Gallant said.

"It's directly connected to the Israeli/South African situation," Hallam continued. "France has linked this new threat from American backed Israel to the necessity of a major re-alignment to prevent the growing threat to world peace. France will maintain a complete no trade, of any kind, boycott with Israel."

"Much as expected," Gallant said.

But Grimly was studying the map, tracing his fingers along a line, shaking his head.

"Make that call to Johannesburg, Hallam."

The map was definitely worrying Grimly. His head was easing a little, but even so, it was hard to think. "You said the test took place here, Gallant?" he queried.

Gallant looked over his shoulder. "So they say."

"But this is part of the Etosha Game Reserve. The South Africans may be inhuman in their dealings with their indigenous populations, Gallant, but I hardly think they'd blow up a game reserve, a tribal trustland filled with Ovambos. The South Africans are obsessed with two things: rugby and game reserves. I guarantee you have either the wrong location, or someone is exaggerating the strength of the blast. As for windborn radioactivity, the prevailing surface winds in summer – it is their summer – would go inland, it's true, but it was an underground explosion, if it was anything at all. You talk as if it were a surface test."

Hallam had reached Johannesburg and called for quiet. "Herman, it's 'open book'. This is Hallam in London. Understand, this is 'open book'." Hallam looked up briefly, suddenly wondering if Gallant knew who the Butcher's Boy was and if he'd tell him. It was something worth bearing in mind.

"I want confirmation, that's all," he bellowed down the phone. "Did they explode the bomb or not? You must know, Herman. Fifty kilotons would shake half the country. We've got reports of thousands lying dead in the desert. Etosha Pan, Angolan border. Yes, of course this is official. Now tell me, what are they saying there?"

Hallam frowned when he received his reply, obviously not enjoying what he heard. Grimly refolded the map. If a bomb had gone off, then there was no hope for Israel or South Africa.

143

One couldn't defend them; equally, one couldn't blame them. Both countries felt abandoned. Particularly South Africa, vulnerable to the continued shallowness of a West weakened by détente.

Gallant took another incoming call. The blue phone, the Relatives at last. "Gallant, Hallam's office," he announced.

"Mitchel," came the familiar American voice. "You boys wanted to know about the South African situation."

"Yes. We just heard the Moscow–Paris pact has been confirmed. I'm pulling my boys out of France, Mitchel."

"Typical of you Brits. We are deeping, getting the Tenderfoots out and old hands in. Washington is in turmoil, deep shit."

"The blast, Mitchel?" Gallant asked, noticing Hallam had disconnected his Johannesburg call.

"Nothing. Got that? Nothing. Our satellites didn't pick up anything. There's no evidence of any radiation at all. No explosion of nuclear type."

"You are saying nothing happened?"

"Just the earthquake."

"Earthquake? What earthquake?"

"The South-West African earthquake, Gallant. Big one. Equals 9 on the Richter scale. Right on the border, whole lot of people injured, but hardly any dead. There's not exactly many buildings out there. No rubble, no deaths."

"But are you aware of the French reports coming out of that area? TASS and the German press all report an Israeli/SA Nuke test."

"We aren't denying it yet."

Gallant caught his breath. He wasn't sure he had heard that right. "Repeat please."

"New policy. The President thinks he can do without the Jewish vote. Let the ZF stew for a while. It's a test."

"But that's crazy. You mean it is convenient not to deny this report?"

"Well translated, Gallant. We will embarrass the hell out of the French next week, meanwhile I gotta go. There's a briefing

144

Tuesday am. Full new policy on Europe will be on show. If you can find two people who are on our side, send them over, that way we can be sure Moscow will get it right first time."

"What is that supposed to mean?" Gallant demanded to know.

However, Mitchel rang off.

"Well?" Grimly asked.

"It isn't true. There has been an earthquake and the Yanks don't want to deny it yet, policy decision."

"Johannesburg admit to an earthquake only," Hallam concurred.

"Then call Sir Charles, Peter. Tell him rumours of nuclear test false. Make sure Cabinet Office tell all the newspapers the same. A full, firm denial. I don't care for the American game. I'll not have double standards, no number games. For once we will tell the truth. Alert our man at the Red Cross. If they start an appeal, it will give it credibility. We will take the initiative on this one."

Hallam dialled Sir Charles' number.

"David, Colin Fielding is under observation and not allowed to leave the Square, under any circumstances. Call in Nolan to look after him and you will find me in Archives." Grimly climbed to his feet unsteadily, dizzy, almost light-headed. "Plateau policy, did you say, David?" He smiled with a knowing despair. "Well, I have no overview. We are a trounced army on the run, David." He looked at Hallam, waiting for an answer. "Peter, you're worried about something, aren't you? I can tell. You always have that furrow in your brow when you're in trouble."

"There's enough to keep it there permanently, Hugh. We were never prepared for more than one problem at once."

Grimly nodded in agreement. "Go and see Colin Fielding. You knew Sir Harold Miller. I want to know a few things. What did Sir Harold know? What did he know about our current defence system, his current briefings? What could he give the Soviets that they flung such attractive human bait at him. I want to know who are his immediate British contacts at

145

Berlin HQ and I'm assuming they are already in custody. Speak to Fielding. He's got a line onto this. He knows why Sir Harold was so important and, more's the point, set up a meeting between Sir Harold and the Soviets in Malta last October."

"He did?" Hallam asked, surprised.

"I don't care what you do to him. But he knows I have a hook into him. If he isn't one of the Second Eleven, then he is definitely a scorer or umpire. I'll send down Dr Sludgeon. He is still our Russian Crystal?"

"Yes," Hallam answered, wondering why Cabinet Office were taking so long to put him through to Sir Charles. He looked at Grimly, showing his impatience. Grimly looked most unsteady on his feet. Gallant picked up his briefcase and left the room.

"Let me know how you get on, Peter. Oh yes, how is little Wendy?"

Hallam started. He hadn't been ready for that one.

"Trouble?" Grimly asked, noticing his reaction. "Young girls can be so headstrong."

Hallam bit his lip, tempted to tell Grimly. Tempted to lay the whole ghastly mess before him. He didn't know what exactly held him back. Grimly would know what to do, but then, he might also decide Wendy was expendable and he couldn't risk that. Never that. Wendy must be preserved at all costs.

"A little trouble. It always comes at once."

"True, always at once. Can't see this blowing over. Tinkabelle has all his claws out. The question is why? Why would they bother, Peter? He has everything going his way. Why does he have to infest this sceptered isle? What do we have to offer anymore? He gets France, Spain and Malta in a weekend, does he expect us to crumble to our knees?"

"I rather think he does," Hallam replied. "Perhaps we are next, Hugh. After all, if we crumble, America will be driven from Europe forever, back to isolation."

"And Germany?" Grimly asked, holding onto the door for

146

support. "Reunification of Germany. The young don't know why we old men cringe at the thought."

"Nevertheless, it is a big possibility now. Paris and Bonn have been big buddies lately. It's written on the wall, Hugh."

"Go and see Colin the Rat, Peter. I'm going to see the oracles. I've an idea our Stationmaster isn't so far away. It's just my tired old brain that has forgotten something, some essential thing, old minds do that."

The phone squawked suddenly. "Ah, Sir Charles, at last. Hallam here."

Grimly braced himself and left the office, his face a desolate reminder of bitter days. He wanted a word with the Butcher's Boy again.

As he took the stairs down to the fourth floor, he wondered if Bettina had located Dr Mowbray yet. He was going to need help soon, no doubt about it. If only he had a grip on this Second Eleven as strongly as Tinkabelle. What was it that made the English such keen traitors? Why, too, had he wasted his life guarding an empty stable door? He needed a grip on the Square only half as strong as old age had on his body. Damn slouching lump of a carcass had him prisoner with no chance of reprieve. And Moscow's threats – did they really believe the West would sit back and take all this? What was it that Strawson used to say? 'There have always been wars; peace is merely a matter of recuperation'.

FIVE

A Small Town in East Germany

Slighty was listening with a distracted ear to the German political officer, a surprise guest from the East Berlin Ministry of Public Affairs. "*Wo ist das Badezimmer?*" he asked for the second time.

"First right, straight on until the skylight, mind your head," Slighty told him, turning to Nibs to ask, "*Wie sagt man auf Deutsch?*"

Nibs, who was trying to make head or tail of a garbled 'flash' coded telegram, looked up briefly, shrugging, "Say it slowly, that always works."

"Bathroom . . . has . . . a . . . low . . . ceiling, mind your head," he explained to the impatient German walking with indecent haste up the stairs towards the bathroom.

"*Ja, Ja,*" he returned, the nervousness in his voice betraying the urgency of his call to nature. He reached the skylight at the top of the stairs, unaware of the expectant eyes of Slighty and Nibs following his every move. They heard him open the bathroom door and both men winced as the anticipated crash of breaking glass reached their ears.

"There goes the bathroom light again," Nibs said casually. The East German bounced back onto the landing, clutching his bleeding head. He seemed most aggrieved and shouted, "*Ich brauche einen Arzt.*"

"He wants a doctor," Nibs said. "Call Hans Honig up from the basement, tell him to bring a box of band-aids and tell him he's a doctor."

Slighty did as he was told. Nothing had been right since the night Sir Harold had defected. Now this German was here for 'discussions', not a good omen in his opinion.

Nibs finished with the telegram and sat back in his chair frowning at the result.

"What does it say?" Slighty asked, still watching the bathroom door.

"All non-essential British citizens and consular staff to be evacuated – with immediate effect. Air or road if car owners. Evacuate with discretion, do not alarm, or inform local populace. All clear by Wednesday 08.00 hours."

Slighty whistled. This was a turn up for the books. "That's the short fuse, Nibs. The whole business is going to blow up in our faces. I'm going to miss Berlin."

"You're not going, Slighty. We are essential personnel. At least officially we are, in your case I sometimes have my doubts." Slighty ignored the insult. "Anyway," Nibs continued, "With Sir Harold gone, we are even more essential."

Hans Honig, the electrician impersonating as a doctor, arrived, his cheerful ruddy face out of place in the Berlin HQ.

"Where is the patient?" Hans asked, grinning. "Same as usual, is it?"

"We'll need a new light in the bathroom, Hans. I told you to put a sign up about that ceiling."

"I did, Mr Nibs. A big sign – in English."

Slighty smiled, "Never mind, Hans, it was only a German head that got dunned. Mind taking your sticky plasters upstairs? Herr Peter Kanter will be dabbing his bloody head in the sink."

"I should get doctor's money, Mr Slighty. Third time since Christmas."

"Last time, Hans, I promise," Nibs said with ease. "We're probably going to have the roof raised anytime soon now."

"Ah, building again. That is good," Hans said, happy to hear that the British were taking positive steps. His friends would be pleased to hear that too. For if they were building, they wouldn't be running away, which was what his friends thought they would be doing now the wall was down. With great cheer he went to attend Herr Peter Kanter.

Slighty looked across at Nibs and shook his head. "You should be careful Nibs, someone might understand your sarcasm one day. They'll panic, you know. I was in Aden when we pulled out. Sheer bloody terror, women beating their brains out on the front door trying to get British protection.

"Let the Germans learn the hard way, Slighty. We've given ground to the Communists ten times out of ten since the war, why should now be any different?"

"I've got work to do," Slighty said, "better spread the word."

"Call a general meeting for 2.30 pm," Nibs said, "make a list of non-essential personnel, but leave us someone to make the coffee, don't be over zealous."

"Righto, Nibs. Have fun with the Kraut."

In session, twenty minutes later, Nibs was less willing to play games with their East German visitor. The man sat on a hard chair, a hand constantly pawing the swelling on his forehead, fingers gingerly touching the large sticky plaster that covered the messy wound.

"I hope they won't think we tortured you, Herr Kanter?"

Herr Kanter smiled. "We know the British torture the Irish, Herr Nibs, but they wouldn't believe you would be so stupid as to start on the East Germans."

"Then you will accept our heartfelt apologies?"

"It is not necessary, Herr Nibs. I was warned."

Which is just as well, Nibs felt. He didn't need a diplomatic row on top of everything else.

"We need not have anything between us, Herr Nibs. May I first say . . . we know where Sir Harold Miller is."

Nibs' heart sank. "Oh?" he said, "you've come to tell me Sir Harold is on a skiing trip in Switzerland? We know. I hear the snow is perfect at this time of year." (This was the cover story, though hardly credible that the GOC would go on vacation in such a crisis.)

"No, I don't disagree with the fact, Herr Nibs, only the

location. Sir Harold is indeed on a skiing holiday, only not in Switzerland, he is staying in Eisenach, a small town in East Germany."

Nibs threw in the towel. Why bother to pretend? They obviously knew everything. The whole security coding and military arrangements will have been blown by now.

"We had an interesting talk with Sir Harold Miller," Herr Kanter stressed, still fingering the plaster on his head.

Slightly popped his head around the door. "It's London, Nibs. New instructions . . ." He stalled, noticing the thin head of their East German visitor sitting up against the wall with the Queen's portrait above him. "Er, I'll call back."

Nibs showed no emotion on his face at all. The East Berliner would be looking for signs of panic, he'd want to gauge the atmosphere. Therefore Nibs was determined not to show any signs of weakness, glad that Slighty had had the sense to withdraw.

"I'd be interested to know what Sir Harold said," Nibs asked at last, "if it *was* Sir Harold?"

"Ach, it was Sir Harold, Herr Nibs. He was with his 'companion', Regina Schmidt. I believe you know her yourself?"

Nibs acknowledged him with the briefest of smiles. The German had all the charm and personality of a ferret. The man must think that he was soft in the head. What sort of foreplay was this? East Berlin had all the cards, what could this meeting be but a cashing in of his chips?

"I do know Regina," Nibs admitted. "A sweet girl. Very strong." Nibs had a flash of inspiration. "I believe Tinkabelle chose her himself."

Herr Kanter was quite taken aback. The damn Britische had just played out one of his cards and he hadn't even opened the pack.

"You knew?" He marvelled at the British cunning.

"Certainly. But Sir Harold is in love with Regina. The English way is to let love run its course. (Or, Nibs thought, give him enough rope until he hangs his friends.)

Herr Kanter shook his head. Love wasn't a word that had

passed his lips since he'd abandoned his childhood for the Party. Yet to judge from the decadent music played over the radio and TV it was all the English and Americans thought about, even to the extent of allowing the Berlin General Officer of Command to betray his country. What strength the Britische must have, what iron will. Yet so much abandoned to the passions must defeat them in the end. The Party will was discipline and that was the difference between good and evil. Freedom to be undisciplined, a foolishness.

"So Sir Harold is having a nice time skiing, is he?" Nibs asked. "You wouldn't like to pass a message to him, would you? From his wife. Regina would understand. His wife wants him to know that it is his daughter Martha's birthday on March 10th, and could he try and be back in time? You see he ordered her a bicycle and his wife doesn't know from which store."

Herr Kanter couldn't believe it. They expected Sir Harold to come back, for a bicycle? What values were these?

"Is he well? How is Regina?" Nibs asked in a friendly manner. "Oh yes, perhaps I could get you some coffee, I could do with some anyway."

The ferret signalled an acceptance and Nibs pressed his buzzer. Five short buzzes meant two cups of coffee, one code that wasn't protected at Berlin HQ.

"Regina is very well, considering her condition," Herr Kanter said, relaxing a little.

"Ah yes, the baby."

"You knew?" Again, Herr Kanter was disappointed.

"Difficult to hide. She had good care, best gynaecologist in Berlin. He thinks it's a boy, though God knows how they can tell."

"She is a pretty girl; Sir Harold, a good looking man. It should be a handsome child, Herr Nibs."

"They like babies over there do they, Herr Kanter? Regina rather thought you'd want to terminate the little fella. She never told her parents, y'know. Told them she was putting on weight with English cooking." Nibs smiled, amused by the idea.

Herr Kanter was only too well aware that the parents hadn't known, such criminal neglect could not be tolerated. Regina had made fools of them all. A punishment would be found.

Miraculously the coffee arrived, in the care of a young British secretary, Fiona, who poured out two cups from a Cona jug. Julian Nibs had been flirting with Fiona for sixteen months, but never once dared to ask her out. Of course, she was dating Monkton, the 6ft scrum-half liaison officer from Private Office, but share and share alike. He'd always hoped.

Fiona smiled, her white face bordered by a pale, limp blob of blonde hair that desperately needed the attention of Sassoon. She had, it has to be admitted, looked a lot more healthy before Monkton had got his hands on her. She withdrew after a moment of stirring sugar into Herr Kanter's coffee cup. He stared mesmerised. Female staff in the Ministry his side of Berlin never looked like this. It hurt him that it was so.

When Fiona departed there was a new camaraderie between them that had not been there before.

"Sir Harold was very naughty," Nibs said, lifting his coffee up to his lips. "The Montag Club are very angry with him, not to mention the British Military Government Pension Fund."

"Oh yes?" Herr Kanter asked, not sure what the man meant. Sir Harold flees the West and all they worry about is his club and his pension fund. The Britische were weird.

"He didn't mention his club, Herr Nibs."

"No?" Nibs replied with disbelief. If the East Berliners were going to get anything valuable at all, the Montag Club members would be the ones they'd want. An anti-Soviet organisation, of which Sir Harold was an honorary member, consisting mostly of secret members of a pro-West alliance dedicated to the division of Germany. Printing leaflets, giving talks in schools, writing letters to the press, all in the name of an independent West Germany and Berlin. With that list, the East Germans would have the most up-to-date hit list to execute on the day of reunification. The first candidates for their own Gulag. Sir Harold had fooled them all with his impassioned speeches on a free Germany.

"He didn't mention his pension fund either," Herr Kanter said. "That is why I am here, Herr Nibs. You see, we don't understand why Sir Harold came to us. We don't understand it at all."

"But you said you had an interesting chat," Nibs reminded him.

"Yes. Sir Harold knows a great deal. Our Martin Luther was living in Eisenach in 1521, you know. Johanne Sebastian Bach was born there, too."

"You mean our Sir Harold Miller defects and all he talks about is Martin Luther and J.S. Bach?" It wasn't credible.

"This is true," Herr Kanter stated. "Very well informed man. Our chief had no idea that Martin Luther was a collector of butterflies. This is interesting. Eisenach has some very fine butterflies."

Nibs swallowed his coffee and tried to understand what the man was saying, trying to decide if it was a play from another angle set to unnerve him. Surely they knew? Sir Harold had absconded with £150,000 in cash. The annual interest on a unit-trust pension fund for the Active Military Forces stationed in Berlin. It was one thing putting his signature to the bank cheque, quite another cashing it in Switzerland. It had returned cancelled and paid out in cash, the very stuff of defectors. It had remained undiscovered for more than a week. What is more, only a special cross check on Sir Harold's office files had revealed this illegal transaction. Gone, too, was the Montag Club members' list. His secretary was under arrest, but he seemed as surprised as the rest of them. So with these 'trinkets' he had fled with his Regina, and now Herr Kanter was trying to say all they talked about was butterflies.

"Now, Herr Kanter, let's have the real reason for your visit."

Herr Kanter looked about himself, confused. His narrow

154

face creased into a frown, instantly reminding him of his bruise.

"But I'm here for your explanations, Herr Nibs. Sir Harold doesn't want to defect. He doesn't want to tell us anything, all he wants is Regina Schmidt. And now we can't find him."

"You said he was in Eisenach."

"He was, believe me, he was. I myself visited him yesterday."

"And today?"

"He went skiing – with Regina. She is not in such a good condition for skiing, Herr Nibs."

"And?"

"We lost him. We rather wondered if he had not come back here."

"Eisenach is a long way from Berlin, Herr Kanter. He might have gone to Frankfurt."

"No–one crossed the border. He would have no visa. Besides he had no visa for the Eisenach exit."

"Let's get this straight. We believe Sir Harold has defected. You say he hasn't. You also say you didn't know Regina was pregnant."

"Correct."

"Yet we both know Regina Schmidt was recruited to lure Sir Harold to the East. Let's be honest, shall we?"

Herr Kanter had difficulty with that word 'honest'. He decided to drink his lukewarm coffee.

"What have we got here, Herr Kanter? One of Tinkabelle's rare failures and a middle-aged army man gone ga–ga over a young girl. A man who has given up everything – well, not quite everything, he didn't give up the BMG Pension Fund."

"What is this pension fund?"

"A ticket to ride," replied Nibs, doodling on his notepad.

"What we wanted to know," Herr Kanter said at last, "is how long has he been ill?"

"Ill?" This was a surprise.

"Surely you know?"

Nibs had absolutely no idea as to what this man was babbling on about. Sir Harold was the fittest forty-six year-old man who had ever reigned as senior squash champion.

"He's never been ill, not within living memory."

"He is a very sick man, Herr Nibs. Regina is a foolish girl. She betrayed herself as well as her own people."

"You've lost me," Nibs said, opening up Sir Harold's file.

"Surely you know about his cancer?"

"Cancer?"

"Cancer of the stomach. He revealed to us that he was afraid we would prevent Regina from seeing him again. Thus he planned to steal her away." Herr Kanter smiled. "He is a romantic man, *ja?* But foolish, for he had not told Regina of his cancer, and now she will have a fatherless child, a burden to the State. It is not something we like to encourage in the German Democratic Republic."

But Nibs, who was studying Sir Harold's last medical report, could find no such hint of any terminal illness at all. He realised that it was not Sir Harold who was romantic, but this East Berliner, Herr Kanter.

"It is not something that a soldier would discuss," Nibs declared with an attempt at sincerity. "It might affect his pension."

Herr Kanter beamed at this confession by a high ranking Britische, and nodded his head vigorously. "Ah, now I understand. He held his secret because Britische Government would dismiss an unhealthy man, a man like that would not like to lose his pension."

"Quite . . . so he took it with him. Smart move," Nibs stated with a weary sigh. "So that's it, is it, Herr Kanter? Neither of us knows where he is. You're not really chasing him, you're cross with Regina for going beyond the call of duty and falling in love, and the East's heart is bleeding for a leading Britische in distress; a man who fled his post in a time of crisis because he wouldn't get his army pension for his loving wife and child."

Herr Kanter vaguely detected sarcastic inflection in Nibs'

voice, but he couldn't be sure. Sarcasm was not a prescribed course at language school.

"Yes," he answered, hoping this was the right answer. "In the spirit of cooperation that exists between East and West, we thought it best we should have this talk."

"Well, in that spirit," Nibs said, "What about the wall?"

"Wall?" Herr Kanter queried.

"You remember, that bit either side of Friedrich Strasse?"

"Ah . . . it is better now, is it not? This city without a wall, I never thought I'd see such a day. They say the Americans are very angry with us, some talk of the Kennedy Trust wanting to rebuild it in Boston. I heard it on your World Service."

"Well, he did stand on it, you know, it meant a lot to him," Nibs pointed out, pushing his buzzer again. "But I don't notice the hordes from Karl-Marx Allee making a rush for our shops or the Café Keese. No reports of a mass invasion of Easterners at the Rheinishe Winzerstuben. Perhaps they heard our little talk about the bright lights, your pretty laser beams."

"You need not play tricks with me, Herr Nibs. There is no truth to the laser beams. No truth at all. Berlin will become an open city. It has been decided."

"When?"

"It is not for me to decide . . ."

Nibs made a guess, interrupting him. "Wednesday 08.00 hours?"

Herr Kanter stood up to leave, ignoring the last remark. "It is a shame, Herr Nibs, you do not look after your Chief of Staff with more care. We have statistics that show a man is twice as likely to develop cancer in the West, as in the East."

"It is the price we pay for democracy, Herr Kanter. Everyone knows democracy causes cancer."

"They know this?" he asked, genuine surprise on his face.

"Know it and vote for it. You know the expression, better dead than red."

Suddenly a broad smile opened up on Herr Kanter's face. "Britische go home!" he yelled, saluting. Then he laughed. "Gott, I miss the cold war."

157

"Me too," Nibs said, with nostalgia. "Fancy some more coffee before you go?"

The East Berliner readily agreed, sitting down once more.

"Never mind, Herr Kanter. I'm sure Sir Harold will send us a postcard, sooner or later."

SIX

The Forty-Two Steps

Mrs Lily Tigre had had to go home. Archives may not function well without her undisputed powers of memory and her innate sense of order, but Grimly had felt that an investigation of such a sensitive subject could, at some point, compromise the Archive Controller and thus, under protest, she had once again returned home to continue her crying there. Basically it was the crying that got to Grimly. It made no difference that your department was suspect, but one should not – and especially a senior should not – cry.

Archives is the kind of building that has history crawling out of the walls, and the odour of a thousand years of books and people trapped in a Pyramid waiting for a lone Egyptologist to cry 'eureka' and dig them out, dust them off and describe them as an important contribution to the world's greater understanding, if only they could decifer what the hell all the hieroglyphics were about.

The mushrooms, growing in almost midsummer profusion from under the skirting boards, lent a colourful appearance to an otherwise indifferent wall. The lighting was subdued, not so much in response to Calon's economy cuts, but more due to a lighting system introduced in 1935, and little modified since. On occasion, when the Relatives had been forced to utilise British records, it always got back to Washington about the official Churchill ashtray, still standing in the Boer Current Affairs section, the stub and ash still there. It rivalled the White House collection of Presidential dandruff and was the envy of the free thinking, museum-conscious world. It was entirely possible that the Churchillian ashtray had remained intact so long, merely because of the lighting system. Some of the staff would use torches to read the ritual records of post-war grief, but most would wait until the 2.30 pm sun first glinted in the far windows, and a spray of direct light source would filter in through the time-honoured, brown dust that had accumulated in the ninety-eight years of the building's existence.

The only stranger to this establishment – some called it a travesty – was the VDU terminal, an offshoot of Central Storage next door in the Square. Its brightly polished aluminium and brilliant green LED display was monstrously alien – on a par with streakers at Lords, Heaven forbid. Alien but necessary, if the Square was to have information at its fingertips.

And on this Saturday night, the world went to bed sure that the Berlin wall was down, that bombs had exploded all over Africa (typically after the gold market had closed) and thousands lay dead. Sure, too, after the Minister of Home Affairs had come on TV interrupting a repeat of *Dallas* to announce that the situation in Europe was tense, that Britons would be safe, for we alone in Europe had made no provision for civilian nuclear fall out shelters. The total expenditure for civil defence of £10.65p in the past decade was a guarantee to the British people that Britain would not readily commit itself to a nuclear war, since 93% of the population would die. This was in contrast to the Swiss, who could accommodate 99% of their population underground (but knowing that, who would want to live in a world in which the sole survivors were Swiss?).

With that reassurance, *Dallas* had recommenced, no doubt calming the defenceless population, most of whom were praying for war, if only to give them defence work to compensate for more than two million unemployed. Out beyond the Archives the world was growing dim, the laymen predicting the worse and young girls' eyes were turning once again to admire a uniform.

And inside, the Emergency Council of Square élite met in

160

privacy, they, too, concerned with war. Not so much its inevitability, but how Tinkabelle and his devious apostles intended to prevent it.

Sussie Sutzman, Doc Sludgeon, Hugh Grimly and Sir Charles Edgeware had sat around the Camelot table and worked non-stop for many hours pouring over mounds of Archive material; reading, making comparisons of reports gone out, those come in; whose signatures occurred most often on which suspect documents; annotating, making cross-checks with microfilmed records and the originals (that were still there). Their concentration was as intense as any they had given Intelligence work in many long years. Time was short and the spectrum of people most likely to be involved, far from a short list.

Grimly checked leave and sickness charts, always looking for the coincidental date, the unusual holiday, the inconvenient sickness prior to a major 'problem'.

Doc Sludgeon studied the activities and leave locations of Soviet Embassy staff, trying to catch the thin thread of coincidence, comparing them to Grimly's charts.

Sussie Sutzman took care of the past eighteen months Archive Moscow course material, all of which was now suspect. She wanted to know who had filed it, who had received it, and, most importantly, what the results were, what was achieved.

Sir Charles read Cabinet Office memo after memo, passing the dubious and downright sinister along the line to Grimly as he came upon them. They were the Woodward and Bernsteins, the Philip Marlowes spending an afternoon in the library, a little research before the major discovery would be made, always on the brink of a breakthrough, but still doubting as logic or back-up failed to materialise. Their arms were in dirty water, up to their elbows, looking for some sense of order to Tinkabelle's puppet mastery.

Tentative findings suggested innocent bunglings. The second generation moles were clever, leaving virtually no traces, like Tinkabelle, invisible to the unbelievers. Grimly had warned them when they had begun: "Suspicion is not enough, facts, we have to be sure it is Tinkabelle at the rudder and not traditional British incompetence. Penetration before obfuscation. The difference between the enemy's work and petty office stabs in the back."

Eventually they thrashed out a background scenario. Doc Sludgeon had painted the picture for them.

"This Moscow–Paris–Madrid axis will only work if Germany falls in with Paris. Our information is that the reunification of Germany will not work at this time. Neither side really wishes it, for much the same reason as Belfast/Dublin mouth the possibility, but abhor the reality. We do see Berlin becoming an open city, however, as part of an experiment and a test of American will. My guess is that a deal has already been made with the Germans themselves. With the wall down and West Berliners' rights of freedom recognised, perhaps tentatively extended to cover access to all the East. If you like, I see Berlin becoming a free trade area within East Germany, much like Hong Kong, say. Used by GDR and Moscow as a financial centre in their run up to re-establishing Berlin as the only capital city of Germany. The US and everyone else out of Berlin, will be the first step. I believe the US will not go to war over this, and I say that because we will back down first, leaving them with no room to manoeuvre, our boys being replaced by West German troops. A German solution. Don't look for an immediate reunification call. Both sides are wary of each other, scared one will swamp the other. Neither side wants to give political leverage to the fanatical fringes of the opposition, particularly the Bavarians."

"So we have to consider war as an impossibility?"

"I think so, Hugh. Not least because successive Governments have failed to provide us with any civil defence, except for the GLC bunker and the Whitehall boys, our population is defenceless. Even without that problem, we are in a no win situation. Germany will not allow us to mobilise our forces there. You have all seen the cable from Bonn?"

Sir Charles said he hadn't.

"In brief, Charles," Grimly explained in a tired, slow voice, "they are speaking to the French President this evening. They are most concerned about our latest report on the situation. We aren't quite in their bad books. For once your department isn't taking the American line."

Sir Charles didn't appear to understand.

"It's easy, Charlie," Sussie called out. "Damn Boché can see that this is just the opportunity they needed to declare a Paris–Bonn Friendship Pact. Y'know, self determination for Franco–German independence from the war mongering NATO Alliance, not to mention the money they would save. It's a way of saying they are strong enough to hold the balance of power in Europe by themselves now. Big Daddy America can roll up the carpet and go home."

"And Italy, Grimly?" Sir Charles asked, thinking of his villa outside Naples.

"Cut off," Doc Sludgeon declared. "She'll bleat for ten seconds, reach for her 42nd Government and reluctantly, but very quickly, join the Franco–German Pact. In the end it will be the old NATO without us or the US Newspeak, Sir Charles, a new alliance to protect the European population from American adventurism and aggression."

"We can't go it alone. What about the EEC?" Sir Charles protested.

"We won't be alone for long, Charlie," Sussie chirped.

"Oh explain, Hugh," Sir Charles complained. "Why won't we be alone?"

"Tinkabelle."

"You keep saying Tinkabelle, Hugh. But he is still our enemy, and as yet our enemy doesn't run our foreign policy – I do."

"I don't think you do," Grimly said, quietly.

And thus it had been said.

"Oh," Sir Charles muttered, looking from face to face, realising what their past few hours of research had revealed.

Doc Sludgeon drew out his notes that he'd made during his interview with Colin Fielding. Notes compiled whilst the Rat had squirmed under Peter Hallam's tender care. He'd come from the Games Room straight to Archives, leaving Hallam to help the Rat recover.

"Eleven men, Charles. As suspected. Pragmatists, the Rat called them. Our Second Eleven. It's a problem, but your department is involved, Charles, no doubt."

"My Colin Fielding told you that?"

"He had little choice. Hallam can be most persuasive."

"But you're saying Colin Fielding is one of your," he lowered his voice, "Second Eleven? A blasted Communist, my Number Three?"

"No, Charles," Grimly said soothingly. "He was far too obvious. Colin Fielding is merely an opportunist. A man who has seen which way the winds blow and bent accordingly. He knows very little really."

"Confirmed," Doc Sludgeon agreed. "He has put together rumours and tiny pieces of gossip. He has also been approached by Moscow Cephal, here in London, by Sverdlosk the Cultural Affairs Officer."

Sussie hooted with laughter. "Cultural Affairs. Did you know he was invited to Eton to give a lecture to sixth formers interested in visiting Moscow. He didn't know any of the ballet stars, couldn't name one artist at the recent exhibition at the Celebration Hall. The only vaguely cultural thing he knew anything about was a dissident author who was sympathetic to Jewish saboteurs in the Soviet economy. All he wanted was to recruit likely sympathisers."

"Must be enough there," Doc Sludgeon said. "It's either Moscow or *Private Eye*, not a place for the wishy-washy."

Grimly frowned. "I didn't know you read *Private Eye*."

"It's sometimes the only way to get to know what's going on in the corridors of power. Find out what's on their minds."

"But, Hugh," Sir Charles complained, not liking these allegations one bit. "What has all this got to do with Tinkabelle? What exactly has Colin Fielding done?"

"One, he introduced Sir Harold Miller to a Soviet contact to enable him to defect. Two, he released the findings on Operation Last Call, our NATO wargame in Norway. They now know exactly how long it will take to get stores and spares to our Norwegian allies and be in battle position. As you know, we have long regarded the outside flanks of NATO, Greece and Norway, as vulnerable to first strike."

"And the Rat gave them that?" Sir Charles was mortified. "Yet you say he isn't one of the . . ." he winced, "Second Eleven."

"That is correct. They are not so much in the position of selling information, but creating it. Colin Fielding sold the report, strictly business, not a scrap of idealism in him. So much for backbone, Sir Charles. Didn't you once say all your men had backbone and breeding?"

Sir Charles glowered at Grimly. Something about an Oxford man you couldn't ever like.

"The Second Eleven are all in key positions, Charles," Grimly continued, his eyes like rocks he was so tired. "Invisible sleepers now awake."

"I can't stand it. Moles all over the place. Eleven! God, to think I thought my golf club was bad."

Grimly gave Sir Charles an uncertain look. Golf?

"The position then is this," Doc Sludgeon rounded up. "We have strong confirmation that we have been penetrated. Not only from the Butcher's Boy, but also Colin Fielding and the suspicious circumstances of one of Gallant's young men being murdered on his first job. Plus documents here which point in quite a few disturbing directions. We have a family tree drawn up," Sussie Sutzman handed him her handiwork, "which includes most likely areas of operation and an operating list of forty-two people who work in highly sensitive, linchpin areas. At this moment we believe no-one knows of our investigation. That Tinkabelle is moving very quickly to activate all his fairy friends to ensure they exercise their influence through the ministrations of Whitehall and guarantee Britain falls in line with Paris and Bonn."

"In other words, America out," Sir Charles summed up.

"Yes," Grimly agreed, "Amercia out and Moscow in, but at a distance."

"We can't do that," Sir Charles protested.

"Eleven little moles say we will, Charlie," Sussie said, with a tiny chuckle. "We just have to find them before that happens."

"But I'm the one who makes decisions," Sir Charles protested. "I will never recommend a pull out of British troops in Germany. We are bound by treaty, we could never let the Relatives down."

"Tinkabelle has laid the ground well, Charles," Grimly warned. "They must have beavered away in Paris for a considerable time. It shows a fundamental shift away from traditional operations. No chipping away at the pillars of our society and sabotage of the economy (if only because there's so little left to ruin), it is a wholesale invasion. They have slipped into management shoes and they are taking over the whole shop."

"Impossible, Hugh. Impossible. No precedent for it and don't throw Afghanistan at me. My God, you might as well say the Prime Minister dines with Tinkabelle every night."

Sussie laughed, but it was an uneasy laugh, for there was many a truth said in jest.

"It isn't as bad as that," Grimly persisted. "But someone in Moscow realised long ago where the true seat of power lies in this country."

"The BBC. I knew it," Sir Charles said spitefully. "Arrest them all. Round up Robin Day, let me shoot him first."

"It's not the BBC, Charles. It's our very own Civil Service. They control the information. They are the seat behind the throne. The invisible, unelected Mandarins who describe every policy and structure our foreign policy."

"Bureaucrats, you're always accusing the bureaucrats, Hugh. I don't think you realise that you are one yourself."

"But we are the Palace Guard," Sussie reminded him in her shrill, much offended manner. Sir Charles ignored her.

"Well, how *do* we go about whittling down the forty-two? Play eeny, meeny, miny, mole?"

"Two ways," Grimly told him, taking time off for a huge drawn-out yawn. His voice was becoming a slur with exhaustion. "One, find out more about what the Butcher's Boy knows and two – lay a trap."

Sussie, Doc Sludgeon and Sir Charles leant foward with interest. A trap was something they could all understand and enjoy.

"We will circulate . . . a highly restricted Intelligence document from Berlin – code named 'Spitfire'." Grimly was definitely slowing down, finding it difficult to string the words together. His mind was spinning wheels, unable to get any grip on an increasingly slippery surface. His body had gone to sleep hours before. The others hung on his words.

"Corroboration between Sir . . . Harold Miller and source . . . sources in Moscow . . . confirmed by the Butcher's Boy . . . revealing that the Second Eleven have all been named and located within Government circles. Suggest that Operation Poppyseed goes into effect."

"Poppyseed?" Sir Charles asked. "Hugh, are you all right?"

"Poppyseed is the Relatives' scheme for putting agents to sleep," Sussie explained.

"Killing them?" he asked, surprised. "Killing them, Hugh?"

Grimly shook his head. "Operation Poppyseed will frighten the real moles. They will try to disappear. They will request urgent meetings with their Moscow contacts and a way out . . ."

"And we will get them running like hares out of the corn!" Sussie exclaimed, clapping her hands together. "Hughie, you're such a genius. Poppyseed, it's brilliant. The CIA used the same plan in Chile once."

"Did it work?" Sir Charles asked, finally getting his cigar to light. Much to Grimly's disgust, though he was much too tired to protest.

Doc Sludgeon shook his head. "Not entirely, language problem. The moles were illiterate, couldn't read the reports 'leaked' to their inner ring. At least our boys will be able to read English."

"Will they run? Won't Moscow smell a rat? Won't they know about Poppyseed?"

"No," Grimly said, with great strength of will, hanging on to consciousness by the slimmest of threads. "No, they won't but there is one problem . . ." He took a deep breath. "It might frighten more than the guilty. There are some, like Colin Fielding, who operate on the fringe, they will get the jitters."

"Just forty-two copies of this document?" Sir Charles verified.

"Doc, you get them out by am Monday," Grimly ordered, closing his eyes, "there's not much time. We think Moscow will make a move on Wednesday. It is the anniversary of the second wave of the Revolution. We can expect trouble . . . then."

Sussie yawned too, fishing out a boiled sweet from her cavernous bag. "We have other business, Charlie. China has been making whispers about your visit there."

"But that isn't until after Easter."

"They won't want it to happen at all if we fall in with Moscow, could cancel all that defence equipment."

"We aren't going to fall in with Moscow. How many times do I have to say that? Really, Sussie, you and China are far too suspicious."

Sir Charles heard a heavy plop on his right. He looked beside him. Hugh Grimly, acting Stationmaster had fallen asleep at the table, sprawled out head first on the polished oak.

"Gawd, old Grimly's had it," he commented. "Better call in Matron, Doc." He turned to Doc Sludgeon, but to his surprise the Doctor was fast asleep too. His head back, mouth open, his cheeks sunken as if in the grip of a fatal disease. It was possible that it was true, that old age was terminal, after all.

Sussie winked at Sir Charles, a giggle escaping her boozy throat. She began to act coy and shy.

"Just like the old days in the bomb shelter, Charlie."

Sir Charles, whose days in the bomb shelters had been

many, but a long time ago, couldn't quite grasp what silliness Sussie was referring to.

"You remember, Charlie, the bombs falling. You grabbing me from behind and saying, "Sussie, make love to me now, the world's coming to an end.""

"What happened?" he asked, still not quite there, not even sure which bomb shelter. Sussie looked quite disappointed.

"You remember, don't you, Charlie? You and me lying naked with the bombs going off." She giggled again. "You were so young and handsome then. I never expected that you'd have such a red nose. You didn't drink so much then, Charlie. You were a fine steed, breaking all the hearts. You broke mine."

"Nonsense, Sussie. I don't believe any of it. Which bunker?"

"St Katherine's Dock. We were visiting the Tower. Your CO had installed some radio listening device in the Tower. 'I think there's a bomb attack coming on,' you said. 'Let's get to the bunker.' How many girls knew it was a personal bomb shelter, Charlie? How many guessed you'd become so important? I guessed. I was so in love with you. You could have done anything to me – you did."

"It was a long time ago, Sussie."

"Yes, Charles, our bodies fail us, but our memories can let us cheat a little. Sussie Sutzman loves Chalie Edgeware. Silly girl, wasn't I? I wouldn't have joined the Square if it wasn't for you."

"You can't blame me for that," he protested, his head sinking to his arms, closing his eyes, trying hard not to remember the past, or the young Sussie Sutzman. What had she been, eighteen, nineteen?

"I was sent to China in '45, then Japan with Mountbatten in '46. I would have gone even further to try and forget you."

"But it was only once in the bunker, Sussie, only once. I made no promises. The bombs were falling, Sussie. If you're not happy now, don't blame me. The war is over." He yawned, really he was too tired to listen to all this.

Sussie smiled. "I don't blame you, Charlie. But if there's going to be another war, do me a favour, don't ask me to the bunker."

When Matron arrived with tea at 11.30 pm, he was surprised to find all four council members fast asleep with their heads on the table. Of course, he'd never expected Mr Grimly to adjust to the pace right away, but with the world expected to come to an end within days, he felt the others could have stayed the course until tea. Nolan felt it presumptious of him to interfere and decided to take tea back downstairs. It probably wasn't the best time to mention his petition, nor the pencil allowance. It wasn't much, but a bit of rooting around in Matron's Archives had revealed that the pencil allowance of 10/6d a year was owing from 1963. It wasn't much, only £8.92½p, but anything to aggravate Calon's office.

He paused at the wet rot and sprinkled some sugar on the fungus. He'd read somewhere that wet rot fungus didn't like sugar. With Calon's cuts, there wasn't much chance of getting things like the wet rot fixed. Especially if they were going to East Putney. Still, he'd been cheered by the news from South West Africa. If there was going to be a war, as the boys downstairs were laying odds on 3–1 for, then no way would Calon be able to push them out to East Putney, not during a war you couldn't.

The day closed on midnight as the four powers that be slept on.

Only downstairs in the Games Room was there any activity still. Colin Fielding wiped the blood from his mouth and accepted the offer of a rinse and clean towel from Peter Hallam.

"You could have made it easy on yourself, Ratty," Hallam said, picking up his jacket and heading for the door. "Nothing further you'd like to add is there? Like Captain Crewk? You wouldn't happen to know who Captain Crewk is, would you?"

"Russian," Fielding answered after a moment. "If you are saying it right, it's Russian and it means hook."

"Captain Hook?" Hallam asked incredulous. "Captain Hook?" he roared.

"Yes, hook. Crewk is Russian for hook, like in fishing hook."

Hallam shook his head and left the room, disgusted with himself and feeling absurdly foolish. They had been playing games with him. Peter, Wendy and Captain Hook. God, he was angry now. They took him for a complete imbecile, playing a silly bloody game with him.

"I'll Captain Hook them, the bastards."

But first he had a name to follow, his first step towards the Butcher's Boy and the last name to fall from Fielding's bruised lips. It had taken many hours, but once the significance of Malta had been established, he had shaved away at the Rat's memory until everything had been exposed. It was just a question of picking through the pieces. A long night's work, no fun for anyone, but he was getting closer to Wendy at last.

*   *   *

The door opened downstairs. A bent, portly figure slowly entered the hallway, closing the stained glass front door behind him, fastening chains and sliding bolts to effect security. Always a worry, always a concern. He drew back a curtain and the dubious, late February, Sunday morning light flooded the quaintly overdecorated hallway, the cold Victorian tilework on the floor briefly recalling days of former glory, when a glimmer of sunlight peeked in.

"Is that you, Willy?" a voice called out from upstairs.

"Ye-es," he answered, in his slow, trumpeting manner.

"Got the papers?" another voice asked.

"*Sunday Times*, *Sunday Telegraph* and the *News of the World*."

Willy placed the papers down on the table and set to work removing his trenchcoat, looking for somewhere to hang it.

The safe house was a curious place. Owned by the Square since '53, and not used since '63 when 'odd things' had been reported going on there, not unconnected to the Keeler-Stephen Ward scandals of that time. For a while, it had become something less than a 'safe' house and a well-known feature of the Sunday gossip pages. But now, eighteen years on and virtually mothballed since that time, it had become a genuine, forgotten stronghold, apparently unnoticed in the row of newly converted family houses as Brook Green was claimed anew by the middle classes. No blue plaque had gone up to celebrate its illustrious infamy, and nothing more than regulation green paint had been slapped on every five years. Still, Willy reflected, they could have taken down the 'Happy New Year 1964' banner from the dining-room, a definite collector's item. It made him feel strangely uncomfortable. 1964 had been a year of hernias. Perhaps that's why he felt this way, he distinctly remembered he hadn't liked the hernias.

He gathered together the papers again and made his way up the stairs. Another thing, the stair carpet was worn through and loose, a positive danger.

Not everything was worn out and early George VI. The two-way mirror in the master bedroom had obviously been a positive asset in '63, now the Stationmaster hung his shirt over it. He wasn't one to worry about being stared at, it was his imagination he couldn't stand. Sleeping in the very bed where 1001 delights (and not so delights) had taken place. It was a strain, his drip drys a good antidote to the meandering excitement of the bygone sixties.

"*Times* for me," the Stationmaster called out from the bathroom.

"*Telegraph* for me," Croc growled from his bed, which he did not feel like getting out of, even if it was his turn to make breakfast. This bed was more comfortable than his own. In fact, the whole house was more comfortable. He wouldn't mind a swop with the Square. Not that he liked Brook Green very much, it was all right in some places, but it was too full of old dossers from the 'home'. Didn't like alcoholics, couldn't stomach them. Seen enough to last a lifetime out in India and the colonies. The world was full of 'em and that didn't make Brook Green a better place in his opinion.

Willy plonked down the papers and headed for the kitchen. He didn't know why the kitchen was upstairs and the dining-room below, but '63 had been a funny year.

"Put the kettle on," Croc instructed him. "I'll be up soon."

"Where's my shaving brush?" the Stationmaster demanded.

"Threw it out," Willy told him, popping his head around the door on the way back to his *News of the World*.

The Stationmaster, who was being very patient with Willy, counted up to ten and then asked him, "Why? Why?"

"Anthrax. Anthrax can be carried on shaving bristles. Big scare about it, Steven. One must be careful."

"I've used that shaving brush for five years, it's never given me anthrax, Willy."

Willy frowned, walking forward to pick up his paper, opening up the front page to reveal a few more bristles on a 'Teenage Sex Report Shock'.

"You can be very annoying, Willy," the Stationmaster called out. "What did you discover for us?"

Willy turned to page five for an in-depth report on Catholic priests running a brothel in Rome – another exclusive.

"The Butcher's Boy is staying in the Newcastle-on-Tyne area."

"Newcastle?" Croc asked, appearing at his bedroom door in a shocking pink dressing-gown with a hand stitched Rupert Bear on the pocket. A present from an admirer, he'd explained the first time he'd worn it. The Stationmaster didn't approve but every man to his dressing-gown, he supposed.

"Why Newcastle?" Croc demanded.

"Safe, out of the way, I imagine," Willy answered. "I've got the bacon out of the fridge, Croc."

Croc took the hint. Besides he was hungry.

"Then we'd better visit Newcastle first thing Monday. Catch the early train."

"But I don't know where, Steven?" Willy pointed out. "It's definitely Newcastle, out in the country though. Could be anywhere. The info wasn't specific. Mr Grimly has him well hidden."

"And does Peter Hallam know that yet?"

Willy didn't want to guess, he wasn't one for guessing. He'd been lucky to get to Newcastle, lucky Matron's Bloater remembered him from the old days. Bloater had always been good for information and had turned up trumps this time – driven the Butcher's Boy to Kings Cross himself. Bought the ticket to Newcastle on Mr Grimly's orders. "Keep him out of sight and harm's way," Mr Grimly had said. "Tell no-one where he is, including Mr Hallam and Simon Caw." It was all right to tell Willy though. Willy was old school, as 'sound' as the Stationmaster. In return, Willy had passed the word about the Stationmaster. "Sanctuary, Bloater. Call off the dogs, he's in Sanctuary."

The word would bring calm to the Square. Reassure those in power that their beloved leader had disappeared with only good intentions.

"Trouble is just lying around on the floor for anyone to pick up and clobber us with," the Stationmaster declared staring at his newspaper. "Berlin. This Moscow–Paris–Madrid Pact, it's the thirties all over again. All we need is Neville Chamberlain, Willy, and it will be complete. What's all this about an earthquake in South West Africa? Is it an earthquake or a nuclear bomb?"

"Bloater said it was an earthquake, Chief," Willy answered, looking for any reference to it in his paper. The only thing about Israel or South Africa he could find was: *Rabbi fined R200 for kiss and cuddle in back of multinational bus. Port Elizabeth C.P.*

"Anything about the power imbalance in your paper, Willy?"

"Hospital had its electricity cut off during a heart swap and patient died of shock," said Croc. "Wife to sue Electricity Board."

174

Stationmaster shook his head. Willy had declined considerably. Four years out of the Service hadn't done him much good. The *News of the World* scored heavily against him. Croc was leading him on, of course, Croc was always teasing Willy.

"What's yours say about the 'Sex-change beauty queen?' " Croc asked from the kitchen.

"Looked better as a sailor," Willy replied, appreciating the aroma of frying bacon.

Stationmaster read the shocking news in his own paper. "Things are getting serious in Berlin, lads, they are already selling off the Berlin wall, brick by brick to tourists, no respect for history whatsoever."

After breakfast, though Willy and Croc were still on the toast and marmalade, the Sunday papers, having been much read and discussed, were abandoned as Stationmaster assembled the order of the day, as he saw it.

"We have narrowed the field down to forty-two possibilities. Our A through DQ files indicate that only forty-two people could possibly be in a position to affect working judgment in classic mole operational moves. We can eliminate all the suspects under twenty-six years-old, or personnel who have worked for the FO or Intelligence for less than and including four years."

"Why?" Croc asked, dipping his toast in his tea.

"We can assume that with our new screening processes and Will Strawson's influence effectively removed, no new recruits were gained in the last four year period. If there were, their potential won't be realised until they have been in the corridors of power for more than ten years, remember they are looking for lasting penetration, not quick flash gains, waste of manpower."

"You can be sure of that?" Willy asked. "Couple of fast bowlers might have slipped in."

"You're right, Willy, we can't be absolutely sure, but for argument's sake, if we limit our suspicions to long termers we will get nearer to our goal. A sleeper, a mole, needs to rest

175

dormant for a long while, he has to build up credibility. Become a pillar of society, if you like. Become the sort of man you'd give the keys of the city to. Someone all of us in this room would put our faith in and perhaps trust with our lives. It takes more than four years to build up that kind of reputation. We are talking about senior people, perhaps late thirties, more likely forties and above. Career men, impeccable backgrounds and club members."

"Bringing the total to?" Croc asked, looking out of the window, noticing a fierce rain shower.

"Thirty-one," the Stationmaster said. "Thirty-one possibles and we don't have time to bring them all in one by one. Not now that the French and Germans are talking. Our moles will be working hard to undermine our position here in London. They'll be applying pressure for the Cabinet to realign with Europe. Sir Charles is with Hugh Grimly, you say?"

"Yes," Willy answered. "Spent last night burning the midnight oil. Sussie Sutzman and Doc Sludgeon too."

"What about Peter Hallam?"

"He went home after midnight. Wendy is still missing."

"But the Butcher's Boy didn't take her?"

"Bloater didn't know she was missing. Definitely not with the Butcher's Boy. Funny Mr Hallam getting that wrong. I mean he was right about Milos. Milos has gone, I realise that now. He must have taken Wendy, but where to and why? Queer pitch, I'll tell you that, a funny queer pitch."

"Does this bear on the case?" Croc asked. "I mean are we chasing moles, or are we looking for lost children?"

"If it connects to the Butcher's Boy, it has a bearing on the case," Stationmaster said.

"Perhaps if I was to have another word with Mr Hallam?" Willy suggested.

"No," Stationmaster said quickly. "Willy, you are on low profile. Croc can handle this. Call David Gallant, he's got no axe to grind. Tell him that Hallam thinks the Butcher's Boy has his Wendy and enlighten him. We can't have the man working at half efficiency with his precious child gone. Find out what he's doing about it, Croc."

Croc made some notes.

"So you're going up to Newcastle?" Willy asked.

"All of us are. There'll be a Ministry connection. They won't be farming him out to just anyone. But we'll need all three of us to flush him out. We have to find him, Willy. He's the one who knows the names, I'm sure of it."

"I remember Newcastle in the war," Croc moaned. "Depressing place."

"It's changed," Willy said with some authority. "I used to get up to Vickers a lot a few years ago. Dolly Bell lives there now."

"Dolly Bell!" Croc exclaimed, his mournful face alight with pleasure.

"Dolly used to be the barmaid at the Dog and Fox in Barnes," Willy explained. "She moved to Newcastle, works at the Blackbird now. Years have worn well, Croc."

"Old Dolly, well I'm blowed. You hear that, Steven? Dolly Bell. She used to do a good strip or two on Saturday nights. Biggest knockers outside of Sweden."

The Stationmaster shuffled his papers. He didn't approve of this sort of reminiscing. He was sure any female called Dolly Bell couldn't have been up to any good. He found the friendship between Croc and Willy very strange. Two men more unsuited to each other, he couldn't think of. Yet together they worked well enough. The past day and a half of concentrated filtering of the A through DQ files had produced satisfactory results. They were definitely close. It was a pity all this should occur whilst the world was bent on chaos, but any decision they might come up with at the Square would be suspect and subject to subtle change, as the moles worked away to cover their tracks. Being outside, working with his trusted assistants, he hoped he could solve the problem with an unbiased eye. He felt they had been hasty to call in Hugh Grimly. Poor man wasn't in any shape to hunt moles anymore. The man was practically dead as it was. A sign of desperation and a signal to the Soviets that the Square was going to be a walkover when the crunch came. All the more reason to get to the Butcher's Boy. His report in November hinted at the coming crisis and that he was working on information that might be crucial to the survival and safety of the whole Square. But Christmas and New Year had gone by and despite a personal letter from Stationmaster to Malta, he had not heard any further. It was his guess that the Butcher's Boy didn't trust anyone anymore, that his appearance in London was to warn, but he had been met by the very people he intended to expose. Even if he was wrong, the Butcher's Boy's suspicions would help set a course and save them time.

"They called in Colin Fielding," Willy remembered to say.

"The Rat? Grimly called in the Rat?" Stationmaster asked.

"Under lock and key."

"He's on our list," Croc said. "I don't know him. One of Sir Charles' henchmen, isn't he?"

"Grimly's moving faster than I thought," Stationmaster muttered. "The Rat was on Malta too. Butcher's Boy and the Rat. Grimly's building. I shouldn't underestimate him."

"No staying power," Croc asserted. "He's too old. Won't stick it."

"But he has drawn the Rat," Stationmaster said. "What did he have to say?"

"Call Simon Caw," Croc suggested.

"Not advisable. He's on our list, Croc."

"Odd game when the Head of Lipsnatchers appears on a witch-hunt list," Croc declared.

"Steven had the Minister of Power on the list in '54. Difficult year '54. Plenty of scandals then."

Stationmaster was looking at the list again. "What is it about Tinkabelle, Croc? Why doesn't he recruit women? Ever thought about that, eh? No women on our list."

"He's a damn misogynist," Croc replied. "If I was recruiting moles, I'd go for women everytime. Born traitors, everyone of them. Always causing trouble."

"Except Dolly Bell. Never caused trouble, Dolly Bell," Willy insisted.

"Time for some more tea," Stationmaster declared. "Whose turn is it now?"

Willy muttered and pushed his chair back.

"You could call Gallant now, Croc," Stationmaster said. "Peter Hallam should be put back on course."

Croc agreed, folding up his newspaper, getting up from the table. "Reserve some seats on the trains, should I?"

"The fastest. We might take the night train, look into it. Second class mind."

"Oh, I never travel first class, Steven. You know me. I like being a peasant."

Stationmaster had to admit that Croc imitated the peasantry very well. It was a hard thing to accept that the security of the nation rested in the hands of two imbeciles like Willy and Croc, but any port in a storm, and two men he could trust more would be hard to find. It was the nature of his business that the only seekers of truth were court jesters and lofty kings.

"Two lumps or three?" Willy called from the kitchen.

*   *   *

If there was calm and a sense of purpose at Brook Green, the very opposite was the atmosphere at the Square. It was one thing for Doc Sludgeon and Mr Grimly to be sleeping through the night in Archives, quite another for Sir Charles Edgeware and Sussie Sutzman to be found lying side by side in the Far East alcove. Sussie was asleep with a broad smile on her face, not seen since the dark days of World War II.

But this scandal was soon forgotten when Bloater, back on duty to relieve Nolan, had tried to wake Grimly up, with no success at all. David Gallant hadn't arrived either. Considering the current emergency, Bloater considered discipline to be something wanting – even if it was Sunday.

"Can't get Mr Grimly to wake up at all, Sir Charles,"

Bloater repeated for the third time, wondering if he should call up a stretcher party.

Sir Charles was trying to work out exactly how Sussie Sutzman, hardly even in her last bloom, had managed to drag him into that alcove for the remainder of the night. His head was woozy, as if he'd been drinking all night, but he knew he hadn't touched a drop. A rare occasion for a Saturday night in his book.

"Hold his nose for thirty seconds, Bloater. If Hugh doesn't wake up then, he's in trouble. Better call up some help. Where's Gallant?"

Bloater tried holding Grimly's nose, pressing finger and thumb together and thumping the Chief with great determination on his back. Grimly didn't show a flicker of life.

"I think he's in a coma," Bloater said.

"Who? Gallant?" Sir Charles asked.

"No, Mr Grimly, sir. He's unconscious, sir, this isn't sleep."

"Oh Christ, that's all we need."

Sussie reappeared from the Ladies Room, all secret smiles and not a glance in Sir Charles' direction. She'd earned her revenge, an unrequited love had been laid to rest. "Hugh needs his medicine, Bloater. David Gallant knows about that. You should call him. Where's Doc?"

"Doc Sludgeon left to draft a report, he's with Philip Oosty downstairs."

"Let's get Mr Grimly to somewhere more comfortable," Sir Charles suggested. "Get him to Stationmaster's office, there's a camp bed there."

"Yes, sir." Bloater rang down for help and Sir Charles made a decision to leave for home. There was no more he could do until Grimly woke up and, besides, they would have to wait for Operation Poppyseed to go into action.

"Sussie," he said, trying to catch her eye, "I'm relying on you to make sure Mr Grimly's suggestions are carried through. After all, we don't want to scare your hares and fail to catch them. We need eyes and ears on them twenty-four hours, all forty-two."

"Yes, Sir Charles," more formal now in front of Bloater. "I'll involve Simon Caw. We don't have the manpower to do it all ourselves."

"No, I don't suppose you have. But it's comforting to know we are narrowing it down, even if it does mean we have to admit they are there."

"They are there, Sir Charles. Little beavers chewing away at the foundations. Pesty little buggers, but we'll get them. We've won before, we can do it now."

"We had better, or we shall all be out of a job."

Sussie knew that. They had to act fast. The war was on, even if no shot was fired. Winston would be turning in his grave. Within a weekend the balance of power tossed like a caper into Moscow's hands. Once more England an offshore island. She could see the lights going out all over Europe, just the British Lion baring yellowed rotting fangs at a Europe already curled up asleep at the Bear's feet.

And Tinkabelle was heading their way, she knew it. She could feel it in her bones. He was coming, not as a spy, not as the king of moles, but open and proud to claim a land he'd been set on destroying for close on forty-five years. Coming not as a visitor but kingmaker, arriving the day the Cabinet fell in with Paris and Bonn. Absurd, impossible, but what else? Why employ *eleven* moles at all unless that was the intended outcome. There was going to be a surprise, something they hadn't counted on. They had to catch them, catch them before the inevitable collapse of British will and the long reach of grasped hands over the Atlantic was severed forever.

"Gently does it," Bloater ordered as the stretcher party took Grimly up and bore him away.

"Mr Gallant isn't at home, Miss Sutzman," Bloater said as he was leaving the room. "Mr Oosty would like a word though."

Quite suddenly Sussie found herself completely alone.

"Oh lor, Charlie," she whispered, "Charlie Edgeware, time has been hard on all of us. But what are we protecting?"

She walked across the worn, wooden floor, realising that

she was crying. No particular reason, no special reason at all, but perhaps it was because she had noticed, and not for the first time, how old and frail all the heroes of all that was right and just were. Old toothless tigers fighting a last, pointless, ritualised battle.

"Silly Sussie," she said softly, "rituals have to be played out. Just like young girls on air raid shelter floors." She sighed. "But he was such a nice boy then, such a nice boy."

Bloater came back into the room.

"What do you want, Bloater? I'm on my way to breakfast."

"With respect, Miss Sutzman, Dennis has been looking for you."

"Dennis?" she queried, studying Bloater's anxious face with tired, glazed eyes.

"Dennis the knife," Bloater emphasised. "I thought it was to do with the cuts. He's got it into his head to pare the service down to a stump, talks about cutting our Hong Kong branch in half, and if he does, it means the PM does."

"I'm not surprised, Bloater. Hong Kong looses more information than they gather. I was there, Bloater. End of the day I was supposed to write 'classified material checked correct'. No-one ever checked – there was always something missing. It's no secret that at the end of every two months they issue a new blank register to catch up with all the information peddled across the Chinese border. It's get rich quick territory, Bloater, not a place for an honest agent. They soon find themselves booted back to Blighty."

Bloater nodded, he'd heard these stories too. "Er, I told Dennis you were in Oxford," he confessed.

Sussie allowed a slow, warm smile to develop, she always enjoyed in-house subterfuge. "Why am I in Oxford, Bloater? I have to admit I don't relish the idea of speaking to Dennis."

"It's Mr Grimly's orders, Miss Sutzman. He doesn't want to open up the investigation to include outsiders, just a precaution."

"Ah, and what am I doing in Oxford?"

"Recruiting," Bloater suggested.

"Naturally," Sussie agreed, though she had to confess it would be a funny sort of recruit who'd be encouraged to join by her. Young men didn't look at her the way they used to anymore. She moved on, then abruptly turned. "What's your opinion of Dennis, Bloater?"

"Formidable, Miss Sutzman. He's the one behind the cuts. He'd have us all in a Nissen hut in Brixton if he could. Told me that an Arab wants to buy this building, thought it would make a good siege-proof Embassy. A man who'd sell this sacred institution to the Arabs, well . . . " Bloater grimaced. "It's a new breed in the corridors of power, Miss Sutzman. Gone are the days of dignity, men like Mr Grimly. I'm glad I'm near retirement, bet you are too."

Sussie bristled, she was still some way off her retirement. Bloater was out of order, that's what comes of encouraging the staff to chit chat.

"Breakfast," she said, terminating the conversation.

"Try the place on the corner of Dean Street, Miss Sutzman, not much else open on Sundays."

"Thank you, Bloater."

She walked on, stalling at the exit as she caught sight of the well-known view of Dennis' grey head in front of the reception desk. She hung back in the shadows, listening in for a moment, unable to see just who he was talking to.

"Do you know how much the Government spends on watering window boxes? Thousands of pounds a year. At least £100,000."

Sussie had heard enough, no big secrets here. She decided to take the rear exit, she didn't want to have to explain why she wasn't in Oxford.

"It's the same with toilet paper," Dennis was droning on. Last year alone it cost us £17 million pounds. It's a major industry, just what is the Government doing in the manufacturing business? I am determined to stop this sort of nonsense. From tomorrow the Government is coming out of the closet."

Sussie couldn't agree more. As long as Dennis concerned himself with loo rolls and window boxes, the Square was safe.

It did occur to her that the scourge of economy cuts was choosing a strange place to announce his plans, but then that would depend on who he was talking to. She understood the need for economy measures. Her generation knew all about making things last longer, nothing new in that. The young hadn't a clue about suffering, they'd had it too good for too long. Yes, overall she approved of Dennis the Knife, it added an element of fear, long missing since the early post war years, couldn't do any harm.

*   *   *

"But I don't know how to reach him, Croc," Oosty protested. "I don't know where you get your information from, but this is the first I've heard about Wendy being missing. Mr Hallam hasn't said a word about it."

"Never mind about that, Philip Oosty. I'm telling you, find Hallam and tell him the Butcher's Boy hasn't got his Wendy, he's looking in the wrong direction. Call Simon Caw, he'll know where Hallam and Gallant are, he always knows where everyone is."

"I'll see what I can do, Croc."

"Make sure you do. Give my regards to Grimly. I hope he's working hard."

"How did you know he was here? Never mind. He's working very hard, all night sessions. It's hard on an old man."

"It's hard on all of us, Oosty. It's not easy. There is something else you could do for me."

Oosty looked at his watch, it was 11 am already. Sunday was flashing by with no results. He was getting jumpy. "Why is it always me that does the favours?" Oosty demanded to know.

"'Cause you are the one with the pretty face, Philip. It's Coetzee in Amsterdam Stationhouse. He's got a friend . . ."

"Sorry, Croc, but Mr Hallam has declared Amsterdam Station a security risk, as from last night 2 am. It has been stood down. Dreyer, Coetzee and Stander have been ordered to London and all records have been placed under deep freeze pending Archive investigations. Violations order."

"Amsterdam?" Croc sounded very surprised.

"Yes."

"But that's our major source, what violation?"

"I can't divulge. To tell the truth, I don't know. But last night he came storming in after talking to Colin Fielding and sent telegrams all over the show. Norway, Denmark and Greece Stationhouses are under the same cloud, all suspect. This is not for dissemenation Croc. I've already told you too much. Everything's in a mess since the Stationmaster disappeared. We heard he was in Sanctuary, but it could be another rumour. I don't suppose you've got him hidden, have you, Croc?"

Croc helped himself to an ironic smile, "No, Phillip old son. Unless he's hiding under a bench at El Vino's. Maybe it's his son again. That son of his is always giving him trouble."

"No, his son hasn't seen him. I have to go, Croc. See you in El Vino's someday."

"Not if I see you first, chum. 'Bye, Oosty."

Oosty replaced the receiver and, still worried about Mr Hallam, called Simon Caw. He was transferred to a remote number in Westminster and told to wait.

Simon Caw emerged from the Cloisters of Westminster Abbey in a pensive mood, disconcerted that he had lost Peter Hallam in the maze of dark alleys beside Westminster School. He saw Jukes beckoning from the Range-Rover parked in the Dean's Square, signalling that he had a call.

They had picked up the 5 am call to Hallam's house and a man's voice, heavily accented, possibly Czech, asked if he wanted his 'little friend' back. Hallam had quite naturally answered 'yes.'

"Then we assume we have some fish for sale?"

"The fish is landed," Hallam had answered.

"11 am Parliament Square. We will find you, Mr Hallam."

That was the extent of the 5 am call.

Certainly Simon Caw was very interested to discover that the Amsterdam Stationhouse had been stood down. The long arm of coincidence, or had Colin Fielding really revealed a few surprises. That they wouldn't know. A rare failure, but the Games Room microphones were on the blink. Been on the service list for three months, of course, but never attended to. Grimly had chosen to make his interrogation in the only 'safe' room in the Square. The whole exchange between Rat and Hallam, a secret between the two of them. They were lucky Hallam's house was fully serviced the day after Wendy's kidnap.

Caw took the phone.

"It's Oosty, Simon. I'm trying to locate Mr Hallam."

"He's in the area. I hope to meet up with him very soon."

"Oh good. Look, pass the word, the Butcher's Boy doesn't have his Wendy. Perhaps you could give us some verification of this Simon, but our info is that Wendy was kidnapped. I find it incredible, but my informant doesn't usually make mistakes. Mr Hallam hasn't said a word."

"It is true, the word is button it, Oosty. Mr Hallam is in trouble. Wendy was kidnapped by the Czechs and Peter Hallam is restricted from entry to the Square from this moment on. Place his office under deep-freeze. Furthermore, Amsterdam is declared safe, and all other houses, until Mr Grimly deems them otherwise. Mr Hallam is no longer Number Two. He is to be apprehended and placed under house arrest."

"Mr Hallam? You can't be serious, Simon. He's senior to you."

"Issue those orders. We will locate Peter Hallam and return him to Kensington."

"This is not a good day for England," Oosty said sadly.

"This is a very good day for England, Oosty. Weakness is a vice. Number Two is out of the game forever."

"If you say so, Simon, if you say so."

"And tell Mr Grimly that I'll be at my office from 1 pm today."

"Mr Grimly is in a coma."

Simon Caw did a double-take on his phone.

"A what, Oosty?"

"A coma. The doctor's here. He's unconscious in a coma. He needs some drug. I'm paging David Gallant, he's got to get down to Petworth and see Lady Grimly. Apparently Mr Grimly gets a daily shot. He's missed two already."

Caw felt a rising anger. The Service was run by cripples, the weak and the insane. The time for a Putsch was very near.

"Get Gallant and if necessary fly him down to Petworth. If Grimly needs a drug why can't St. Stephens or St. Thomas's supply it?"

"We don't know what it is. I can't locate Lady Grimly either and the local bobby won't go round because he's scared stiff of her."

Caw cursed everything and everyone. "Find Gallant, fly him down to Petworth. We can't have the bloody Square paralysed like this. There isn't anyone else left in mothballs."

"I'll continue paging."

"You'd better." Caw slammed the phone down and jabbed a few words into his portable transmitter. "Hallam located yet?"

"No sir." Five separate 'No sirs'.

"Haines," Caw barked, "who's covering the St. Margaret Street exit?"

"Barrie and Birkin, sir. Nothing from them at all."

Simon Caw threw the instrument back into the car in disgust.

"Shit, how the hell did we loose him?"

"He'll probably head for the Square or home, sir. I can't see him doing much else," Bill Jukes offered by way of encouragement.

"Any man who's just been through what he's just been through wouldn't go home, to the Square or anywhere normal. Tell me again what happened."

Jukes lit up a menthol and looked back through the tinted glass at the tourists walking the Dean's yard. He didn't like

187

courtyards, even big ones. Trouble with the equipment, sound bouncing off the walls in all directions. Hard to pinpoint conversations.

"Well, we had seven men posted around the Square and two up there with directional mikes."

"Why do you think they chose such an obvious place?" Caw asked.

"Cheeky, sir. Just being cheeky. Anyway, I saw Mr Hallam arrive by taxi. He got out on the Great George Street side, having come along Victoria Street. He walked back on the Little George side, past the Institute of Civil Engineering. We had his range already and could pick up his breathing. What happened next was quite sudden really. A man, now identified as Captain Crewk, or Hook, came out of nowhere and made a great show of being old friends with Mr Hallam. You could tell Mr Hallam didn't know him from a bar of soap, but he fell in with the idea quickly enough. They walked up Broad Sanctuary and crossed the road to join the tourists gawping at Westminster Abbey. I can play the tape."

He flipped a switch and immediately conversation, mingled in with the sounds of London traffic, filled the car interior. Simon Caw leant further in through the window to listen.

"So, Mr Hallam, you have something for us?"

"Where's Wendy?"

"She is safe – perfectly safe."

"No, I want to see her. I'm not giving you anything until I see her."

A bus goes by drowning the conversation.

". . . have all the information?"

"I have completed all the requests, exactly as you required. I will not give you the rest until I can see Wendy with my own eyes."

"Amsterdam is down?"

"Yes. Deep-freeze, just as you requested. You have a clear field. And don't stall me, Captain Hook. You see, I know your silly name. I don't like childish games. And don't take me for a fool."

"Oh we don't, Mr Hallam. We know you didn't tell anyone. You have been very well behaved. You must excuse my
little joke. It's amusing me very much, your British obsession
with history. Wendy chose the name, she thought it most
amusing."

"I'm sure she did."

"Oh she did. She said you'd understand all about Captain
Hook."

"Where the hell is she, man?"

Traffic noise again.

"The telephone booth, Mr Hallam. See the lady with the
flowers? You remember her, don't you? She was your first
visitor. Little Wendy is inside the phone booth. If you do not
give us the name and location of the Butcher's Boy we will
have to take her away again. Regrettable, but that is the way it
will be. She misses you, Mr Hallam. She misses you a great
deal."

"I can't see into the telephone booth." (Hallam's voice
irritated and harsh.)

"I'll signal for our friend to make Wendy wave."

Pause.

"See, Mr Hallam, she waves."

"All right, all right. The Butcher's Boy is Henry Betand, the
artist, and he's staying at . . ."

Traffic noise once again.

"I don't know which house. I don't know why there. But
it's a small village. He can't be hard to find."

"Henry Betand, the artist? The one in Malta?" (Much surprise.)

"The same."

"Your Wendy waits for you, Mr Hallam. It has been a
pleasure doing the business with you."

More traffic noise.

Jukes turned off the tape, explaining, "Mr Hallam ran across
the road. The woman passed him on the way running to join
Captain Hook as he cut into the Dean's yard here. Mr Hallam
opened the phone booth door and –" Jukes shuddered slightly,

189

re-living the shock he'd felt – "it was quite a bloody surprise, sir. The figure in the booth fell forward and the head just rolled off onto the pavement. I thought it was Wendy at first, thought they'd decapitated her, but then I saw Mr Hallam turn away, looking really angry, madder than hell, I can tell you. It was a dummy. A fucking dummy. He'd really been tricked out. I'll say this for him though, he reacted like lightning. Didn't stop to look at the bloody dummy. He ran back across the road, dodging traffic, shouting blue murder at Captain Hook, chased after them right through the portals and across the Dean's yard, disappearing into the cloisters. I had the area sealed off in seconds. All the exits, there's no way, short of a secret passage, they could get out, sir. No way."

"So Hallam got the dummy. When was that trick last used?"

"Strawson and Blanche, Rome. The Italian Ambassador's wife kidnapped by the Red Brigade to get the Red Mole out of jail."

"Been doing some homework have we, Jukes?"

"Just happened to remember it."

"Nevertheless, we checked out every apartment in the cloisters, all the tourists, every damn nook and cranny and there's no sign of any of them. How do we account for that?"

"We don't, sir. They have to be in there. Have to be."

"And the Butcher's Boy, Henry Betand? Where is he? I didn't catch it."

"Me neither. I'm checking with the Square, but for starters no one knows anything. No Henry Betand on the Archives computer. Doc Sludgeon doesn't know, though everyone has heard of the Butcher's Boy. Grimly's got the wraps on him, sir."

"Call Calon and Gallant. They'll both know. If they try to pull rank tell them the Butcher's Boy has been blown by Hallam and his life is now in danger."

"I'll get to work on it."

"And I'm going back into the cloisters. Tell Haines to meet me at the choirmaster's lodge."

The radio-phone buzzed once again and Jukes answered it, stubbing out his cigarette on the window sill.

"Bloater, the Square."

"Go ahead, Bloater. Bill Jukes here."

"It's Colin Fielding, Mr Jukes, he's dead, sir."

Jukes took a moment to react. "Dead? How dead?" Jukes turned to Simon Caw and mouthed, "Fielding's dead" to him.

"I was taking him to the Annexe, Mr Jukes, in Euston Road. For security, sir, he could be better provided for there. Anyway, we were crossing the road just outside the Square, going to the car, y'see, some fool bumps into him and before I knows it, Mr Fielding is down on the ground clutching his leg. He was yelling about being stabbed in the leg by an umbrella. Well I can understand it hurting a bit. I mean, umbrellas can be a bit sharp, specially these Japanese ones, but he was only on the deck a moment when he shouts again, 'Bloater, I'm dying man. Blighter got me with the umbrella. Poisoned, Bloater, I'm telling you, it was poisoned. Get an ambulance.' He died immediately, sir. Right before my eyes. I couldn't believe it. I know Mr Caw was expecting a report from me, but honest, Mr Jukes, I couldn't do a thing. He died instant-like. Funny thing is, there's not a mark on his leg. Nothing."

"You get his leg X-rayed. Then call for a standard autopsy, Bloater. Get Philip Oosty to call his family, he's good at that. Everyone in the Square know?"

"Everyone is in shock, sir. What with Mr Grimly in a coma, Mr Fielding dying and the new order about Mr Hallam, it's more than we can take, especially on a Sunday. They won't need the cuts, Mr Jukes. The Square will be nothing more than a skeleton soon."

"A what?" But he realised what he meant as soon as he asked. "Don't give up, Bloater. You and Nolan do a good job. Things are only just beginning. If you sight Mr Hallam, get right back to me, OK?"

"Yes I will. I most certainly will. I'm sorry about Mr Fielding, I really am."

"It wasn't your fault, 'bye Bloater."

"What was that?" Simon Caw asked. "Fielding killed with an umbrella?"

"Left it a bit late, didn't they, sir?" Jukes said, looking for another smoke. "Should have killed the Rat before he talked to us."

Caw cursed bitterly. "I don't understand it. They must think we are daft in the head. There's going to be a scandal about this. Bloody umbrella. Well, it confirms his guilt and the likelihood that it is Czechs we are dealing with. Documented fact, Jukes. Czechs have a thing about poisoned umbrellas."

"I'll bear that in mind, sir."

Simon Caw angrily snatched up his radio contact and ran off into the cloisters, annoyed and embarrassed that they had slipped up so badly. He was almost ready to feel sorry for Peter Hallam, betraying your country and your whole way of life for a bloody dummy was a very poor exchange. What was the connection to the Rat though? But still, why worry about the Rat now he's dead. He still had bigger fish to fry.

*　　*　　*

Still naked, she came back to bed with two bowls of cereal and an amused smile growing on her white face. "Do you always yell like that when you come?"

"Yell, I don't yell. You're the noisiest female I've ever met. No wonder your husband threw you out."

"Well, it was either me going, or losing the council house, thin walls you see."

"Curse of modern civilisation. I had a room in the new wing of St Mary's, rugby player next door. I knew exactly when it was 10 o'clock every night, that's when he took his front teeth out and plonked them into his bedside glass. It was disgusting."

She laughed. "Oh it must have been so hard for you at university, David. We had a choice of Tesco's or the Woolite factory. I always wanted to be different, so I went to work in

Marks and Sparks, five years in woolly sweaters and pom-pom hats."

"Do you regret it?" Gallant asked, stroking her arm.

"Not really. I've got a nice lot of sweaters. Wish I hadn't married Bill though, he was always boring."

"Bill's all right, he works hard. Simon Caw thinks the world of him."

"He doesn't have to sleep with him. He just lies awake all night thinking about computers and microphones. The house is wired up. Even next door's mouse is on tape, poor little sod."

David Gallant smiled, ignoring her offer of cereal. He snuggled down beside Mary Jukes, stroking her flat tummy and pressing his face into her side.

"Aren't you going to eat your cereal?"

"Later, I'd rather eat you."

"Not again, David. There won't be anything left of me soon. Anyone would think you'd been away at the Antarctic for a year, the way you carry on."

"You said we could meet last weekend."

"Bill had his mother round. I had to entertain."

"But you've left him, Mary. You don't have to entertain mothers."

"I know I've left him, but it would break her heart to know. She's old, you see. Anyhow, I had to stay, I was on the rags anyway. I'm never at my best then."

Gallant lay back, looking up at his weekend woman. She had her hair pinned up and, even with milk dribbling down her chin, she still looked fresh and uncommonly glowing with some inner vitality. Bill Jukes had lived with this woman for four years and never noticed she was sexy, exciting and clever. She wasn't exactly pretty, her nose was perhaps just a little too big, but her intense brown eyes enchanted him everytime he stared at her, that and her crooked smile.

"You're staring again."

"I can't help it. I'm in love with you and you're beautiful."

"You're still drunk, Gallant. I'm thirty. You hate women of thirty. I've never seen you with anything other than some dumb eighteen year-old."

"You have opened up a whole new world to me, Mary. From now on I'll never look at another eighteen year-old. How do you keep in such good shape? I mean, look at you, perfect, everywhere."

"Surgery. I was eighteen stone two months ago. The whole lot was cut away by a surgeon. He used to work in a whaling factory in Iceland before that."

Gallant laughed, kissing her again.

"Come eat your cereal, they'll be ringing for you soon."

"They have probably been paging me since I left the Square, but . . . " He stretched a hand up to her petite breasts, "even if the country is going to the dogs, I'm entitled to a few hours with my sweetheart, aren't I?"

"Sweetheart? Where did you dig that word up from? I'm just a flag of convenience to you, David Gallant. Somewhere to stick it when there's nothing else around."

Gallant frowned. "That isn't true, Mary. You're living in my flat and I've got you a good job. I care about you, you know I do."

Mary sighed. "I know you do, David. But it won't last. I'm too working class for you. I can see you wince every time I open my mouth. You can't help it. You like me, you even think this body I've borrowed is beautiful, but you still patronise me." She put a hand to his mouth. "No, don't protest. You're everything Bill Jukes isn't. Generous, intelligent, kind and considerate, a good lover, but you're slumming, Dave. It kills you to think you've fallen for a girl like me. I know it. I mean you practically throw up when Janet Street-Porter comes on the telly and I don't exactly speak a whole lot posher than she does, do I?"

Gallant didn't like this sort of conversation. "You're only putting words into my mouth, Mary. I like you and I love you. Your bloody accent is part of you. You have to live with mine, just like I live with yours. I never liked Sloane Rangers, I've

194

never thought a Deb remotely sexy and you are – very. So shut up, lie down and let's make love."

Mary shook her head. "Three times is enough for you and me. I want a bath. Anyway . . ." she reached down and reconnected the phone, smiling as it instantly began to ring, "you're wanted on the phone."

"That's not fair Mary. I said we should have the morning together."

"We have, David. It's 11.30 am and you've got to go to work." She jumped off the bed and ran to the bathroom. "Me first."

Feeling cross, Gallant rolled over the bed and answered the call, irritated Mary had handed him that snob stuff again.

"Hello," he snapped down the line.

"Oh thank God," Oosty sighed. "Gallant, all Hell's broken loose. Where've you been?"

"Nowhere, phone must have been out of order."

"And your pager?"

"Battery's dead."

"Typical. Just when we needed you most. You've got to fly down to Petworth right now."

"As fast as my Triumph may look, Oosty, it does not fly."

"No, Calon has laid on a Ministry helicopter. It's standing by at Vauxhall Bridge, at the wharf."

"And what am I supposed to do in Petworth?"

"Find Lady Grimly and Mr Grimly's doctor."

"Why? Are they to be put in charge of Intelligence now?"

"No, silly. Mr Grimly's in a coma. He needs his drugs. It's your fault for not checking he had everything when you brought him in."

"Checking to see if Hugh Grimly was a drug addict wasn't on my list of instructions."

"Anyway, that's your task this morning, there's been a whole lot more. I haven't had a moment's rest. Mr Hallam has been sent off."

"Sent off?"

"That's all I can say, except the Stationmaster is in Sanctuary, but that might be a rumour, ignore it. It has been hectic, David. Be as quick as you can. The helicopter's been on standby since 10 o'clock. Calon is upset about the overtime."

"Just for Calon, I'll wet shave this morning. You can bet I'm putting in for overtime."

"No, don't wet shave. Please hurry, David, Mr Grimly is in a very bad way."

"All right, Oosty, all right, don't get your knickers in a twist."

Gallant replaced the phone. Mr Grimly in a coma was not good news. Poor man, he should have said how serious his condition was. And Stationmaster in Sanctuary, that was interesting, very interesting. But first he had to wash and shave.

"Will you wash my back?" Mary asked, as he entered the bathroom. She was sitting in a foam bath, steam billowing up in great clouds towards the closed window.

"Yes, I have to fly down to Petworth. My Chief's gone into a coma."

"A coma?" she laughed, splashing water onto her face. "Typical of your lot. Things don't seem to be going too well for you, Mr Gallant. I hope he wasn't got at by the Russians."

"Mr Grimly wasn't got at by anyone except old age. It's criminal the way they dragged him out of retirement. He's a good man, Mary, but he's past it. They need someone younger."

"My Bill. My Bill would like to be the Chief. That's his personal amibition. If he had his way he would have every man, woman and child under surveillance, every skinhead roasted alive in public and televised hangings in all the jails. He's what you'd call a lapsed Liberal."

Gallant smiled. "Bill's not so bad. He does his job well, he's got a long way to go yet. Simon Caw wants to be Chief too."

"He'll be Chief. All my instincts tell me that. I'll tell you one thing though. I'm emigrating if he becomes Chief. I've got enough life left in my fanny to get me around for a few more years yet, I'm not going to live here with a man like that

running things. Bloody police state already without him linking up with all the fascists."

Gallant didn't comment. He knew the word 'fascist' would
activate the Lipsnatchers tapes. He hadn't found Caw's devices
in the flat yet, but he knew they had to be there. Still, he wasn't
going to disagree with Mary either. He discharged shaving
cream all over his face, searching for his razor.

"You'll need this," Mary said. "I was going to shave my
legs."

Gallant turned and grabbed if off her. If there was one thing
he hated it was a woman using his face razor to do her legs.

"Now you're angry," she said, lying back in the bath,
soaping her long, firm legs.

"I'm not cross. I refuse to be cross. Actually I was thinking
about when I was a kid."

"You were a kid?" she mocked. "Not you, Gallant. You
were born six foot high with muscles and everything. I don't
believe you were ever a kid."

"Well I was. I was thinking how I miss the ruins. Just after
the war it was, for quite a long time really, ruins seem to have
been a big part in my early years. My father was in construc-
tion then, reconstruction. My favourite pastime was to crawl
down into the bomb sites and explore, you know? I used to
scrabble through the soil and debris and uncover toys, cups,
pens, books anything. I thought it was treasure. I used to bring
armfuls home all during the holidays. When I was older, I used
to go and walk in the empty streets where all the houses had
been flattened and imagine I knew the people in No. 4 or 6.
Wherever there was a crater. I'd crawl down and look for
letters, diaries. I believed that I'd find whole family histories. It
was as if I felt their deaths personally. For years, until I was
eleven or twelve, that's all I ever wanted to do in the holidays,
visit the building sites, or the abandoned docks, sift through
the past. It was never morbid, or anything. It just felt natural
and right someone should still be interested in them, even
though their whole communities had been wiped out."

"And that's why you joined the Square?" Mary asked.

"No – yes. I wanted to make sure it didn't happen again. Becoming a soldier wouldn't help, I'm not the hero type. I wanted to be in a position where deed, or word, could diffuse tense situations, prevent mass bombings and slaughter."

"And the Square does that?" Mary asked, full of doubt.

"According to its Charter it does. But in reality, no-one can stop wars forever, Mary. There's too much vested interest in them. Too much profit. I should have studied archaeology."

"Poor David Gallant, took the wrong road," Mary said. Then turning to him with a soft smile added, "Come into the bath, Mr Headhunter, let me hug you. Then you'd better go and save that Mr Grimly, or you'll be missing one more ruin."

Gallant smiled, washing away the remaining shaving cream. He switched on the radio, permanently turned to Radio Moscow, part of Headhunters regulations. The Kremlin were attacking the Government again, the daily ritual of hatred and poison. It was amusing, but it more often hurt than amused.

Gallant was parking his Triumph, signalling to the chopper that he was coming, when a diplomatic Chevrolet bounced into the carpark. Mitchel from the Relatives jumped out and approached Gallant. The chopper's blades were starting up, the turbines screaming in protest.

"Gallant," Mitchel said greeting him, shaking his hand. "God, you are a hard man to find."

"Hello, Mitchel, I thought you played golf on Sundays?"

"Golf? I'm scared to go outside these days. Scared the damn bomb is gonna wreck my handicap forever."

"Come on, it isn't as bad as all that."

"The Hell it is. Now tell me, David, what the fuck is going on in this town. This Moscow–Paris–Madrid shit is for real, man. I mean the German Chancellor is really talking about getting us out of West Germany. Can you believe that? We gave them everything, the Marshall Plan, we bought their lousy Volkswagens and now they want to kick us in the teeth. What is going on at the Square? My informant tells me it's chaos. Grimly's sick, Fielding murdered, Hallam disappeared and on the wanted list. Look, you are one of the few sane guys down there, I want to know something."

"Mitchel, I'm flying down to Petworth, urgent business, can't it wait?"

"No it can't wait. Look, David. I want to know. What are Cabinet Office's intentions. Are you with us, or against us?"

Gallant looked at the helicopter, then back at Mitchel, appearing comical in his pork pie hat, trying to hold onto it as the wind built up from the chopper's blades.

"Mitchel, we still support NATO. We have not been approached by any of the principal parties to change our minds. The Cabinet is still firmly opposed to Moscow. Especially whilst Sir Charles is in the chair. But we are under threat. The Second Eleven do exist. Mr Grimly is getting close. It is my guess that if Mr Grimly succeeds in finding the moles, our policy will stay the way it is; if he doesn't, anything you can dream up will be only half as bad."

Mitchel nodded, it was the way he saw it too.

"Meanwhile, you could help the situation by announcing that Israel/South Africa bomb test didn't happen. You may find Israel is the only friend you have on this side of the ocean soon, best not to throw that card away."

"The President has decided he has to make a statement after all. It was announced at noon your time, gives New York something cheerful to wake up to. A full denial. After all, once you had denied it, we couldn't sit on the fence for long."

"Tell Washington that the Square is still with them, but we have problems. It's us that lives next to Europe. We don't want France's nuclear missiles pointing at London, do we?"

"It's going to be a pull out. I can see it coming. That or war, and if you don't opt for war, we can't fight this one without you."

"Which is quite an admission, Mitchel. Now, if you'll excuse me, I've got a chopper to catch. I'll see you Tuesday. If you really want to help, share as much as you've got on

Tinkabelle. I'd like to know your source, we need all the help we can get. Grimly's sure 08.00 hours Wednesday is our deadline, that isn't much time."

Mitchel nodded. "I'll think about it." He walked quickly back to his car, leaving Gallant to run to the chopper.

"Train fast – flight easier," the pilot said with a cheerful smile.

Gallant looked down at the Petworth Estate and shuddered. He had never liked helicopter travel, just couldn't trust it.

"I'm going to put you down outside Lady Grimly's manor then?" the pilot, Collins, queried.

"Yes, just follow the road out of town towards Fittleworth. It's a large stone mansion with a row of pine trees leading up to it. There's a big field in the front, plenty of clearance."

"Good, I'm not one for parking on trees."

The chopper swung round and headed across the fields and woods for Fittleworth.

"That's it," Gallant pointed out, hoping he wouldn't have to traipse around too much to find Bettina Grimly. She was always a hard woman to find. A penchant for hide and seek that was quite infuriating.

"I'm going down," the pilot informed him.

The chopper descended, sending a lone, miserable horse running for cover to the far end of the field. For some reason Gallant indentified with that horse.

"Smooth as a baby, Mr Gallant. You take all the time you want doing what you have to do. I'm going to take a leak and read my book. Ever read Hermann Hesse, Mr Gallant? Makes me laugh a lot he does. Haven't enjoyed reading so much since I gave up Captain W.E. Johns."

"Hesse makes you laugh?"

"Well, he's not as funny as that other fella Böll, but they are both funnier than Kafka."

Gallant nodded, a puzzled expression on his face. "I have to admit, Collins, I've never found Kafka a barrel of laughs."

"Me neither. I thought it was me at first, missing the punch lines. That's what happens when you come back to reading late."

"Yes, I know what you mean," Gallant lied, though he hadn't read a work of fiction since leaving college. He was a biography man, always had been. "I won't be long . . . I hope."

In actual fact, it was not going to take Gallant long to find Lady Grimly. Nor was she unaware of his sudden arrival. Quite naturally, she had witnessed the helicopter come down in her paddock and she knew from past experience that helicopters only brought bad news.

"You'd better hide, Igor," she suggested to the snow-white haired man lying in her bed. "It's them."

"Them?" he asked, bored, struggling to exit a self-induced stupor. "Who are 'them', Bettina? Your English friends?"

"It's the Square. They've come for something. It isn't Hugh, it's young Gallant, his swordbearer."

This Igor looked up past Bettina at the window, really his head was far from clear; this crazy reunion with Bettina had gone much further than he could have ever imagined. It was one thing being an old flame, quite another when Bettina filled him so full of something that he was ablaze with passion for the best part of the night and morning, uncontrollable, insatiable and he was sure he had aged ten years in that one night. Bettina, of course, had showed not the slightest damage and, sickeningly, positively thrived on a night of love. It was as if she was determined to get all she could out of life, sure that at any moment it could end. A dangerous state for a woman at any age. The English were incredible, so strong, so unwilling to bend. No wonder Moscow had ordered out the best on this job. The last call for the old boys.

"Do you think they know I'm here?" he asked, wondering why he was unable to think clearly, command his leg muscles to work. Disconcerting, but not unpleasant. He needed another dose of whatever was in that syringe she had forced on him. That would get him going. Certainly he couldn't allow the Square to find him at Lady Grimly's. They would know the worst if they found him . . . but he was so tired, just a little nap . . .

"I said it's Gallant," Bettina called out from the window.

Igor stirred, running the name Gallant through his sluggish memory. "I know him. He is Headhunter, a loyal man."

"A fool. To be loyal to my son, one has to be a fool. Now please be a good boy and go and lock yourself in the bathroom. I can't have Mr Gallant in here sniffing out Russians. They are trained, you know. Gallant can smell out a Moscow agent at 400 yards."

"I'm not so sure I like what you are saying, Bettina."

Bettina whipped around, instantly angry, glaring at her overnight lover. Really, the man was too much. Not only had she had to give him an entire week's supply of her sons's health serum just to get it up, but it was quite obvious to her that Igor was at death's door. How Moscow could reactivate him of all people; why it was more absurd than dragging Hugh up to London. Igor had retired in '64. Tinkabelle must be senile to think of sending this relic to England on his behalf. It was all very well to activate sleepers, but waiting until one is ninety-three is ridiculous. Yes, she had been there with the boys on the steps in '17. Yes, she had helped in the decline of Trotsky and Joey had grandly made love to her five times before sending her back to London after a dramatic winter in '31. But for all her fondness for Joey, even through the purges, she had only spent the sum total of three years in Moscow and Leningrad. Little Hughie had been born in China. Children didn't know what life was today. Without an Empire to roam what was the point of it all? Her father, Rt Hon. Lord Fairley-Orr had dragged her all over the world. The Russian Revolution has been so terribly bloody, but so dramatic, she wouldn't have missed it for the world.

It was unfortunate that they had killed her first husband Kerry Grimly, Ambassador to Turkey and God knows where else; and more than natural that little Hughie had grown up with such a determined hatred of the Russians. Of course, he'd only been twelve in '17, he wasn't swept up in the grandeur of it all. He just saw his dead father and drew the inevitable conclusions.

"Igor Alexander Puttin, you will leave my bed and go to the bathroom. You are getting on my nerves."

The Russian, no mere strip of a lad, wound up his mainspring and eased himself out of bed, taking his thin, frail frame, inch by inch into the bathroom, the old scars still very much in evidence. The war horse to the stable to await further orders. He had no choice. She had been there, been on the steps with history. One didn't argue with history. Bettina watched him go with some apprehension. "You should eat more, Igor. Hugh does keep his weight up at least. You aren't much older than him, why can't you look after yourself more?"

Without turning around, he answered with a curt, "I have not succumbed to growing cabbages."

Bettina's lip curled with contempt. The man was too weak to grow cabbages, probably couldn't turn the sod. Come to think of it, he'd never been able to do much of anything. Igor's sole, useful role in life was survival, no mean feat, but had it been worth it? She shook her head, wrapped her flowing nightgown about her and waltzed out of the room.

"Is that you, Gallant?" she called, walking along the gallery until she came to the head of the stairs.

"Lady Grimly?" Gallant was calling from downstairs, his voice echoing along empty, marbled corridors, and then fading into some damp room.

"I'm coming down," she announced in her royal voice, which was rumoured to have, more than once, cleaved a social climber in two. A shaft of ice, long honed and polished by time to perfection.

"No, no, Lady Grimly. I'll come up."

"I'm not infirm, Gallant. I can climb and descend stairs just as well as you."

But Gallant was already half way up and approaching her. "Good afternoon, Lady Grimly, how are you?"

"I was fine until you turned up. You frightened my horse, Gallant. I think an apology is in order."

"I'm very sorry, Lady Grimly. Your horse is all right now, he's quite a jumper, I've never seen such a clean jump, must be all of seven foot high that greenhouse. Puts Red Rum to shame."

Lady Grimly scowled at him. "Chester has never jumped as much as a mushroom, Gallant. I shall have to make an official complaint. Where is Hugh? Where is my son?"

"I thought you knew. We have tried to reach you by phone, you know." He could hardly believe his eyes at the change in her.

"I have been busy. I can't be expected to be at Hugh's beck and call twenty-four hours a day. I'm his mother, not his slave."

"He's in a coma, Lady Grimly. Hugh is doing work of great national importance. It is vital he is kept at full strength. He blacked out sometime last night. He had mentioned a Dr Mowbray?"

Bettina suddenly understood the seriousness of it all.

"The whole nation needs him, Lady Grimly, he isn't much use to us in a coma. Where do I find Dr Mowbray, or Hugh's pills?" Gallant wasn't sure he was getting through. "What do I need, what does he take?"

Bettina felt a malicious smile fix itself onto her face. Hugh Grimly, her brave son the masterspy, in a coma. Well, it served him right. The boy had retired, he should know what was good for him and stay retired.

Gallant looked at this tall, elegantly thin woman and kept his earnest smile plastered to his face. In reality, he wondered how it was possible for a woman of Bettina's age to look so young and healthy. Her face was full, yet the last time he had met her she had looked like Gladys Cooper on her last legs. This woman, impossibly young and vital, didn't look a day over fifty, impossible to say she was older, but she most certainly was. She was still a beauty after the Elizabeth Taylor fashion, only drugs could have engineered this transformation, a miracle of post-war reconstruction. The red hair was a giveaway, no-one her age would have such fine, strong red hair. Bettina flashed her eyes at him.

My God! Gallant thought, she's making eyes at me. The bloody bitch! Not a thought for her son?

"The nation needs Hugh," Gallant appealed once again.

Bettina leant back against the gallery wall, her shoulders nudging an Edward Burra dedicated to her. Sunlight lit the back of her head; it was as if she had melted into a Hollywood movie and he was a panicky Leslie Howard, and she a calculating Vivien Leigh.

"Stuff the nation, Gallant. It went to the dogs the day Edward married Mrs Simpson. If the Russians want the place, let them have it. Do you know any other way to get them back to work? Let them take over. The combination of Soviet politics and British incompetence will be a glorious sight to see. What will the British worker do when his strikes are smashed with tanks, and dissidents sent to the Outer Hebrides to dig for oil, by hand? Best thing that could happen, Mr Gallant. If withholding Dr Mowbray's Battery Charger brings the revolution forward by a few days, then so be it."

Gallant couldn't believe it. This was Hugh's own mother talking like Winifred Wagner (or was it the Mitford sisters?). "Your son is in a coma, Lady Grimly. Whether there's a revolution, or not, you wouldn't like him to suffer."

"Why not? He's made me suffer enough. I vowed I'd outlive him, if it was the last thing I do. Look at him, still alive at seventy-five. He looks like death. He isn't well, he doesn't remember things even half as well as I do."

Gallant could see he wasn't going to get far with Lady Grimly. "Does Dr Mowbray live in Petworth?" he asked.

Bettina turned away, silent, resolute. This was a way to reward Igor. The power of silence, Joey would appreciate it, applaud it.

"He's a doctor. He'll be listed, Lady Grimly. It would save me time if you'd oblige me."

"Oblige you?" She laughed, throwing her head back with a

dramatic sweep of her hair. "Oblige you? Damn you, Gallant," she said with great savagery. "It's people like you that have kept my Hughie going these past years. He should have retired years ago. He is a sensitive boy. He shouldn't be out and about in London at all. Your flattery makes him believe he has a duty to this God-forsaken island. It's not true, Gallant, it is simply not true. He hasn't lived his own life. He hasn't known what it is like to be alive. It has been vengeance, vengeance. You all killed him. If he's in a coma, good. He has always been in a coma. For more than fifty years he has been in a coma."

Gallant didn't feel he had to waste any more time. "Goodbye, Lady Grimly." He immediately about turned and descended the stairs. Almost at the bottom he looked up once again. She was standing at the top, her back to him, a chit of sunlight stroking her shoulder as she disrobed. In one continuous motion she stepped from her clothes and walked back towards her bedroom – and a lover?

But as Gallant stepped out into the fresh air, he had a feeling of death weighing heavily on his mind. The mansion shrank from it but, nevertheless, it was there, waiting in the wings.

He walked across the ornamental garden towards the paddock and the chopper. Chester the horse was grazing in the shrubbery. One leap for horse, one change of diet for horsekind.

"I'm going to drive into Petworth to look for Dr Mowbray, Collins. Not much co-operation there, I'm afraid."

"How will you get to Petworth?"

"Borrow one of the Grimly cars. They won't miss one."

"What shall I do?"

"Fly to Petworth, put down at the nearest open space to the Milford–Goldaming road."

"Righto. I'll leave in a minute. I just want to finish this chapter."

"Funny, is it?"

"Hilarious."

Dr Mowbray was in, but sick. He lived on the downside of the town in a tiny cottage, probably considered 'chic' by city folks, but looked cramped to Gallant. The doctor's wife let him in, looking nervous and upset.

"Ossie hasn't been well for some time actually. On Sundays he likes to rest as much as he can. Is this an emergency?"

"Yes very." He told her about Hugh Grimly's condition. She went upstairs to let the doctor know, leaving Gallant in the living-room watching the doctor's children playing outside with a large alsatian, who was playfully trying to bite their heads of. It was a very mediocre room, desperately chic but cheap, filled with Sunday Magazine special offers, fanatically well dusted. It was cold and lifeless. Like most people, he imagined that they lived most of their life in the kitchen.

"Ossie says he'll see you now," the mousewife whispered behind him. He whipped around, surprised she had been able to enter the room and creep up on him like that. He took a breath to recover.

"Thank you, Mrs Mowbray, thank you very much. I'm sorry I had to invade your Sunday like this."

"Oh that's all right. We don't have many visitors these days, and Ossie always has a kind word for Mr Grimly."

Gallant smiled and walked through the archway and up the stairs.

"First door on the right," Mrs Mowbray called out after him.

But when Gallant opened that door and walked into the bedroom, he thought he had made a big mistake.

"I'm sorry," he stammered," I . . . I was looking for Dr Mowbray."

"I *am* Dr Mowbray," the woman returned, flicking back her long, full bodied head of red hair. "Or, at least, I was."

"You're Dr Mowbray?" Gallant couldn't conceal his surprise. He/she nodded sitting up in the bed, a well formed naked breast flopping out of his/her pyjamas.

"Sex-change?" Gallant asked (or lesbian, he wondered). He'd read all the scandal sheets, of course, but he'd never seen one in the 'flesh' before. Hughes in Cabinet Office had taken a long leave once to have the op. but had changed his mind for some reason, probably because it wasn't available on National Health.

"No, not a sex-change, well, not intentionally anyway. This is all rather sudden to tell the truth. Five weeks ago my hair started to turn red and grow thick again, then," he indicated his breasts, "these began to sprout. My wife is in shock. I had to shave off my beard. In fact, I think I'll have to have electrolysis."

"But why?" Gallant asked, half repulsed, half fascinated.

"It's the serum. It worked so well on Lady Grimly, boosted Mr Grimly's health so remarkably too that I decided to use it myself."

"Just like that? I mean, one injection and your hair turns red? Not to mention the rest?" Gallant was glad he wasn't on the stuff, drugs scared the Hell out of him as it was.

"No," the doctor explained, emitting a high pitched laugh that didn't seem natural to him at all. "This is after a year. My skin changed first. It became softer, my wife noticed it. Then the hair . . ."

"But Mr Grimly? Could he . . . " Gallant enquired, nervously. Dr Mowbray arched his plucked eyebrows, thus revealing that anything was possible, anything at all.

"Mr Grimly is in a coma," Gallant told him, standing back against the wall, wishing there was somewhere other than the bed to sit down on. He was not going to sit on the bed. He was nervous enough without getting too close to sex freaks. Nevertheless, he found he could not take his eyes off the doctor. The man/woman was in his/her forties, but Gallant noticed that Dr Mowbray had developed this same sheen, that vital, filled out look of a *Cosmo* cover girl, a young, almost plastic expression that had occupied Lady Grimly's face. The serum seemed to abolish wrinkles, which was terrific if one was a woman, a drug more important than Interferon, a miracle drug. But if you were male, it was a locker room nightmare.

"And Hugh Grimly is in a coma, you say?"

"Yes. It's very inconvenient. He's conducting an investigation."

"I thought he was in retirement?"

"We took him out of mothballs. I need at least five days supply of the serum, but if this is what it does . . .?" Gallant suddenly wanted to laugh, it was all so crazy. Everyone had gone stark raving mad. Did the Russians really want all this?

"Mr Grimly is a lot older than I am," Dr Mowbray pointed out, somewhat needlessly in Gallant's opinion. The doctor's voice was obviously in trouble, deep one moment, squeaky the next. No female impersonator could have achieved such accuracy, it was almost as if the man's bones were softening up into a new shape – impossible, but the impression was there.

"I don't think there will be any problem for Mr Grimly. His body settled, any imbalance in his hormones might make his hair grow again, or fatten him up a little, but I don't think a man of seventy-five will start to look like Sophia Loren overnight."

"Unlike you," Gallant said, unkindly.

"On the contrary, I always looked like Sophia Loren," Dr Mowbray said. Then, with a sudden shudder, he buried his head in his hands and cried, tears appearing from nowhere. "It's not true, I never looked like Sophia. Oh God, how can I go out and see my patients like this?"

Gallant could imagine their surprise, especially in a small country town like this. "You could go as a locum," he suggested, trying to be helpful. "Tell them Dr Mowbray got called away to his dying mother in Brisbane, or somewhere."

The doctor seemed to cheer up at that suggestion. "A locum? Yes, it might work. I could always inhale nitrogen to lighten my voice before surgery."

"Good idea. Now . . . I do have to get back to London actually. Do you have a batch of the serum ready?"

Dr Mowbray nodded that he had, climbing out of the bed. Gallant almost whistled. Dr Mowbray had the best pair of legs he'd seen on a woman since Cyd Charisse, smooth too.

"My wife, she's a little disturbed by all this. She's catholic in taste, finds it difficult to adjust to being in bed with a woman. Sex is right out the window. Can't get it up at all, all the feeling's gone. Waste really."

"It's a tough world, Doctor. Personally I wouldn't want to become a woman at my age, can't grow old with dignity if you start at forty."

"Don't I know it. I suppose you mean Bettina?"

Gallant smiled briefly. There was never any growing old with decency with her. He watched as the doctor opened up a small fridge over by the washbasin. He took out something that looked like an egg carton and placed it in a cool-bag.

"Should stay at the right temp for eight hours, but get it to a fridge as soon as you can, to be on the safe side. I'm going to give him a booster dose first, then there is a normal week's dose. He can administer it himself when he's normal once again. This is confidential, Mr Gallant, I mean . . . I don't want to loose my licence as well as my sex."

"Isn't it reversible? You could stop taking it."

"And spend the rest of my life in a coma? I never had the funds for research, you see. I couldn't get them, people thought I was a crank, just another MD with a lively imagination. Lady Grimly helped me, of course, she saw my serum for the brilliance it is, she knew I had found the fountain of eternal youth, but her money wasn't enough. I need laboratories, incubators, all the equipment everyone else gets. You think I can be a genius on £8000 a year? It's the antidote, Mr Gallant, I can't afford to experiment and I haven't found a way back. Lady Grimly isn't interested, she just wants to race forward to her youth. She looks younger now than when she was fifty."

"Does it stop? Will she continue to get younger?"

"Your guess is as good as mine. Frankly the laws of nature are being refuted here. My intention was to make old age more tolerable and middle age less aggrieved. I made a miscalculation somewhere."

"It certainly looks like it. Still, if you do find it difficult

remaining a doctor, you could always try *Penthouse* cen-
trefold."

"You really think so?" he asked, happily surprised. "I do
have nice legs, don't I?"

Gallant smiled, blushing for the first time in many years. He
took the cool-bag with the serum in it and tucked it under his
arm.

"Give my regards to Mr Grimly. It will take approximately
five hours for him to come back to normal, so be patient. He'll
be hungry, too, try and get him to eat steak, something with
high-protein anyway."

"Thank you, Dr Mowbray. Who knows, if Mr Grimly
succeeds with his investigation, you might find yourself on the
Honours List."

"Oh God no. I wouldn't know whether to bow or curtsey."
But still, he brightened up and decided to dress. "I think I'll
take a walk around town, try your locum theory out."

Gallant gave him an uncertain smile and ducked out of the
bedroom. The things he had to do for Queen and Country.
No-one would believe his memoirs, that was for sure. Funny
thing was, he didn't feel shocked; it disturbed him that he
wasn't disturbed.

He left the Mowbray cottage and rejoined the Grimly
Mini-Estate. The sky was clouding up, dark, menacing purple
in the far right hand corner. That was all he needed, a rain-
storm and to get struck by lightning. The complete absence of
any wind was a giveaway, it was going to be one hell of a
storm. Best to get to the chopper before it was too difficult to
take off.

As he drove through the town he felt happier, at least Mr
Grimly would be able to carry on now. Trouble was, how
long before he would start to look like Sophia Loren? Or
Sophie Tucker in his case. Gallant laughed out loud. It was
crazy. It didn't bear thinking about. The Service would
become the laughing stock of the world. It couldn't be allowed
to happen. Mr Grimly would have to be weaned off the drug,
no question about it.

He drove around past the church and down North Street on his way to the rendezvous. The stormclouds were spreading from the horizon to above his head, it was going to be a grand affair.

The chopper was waiting in the distance, in the middle of a local field, a village policeman standing alongside with his bicycle. Gallant's heart sank. Local police could be an awful bother. He abandoned the car with the local garage, giving the pump attendant a fiver to take it back to the Grimly's some time that day. Then he struck out across the road, over a fence and into the field.

As he approached the chopper, carefully holding the cool-bag steady in his arms, he overheard the pilot and policeman's chatter.

"Personally I prefer Gerald Durrell. I like animals you see."

"But you *can* see my point?" the pilot asked. "The exchange between worker and policeman is not one of mutual interest. Karl Marx saw the worker as the policeman of society, he didn't believe they should be used as a tool to separate and divide the rich from the poor."

"Or there again," the policeman said, "I quite like the *I-Ching*. I often consult the oracle before setting out on my rounds, sharpens the eye, it does. You'll be taking off before the storm then?"

Gallant climbed in. "OK, Collins, London." He turned to the policeman, who was backing off with his bicycle.

"You should try *Origami*, much more practical than *I-Ching*."

"That so? I never got much time for Eastern esoterics."

Collins started up the turbines, the policeman fled, concerned for the safety of his helmet.

"What did he want, Collins?" Gallant asked, strapping himself and the serum together.

"Wanted to give me a parking ticket, silly sod. Said it wasn't an official helicopter pad. I told him, didn't I, the day Petworth gets an official chopper pad, I'll be Archbishop of Canterbury."

"What did he say?"

"He said they already had an Archbishop."

The chopper took off. Gallant held his breath, as the ground fell away.

"London, is it?"

"Direct," Gallant said, sweating. He still hated flying.

"Nice storm up ahead, Mr Gallant. Let's hope visibility doesn't get too bad, the radio's on the blink."

"Just fly, Collins, spare me the details. I don't want to know about any problems."

"No problem. I could fly back to London blindfold."

Which was precisely what Gallant didn't want to hear. Navigation 'firsts' weren't one of his favourite entries in the *Guinness Book of Records*.

SEVEN

Midnight On The Hibernian Express

The Connaught Hotel is, perhaps, the holy ground of London hotels. It is a preserve for those in play only, attracting the exclusive who gain entrance by some extraordinary subtle initiation process, invisible and incomprehensible to the great unwashed, whose idea of sophistication is a stray hand on the sweaty thigh of a limp rag Playboy Bunny during lunch at the Casino. The Connaught is not for those who savour the Waldorf or revel in the Dorchester. It is the extra-dry, red label champagne, the quiet, superior dullness that is the quintessence of the English. A place for the mildly grand who come up to town for the day, to be reassured that there is a bastion of the pre-Suez Empire lurking in Mayfair. As Thurber was to the Algonquin in New York, Osbert Lancaster would be to the Connaught, irrelevant, but something dimly recalled as a special time.

Injected into this rarefied atmosphere were senior personnel from the Square and (only just tolerated) the Relatives. It wasn't actually the FO's bag, they had the Savoy and Simpson's of the Strand; Mayfair was altogether too much of a walk for them.

And it was Sunday evening, the night cold, the sky clear, promising to be rain-free, but zero temperature in the city. Peter Hallam emerged from the cloakroom in a long overcoat and scarf, both much too big for him; his hands carried a battered brown felt hat, altogether completely out of character for the usually suave Number Two. He was nervous, not least because he'd swopped his blue mohair overcoat for this plain

214

black wool in an attempt to disguise himself. He knew the
Easton training manual well enough to know that an effective
disguise was virtually no disguise at all. Everyone knew him as
a smooth, impeccable dresser. With a scowl and shapeless coat
he would join the shabby multitude and escape detection, he
hoped.

He was irritated, not least because his emergency rendezvous with Doc Sludgeon had come to nothing. He'd waited
from 6 pm to 6.45 pm, but Doc hadn't turned up. A brief call to
the Square Archives had revealed why. Simon Caw had Hallam in chains already, a wanted man, *persona non grata* at the
Square. A lifetime of service tossed away on a dummy – for
what? The fact that he had stood down Amsterdam Stationhouse wasn't anything to cry over. The Dutch couldn't wait to
leave NATO anyway, damn pacifists would just roll over and
let Moscow rub its tummy the moment trouble broke out.
The Dutch hadn't much choice anyway, sooner or later they
were going to request Britain to cease Intelligence operations
there. Their left wing were already sharpening axes and polishing their bulldozers. Forget the barricades, the dykes were the
prime target and why get involved with Europe's troubles if
you stand to loose half your nation to the North Sea?

So he hadn't got Wendy back and he'd betrayed the
Butcher's Boy. Simon Caw would be looking for him, certainly he could expect to lose everything: his pension, his
status, his freedom. It was not a promising future, nor did he
have a suitable escape plan (though he was fortunate he had a
joint trust fund set up for Wendy in Switzerland, enough to
keep him going for a while).

"Mr Hallam?" A hesitant voice enquired.

Hallam was in the lobby, aiming for the revolving door. He
attempted to bluff his way through, pretending not to hear.

"Mr Hallam, wait, it's me. Peter, it's me, Sandy Bleak."

Hallam turned in surprise, staring at the Paris courier.

"Sandy?"

Sandy broke into a smile, very pleased to see his Number
Two.

"Drink, sir?" Almost pleading in his tone.

Hallam thought about it a moment. It was probable Bleak didn't know he'd been struck off. "Been back from Paris long?"

"Just this afternoon, sir, I . . . ."

Hallam cut him off. "I have a visit to make, Sandy. If you'd care to come along, we could pop into Richoux for half an hour."

"Fine, sir, fine. I'll just get my coat."

Hallam spent a nervous couple of minutes outside on the pavement until the young courier rejoined him. They walked away from the hotel with a briskness in their step.

"Can't find any of the regulars, Mr Hallam. It's all very odd, but London is like a ghost town this weekend. The Square is off limits and the Relatives are being pretty shirty. I called a friend of mine there, Tim Hanson, in Language section. He said – well, pretty strongly hinted anyway – that the Square and Relatives weren't on speaking terms. Philip Oosty is desperate, can't see his boyfriend."

"It's difficult times, Sandy," Hallam said, walking alongside, guiding them towards South Audley Street.

"What's happening? David Gallant has pulled the plug on France, closing down everything. Paris is very nervous. This new pact with Moscow has frightened a lot of people. Paris gold has gone sky high. Everyone thinks the President has taken a very high risk gamble, difficult to believe Moscow will keep a 'hands off' approach to French politics. They look at our increased military spending and think that it is going to be 1940 all over again."

Hallam sighed, repeating that well used, half serious joke bandied about Square corridors: "I never discuss business during business hours, Sandy."

Sandy smiled weakly. "Things are bad, aren't they?"

"The Warsaw Pact has to try this peaceful expansion gambit. There is so much trouble in the Soviet heartland, they need to feel safe. Getting us and the Americans out of Europe will make them feel very safe."

"Safe enough to crush internal trouble. I'd heard there was trouble in the Balkans. It's all the Olympics fault, the damn Eurocrats have shooed in on this détente spirit. It's sickening, Mr Hallam, the European papers are all for it. Extolling Moscow's virtues, claiming this peace initiative will bring about a new order in the world. Millions of people are having a love affair with that little runt, Mishka the bear."

"Said the spider to the fly, Sandy. Remember the story of the Fox and the Crow?"

"No."

Hallam frowned. He thought everyone knew the story of the Fox and the Crow. "Well, our friends in Europe will soon find their new bed-fellows will want all the sheets."

Sandy understood that. If there was one thing you couldn't get in Russia, it was good sheets.

"I need something here," Hallam said, coming to a halt outside the Counter Lipsnatchers shop in South Audley Street. "You go ahead to Richoux, if you like."

"No, I'll come in. Always like to see what's new. This must be Simon Caw's favourite shop. You wouldn't think there were that many laymen interested in anti-bugging devices. They've even got exploding briefcases here."

Hallam smiled, it was highly probable. But he didn't stay long. Just time enough to obtain a phone number he needed. Outside again, aware that it was growing colder still, they hurried along to Richoux, a chill wind cutting through their coats.

"I never knew you used that place," Sandy said, putting up his collar.

"I don't, but they like to co-operate. We can put a lot of business their way. Look, go ahead, Sandy, I have a telephone call to make. There's a call box on the corner of Grosvenor Square."

"Coffee? Or something stronger?"

"Coffee and a lamb chop or something. I'm quite hungry, it's been a busy day and I haven't eaten a thing."

"Fine, fine. I'll get something ordered then."

They parted outside the restaurant, Hallam hurrying to the call booth, thankful to find it empty. He had a little burglary in mind.

"Hello?"

"Mr Curtis, Mr Francis Curtis?"

"Yes?"

"Mr Leeds here. The Tate isn't open on Sunday mornings."

"I know, only after 2 pm."

Code exchanges over, Hallam got down to business, pushing in another five pence piece.

"There's a house in Bolton Gardens, no. 12. I need two passports, contained in a sealed OHMS envelope in the third drawer down of the recessed dresser in the white first floor bedroom. There is some cash there and a .22 calibre gun. I can tell you where the keys are hidden to the basement door, your problem is getting in past the guards. The house is under twenty-four hour surveillance."

"No problem, Mr Leeds. You know my fee?"

"Your fee can be taken care of with half the cash in the bedroom. Can you do it now. I mean tonight?"

"I'm free up until midnight. Delivery?"

"Victoria Station, Platform 9. Ten o'clock."

"Ten? That's a bit early."

"As near as you can then. I can't risk visibility for long."

"Make it ten–thirty. How will I recognise you?"

"Copy of the *Field* in my hands and a brown felt hat."

Hallam told the man where to find the keys, repeated the instructions and hiding places, and warned him about the housekeeper, who would be returning from Bingo at 10 pm. It was a peculiar thing, but he quite enjoyed employing a burglar to rob his own house. Simon Caw would be amused, too, but he wasn't going to find out. He had been assured Curtis was the best. For £500 he would have to be.

He left the phone booth, sneaking a look up at the third floor of the American building. Mitchel's office, lights on. Either working, or just trying to impress the opposition.

"I ordered you a ham omlette au gratin, hope that's all right, Mr Hallam."

It was dull, but he accepted it with good grace. "You ordered the coffee yet? It's cold out there. Wouldn't be surprised if there was a frost tonight."

"Bound to be. It was warm in Paris. London always freezes when I come home. The Bleak family has more drag coefficient than the moon. If they sent me to the Sahara, it would rain."

Hallam listened. He had to remain invisibly visible for four hours, keeping company with Sandy Bleak would be unexpected. Easton law, 'Hide out in the open – under their noses.'

"To tell the truth, Peter, I'm pretty surprised to see you in England."

"Oh yes?" Hallam asked sharply.

"Well, I would have thought you'd be in Paris with Wendy. Bit young to be out on her own, isn't she?"

Peter Hallam wasn't at all sure he was hearing right.

"Paris?" he asked calmly, wanting to reach out and beat the information out of Sandy Bleak.

"I saw her, on her own, walking into le Forum des Halles, looking very pretty, Mr Hallam. I would have said something, but some people came between us and I lost her. School holidays, is it?"

"No, no – I mean yes, Sandy. She went over with her school." This was amazing. Wendy in Paris!

"You look surprised," Sandy said, playing with the sugar.

"Oh, do I?" He affected a cheerful smile. "I miss her."

"Well she looks well enough. The Forum is always full of teenagers – bright lights and all that."

"When did you see her exactly?" It was hard for him to be calm, his hands had begun to shake again.

"Last night, er . . . around eight. I was having a bite to eat with a friend, farewell actually. Paris Stationhouse a bit upset about the change of policy. No-one wants to leave Paris. London a bit on the dull side to be honest."

"Quite, know what you mean," Hallam agreed, trying to sound as unperturbed about Wendy as possible, yet thinking all the time of his next moves. With his reserve false passports and £500, he would have enough to get to Paris and look for Wendy. He could catch the night train to Paris if it was still running, or fly. The thing was, where to find her? Bloody needle in a haystack. Certainly he could watch the damn Czechs in their Embassy and homes. A long job, but Wendy was there and she was alive, apparently well and he had everything to gain by leaving England.

"Isn't that Lord Carlingford and his aide?" Sandy pointed out suddenly.

Hallam swivelled around, his heart missing a beat. It most certainly was the Minister of Defence himself. Hallam shrank into his seat, glad they had a dark spot by the wall. Instinct had them both tuned in to the Minister's conversation with a practised casualness; strangers looking at the two would have assumed them both to be lost in thought, years of friendship commanding the respect of silence.

". . . likely that Moscow Cephal will slip a few agents into the Balkans, stir up a bit of trouble between the Serbs and Croats. They don't need to invade Jugoslavia, just watch them tear the place apart, set state against state, pit the poor South against the rich industrial North. It's an old game and they are past masters at pulling the house down over people's heads. I'm telling you, Ron, they will be invited into Jugoslavia by the spring of next year, to bring stability to the region, a complete re-run of Afghanistan."

"So that's why they kept Tito alive for so long."

"He would be alive now, if it wasn't for a damn power cut."

"Tricky business, European politics, damn tricky. I hear there's been trouble in Dubrovnik already."

"Adriatic was always a hot spot, as the Victorians found out only too well."

"What about Austria?"

"Worried I'd say, very worried."

Hallam smiled. It was his opinion that if every Russian,

220

American and British General had half his salary paid in Switzerland, they would be less inclined to declare war in Europe, but that was heresy, of course. Contrary to popular opinion, it was exactly the Minister of Defence's brief to find a way for war to break out. The push from the combined forces had always sought a 'military solution'. Who knows, perhaps this Moscow–Paris Pact was a good thing, if it blocked a rash of bloodshed. He shook his head.

"God save us from old Generals, Sandy."

Not quite following Hallam's drift, he anwered, "Rather, never quite got on with Generals actually."

"So what was Wendy wearing?" Hallam asked, curious to know for practical reasons.

"Red. Red top, red jeans. That's how I noticed her."

Hallam's face displayed momentary anguish. She didn't like red, she'd never liked red. But she was wearing red. He forced himself to think of all the haunts they had shared in Paris. The cafés she liked, the skating rink. He had a host of places to hunt her down, but at least he had the city and hope. Now it was possible to find her. For the first time since her abduction he allowed himself hope that he would see her again.

"Have you seen Mr Grimly?" Sandy asked.

"Yes, looks terrible. It's very sad. He's too old. It's a shame to force him back on the road."

"Bad for morale," Sandy said forcefully. "Plenty of younger men. Can't understand the Stationmaster going off like that. Where is Sanctuary?"

Hallam shrugged, quite frankly he didn't care a damn about anything anymore. Just his Wendy.

"Your omelette, sir," the waitress said, slipping a plate of food under his nose.

For once Peter Hallam had an appetite. "Better bring me a small salad as well," he told her.

*   *   *

10.45 pm is a busy time at Kings Cross Sation. The late arrivals from England's hinterland converge, expelling the weary travellers, exhausted from peeling the plastic from slim, chemically pure sandwiches and vainly attempting to prevent tea slopping from collapsible cups. Travelling by rail is not, as they say, what it used to be.

The night train, the euphemistically named sleeper, known as the Hibernian Express, was standing at the platform with a few minutes to go before departure. The mail van was still busy loading, as were passengers with their assorted luggage, and a couple of MPs on a lonely vigil to their constituencies in the North, the weekly ritual to prove they cared.

And in the midsection, in a first class compartment, a passenger lay asleep already. Not unusual, save that this passenger was fully clothed and was not asleep, but in a coma. This rotund figure, partially hidden by a British Rail blanket, looked pale, decidedly ill, possibly destined for a funeral – perhaps his own – for Hugh Grimly, having been injected with Dr Mowbray's booster and placed on the Newcastle train, showed absolutely no response whatsoever. It was even doubtful whether there was any purpose to the whole trip. Neither Bloater nor Nolan knew where the Butcher's Boy was. Just Newcastle. That was the sum total of their knowledge.

Doc Sludgeon, who had substituted for Grimly at the Square, was busy ensuring that the 'leak' of Operation Poppyseed went according to plan. The carefully worded document marked: 'Highly Restricted. Most Secret (issue of ten copies only)' was a lie, but no-one was to know. The whole pink document was distributed to the in-trays of the suspect forty-two, and to each document two men and the full back-up of Lipsnatchers was put into operation. Time would tell, patience and a modicum of luck. There was no doubt in Doc Sludgeon's mind that Operation Poppyseed would work, that Grimly's plan was sound. It was just that he would have preferred it if Hugh Grimly was around and fully conscious, and Simon Caw's mob were not involved. Grimly would be able to tell which were the rats leaving a sinking ship and which were the rats suffering from paranoia, believing a purge was on its way. Paranoia was rife, only an inch below the surface since the Will Strawson days, a dangerous ingredient, hard to irradicate.

The wisdom of sending Hugh Grimly on the night train was shared between Sir Charles and David Gallant. They had reasoned that if the Butcher's Boy was up there and he really did know something, then it was best to pursue the matter, a fallback operation if Poppyseed was stillborn. Nothing could be done in London in any case until the forty-two reacted. It was a gamble, but Hugh's recovery would be considered a bonus – if it ever happened at all (about which there was some doubt).

The Square could only wait, listen to the world in a panic, for no policy decision would be made by Sir Charles until he was sure his office and those of his colleagues had a clean bill of health.

Apart from Mr Grimly, secure in his coma (one of the few guaranteed a quiet undisturbed ride), others were gathering on the platform, luggageless and in a lather about cabins, astonished at the cost of their tickets. They were worried that if they didn't find and unmask the Butcher's Boy, discover the names of the Second Eleven, no-one would reimburse them, a strong deterrent if ever there was one.

"Get on the train, Willy, no use fretting about your trench-coat now, you can clean it in Newcastle."

"But it was a filthy taxi," he protested vehemently.

"I've seen worse," Croc said, opening the door, "in Burma." But he didn't elucidate, for his eyes had settled on the back of a tall, grey-haired man and a short camel-coated female climbing onto the next carriage of the train.

"Don't look now, Steven, but that's Zavrel and Cosmo."

The Stationmaster looked down the platform with narrowing eyes, his heart skipping a beat as his gaze fell on the tall, bearded Zavrel helping Cosmo into the train.

"Tinkabelle's assassins. Why this train?" It was very disturbing. "Willy, get along, get along, find out which cabin they are in."

Willy, nothing loathe to add to his knowledge of foreigners, hunched up his trenchcoat and insouciantly ambled along the platform, blending so well into the bustle of a train about to leave, that neither Stationmaster nor Croc could see him from the moment he left their side.

"I don't know how he does it," Croc muttered, boarding the train.

"But what are they doing on this train, Croc? What are they doing?"

"Edinburgh? A holiday perhaps? Bloody cheeky if it is."

Stationmaster closed the door after him, a heavy depression sinking in. If ever there was proof of a leaking ship at the Square, this was it. As far as he was concerned, no-one at the Square could possibly know of their sudden decision to go and seek out the Butcher's Boy. If it was coincidence, it was the most absurd and impossible of coincidences. He didn't like it one bit. Zavrel and Cosmo were Tinkabelle's best assassins, the most successful team known, never apprehended. Their photographs were on constant display in the Square's Operations Room. It was every agent's dream to capture this elusive legendary team. How incredible that they should be on the train. He had to know why. Capturing those two would be a feather in their caps, but there could be no contact, no identification at all. Sanctuary meant Sanctuary – therefore they simply did not exist. Who would be fool enough to expose themselves before the moles were unmasked? Not his team, not whilst the Stationmaster was in charge.

Croc moved him into their cabin. They had taken two. One for Willy at the end of the carriage (his snoring would be too much for a rough night on the rails) and theirs midsection.

"I never knew second class was so cramped," Stationmaster moaned, staring at the narrow bunk and miniature basins.

"This was built for an invasion of Japanese tourists who never came. So we get stuck with them."

"I miss the tourists," Stationmaster said wistfully. "They used to make this city so international, one could almost imagine London was truly cosmopolitan."

Croc's sympathies tended towards a different direction. London was for Londoners in his opinion and that didn't mean Midlanders or Scots either, never mind planeloads of foreigners littering the parks.

"That's one thing that silicon chip can't replace, Croc. You won't find chips touring the Tower or watching the Changing of the Guard. Did you remember to bring the Bell's along? I don't think I could stomach this journey without a nightcap."

"It's coming up, sir, just let me unwrap the toothmugs." Croc busied with the whisky as Stationmaster prepared his bed and removed his jacket.

"This incognito business reminds me of the war, Croc."

"Everything these days reminds me of the war. That blasted silicon chip has destroyed more industries than German bombs ever did."

"Travel was cramped then."

"The blackout was fun though. Can't get a decent blind these days for under £55."

"The war was hard, but an adventure, miss the spirit of it all."

"The young don't know what they missed. But how can you get them interested if the damn Russkies want to use chemicals and nuclear weapons. No John Wayne or Errol Flynn needed in modern war. It's chip to chip, warhead to warhead and poof – there goes Birmingham."

"And they call it progress," Stationmaster wailed.

Three raps on the door signalled Willy's return. He pulled open the door and wedged himself in the doorway, his red face even redder from sudden exercise, his hair glistening with sweat as he stared at Croc and Stationmaster, gathering himself for a report.

Croc thrust a nip of Scotch into his hands and watched as Willy tossed it back, swallowing hard, allowing the fire to ignite his stomach, leaving his throat untouched.

"Been doing some fielding, Croc. There's more than just us and Tinkabelle's advance men on this train."

"Oh?" Stationmaster asked, ever suspicious, glad he had sent Willy out on this mission.

"David Gallant is on the train, too. Caught sight of him in the mail van."

"Headhunters?" Croc asked, raising his eyes to the roof of the carriage, trying to think this one through.

"Perhaps he's tailing Zavrel and Cosmo?"

"Perhaps, Steven, but they are headed for Durham."

"Durham?" both men exclaimed with surprise. "What's in Durham?" Croc asked.

"World Disarmament Convention, I think," Willy replied. He didn't know for sure, just counted himself lucky the train attendant was writing down early calls for people getting off in Durham and Newcastle.

"Well, one of us better get off at Durham and follow them, in case. Typical of Moscow Cephal to send agents to the World Disarmament Convention, as if there weren't communists there without them."

"University got an active communist society, d'ye think?" Croc asked. "Should have thought it was prime territory."

"Tapered off into anti-nuclear activity and Jane Fonda Fan Club," Stationmaster declared thoughtfully. "Willy, you must follow them. Hire a car if need be, but you're the best, Willy. I know you can do it."

"Bit short of ackers for hire jobs," he pointed out.

"Croc, give him a Ministry chit," Stationmaster ordered. "Show the chit and they'll sort you out. Better stick to Godfrey Davis though, we don't have an arrangement with the others."

"And Mr Gallant?" Willy asked.

"If he gets off at Durham, ignore him. He'll be too busy following the visitors to worry about you. He could be making a visit to the Butcher's Boy himself. We might find ourselves following him."

"No-one else in the train, is there, Willy?" Croc wanted to

know, a mischievous smile on his face. "I mean, the Red Army isn't in the baggage van or hiding in the caboose?"

Willy frowned. "No-one else. Train's full, you know. I have to share my cabin. I hope he doesn't snore, can't stand people who snore."

Suddenly the train lurched forward. The Hibernian Express was off and running.

"Cheers," Stationmaster offered. "Here's to the Butcher's Boy."

"You're on," said Croc, pouring Willy another nip.

The train pulled through the grey, riot torn northern suburbs, the rain damping down the heated passions of tropical blood transferred from the outer reaches of the Commonwealth. London had always been a myth, attracting the optimistic hopefuls to its bulging skirts, yet never attempting compensation for the lush greenery so casually abandoned for the dismal streets of Islington or sunny Clapham.

Gallant stared out at the disappearing city and tried to dispel this overwhelming depression that gushed over him in waves whenever he looked out over his London. It was the same every time, row after row of houses. Just what did all these people do and why? Simon Caw probably knew, and he'd like to keep them there. Caw's ideal city was a dead one, a city asleep at 4 am, still, everyone locked in and accounted for. The gaoler of the future with a computer system for a key.

He looked over at Hugh Grimly. Even with the injection, Grimly looked as though he'd been embalmed and this was his final journey. A former Chief, lying in state for members of the public to crowd into the cabin and kiss the ring on his hand, touch the robe. It was worrying, the callous way they had injected him, pushed him on the train in the hope that he'd recover.

Everyone had had their say about the situation. In Bloater's book Colin Fielding might have known more, but below stairs people always saw conspiracies and spook. Nolan was saying there was a link between Mr Grimly's coma and the umbrella attack. Gallant saw no such connection at all. He was just surprised they'd killed the Rat. If the Rat knew people like the Butcher's Boy – *if* he knew – then why kill him? He'd be more use to them alive. Besides, from what Simon Caw said, Peter Hallam had got everything he needed out of the Rat, enough to sell out John Welland to Tinkabelle. Everyone had been most surprised to hear about his Wendy having been kidnapped. Not a few, including Sussie Sutzman, were sympathetic to him. No-one knew the Butcher's Boy, so his betrayal didn't seem to count. And as far as Amsterdam was concerned, wasn't Holland the weakest link, their information quite often interesting but suspect? Simon Caw, quite naturally, didn't see it that way. He wanted Hallam's blood and he intended to get it. Gallant's money was on Peter Hallam. Wendy was a good kid, it was probable that she was worth twenty times the Butcher's Boy. But Simon Caw would be implaccable. The man had lost his heart to a robot, his veins went with the electronic flow. The man was the way of things to come. The day of human spies was rapidly coming to an end and the Second Eleven was only one more nail in the coffin. Caw's maxim: Machines don't leak, discs do not playback to all comers for a few ounces of cocaine and a paltry thousand pounds strapped to the back of an instant blonde.

The Square and the FO were always vulnerable, but what about the oil companies? Did the public realise, did the Minister realise how many ex-Square, FO personnel they had on their books? Damn oil companies had more spies than the Relatives and Square combined, and they had more money with which to buy the information they wanted. If there was a clash of interests, they won every time. Patriotism had been bought, framed and slung into the basement of the Natural History Museum, along with Drake, Nelson and Churchill. An embarrassment.

The train was moving very quickly now, a sway and rhythm that would last for many hours. Gallant decided to turn in. Might as well arrive fresh; it would, no doubt, be yet another long day ahead.

"It's the style of men who operate Intelligence organisations, to aspire to a place in history," Grimly said clearly, as if Gallant was at Easton attending one of his training lectures.

He turned to face Hugh Grimly, but didn't know whether he was surprised because his Chief had spoken, or because he hadn't moved, showed absolutely no sign of having spoken.

"Few make it to history books. Our own Burgess and Maclean, and possibly Blunt, will make it because they were caught out. But for the Stationmaster or Tinkabelle, who both want to be remembered *and* good at their jobs, how can they ever reach the history books, who would ever know their names?

"Our Tinkabelle, whose name was Larianov once, has always wanted a place in history. We have only sporadic details on his life. He has dipped in and out of all the major events of world history since the early thirties. If a biographer were to attempt to reconstruct his life, he'd find no-one left with long memories, and all the ones who'd worked alongside him either monotonously dead, or effectively silenced in a pet psychiatric ward."

Grimly sighed, still showing no sign of being conscious. Gallant found it eerie, but he sat down on his own bunk and listened, for practically no-one knew the history of Tinkabelle and if this was a lecture on that subject, he wanted to listen. This, at least, was one place in the UK that was safe from the never tired ears of Lipsnatchers.

"Larianov's father was a senior officer in the Cheka, though never actually proven to any satisfaction, nothing ever is. One story is that Larianov learnt his craft from Breska, which is like a soldier having Bismarck as a tutor.

"But my point of contact is Franco's war in '36. Larianov appears in Archives from May '36 onwards. He was there as a correspondent for Czech and Balkan news sources. In reality, he was keeping an eye out for German agents, recruiting doubles, always thinking ahead, a difficult operation, and from the energetic way he went about it, the one where he earnt his spurs. I met him in Madrid, only once that time. We were aware of each other, but rivals, even then. Our meeting wasn't arranged, merely a tipping of hats really. During the Berlin Olympics we were invited to a film show by the Germans, flown in direct from Berlin. Larianov was there with his German friends. I was surprised he took the time, but he came up to me and poured me a glass of wine. 'You like history, Mr Grimly?' he said. I didn't understand really. 'We will be in the history books, Mr Grimly, perhaps only like athletes with momentary fame in the Olympics, Mr Grimly, but I should like to know, which one of us do you consider to be Achilles?'

"Larianov always had this sense of destiny, which was his most extraordinary capacity, considering the volatile politics that have so bedevilled Moscow."

Another long drawn out sigh came from Grimly. Gallant shot out of his bunk and felt for the old man's pulse, a moment of panic there as nothing came and he was sure the Chief had given up. The booster, the damn drug, had been too strong, his old heart was giving up the struggle. He slapped Grimly's face, loosening his shirt collar, shouting, "Mr Grimly, Mr Grimly."

Grimly abruptly took in a deep breath, arching his back, his right foot going into violent spasm, thumping up and down with astounding ferocity, Gallant trying to hold it down, but only succeeding in vibrating along with the rest of the bunk. As abruptly as it began, it subsided and Grimly relaxed once more saying, "Larianov was in Britain in '36 and '40, possibly as long as nine months in total. Our First Eleven was recruited then. Even when we finally uncovered them, they couldn't or wouldn't, tell us what name Larianov used, then or now."

Grimly smiled. Perhaps he actually did think he was giving a lecture. Perhaps he imagined he had a new bunch of recruits with him and this was his little talk to give them insight into the length and depth of the enemy. To let them know just how far back the struggle had begun.

"In '49, as a reward for setting up a devastatingly effective spy network in Central and Northern Europe, he was summoned home and thrown into prison, and according to an acquaintance of a certain celebrated Soviet exiled author, was placed in an insane asylum, along with all the men he had betrayed and sent there. One of Stalin's fits apparently. Tinkabelle's face suddenly didn't fit.

"He didn't reappear, as far as we know (and this is Doc Sludgeon's field really), until the early fifties and then, although we weren't sure it was him and he was known only as Tinkabelle, I recognised the footprints immediately. He was involved with that Fuch's Rosenberg affair, tying America in knots. This was a comeback of a preposterous ego. He had the Philby quartet and the Washington Seven serenading him morning, noon and night. But he made a mistake. Like Shirley Temple, he peaked too soon. Jealousies at home; talk, not of awarding him the Lenin Medal of Honour, but of incarcerating him again. Kruschev was sharpening knives and Tinkabelle had not kept his seat warm.

"He was run to ground in Cairo, probably holding up a crystal ball to young Colonel Nasser, tempting him with all kinds of goodies. But in '55 Moscow Cephal was not a healthy house. From top to bottom, top brass to cypher clerks and tea-boys were being gunned down, flung into asylums. Suspicions and mania were as rife – far worse even – than in London now, a case of loving Russia less and Stalin or Kruschev more. There were no noble men or deeds in those months of chaos. There was a rich harvest of deluded, frightened defectors of Cephal personnel stationed outside Soviet territory, US and Northern Europe stations in particular. In a way this exodus was the inspiration for the Berlin wall built five years later. Moscow has never been loathe to scar a city, to teach a minority elsewhere a lesson; and whatever romantics might say, the East Germans had always looked east. The wall was as much for home consumption as it was for President Kennedy.

"I was in Headhunters then. Flying out to all sorts of remote places to verify the 'catch' was the genuine article (not a lot were), offering the usual contracts and lies about the cars and swimming pools that would go with their cottage in the country. I used to say, 'You'll live as well as I, better probably.'

In those days I lived in Barnes on the river. The roof had bomb damage, even in the fifties; it rained onto the top floor and my car was a '37 Austin 12. The Grimly money took a long time to recover from the war.

"And there was Larianov, our Tinkabelle. Not offering drinks this time, but, so I was informed, interested in defecting to the British and in particular, me."

Grimly paused, his face took on a ghastly impression of a smile, almost a deathmask.

"But he had them all fooled. Tinkabelle was not in the least bit interested in defecting to us. We were downstairs in the British Embassy, the old one with dry rot. The temperature would have been 110–120 Fahrenheit down there. I was exhausted, the plane I'd flown in on must have touched down eleven or twelve times out from London. Not only exhausted, but I had gyppy tummy, and that from the meal on the plane. I had had no time to drink as much as a glass of water between the airport and the Embassy. Tinkabelle himself was dressed in white, he looked cool. I must have looked like a pig, a gross, unpleasant, foul-smelling and ill-tempered pig. I knew him the moment we met and I saw his contempt. He'd aged, we had both aged. Whereas I had grown fat, he had a cheerful, plain, yet ungiving face, and he was thin. In another century he would have forsaken his role as gadfly and been a teacher or priest, perhaps an angry artist. Tightly wound, high energy sort of fellow with white hair. Not in the least distinctive, except for his urbane manner. A man who offered nothing, no first impressions, no last impressions, calmly sitting there watching me sweat, with his pale brown eyes.

"I sat against the whitewashed walls in my stained and shabby tropical suit, my head aching, my stomach turning, and he stared at me with a slight mocking smile. I knew from the moment I'd entered the cellar that he had come, not to defect but to recruit, and it was no accident he'd requested to see me.

"We sat facing each other for almost half an hour, neither of us saying a word. He didn't smoke, just stared at me. I sat and forced myself to think cool, removing my jacket and tie. The break came when Chancery sent down some cold orange juice. I fell upon it with great enthusiasm, I can tell you. At first Tinkabelle wouldn't touch it, but I think he must have noticed the effect it was having on me and relented. 'I thought I would get tea,' he said."

Grimly coughed. Gallant stood up again and tried to raise the old man's head, building up the pillows. He didn't want the Chief to choke to death whilst coming out of his coma. Grimly licked his lips, his throat most likely dry. Gallant looked around for the hip flask in his briefcase. Sussie Sutzman's idea, an emergency supply of Scotch. "If he shows the slightest sign of revival, Gallant, pour it in. He'll react, I know old Hughie, he's never liked Teachers."

Gallant tipped a capful into Grimly's mouth and held his nose to help him swallow. With the second capful, the coughing stopped and Grimly seemed to relax more, sinking back into his bunk, his face much softer, his eyes moving with more activity behind the closed lids. Gallant felt sure, for the first time since returning from Petworth, that his Chief would recover. He put the Scotch away again and switched off the main light, believing Grimly would sleep now. He, himself, undressed and climbed into bed, pleased to be getting some shut eye. And it was true he had gone a long way to relaxing his body, lulled by the rhythm of hi-speed rail, nearing sleep and 4999 sheep when, abruptly, Hugh Grimly's voice filled the cabin once again.

"Jove, it was hot in that basement. The orange juice seemed to evaporate faster than I could drink it. I think I was supposed to be feeling sorry for him, after all he was, officially, contemplating leaving his Motherland, and head office was very keen to have him. It was impossible to play him back to Moscow. Tinkabelle was not the sort of man you could trust. I didn't ever seen him coming over to us with any genuine heart. He wasn't – couldn't – ever be a traitor. Not a man aiming for the history books. No, in as bad a state as I undoubtedly was, I knew Tinkabelle for the cunning fox he was and that any trouble he was in, back home, would pass and he'd scrabble to the top of the heap again. It could be that I just didn't want him to join us, not my arch rival, for even then I knew him to be my *raison d'être*. The old saying, better the devil you know. I didn't want someone new over, I didn't want to learn a new alphabet. We had a neat and orderly battle, a constant war with undeclared, but understood rules. I felt cheated that he wanted to come over to my side, cheated and slightly afraid.

"But, as I've hinted at before, he didn't refer to his request for political asylum, not once. Nor did I trot out the usual picnic basket of contraband goodies. He was not some lowly Indian who'd settle for beads.

"I remember his hands, lying flat out on his knees. The flattened nails, as if someone had smashed the ends with a hammer, difficult to avoid staring at something like that. But still this disquiet, the heat and the sour smell of a nearby sewer; even more unnerving, his apparent calm. I even wondered if he was trying to unnerve me. I couldn't get comfortable, all I was thinking of was the swimming pool outside, though I hadn't been near one in years. I felt the heaviness, the full gravity of the world weighing me down, deluded myself that the balance of world peace was in my hands right there in that whitewashed basement. Silly really, just vanity. If the roof had fallen in at that very second, others would have replaced us, but in the heat of the moment . . . I was reminded of the Bard: '*As he was valiant, I honour him: but, as he was ambitious, I slew him.*' It would have been easier for all of us had I done just that, but we live by a code, I could not take offence and let the great axe fall."

Grimly swallowed, trapped in a memory insisting on reliving the past with an intensity that often comes with complete exhaustion. He was still, unveiling his most deeply buried secrets, long thought submerged on a long forgotten manuscript, grown mouldy in Archive vaults.

"He could see I was ill and thus had the advantage over me. He'd been in Cairo for six months, I'd not had six hours. I should have gone to bed and tried this 'historical' meeting when I was rested. Instead – and I must confess it is something I am still ashamed of to this day (an embarrassed laugh interrupted the flow) – it still makes me wince.

I began to talk about my mother, or to be truthful, his mother, asking him when he would see her again, whether he could part from her, wondering if she could make a new life for herself without him. With him with us, they wouldn't let her leave Moscow, could even lock her up in reprisal. But then, if there was any truth, it wasn't his mother I was talking about – it was mine. Who was sleeping with her? Who would protect her from her follies and excesses? I knew he had a mother alive still, but the mother I was describing could never be a Moscow mother. It was mine, wholly mine, and my worries of whether I could leave her. Even as I was saying, 'Perhaps we could get your mother out,' I was thinking of my own Bettina.

"It was at this point I produced the standard Square document, the: 'I volunteer to tell all and will not withhold any information. The British Government has treated me well, asking nothing I would not voluntarily offer.' It has always amused me. Form 105A we call it. Some remnant from the last Liberal Government. I gave him my pen and, although he took it, he did not sign the form, just stared at the inscription on the pen, 'To Hugh with affection – Bettina'.

"It was then he produced his form. Their 'ID II. Intention of Defecting proposal II.' He offered it to me. 'Enough,' he said, 'we are tired. It is hot. This is your chance for history, Hugh. Sign this, come over, leave the war. You have played your part, the October woman, Bettina, will follow. We could not leave Bettina behind.'

"I must confess, leaving the Square, all the damn nonsense for a comfortable Dascha in the country, to retire with Bettina and forget everything, finally admit the inevitable that we had to lose, was tempting. I looked at him and that form for a long five minutes. His eyes never left my face, we were two cats, kings in our own territory, daring each other to cross the dividing line. Two old knights whose lives had been diverted into searching for the chinks in each other's armour, neither side believing in their rightness, the justness of their cause. Two compulsory liars faced with an undeniable truth. His side might reclaim him and return the throne, or they might have used his crushed bones as fertiliser on the Moscow rose garden. I believed that his number was up back home. He believed that I was ready to quit, admit the cold war was won by him. The great truth, the world view, had been lost to us from working too many years preparing poisons in the cellars.

"With sadness, I realised there was little between us. We had become the same man, taken different routes, but we had arrived at the same destination and time, in an identical frame of mind. Our devotion to duty, honour, political and ideological committment was nothing more than habit. The world we had fought for, dreamt of, had been cut off in its prime by politicians and purges, weaknesses and sheer stupidity. Potsdam had sickened me, just as Yalta had. Roosevelt thought Stalin a saint, would do anything to enrage Churchill. Tinkabelle must have been fascinated by the peace and the massive Soviet land grab after the war. It is easy to say it now, but we should have gone to war in '45, taken Moscow whilst we could.

"Tinkabelle has spent a lifetime on the winning side, his setbacks were temporary, mine were always permanent, and cut-backs had made us cripples in the capitals of Europe. That's all the Square has ever been, begging cripples. And now we spend 60% of our budget on compiling information against the British public, rooting out nuclear dissenters. Had I known that, thirty years on, Britain would become a more efficient police state than the USSR, I would have signed. I would have signed. Why save a creature from extinction? I was a curator of a fast diminishing species. Free thought, free spirits had died in Russia. I could never believe it would die in Britain, but it has and once again I preside at a ceremonial funeral.

"But I didn't sign. He wouldn't sign. After a while I signalled for the guards to take me up top. Tinkabelle withdrew his request for asylum that afternoon and was returned to the

Soviet Embassy. It was only a few hours later that I realised he had my pen.

"Tinkabelle is not just our enemy, he's our judge too. He's fanatical. The Square has been his playground for years. I've tried to beat him back, but he's like a forest fire contain him in one part of the forest, he bursts forth anew in another. But his habit and dedication will trip him up one day. Perhaps now is that time, perhaps there will be a showdown after all."

And then, all there was to hear was the sound of the train rattling through the night.

Gallant was awake, thinking through, considering the implications. The main thing was Tinkabelle and Grimly had remained implaccable, pledged to their fight. And if the Butcher's Boy had the names, perhaps this time Grimly really did have a chance. The Square would be cleaned up once and for all. Gallant drifted off to sleep. He couldn't help but wonder if perhaps there was no way to beat Tinkabelle, something he didn't want to believe.

Thrusting aside a light northerly wind, the dark stream of metal and sleeping people pierced the moonless night at 125 mph, rushing through empty stations and bare March frosted fields. The Hibernian Express was on time and already a long way past Doncaster and York, making for Durham City.

And Willy was keeping vigil over his wards from Moscow Cephal, a little bit worried about the Kings Cross meat pie he'd managed to slip down before the train departed. Something dreadfully suspicious about the way his stomach was preventing him from sleeping. It was one thing keeping an eye open for activity from Moscow's angels, quite another being kept awake by meat pies, not the same thing at all. In fact, the more he thought about it, the less comfortable he became.

It was some time after Darlington that he couldn't do anything to avoid it: he had to visit the toilet.

When British Rail redesigned their trains to go 125–160 mph on existing track, they made no such adjustment to their ablution arrangements. Willy made it down the corridor all right, opened the door and closed it, locking himself in. Only to be thrown against the window, pursued by half a gallon of water as the train banked around a steep gradient. It was a true modern miracle that the hi-speed train could get around the corner with such stability and adhesion. It would have been more of a miracle in Willy's opinion if the designers had eaten a Kings Cross meat pie and had planned for high speed access to their loos.

He looked around for the usual soap, paper towel and toilet paper. Nothing. Nothing save three hundred and thirty-one paper towels strewn on the sopping wet floor, showing signs of beginning to float.

But meat pies had no time for niceties. It was just fortunate that he had half a dozen WH Cullen's bags stashed away in his jacket pocket and, as he sat down with a grim determination, clinging to the hand rail to keep his body in place, he was once again glad he had had foresight to pack away a few paper bags for emergencies. It was gratifying to know one's hobby could be so useful; he made a mental note to stock up at Binns or Fenwicks once he reached Newcastle.

But such was the intensity of the pain and the discomfort of the hi-speed toilet, it was with extreme surprise and horror that Willy felt the train begin to slow. Approaching Durham and he was not in the least bit prepared. Not only was he in the loo, but his trenchcoat was in his cabin and not even Queen and Country would make him part from that.

In panic, he removed the elastic band from the paper bags, but it was a race against time. The train slowed with unnecessary haste and slipped into Durham Station, coming to a less than smooth stop. Willy could hear doors opening and slamming shut, people with luggage shuffling down the corridor. He even heard the Czechs announce, "No, we are being met, thank you for your kind offer, sir."

Willy's heart sank as he pulled up his trousers, desperately washed his hands, remembering not to flush whilst in station. Still in pain, he pulled at the door lock, a frantic haste not seen in Willy since the day he was late for his disasterous wedding in '39.

The lock came away in his hands.

This was the end, a conspiracy against him. Not only were his feet wet, but he was locked into the damn loo for good measure. He began to beat on the door shouting for help. After a good two minutes of banging and shouting, a voice asked him to calm down and, much to his relief, opened the door. Willy was confounded to discover that Zavrel was standing behind the guard.

"Lucky for you this gentleman heard you, sir. Could have been stuck in here all night."

Willy was too surprised to say anything.

"Bit of a mess in there, too, by the look of it," the guard commented, looking at Willy's sodden trouser legs.

Zavrel took his last case off the train and closed the door. Willy regained his sense of panic and raced for his cabin, retrieving his trenchcoat.

"You getting off, sir?"

"Yes," Willy returned. "I can't stay like this. I need a wash and a change of clothes."

"I'm sorry, sir. Door sticks like that. Should have been fixed in '78, but what with the cutbacks. . . ."

But Willy was leaving already, not in the least interested in the guard's explanations. Trenchcoat on, he opened the door and jumped down onto the station platform. Immediately the whistle blew and the train pulled out of the station. No sign of the Czechs.

He began to hurry, the ticket collector had already gone off duty, he rushed out of the station to the main entrance to see a lone Ford Granada disappearing into the distance.

"Taxi?" Willy shouted, somewhat optimistically. None of the cars replied. All were empty and looked as though parked for a considerable amount of time. His eye caught a chalked sign on a notice board. 'Owing to dispute with local authorities, there will be no taxi service from station.'

And as Willy stood in the cold, mist coming in at him from either side, he knew that he'd been beaten for the first time. It was 5 am. The Czechs had been collected, snatched from him, all due to a meat pie he shouldn't have eaten in the first place. There was only one thing for it. He began to walk towards the hotel. He needed sleep, a wash and breakfast, time to think as well. Check on that Disarmament Convention, do something useful. He didn't want the Stationmaster to get angry with him, didn't want that at all.

*   *   *

Simon Caw was in the second stage of exhaustion. Not only had he not slept, but the crises were piling up in such grand proportions, it was beyond his belief and comprehension how fast British Intelligence could deteriorate.

Latest information to hand showed Soviet activity in Holland and Belgium. There were signs that their Governments were following in the wake of Paris and Madrid. Berlin was already showing signs of moral collapse with clashes between the military police and irate, unsure citizens. Added to which, the Square was in total paralysis. All right, they had the Poppyseed plan, it showed promise and there were monitors on each of the suspects, but what was worrying him the most was Grimly and Gallant's trip to Newcastle. Surely they knew of that invention, the telephone? It was inconceivable to him that it needed Gallant to stow a half dead Grimly onto a train and transport him all that way North. Not only that, but the telegram awaiting Grimly's return, from Triple X (yet another private Grimly code), stated that Tinkabelle was in Paris, actually seen in Rue Bachaumont, a known Moscow 'safe' house. Next stop Amsterdam or Brussels? Or even London? It really worried Caw to think Tinkabelle might reach British soil and he not know about it.

But what got him down the most, was this obsession with the Butcher's Boy. The Czechs knew where he was, thanks to

Hallam. Neither the Square nor Lipsnatchers could find either the Czechs or Hallam, didn't even know which city he was in. But it was ridiculous that, apart from a comatose Grimly, no-one in British Intelligence knew where the Butcher's Boy was. Worse, Poppyseed was likely to begin operations at 08.00 hours, roughly three hours away. The list had some very sensitive names on it; he had a bet placed with himself that more than a few would take offence at inclusion. One name he was interested in was Hacking, the postman. His duty was to distribute all incoming mail via the VDU system, diverting sensitive material to Archives. He was a vulnerable man in any investigation. Caw wanted that man to be cleared, it would be too easy and probably wrong if he was one of 'Them'. But it was a daunting prospect and, apart from Bill Jukes, he couldn't trust a soul. Not a good position for him to be in. He dialled 'information' on the Archives line, watching the VDU screen as it cleared itself. He typed in: 'Square residences and man-power—Newcastle on Tyne.'

All that came back was: 'See Oxterby. Gosforth 7190'. But when Caw dialled Gosforth no-one answered. He was still no further. He couldn't fly up there as well, that would be absurd, apart from being against the regulations. All the technology in the world couldn't save the Butcher's Boy, all because of a lack of trust, something Tinkabelle must have forseen. Caw couldn't blame Grimly for hiding the man. If Henry Betand, or whatever his name was, knew the names, he was a valuable man, but if he knew, why hadn't he told Grimly? Why hadn't he told Calon, or written to the Stationmaster? It was entirely possible that this oddball from Malta didn't know a damn thing and it was just wishful thinking on their part. A mad hope that it was simply a case of them being frightened into silence by suspicion, that, in reality, everyone knew the truth. But Simon Caw had his fears that British Intelligence was rapidly going the way of Australian Intelligence – up the spout – about as reliable as a Wombat in heat.

Caw made himself some coffee and stared out over Putney.

241

Dawn was spilling over East London, promising nothing but hell. The phone rang, startling him. An unsteady hand reached out and pressed a 'broadcast' button.

"Simon Caw," he answered.

"Smith at HQ, sir. There's a military shuttle leaving from Heathrow in 45 minutes, sir. I could have a helicopter standing by, we could have you picked up off your roof in approximately ten minutes."

"It's too late, Smith, I don't know where to fly to. No-one except Mr Grimly knows where to go and he's not telling. I need a good medium, not a military shuttle."

"Oh, but I thought . . . ."

"Thanks for calling, Smith, but until Gallant reports in we don't know where to go to. I'm going to put some reliable people into the field up north, I don't want Grimly unprotected, not with the Czechs around."

"I'll keep in touch, sir," Smith said, ringing off.

The phone rang the moment Smith hung up. Caw sipped some of his coffee before answering it.

"Caw."

"Oosty, sir. I'm back on duty. Flash calls came in during the night, sir. I thought you'd like to know."

"Go ahead, Oosty." Caw had underestimated Philip Oosty. He was a namby-pamby pretty boy all right, but at least he showed dedication, a remarkable trait, one that deserved consideration in the coming shake up.

"Our man seeing off Mr Grimly at Kings Cross observed the following passengers get onto the Hibernian Express. The report was filed at 11.49 pm, put into the routine box, sir. I can't understand it, it's coded High Priority."

"But what does it say, Oosty?" Caw asked sharply.

"That Stationmaster, Croc Tate and one unidentified male in a trenchcoat boarded the sleeper, along with Mr Gallant, Mr Hugh Grimly and – this is the interesting bit – Stery Zavrel and Hellena Cosmo, all independent of each other I must hasten to add. My list shows Zavrel and Cosmo to be . . . ."

Caw cut him off. "I know who they are. Alert British Rail.

Hugh Grimly and Gallant have to be warned. I hope we aren't already too late. I'll get onto my boys in Newcastle, wish I could get hold of Oxterby. Grimly would know him."

"Oxterby? I'd forgotten about him. He might know the safe house list, the Butcher's Boy is bound to be in one."

"We didn't know where the Butcher's Boy was. I'm not even sure Oxterby is still in business. He's a veteran like Hugh."

"Of course he's a veteran, who else would Grimly trust? Now you said two messages."

"Sandy Bleak, Paris Courier called in. Had a meal with Mr Hallam before he knew Mr Hallam was *persona non grata*. Seems Mr Hallam has gone to Paris, flew there late last night. Sandy saw Wendy there, walking alone."

Caw frowned. He couldn't do anything about that now. Hallam would have to cope by himself. As long as he didn't find his Wendy, the Square still had a chance of catching up with him. A thought did flash through Caw's head. "Oosty, put up an ID picture of Zavrel and Cosmo on the screen. You do have one?"

"Yes, sir. I have already put their file on standby. Section 7 should be coming through right now, sir."

Caw flipped a switch to the right of him and a green picture of Zavrel appeared on his screen, his personal details alongside. Cosmo followed. It was the other woman all right and Zavrel was, as he had suspected, Captain Hook. It was inexcusable that neither Hallam nor Jukes had recognised him – Zavrel's face should have been as familiar to them as their own. Here was proof that Wendy's disappearance and the engineered betrayal by Hallam of the Butcher's Boy was a Moscow directive, strong evidence that the Butcher's Boy really did count in the Second Eleven exposé.

"Oosty, I'm going to be busy. Stay in control, give all the help you can to Doc Sludgeon. It is going to be a long, busy day – and thanks, Oosty."

Oosty was stunned. Simon Caw had said 'thanks'. Another first for the Square scrapbook.

Simon Caw dialled Newcastle CID. He needed help, he obviously couldn't rely on this fellow Oxterby, probably drunk with some tart from the docks anyway. No, now it was life or death. The Czechs were on an assassination run and walking right into the trap were all the leading Square hierarchy. No matter what his personal ambitions for power were, they were not, in his opinion, furthered by allowing Stationmaster, Grimly, Gallant *et al*, to be slaughtered once they reached their goal. There was just time to contact Smith and get himself on the helicopter.

It was only 5.17 am and the day was already a potential apocalypse.

*   *   *

The station clock pretended to 9.20 am, but anyone with any intuition of British Rail stations would have known from the existence of fresh tea in the Travellers Fare café urn, that it was still only minutes past the no-man's-world of 6 am.

The Hibernian Express was already standing in the station, changing crews, passengers stumbling out in a daze, leaving others still in their cots, hanging onto a flimsy sleep before they, too, would be expelled in Edinburgh.

On the platform, assorted Square personnel stood blinking in the glare of daylight. Hugh Grimly was inhaling a strong distillation of diesel and Newcastle City air. He'd never felt better in all his life, or at least the last ten years.

"Just up the platform, around the corner, David, there's a small local diesel that will take us there." He looked down at Gallant tying up his shoes. The man looked terrible, needed a shave, quite obviously hadn't slept a wink.

"You should learn how to relax, David. You look a mess. Come on, there's an early train at 6.45 am. Perhaps you will go and get us some tickets and a *Daily Telegraph*. Then I hope you will explain to me exactly how we arrived in Newcastle on a Monday morning or, to be more precise, what happened to Sunday."

Standing up, Gallant yawned, picking up his briefcase and staring down at his Chief with more than a casual inspection. "Er, Hugh?"

"Yes?" Grimly returned, walking briskly away from him along the platform. "I'm going to have some tea, Gallant. I'm ravenous."

Gallant caught up with him. He didn't quite know how to break it to his Chief, but Hugh Grimly was sporting a fine crop of newly sprouted red hair. Gallant decided against it. Afterall, it was a bloody miracle that Grimly was alive and looking so well. Why spoil his morning?

"I'll get the tickets and paper then. Order me a bacon sandwich, or something, to go with tea."

"Two bacon sandwiches. My goodness, I do feel hungry today. Best night's sleep I've had in a long time."

Gallant left him to his own devices and cut through the station barrier, looking for the ticket office.

It was a less joyous occasion for the Stationmaster. He was tired, had slept intermittently and was worrying about two things. One, the garbled story of Willy's night in the train's toilet, which smacked of uncommon ineptitude on Willy's part; and the other was the sight of Hugh Grimly, far from looking a decrepid wreck, strutting past himself and Croc, looking twenty years younger and sporting a youthful crop of red hair. Surprise, envy and, in other circumstances, amusement had all occurred to him on seeing the man. But one thing was certain: if the Square was putting out information about Hugh Grimly being in a coma, portraying a man near death's door, it was a damn queer way to go about your business.

"It's bloody odd, Croc. Hugh Grimly wearing a red wig. Who does he think he is, Benny Hill?"

"I'm going to follow Gallant," Croc said quickly, shaking the sleep out of his slow, bloodshot eyes. He'd had a good night's sleep, helped in part by the Bell's. Sleeping on trains was quite a luxury for him. Reminded him of the war again, that was a time for learning how to sleep on trains and a time for praying some bugger in the Luftwaffe wasn't in a mood for straffing.

Stationmaster was alone. He, too, could have done with a cup of tea, but he couldn't reveal himself to Grimly – not yet, it wasn't safe. Follow him, that was the plan, keep back and out of sight until events unfolded, and only if it was justified and convenient would he risk exposing himself. So he stayed where he was, sinking into a stupor, his body still in rhythm with the night train. The train itself gave off a wild shriek as carriage after carriage clattered into each other before sailing out of the station northbound, ensuring every passenger was duly warned that daylight was upon them and early morning tea was on the boil.

Gallant, dogged by Croc, passed by the Stationmaster's unseeing eyes. Both men slid into the tiny station cafe, Gallant to join Grimly, Croc hanging back, invisible, true to his trade.

"Two teas and two bacon sandwiches for the gent with the hair, hinny," the lady was saying from behind the counter.

"Chief, the station is crawling with cops. Special squad, CID – they're out for someone. Two tickets for Riding Mill."

"Well, at least it isn't us they are looking for. Thank you, Gallant. You know, I'm looking forward to our chat with John Welland. It's a pity Stationmaster isn't here with us. They got on so well y'know. Did they find him yet, by the way?"

"There's a rumour he is in Sanctuary, but no-one quite knows where it is."

"That's the old Brook Green house, you remember that, don't you?"

Gallant didn't remember, but if Grimly did, he thought it worth a call to London.

"What's the precise address, Hugh? I'll call Oosty at the Square."

Croc slipped out. He'd heard enough. Besides, he had two tickets to Riding Mill to buy. He'd have liked a cup of tea, but it would have to wait. As he scurried away, he thought of Willy, wondered how he had got on in Durham, hoping he was on their tails. The announcer drowned out any further thoughts.

"The 6.34 express for London is now leaving Platform 3."

246

EIGHT

A Sunny Morning Stroll

Although he had risen later than usual, he still bathed, shaved and chose his clothes with his customary leisure. Riding Mill wasn't Malta, but it was pleasant enough and quiet. Quiet enough to get some new work done. He hadn't ever really appreciated the English countryside and, at last, he was able to walk amongst the fields and get to know it well. He liked what he was painting too; it was developing into a new period for him, a new naturalness he'd not seen in his work in a long time, perhaps never.

It was one of those rare, sunny days that early March can throw in as a surprise, promising greater things for summer, but only in rare instances ever delivering, nevertheless astonishing the English who had a history of 300 failed summers, and had not yet adjusted their calendar. John Welland, alias Henry Betand, alias the Butcher's Boy was taking his daily stroll up to the village shop to buy his *Daily Telegraph*. Each morning was an event: would it be there or not? Welland had reflected on the suspense and decided that he liked it that way. The unions had introduced a modicum of stimulation to his Riding Mill mornings that was quite exciting.

He observed the large houses, their owners away in Newcastle, the wives left at home to tend the children, or their lovers, locals in Hexham or Corbridge, something more accessible than their husbands. He smiled, looking through the bare, sunlit trees, a time when he considered trees were at their most glamorous, no thick foliage obscuring their sinews. The true artist always preferred a tree or bush naked, the real beauty was an unpolished diamond, a woman beside you stripped of her clothes, her pretences. A village in winter spoke the truth, no deceits; it became what it was, houses planted in fields and hills. Summer tried to disguise that, he wasn't a summer man.

He crossed the main road and entered the shop. He handed over his 12p and, with the ease of modern commerce, escaped from the place without exchanging a word. Another pet hate: he didn't like shop conversations, or any meaningless exchange. He wouldn't discuss the weather or give the time of day, or comment on the season, unless it was to an expert. Conversations had to be important, at least have potential, or else be ignored. Inevitably, he'd be trapped by someone into some trifling matter, but he wanted it noted on his gravestone: he didn't enjoy gossip. He was a man with destiny on his mind, no lightweight he.

He passed by the small police station, nodding to the man in blue out polishing his moped, and then continued down to the small narrow valley in which he resided. He was thinking it a shame that new houses had been allowed to creep into this village, spoiling the trees, filling the narrow roads with Cortinas and Escorts. A tragedy that was killing all the villages.

He scanned his morning paper headlines: *Riots in Berlin as British withdraw. PM claims British withdrawal will put £10 in the pocket of every man, woman and child in the UK.*

And further down were reports on trouble in Iran, Israel, Eygpt, Jugoslavia, Belgium – and this was only the front page. Hardly worth reading the damn thing, only resulted in reaching for the aspirin, as usual. He looked up from his paper, noticed a Durham-registered Ford Granada, and wondered why it was parked in the middle of nowhere, far from the nearest house. Welland wasn't so far removed from events in London that he wasn't aware that he could be a target. He knew only too well that he was vulnerable; he kept an eye out for strangers. It was that sort of village, strangers were easy to spot, being one of the few objects of interest to the bored housewives.

Welland had been surprised that no-one had come for a second helping, surprised and puzzled. He felt sure Grimly would want to know more. Grimly he could trust, not that it would do any good. What he knew wasn't going to be of any use to anyone in Grimly's position. The Square was in its last days. Cognisant of that fact, he'd held back. Not out of any malicious contempt for England and the Square, but out of kindness really. He'd had to tell them something, but other than an oblique reference to the Second Eleven, he'd held the big stuff in reserve. Giving a weak Square the information he had would be like giving a .45 to a two year-old. He wouldn't know how to use it, but it just might go off and hurt someone.

The names wouldn't be acceptable. They wouldn't swallow it, and the PM wouldn't believe it, nor risk the bad publicity. There was a faint hope that the main contenders could be asked to resign, but the Press was bound to get hold of it, wasn't the sort of thing that could happen in secret. Probably be a feature on the JY Prog and then everyone would know. So, the impossibility of it all notwithstanding, he was nevertheless disappointed they hadn't come to see him. The country life was all very well and he liked snowdrops and daffodils, was learning to adapt to the incessant cacophony of early birds lining up for the worms, but they had isolated him and forgotten him. They were giving him too much time to think of Nina back in Malta, hoping she had received his latter, which he had sneaked out to a neighbour who had promised to post it in London during a visit.

The sun was warm now and he took off his jacket, deciding that it would be a good day to go sketching out on the farm, or down by the brook. One thing he enjoyed was an English brook at full winter strength.

There is a long uphill driveway to the Square house, itself a long, low, ranch style building with an ugly extension tacked onto the side. One time it had been a family home with many daughters: now it was empty. One of Mr Grimly's colleagues had died and it stood awaiting sale. Mementoes to those daughters lay all around the house; pin-up posters, boyfriends' photos strewn in abandoned bedrooms. God knows where they had all gone, the last mail delivered was more than eighteen months old. As if the whole family had disappeared overnight, taken by the aliens. The Square did that to families. Daddy dies in the Service, get the family out of the house, to somewhere safe, but boring. This was quite a house, must have been a happy home one time. But houses didn't stay happy homes if the Square could help it.

Welland stood in the road looking up at the house. He was staring hard, for he couldn't recall whether he had pulled the curtains in the living-room, or not. It wasn't important but, nevertheless, it worried him that he couldn't remember a detail like that.

He started up the driveway, his paper tucked under his arm, deciding at the last moment to cross over the lawn and enter by the French doors. He was tense, something was amiss. Some subtle changes had taken place, he couldn't put his finger on it, but the atmosphere had changed. He stopped twenty feet from the house, sensitive to his fears, a sixth sense that kept a good agent alive. There was either someone in the house or in the woods to his right, watching him. It could be kids, there were a lot of kids in the village. Some even played in the garden, rolling down the lawn to the road below, but if it was kids, he shouldn't be so afraid. One thing was certain, he couldn't stand out in the open like this, not knowing which way to go. He could taste fear, his own. He called out, "I know you're there, come out of the house with your hands up." A silly bluff, he didn't have a gun, but did the stranger know that?

There was movement in the corridor between main house and extension. Welland's heart began to pound, praying this wasn't a showdown, when all he had to fight with was a rolled newspaper.

The French windows opened. Welland took a step back as a figure emerged. "Hello, Henry," the Stationmaster said with such innocence he might have been a permanent houseguest. Before Welland could reply, or even get over the shock, he was addressed from the open bedroom window to the left of him.

250

"Hello, John," Hugh Grimly said, with a warmth in his voice, but causing Welland some consternation as he caught sight of the red hair.

"Hello, John," Gallant boomed from behind him and finally a, "Does he take sugar?" from Croc in the kitchen.

Welland began to laugh. Not so much at his own surprise, but at the possé come to see him. Stationmaster, Grimly and Gallant in tow, just as it always had been, like he'd caught up with a travelling circus twenty years on and found Blondini the skywalker was still doing his nightly act on high.

"Well, good morning, gentlemen," he replied, walking inside to the kitchen. Croc handed him a cup of tea saying, "Just one sugar."

Welland pitched his paper into the corner of the room and sat down at the long dining table, amused and pleased to have company. "Better call the conference to order, Croc, there's biscuits in the tin marked Flour above the fridge. Did you bring me a card from Malta perhaps?"

Croc shook his head. Grimly walked in, a mug of tea in hand and sat down at the top of the table.

"Been enjoying your rest, John?"

"Pleasant spot, Hugh. Never thought I'd get to enjoy the countryside, but I do. Did you come in a Ford by the way?"

Grimly shook his head, thinking it an odd question. "Train. You know, the countryside took me by surprise, too. Took to growing cabbages this year, funny how much pleasure there is to be derived from watching them grow."

Welland smiled. He was still amused by the sudden visit. Outside Gallant and Stationmaster could be heard arguing.

"I thought the Stationmaster was missing, but then I thought Croc had gone to pasture years ago. I think I'm in shock."

"Just cover," Croc said, coming to the table with the biscuits. "Petite buerre and chocolate fingers, takes you back a bit, eh?"

Grimly smiled, sampling his tea. He passed up the biscuits, and then looked across at grizzled old Croc with a penetrating curiosity. "I'd like to know where you fit in, Croc, but it can wait. I have a few questions for young John Welland here."

"Evens they are the same questions Stationmaster had in mind," Croc countered, not about to be banished from the room.

"It's possible. It is difficult to assess what Stationmaster's questions might be, he has not been at his desk for a few days. His star has fallen, Croc, a man who deserts the top desk in such a crisis, is in trouble."

"How else, Hugh? The contamination is there. The Square has got another outbreak of moles."

"I know what it has got, Croc. No, if you would just run off and bring back the Stationmaster and Gallant, perhaps we could get down to business."

John Welland retrieved his newspaper. "Lots of trouble in Berlin, Hugh, true we are pulling out?"

Grimly nodded. "It's not my decision, taken at Cabinet Office. I think it is a mistake, but we don't run the show."

"Did we ever?" Welland asked, a hint of a sneer.

"I sometimes wonder."

Welland stared at Grimly's hair. It wasn't a wig, that was the real surprise. It looked natural. However, he didn't think he knew Hugh Grimly well enough to bring the subject up. Coming out of retirement was one thing, rejuvenation was taking it a bit far. A lot of men couldn't take the stress of ageing. Grimly was mocking it, not a good sign.

Gallant and Stationmaster entered the room, a black cloud between them. Grimly knew Gallant's opinion surrounding the Sanctuary business. He didn't approve of Stationmaster leaving without notice with important files, whatever the reason. The phone call to London had revealed the files stored in the 'safe' bin, intact save for forty-two names. It had taken no imagination to deduce Stationmaster had the same forty-two names – and that was the trouble. Stationmaster had chosen only twelve names that corresponded with Grimly's list. Grimly was very interested in that overlap and hoped that John Welland would now clear things up for them.

Stationmaster was sulking. Gallant had been impertinent, bloody rude, in fact. He would have words with him at a more auspicious occasion, but right now he was just glad to have reached the summit table.

"You're looking well, Hugh," Stationmaster said, admiring his red hair, thinking that it didn't fool anyone. "Your retirement must suit you, never seen you look so well."

Grimly smiled. He really did feel well, though he was very worried about this red hair. Dr Mowbray had warned him it might happen, but so sudden? Looked like a damn woodpecker. He knew Gallant had noticed, but there had not been an opportunity to discuss it, too much was at stake to worry about his hair. He finished off his tea and sat back in his chair.

"Any discussion about the events leading up to this meeting must be set aside for now. We have all come with the same purpose in mind – to discover what John here knows. Gallant and I have already had a little chat last week, but – and I must say, I am cross with you, John – we have all come to the conclusion that you know a great deal more. As to why you withheld the information, only you can tell us. But I can promise you – and if I'm wrong, I'm not sure I want to know – that this quartet is sound and friendly. We are clean and all of us are dedicated to rooting out the moles, as soon as we can."

John Welland leant forward, resting his moustache on his cupped hands, a man relaxed, comfortable in these familiar surroundings. "I've been waiting. It occurred to me that you might come, but my orders last year were to reveal information to the Stationmaster only. I was uncomfortable in Calon's home, Mr Grimly. No disrespect to you, but I couldn't reveal all the cards in my hand in that room. I was unsure of your role, sir, and didn't understand why the Stationmaster was unavailable. As it was, I overtipped my hand."

"You mean, you couldn't trust Calon?" Gallant asked, looking for a much needed cigarette.

"I mean, loose talk costs lives. Calon is basically sound, but he likes to drink and he trusts too many people."

"Accepted," Stationmaster said, looking for another biscuit. "Calon's a blabbermouth and I'm laying odds on one of the moles is in his office, sticking to him like a leech."

"Gallant's going to show you a list," Grimly said, "two lists really. Stationmaster's forty-two and our list of the same number. You'll see there's an overlap of twelve names. Total list therefore has 72 names. I'm particularly interested in the double twelve, all underlined in green ink. Gallant handed over the list.

"How did you know?" Stationmaster demanded, surprised that Grimly knew anything at all about his activities, let alone his suspect list, which he would have guaranteed was secret.

"We found your files at the Brook Green house. Still a hot bed of sin, is it?" Grimly enquired.

"We woke London up. Ran the A through DQ files through the computer this morning and it coughed up the missing names," Gallant explained.

Stationmaster flushed. They'd known. All the trouble they had taken to stay invisible, and the Square had known. Grimly was a tougher customer than he remembered.

"Anything familiar to you," Gallant asked Welland, offering round his packet of Rothmans.

Welland took one and returned a laconic smile. "It's not bad, David, not bad at all. The Second Eleven are all here. You've all worked hard. I'm impressed. I didn't think you could have done it, Stationmaster, Mr Grimly, but what I'm really impressed with is this name." Welland pointed to a name half way down the list and heavily underlined in Grimly's green ink. "The twelfth man, David. This is the joker in the pack. You could knock the whole team out, but unless you get the twelfth man, you've only got a draw."

"Who is it, John?" Grimly asked impatiently, straining forward.

Gallant whistled, as did Croc who began to laugh. Accusing that man was like turning to God and telling him his one and only son was bent. There wasn't any way the Square could approach that name.

"No, John, tell me you're joking," Grimly protested, staring at the list like it was some snake.

"Who, who?" the Stationmaster demanded to know. Croc was still laughing and Welland was already pointing to another name when quite suddenly the kitchen door was kicked open and burst onto the glass cupboard, sending glass everywhere. An armed man leapt into the room, firing as he spun and landed.

"Freeze," Grimly ordered, who'd seen enough men killed in a panic. Gallant lay flat on the table, Welland's face was fixed in surprise and shock until the second shot of the .38 practically tore his head off, twisting him sideways, dumping him on the floor as his legs caught underneath the table. One . . . two seconds, that was all it had taken.

A woman, also armed, entered the room from the other side. Stationmaster recognised Zavrel and Cosmo. He remained silent as Zavrel's gun levelled with his head.

"I'll take that list," Zavrel said, pointing to the piece of paper on the table. Blood was heading for it, forming a little pool at the edge. Zavrel looked cool, his eyes and hand steady, almost as if he knew the Englishmen weren't armed.

Cosmo came forward and snatched the list from the table top and pocketed it, immediately leaving the room with the cold indifference of some super efficient secretary.

"Mr Grimly," Zavrel said, acknowledging the Chief. "Nice to see you looking so well. I'm sorry the Butcher's Boy was not able to tell you more. I, too, hate wasted journeys. Oh yes, this came for him, I'm sorry he was not able to read it." He placed a postcard depicting Valetta on the table and quickly left the room.

Gallant was up in an instant. He was thinking how difficult it was to get out of Riding Mill. He could have the roads sealed off to Corbridge and Hexham within minutes. Tinkabelle's twosome wouldn't escape. They would live to regret this escapade. He was out through the kitchen and French windows before Croc had unclenched his eyes. The Stationmaster knelt down beside Welland, but there was not the remotest chance of a dying breath, a last word. The man had died instantly.

"Find the telephone, Croc," Stationmaster ordered.

"There isn't one," Grimly told them. "Calon thought it an unnecessary expense."

"I'll go next door," Croc said, rushing out through the kitchen, glad to be useful.

"A Ford Granada, that black one," Grimly was muttering. "Welland asked me about it. I noticed it on the way up."

Five minutes later, Gallant came back out of breath. His cheek was grazed as if he'd fallen. "They got away. It was a Ford Granada, Chief. I tried to cling on, but they shook me off. I didn't get their number, it was a hired car from Durham. Where's the phone? I'll call Newcastle CID."

"No phone, try next door. "Call Oxterby in Gosforth. His number is in the directory. If Zavrel and Cosmo are going by the book, they will have changed cars by now. No use starting any roadblocks."

The sound of a car coming up the steep driveway reached their ears.

"Who the hell is that? It's not them coming back for more is it?" Stationmaster asked, fearing the worst.

Grimly followed him and Gallant outside to the garden. Croc was sitting on a stone bench in the sun, nursing a painful ankle. "Fell over the bench, chaps, not as fast as I was."

But no-one was interested in Croc anymore, all eyes were on the Vauxhall Astra parked outside the house. Simon Caw stepped out, accompanied by the local Square antique, Oxterby, who gave Grimly a discreet, guilty wave.

Afterwards, no-one was quite sure who was the most surprised. Simon Caw, seeing Stationmaster and Croc, or vice versa. "The Czechs," Caw explained, "Tinkabelle's flying crusaders know he's here, Mr Grimly. Hallam told them."

"Next time, send a telegram," Grimly said, turning around, and angrily heading back to the house. "I need another cup of tea."

"What happened?" Caw asked, studying their white faces.

"We lost the Butcher's Boy," Gallant told him, following after Grimly. "Wasted journey, Simon, should have stayed with Poppyseed."

"Poppyseed?" Stationmaster blurted out. "Not that old tart of a trick. Old Grimly dredging the barrel a bit, isn't he? I last used that in '58."

Simow Caw frowned. He'd thought Grimly's idea sound, but he wasn't aware it was such an old idea.

"Old dogs don't like new tricks," he said realising that it was too late to change anything now. "It went into operation last night. Doc Sludgeon is running it."

Stationmaster nodded. "Then we have a chance. What was the name, Croc? What name did Welland point to?"

Croc couldn't answer. It wasn't his place to answer, not in front of Simon Caw and Oxterby. "Better speak to Mr Grimly about that, Steven. I've got my foot to worry about."

Stationmaster didn't appreciate the evasion, it was important to impress Simon Caw at this juncture, not play dumb.

"Where did the Butcher's Boy go?" Caw asked impatiently.

"In the dining-room," Stationmaster answered quietly.

Simon Caw turned to Oxterby and snapped, "Call the Square and tell them I have the Stationmaster in view. Then call Newcastle CID and call off the dogs. Codeword 'Orange'. Orange is stood down. Got that?"

"Yes, Mr Caw," Oxterby droned, still resentful that he'd been woken so early and ordered to reconnect his phone.

As Simon Caw passed by on his way into the house, Stationmaster couldn't but help feel that events had passed him by and that his worst fear had come true. Simon Caw in control of the Square. It was worse than moles in his opinion. He just couldn't predict Caw and that gave him a very uncomfortable feeling indeed.

"Think I've done it in for good," Croc said, staring at his swelling ankle.

"Oh bother your ankle, Croc, bother it, and go to hell."

Something told Croc that Stationmaster was not a happy man, but then, what could one expect? No breakfast. It wasn't civilised gadding about Northumbria without breakfast, not surprising the morning hadn't turned out well, not surprising at all.

*   *   *

But this axiom didn't always ring true. At least not for Hallam. But if asked, he would have had to admit that it had been a very poor breakfast and, therefore, taking that into consideration, the morning's events could be assumed to have been only partially successful in direct proportion to the inferiority of his light repast.

It might also be assumed that looking for a young, barely teenaged girl in metropolis Paris would be a difficult and arduous, unrewarding task. That Hallam, unused to the ways of the young, would not know where to begin. Indeed, he could search Paris from top to bottom, and always in the right places, yet never coincide with Wendy.

It was lunchtime and the city was absurdly full with visitors, but not as full as it might have been. Peter Hallam counted himself lucky that it wasn't Easter. With the children all at school, at least he could be assured that any children on the streets were visitors. Out of the thousands, it did at least narrow it down.

Hallam had arrived in Paris at 2 am. It should have been 12.30 am, but a tactical strike by baggage handlers had delayed the flight at London's Heathrow, and a ceremonial indifference at Orly had lengthened the in-cabin flight time somewhat and stretched Hallam's tolerance to a very fine limit indeed.

He had found the small hotel that he and Wendy had shared many times in the past three years, hoping that she might haunt the familiar. Then he slept. Glad to be out of England and the Square. He supposed that they could try an extradition from Paris, but in the new mood, would Paris grant it, once it knew the truth? He doubted they would hand back a man who'd performed such a service to Moscow, not in their new euphoria. Hallam decided he needed a Mishka the Bear badge.

After the debacle of the Olympics there were millions still in circulation going cheap. Now it was a symbol of accord, a with us or against us signal. Mishka was decidedly with and he needed a badge.

Coincidences happen only on TV movies, yet Hallam was a true believer in them. He had seen too many of them to believe otherwise. Once he'd gone looking for a Czech spy in Luton and sat right next to him on the bus the moment he arrived. Had he not once taken a holiday in Rome, hating every moment of it, wishing he was back at the Square, when the Square came to him, embroiling him in a scandal with SOI trying to keep the lid on oil stolen from Iran. Rome had become considerably more interesting.

And so it was with Paris. But it wasn't Wendy coincidence put Hallam's way. He was at the Hotel George V, paying a courtesy call to Lord Leech, a refugee from the British tax system and sometime friend of the FO. He was one of the many who passed on information from time to time, for a large consideration in his case, as he made quite a business of it.

The gilt baroque grandeur of the lobby was filled with businessmen seeking alms from the rich and the usual lend lease Arabs occupied the corners, no longer a freak show, but still unacceptable to the establishment. Oil money versus class. Paris preferred class – and at least, in private – Hallam too, as did Lord Leech who had spent two hours raving about the insanities of Islam and European politics.

"The French are whores, Hallam. They will sell out to Moscow to keep their natural gas and hang onto the Arab oil. They even kiss Islam's arse, anyone who wants to suck her tits dry. A whore with a heart of stone. They take my money here, and do I get good service? Do I hell."

Hallam had listened with patience, let the old man ramble on, hoping that he would get to a point where he could jump in and ask for help. He recognised the fact that as he was blown in London, he was going to need work, or regular money to be more precise. He wasn't a rich man: bringing up Wendy hadn't been cheap and it was almost a certainty that they

259

would freeze his assets in Britain. Lord Leech ran a small, but highly effective industrial espionage company, mostly selling new product developments to rival companies. His organisation had saved many major chemical companies years of research and capital outlay, and had built up a cash mountain for the exiled Lord. Lord Leech wasn't so sure about Hallam. If the British didn't want him, why would he? However, Hallam had left the Lord's suite almost sure he had a helping hand. It wasn't the Lord's way to commit himself to anything. A rich man could afford to keep people guessing.

And there in the lobby of the hotel, standing under the dome, stood the Lord and Master of the underworld. Tinkabelle. Talking to a hotel employee, a woman. Hallam was feeling less than charitable towards this man. After all, he was now sure that Tinkabelle was behind Captain Hook. That man under the dome had flushed a lifetime career down the toilet, Hallam's life and career. No more Peter, no more Wendy and all at the whim of that old warhorse. Hallam felt a surge of anger, a tension rising within him, going quickly out of control. He had no doubts that it was Tinkabelle – the same bland face. The photo behind the Stationmaster's door was accurate, failing only in one respect: his age. Tinkabelle looked older than Grimly, a skeleton. The white hair and badly fitting suit was unmistakable. Hallam would have liked to have gone up to him; he wished for a gun, or dagger. A George V assassination would have been a satisfactory finale to the Wendy abduction, a crowning glory to a spymaster's career. But, and Hallam was aware of this as he stood transfixed in front of the elevators, one did not shoot a man as important as Tinkabelle. It would be a shot heard all around the world, as significant as an assassination of the Czar. He wouldn't solve anything by putting a bullet in Tinkabelle's head, and he could be sure that he would never see Wendy again. He would be shot down by the guard dogs never more than ten feet from Tinkerbelle's side.

Hallam's eyes tried to pinpoint the goons. He spotted one leaning on a sofa, standing out like a sore thumb: the only man, aside from Tinkabelle, in a Moscow tailored suit, standard coarse fitting, cheap, an eyesore in such opulent surroundings.

Habit, possibly a lifetime's loyalty got Peter Hallam moving again. He forced his legs to move and found his way to the public phone, penetrated the many barriers to comprehending the Paris telephone system and eventually made a transferred charge call to the Square in London. Whatever Hallam's status, his information on Tinkabelle's whereabouts would be appreciated. With the Square in chaos, it was the least he could do, they'd need to be able to pinpoint the enemy.

After completing his call to the London answerphone, he was on the point of leaving the George V for good, when a casual glance back towards the dome rewarded him with another bonus of information, sending a shiver down his spine. The elevator doors rolled open and the squat, overweight body of Lord Leech stepped out into the lobby and immediately into a welcome embrace of Tinkabelle. They greeted each other as old and genuine friends. Yet nothing in Leech's records showed that he was even aware Tinkabelle existed. Hallam knew that he sometimes sold to the USSR, but he sold best price to all-comers. After all, information is a commodity like any other. But a special relationship? Hallam was regretting he had made the call to London with so much haste. Grimly would be interested in Lord Leech's friend.

As he left the hotel, boarding a waiting taxi, he knew there wouldn't be any offers coming from Leech's crowd. Tinkabelle would see to that.

It was time to seek out Wendy once again. He left the taxi at the left bank of the Seine, the inevitable Notre Dame in the distance. He was looking for a narrow street headed by a sleazy movie house. The sky was an indifferent grey, the air turning cold, though shafts of sunshine could be seen in some places. The streets were filled with budget tourists, searching out mythical cheap restaurants and window shopping in the disposable boutiques; displaced Algerians trying to catch their eyes, selling coke-hash-acid-speed, the hard currency of the underground economy. It was probably ironic that when the

Czechs bought their 'safe' house in the quiet quarter twenty years before, they had chosen it for its proximity to the peasants living in the area, a sympathetic environment for diplomatic subversion. Now that the peasants had been driven out by rocketing prices and replaced with the tourist invasion and the night economy of whores and drug pedlars, the marching drum of the Czechs fell on unreceptive ears. If the subversion of the West cut them off from their roots, it was a lesson that could stand being learnt.

It was to this address, along the narrow, cobbled street, that Peter Hallam approached. Nervous, instincts finely tuned had him remembering Paris Stationhouse mentioning in dispatch after dispatch that 19 Rue Aaron was the transient address: the place where agents passing through would board. The Czechs were his territory by right. Besides, where else could he start? This house would be as likely as any, with its shuttered windows and crumbling facade.

Hallam took the opportunity of getting something into his stomach. There was a café opposite the house and he fancied a coffee and light snack, excusing the inactivity with the Easton maxim: if you want something to move, watch it.

Hallam knew that when it came to houses, doors had to open. Only he hadn't even placed an order with the waiter when a hand slipped on his and a red jeaned bottom perched on his lap.

"Peter, Peter. What are you doing here?"

With shock and surprise, Hallam looked into the eyes of his Wendy. He couldn't even attempt to say anything.

"I've been following you," she said with pride, a bright pert smile on her face. She flung her arms around him and hugged him, burying her face into his neck, making familiar happy snorts like she always did.

Hallam inhaled her body scent, his heart somersaulting with joy. He wanted to grab her, hold her tight against him and rush out of the café, but he was conscious of causing enough interest with the café patrons with this child on his lap. He had to remain calm, impossible, but essential.

"Wendy, my love, Wendy," tears welling-up in both pairs of eyes.

"I saw you get out of the taxi, Peter. How did you know I was here? It was *me* you were looking for, wasn't it?"

She was teasing, at ease, comfortable in familiar arms. Her eyes, though drowned, were excited, her hands rushed about his head, stroking his hair and neck.

"Why are you here, little one? Why haven't you called me? You know you could have called home, reverse charge. I have been frantic . . . ."

She placed fingers on his lips. "Come on, Peter. Let's go for a walk. We can go down to the river."

Hallam was so confused. "But I don't want to go to the river, Wendy. Let's go away. I have a friend in Switzerland."

Wendy frowned, pulling back and looking at her Peter. "Let's go for a walk," she insisted and he knew her well enough to know that she meant she wasn't going to explain anything right there, not in the café. He saw the café owner reach for the telephone. To call the house across the road perhaps? Was he a babysitter? Suspicion everywhere, about everyone.

"All right, but you'll explain? Wendy, you're my girl, you're breaking my heart, little one. I couldn't believe it when they stole you away . . . ." His voice trailed away, full of doubts.

She shook her head, slipping a hand into his, pulling him up off the chair and out of the café. In the street, her mood changed again. "Come on, quickly. I want to talk to you but they might be watching. Through here."

Secretive, in charge, their roles reversed. He followed with expectation and a rising irritation. She led him up an alleyway, filled with the stench of urine and garbage. "Wendy," he complained, not enjoying this cat and mouse game. "Wait."

She stepped out of the alley ahead of him, turning into another street, filled with tired looking youngsters, off-duty pimps and whores, or Dutch tourists. Hallam couldn't tell and wasn't looking. His eyes were on Wendy.

She was smiling again, at his side, gazing up at him with her familiar look of longing. "Peter, I've missed you so much." She took his hand again, leading him along a narrow street towards the riverbank road. The shops were re-opening after their lunchtime break.

"I've missed you. Who took you, Wendy? I knew it would be the Czechs. It was too easy, I came by you too easy."

Wendy stopped outside a Pattiserie looking up at him with an impish smile. Always before he'd had to buy his answers with chocolate, or sugar almonds, her favourite sweets. Hallam noticed what sort of shop it was and responded automatically to the Greek shopholder. "*Chocolat Lindt, monsieur.*"

"No, I want those." She pointed to the stickiest toasted coconut marsh-mallows he'd ever seen.

"God, not those, Wendy, you were sick last time."

She grinned. "Come on, Peter. Please, I've said please."

He bought the marsh-mallows and watched her make a pig of herself as they completed the walk down to the river. "So will you tell me now? And are you coming back to me?"

He was pushing too hard, she would have been through a traumatic time, best to hold himself back. He stood beside her when they reached the river side and watched her greedily finish the gooey sweets, a chill wind sweeping off the river, neither of them dressed for such a day. She buried her back into his unfolded coat, brought the flaps around her with sticky hands and snuggled in. She was smiling and he just fooled with her hair, very happy they were together, mortified that it might not last very long. Suddenly she threw the sweet pack away and stooped down to the river, dipping her fingers in, bouncing back up inside the coat, facing him this time, giggling in the cold. Things were still completely natural between them. It was as if nothing had happened at all.

She stole his clean handkerchief to wipe her face. "I'm a pig," she said. Then, hooking her chin into one of his waistcoat pockets, she looked up at him and asked, "Are you cross with me?"

Hallam looked away, out across the river and the distant

Notre Dame spires. "No, you know I can never get angry with you."

"Good," she said, reassured. "I couldn't stand you being cross with me as well."

As well as whom? Hallam was thinking as he looked down at this waif – half woman – the hunger in her face only part of its beauty. It was no good. Still, after all this time, she was such a source of wonder to him, so magical, she could take his breath away.

"Pa says you knew all the time, Peter." She looked at him with earnest, pained eyes. "Pa and Mother. She isn't well, has a lot of headaches."

Hallam knew he hadn't misheard. "Pa?" he whispered.

Wendy narrowed her eyes. "Pa and Mother . . ."

"Now wait a minute, girl. Wendy, listen to me." He knelt down, collapsing onto a stone step, placing her on his knees and wrapping the coat around her again, his hands on her shoulders.

"Wendy, your mother and father are dead. We both went to their funeral. They were blown up, you know that. It's true, little one. Don't look at me as if I'm crazy. The Kostavitzs died, there were death certificates and everything. Witnesses. Don't play this game with me, Wendy. I love you. I've never lied to you. Now explain."

She bit on her bottom lip, still unsure. "Pa and Mother want me back now, Peter. I'm going to Moscow and then to their home in Copenhagen."

Hallam winced, blinking his eyes, a new pain, like that of a knife entering his shoulder, began to worry him. Either she was fantasising, or someone was playing yet another foul trick on him and her.

"Wendy . . . ." He fought back tears, his voice breaking up with emotion. "They are dead. It's documented. Who's got you, little one. Who's filling your head with all this silly nonsense?"

"It isn't nonsense, Peter, honest. Pa and Mother *are* back at the house." She shook her head suddenly. "I mean, they were.

They had to go to Prague on Saturday and I was left here with a guard."

"And you didn't call me? You know how much pain . . ?"

"Peter," she shouted, not knowing how to explain her feelings. "It's Pa, they came to get me. You knew they were alive, you did, Pa said so. It was you who wouldn't give me back to them."

Hallam couldn't believe this. It wasn't happening.

"Wendy, listen. I don't know anything about this, nothing. If anyone has filled your head with lies or rubbish, I know nothing. I cannot believe your mother and father are alive. The car blew up, no one could have survived the blast."

"Pa said it wasn't him. It *is* my Pa, he doesn't have the third finger. Mother still has the scars on her back. It is them, it looks just like them, sounds like them, though I've forgotten so much of the language. I know my own parents, Peter, you'd know them."

She pulled away from him, escaping from the coat, walking to a position about five feet away.

"I'll be in trouble for speaking to you. They told me I wasn't to speak to you again. I tried to call you at the Square, honest. But I haven't any money and I don't speak French. I can't get anyone to understand me. School French is hopeless." Then coyly, looking sideways at him, "But I knew that you'd find me."

If she knew that, there was hope, he thought. He tried for an explanation again. "Wendy, you were captured, taken to the Czech Embassy by Milos, what happened then?"

She looked away, suddenly catching her breath. "Pa was there. I was so shocked, I couldn't say anything. I just fainted. When I woke up, I was in Paris. I'd slept right through a whole day and night. Mother was at my side. I was in such shock, I cried and cried. I couldn't stop for days. Then Pa explained how they had wanted me back for two years, but you'd blocked all the proposals, refused to cooperate, kept me under guard, destroyed their letters . . . ."

"Wendy," he wailed. "Listen to yourself. Did you, or did

266

you not have your own key to the house? Weren't you free to go out to rock concerts or the roller disco whenever you liked after homework?"

She nodded. "They said you never answered their letters."

"What letters, Wendy? The mail comes after I leave in the morning, you get the letters first."

She looked confused. "They said so many things I. . . ." She walked towards him again, frowning.

"They'll say things to make you doubt me. They have to realign your basic loyalties. Your parents are using technique on you, Wendy – if they really are your parents."

"They are, they are!" she yelled, stamping her feet. A tourist boat glided by, a barge following in its wake, sending a series of waves towards them.

"If they are alive, then I'm beaten, I can't keep you." He reached out a hand for her, she came to him. "I love you, Wendy, but I can't compete with your parents."

"They said you were working for them."

"First they say I'm against them, then they say I work for them. The least they could do is get their story right." Hallam smiled. "In a way it's true, sad to say. After you were taken I was persuaded to betray a man, most likely he's dead now, a man I don't even know. An old man's folly, Wendy. I thought I could win you back with bargains. I was naive," he laughed to himself, "I should have known you can't trust a Czech. Moscow doesn't have a word for it in their dictionary."

She regained the inner sanctum of his overcoat, burying her head into his warmth. "Peter, what's happening? Why do you look so ill?"

He laughed again, mirthless, for he felt like crying. He wanted to throw himself into that river. "How did you get out of the building, Wendy?"

She smiled, looking up at him into his eyes. "There's only the guard and the French lady who comes to cook. The guard drinks at the bar on the corner and she doesn't come to cook until tonight. Pa and Mother will be back tonight."

"And you have all this freedom? I find it hard to . . . ."

"I promised to stay. They don't know I'm out, but I was bored. I come back though. It's Pa and Mother. We'll all be together again, just like before."

"I didn't know they were alive, Wendy. I can't believe it still. You will have to believe me, your father is still listed as dead. It is *I* who have been used. I who was useful to them when they needed to get at someone in a hurry. Your parents gave you up so easily before, what happens if they do it again?"

"They won't, they love me. Mother needs me." She snuggled up to him again, kissing him full on the lips, pressing herself into him, her hands winding around his shirt waist, his hands pulling her tighter to him still.

They stayed that way for ten, twenty minutes, silent, just kissing and loving, a farewell song.

"I love you, Peter," she whispered finally. "I love you, honest."

"I know. I'm hurt, but I understand." He sighed. "You've a life to live, might as well live it on the winning side."

"Oh Peter, we can still write. It can be like it was before. Look, I promise I'll come back once a year and clean the house for you; and when I have a child, I'll call him Peter. I promise.

But Peter couldn't bare to smile at her little girl plans, she didn't know how cruel she was being.

"Oh God, Wendy, I just want to throw myself into the river."

"No," she said. Then looking back at the water, "not this river anyway, it's disgusting."

"All right, you choose the river," he said, attempting a brave laugh.

"I should go," she said. "They are so happy to have me back, Peter, they really are."

"I don't want to see them. Wendy?" he asked sharply, "there's not the slightest chance you'd want to make a choice?"

She frowned, kissing him on the forehead, noticing a courting couple wandering by. "I love you, Peter, but . . . Oh, don't make me choose, please."

He kissed her again, running his hands down her body, resting his hands on her thighs, resisting a temptation to go further, suppressing a rising intensity of desire, stronger than any he had experienced in many months.

"You'd better go then. Think of me, Wendy. Don't listen to any lies, I've loved you all your life, given you everything I could. I didn't know they were alive, you must believe me. Your father lies to win you back, one shouldn't have to lie to win back a daughter."

Wendy half smiled, wistful. She reached behind her and took one of his hands, rubbing herself in the place she liked him to touch. "I'll miss you, Peter. Mother says it was wrong. She says you are sick. She's wrong. I love you and I do know you love me."

Then she was free of him, running across the concrete to the steps up to road level. He didn't watch her go, he couldn't move, couldn't think, breathe. He just wanted to die, a bolt from heaven to strike him on the head, perhaps one to strike her parents too. It was a typically momentous Moscow trick. Were her parents so fanatical that they could have given her up for so long? Was the Butcher's Boy worth the wait? He'd always underestimated the enemy. Would they now pro-gramme Wendy, aim her in some other direction? Were they that sure of themselves that Wendy's life was expendable? How soon before they extinguished her love and replaced it with the logic of cold steel? And now, what was going to happen to him? What was the next surprise Tinkabelle had planned?

The night would fall before Hallam moved again.

*   *   *

Monday proved to be a momentous day at the Square for another reason. Monday was the day the Square realised just

269

how far things had deteriorated. Nolan had organised the cabal in the basement refectory. Bloater, Carter from records, Oosty, anyone he could get to listen was there.

"In short, this can't go on," he was summing up. "I thought at first a simple work to rule would do it, bring the great minds at the top to their senses, enable them to perceive that a 31% cut is ludicrous, likely to do more damage to us than anything the Germans threw at us in the last war. However," and at this 'however' Nolan looked his most angry, "this latest cut, this savage, base, most insensitive callous cut is the camel that broke the Arab's back."

"Er . . ." Oosty attempted a correction, immediately thinking the better of it.

"Refusal to supply toilet paper is an immoral act. They'll not get away with it. I've already talked to the other divisions, we're all agreed. We will mount a non-cooperation month with Whitehall. No paperwork will move, not a scrap, and the technicians will not maintain their computers, subject to ratification from their union. We will gum up the works until our demands are met."

"But is this all worth a roll of loo paper?" Oosty asked. He'd never liked Government loo paper. Never understood why they continued to make that sandpaper-like substance that positively refused to tear, always ended up around your trousers in a heap of confusion and more often than not left a nasty imprint of the words Government Property on one's behind (a disconcerting moment for the rough traders). In his opinion HMG was well out of such a dubious trade.

"It's not about loo paper, Oosty, it's principle. 31% cuts, transportation gone, loo paper, East Putney – you watch, it will be tea-breaks next. It isn't about paper, Oosty, that's just the thin edge of the stick."

"Ah," Oosty said, getting the picture.

"What about a relocation allowance?" a voice piped up.

"We don't need a relocation allowance, Carter. We aren't going anywhere. They'll not get us to East Putney, Woolwich or anywhere. We are staying here. Tradition, lads, we have to maintain tradition, standfast."

Oosty observed the resolute expression on Nolan's face and knew the man was sincere.

"Now," Nolan said, changing the mood, "just to show that we look after our own, Bloater here has arranged for loo paper to go on sale in the tuck shop at hours 9–10 am and again 4–5 pm. At a fair price and I advise you all to keep your own, can't have the top floor thinking they can get away with this travesty, this obsession for penny pinching."

A muffled assenting cheer rippled through the small assembly.

"Now, since it's nearly tea time, may I suggest we disband, but take care, lads. They'll be charging us to work here next. We have to stop this rot the moment it starts. Be on guard, pass the word to me or Bloater the instant a new cut is implemented and, above all, solidarity. Remember we could be joining the three million unemployed unless we stand on our rights. No redundancies and no cooperation."

"We're wiv you, brother," a sarcastic voice declared from the back.

Nolan missed the attack and beamed with delight instead. "I never doubted it, Dancer, I never doubted it."

But it was a battle already lost for Nolan. Events beyond his control were at that moment in play and, although the Square hadn't realised it, they were about to pay for their failure to unmask the moles and keep the Butcher's Boy alive.

NINE

Snowdrops Are White, Moles Are Red, Grimly Is Blue

Traditionally, Tuesday morning meant the weekly briefing with the Relatives at Grosvenor Square. This Tuesday was no exception, but the atmosphere was glum. Mitchel was doing his Nixon impersonation, a man whose thinking was currently under rivival in Washington.

"Moscow had threatened, bluffed, schemed, plotted, undermined, bribed, bullied, terrorised and murdered in the name of détente. It is lying, cheating, thieving, brutal, callous. It continues to train terrorists, rig elections, destroy private property, disrupt labour relations, sponser coups, poison refugees and deprive millions of their human rights, yet we are still turning the other cheek. We still meet like stooges, pretending that Moscow will stay in check, stay somewhere over the horizon, out of sight, leaving us to live our lives in peace. It's all shit and you British make me sick. The chips are down, boys, where are you? What's happening? Lost your balls? Where were you when Afghanistan went down the tubes? Where was your support when our people were captured in Iran? When will you realise that the war has not only begun, but it is very nearly over without a shot being fired. And don't bring up Tabas – at least we tried."

Grimly scowled, he had no defence. Stationmaster stared out of the window daydreaming. Gallant was reading a memo from Doc Sludgeon about complications with the distribution of the Poppyseed document. Some had been intercepted.

Meanwhile, Oosty chatted on the phone to Peter Hallam. He'd turned himself in to the British Embassy and Grimly, perceiving he needed help, suspended any charges on him (temporarily), keeping him in Paris as an official observer. It wasn't as foolish as Mitchel had (off the record) declared it to be. Hallam had betrayed them all, but it was for Wendy, and the man was more than repentant. There was no question of acquittal but, in an emergency, it had to be remembered that he was one of them and without Wendy, his word could be trusted. Especially now, as Tinkabelle knew him to be busted. In short, Hallam had a sort of immunity from Moscow; he could be useful monitoring events in Paris.

Mitchel wasn't finished, he was angry with the Square. "We've gotten so used to seeing Moscow's arm around Hungary, Czechoslovakia, Jugoslavia, Rumania, Bulgaria, Albania, East Germany and Latvia that we have come to believe it's natural, that it has always been that way. Yet it isn't so. 1945 is not so long ago when we were all alive and active, except Oosty and Gallant here. Now in its most sinister move yet, it's poking us in the eyes and taking France, Spain and Malta. They are destroying NATO, you are moving out of Berlin, tearing up the Potsdam Treaty. How long will West Germany take to realise the game is up. Another day? Another hour? You pulled out, Grimly. Britain pulled out of Berlin, like she was suddenly turned Catholic and you were afraid of getting her pregnant. It was our only ace up our sleeve and you bastards pulled out. It's over – you think our President is going to lay his balls on the line for Europe now? He's going to have to pull out, you know it; and then what? You think Holland, Belgium, the Danes or Norwegians will stay secure? Moscow is going to grab and grab hard. Our assessment is of a neutral Europe by the end of the year, it all depends on you. You're the Square, you've got the ear of Cabinet Office. Reverse that policy, get Sir Charles or Calon to say publicly that the Rhine army stays. Do it today. Heaven knows there isn't much time. I wouldn't like to be in the German Chancellor's shoes.

"England can't go neutral, Stationmaster, Grimly. It can't, you can't give up everything. Jesus, I'm up here sounding like a preacher, but look at it, guys, look at the situation in the face.

They get a neutral, or anti-American Europe. They have already killed off our 'two-pillar' policy in the Persian Gulf and why? They need oil. You're all right, Jack. North Sea oil may have destroyed your heavy industries with a strong pound, but at least you can buy all you want with it.

"Moscow is going to take the rest of the Gulf next. Cut off supplies to us and Japan. And won't Japan scream. None of us care, of course. Japan has done more than any other country to wreck our mutual car industries. Japan can die, it has always been expendable. They have to realise that they've got to defend themselves. We can't afford to have that monkey on our back any longer. And if France and Spain, the rest of them believe they are going to get guaranteed Gulf oil supplies, they are damn fools. Moscow needs that oil. Her need for oil is rising almost three times faster than her ability to supply. We are talking war here boys. We are standing here with our pants down pissing into the wind whilst Moscow isolates us – what are you doing about it?"

There was nothing but guilty silence at the table, until Oosty chipped in with, "Hope you get your oil men out of Siberia, Mitchel, quite a colony of Yanks there I believe."

"I'm going to ignore that. Technical aide is different to politics. What's going to happen to shipping if Moscow controls the routes? They are already talking about blockading South Africa for that nuke test that never was. Western Europe imports 80% of its minerals from there, Japan 95%. We import 92% of our chrome from that region and you know what's made with chrome, Gallant? Military aircraft and ball bearings. What are we going to do when they cut off our balls? National Research Council says we are more vulnerable to chrome disruption than oil.

"Are you prepared to see your children sent to Moscow for their education? Do you want to be colonies again? Remember Caesar, Hitler? That's where this is all headed.

"Act now, Stationmaster, or we are on target for war and, with our new President itching to make his mark in the saddle,

274

you, the whole damn world is a potential target if you start kissing Moscow's ass."

"Have you finished?" Grimly asked, as Mitchel sat down reaching for a glass of water.

"No. We gave you a tip about the moles. What have you done? Promoted them. Given them a royal pension and a Knighthood?"

It was no use telling Mitchel that most of them already had Knighthoods. Grimly, intensely irritated by Mitchel's lecture, was, nevertheless, unable to counter the last swipe. "I think we should warn you, Mitchel, that however hurt and depressed you might feel about the current European pragmatism, I cannot offer you even the remotest encouragement."

Oosty put the phone down, smiling at Leon, happy to be reunited with his Romeo at last, hoping he had not found new conquests. Hoping, too, that they could take a long holiday in the US, get out of the mess London was in.

"Mr Hallam had bad news for you, Mr Mitchel. Lord Leech and Tinkabelle are big buddies."

"Our Lord Leech?" Sol Guss asked. A late arrival for the meeting.

"Our Lord Leech," Oosty answered, pushing over the notes he'd made to the American's side.

"Shit, I'd have thought we could have counted on him."

Grimly smiled. The Americans had a childlike innocence that amused and disappointed him. Lord Leech was a tax exile, suspect since the '76 honours list and his life peerage bought for him in Cabinet Office. No surprises there. There would be many more who'd percieve the winds of change and defect for a momentary gain, for that is all it would be, momentary.

"I want a discussion about the moles," Mitchel was insisting. Grimly perceived that he had a right.

"And you shall have it," Stationmaster said. "Mr Grimly has pieced Poppyseed together and Doc Sludgeon has already made a preliminary report, not entirely favourable, but it is still early days as yet.

"We don't have a season for this," Mitchel snapped. "You've got to get a clean house now. We shouldn't be talking as it is. I'm only continuing the Tuesday briefings because we're so darn isolated up here we go crazy for a bit of company."

"We know the name of the twelfth man." Grimly said at last. But the phone rang interrupting him before he could say more.

"It's for you," Guss mumbled, sliding the phone down the table towards Grimly, who wearily picked up the receiver and announced himself. "Hugh Grimly."

"This is Dennis, Hugh. I think you know which Dennis."

For a moment Hugh Grimly didn't have a clue, there were no Dennis's in his book. Then it clicked into place. Dennis the knife, the Cabinet hatchet man. One of the names on Stationmaster's list. The most important name the Butcher's Boy had said.

"I got wind of a little list, Hugh. Lot of names on it, mine was underlined several times. I didn't know you cared so much. I was very interested to learn about Poppyseed, it is a good idea, might have worked if your system was a bit more reliable. Let me see, ten copies in all, is that right? Convenient of you to let me know exactly how many copies you printed. Sorry to hear about John Welland. I'll try to get to his funeral, had no idea he was the great Henry Betand, such a good artist, a loss to us all, but at least his stuff will go up in price now. Still, when all is said and done, he was only the Butcher's Boy, eh?"

The others could see Grimly had turned pale, the famous stern face was rigid with anger again.

"Dennis, we shall continue with our investigation. I'm not afraid of you," Grimly threatened.

Dennis wasn't perturbed. "That's just it, Hugh, bit awkward to come right out with it, but you won't be going on, nor will Doc Sludgeon. He's had a nasty accident I'm afraid, I don't know the details. However, the PM agrees with me. We feel with the way things are in Europe now, well . . . having an

276

organisation like the Square is a bit dodgy. On ice actually, the whole bang shoot is going on ice. Simon Caw will keep his section going, after all it was set up for internal operations, got to give the 'RX' something to do. But think of it this way, Hugh, you can go back to your cabbages. Can't think what Sir Charles was doing dragging you out of retirement . . ."

Grimly slammed the phone down on him, despair and urgency written on his face. "Oosty, get over to the Square, find out what happened to Doc Sludgeon. Gallant, find Sir Charles and tell him to meet me at the Admiralty in half an hour. I'll beat them yet, y'hear." Mitchel and the others looked startled. Grimly shook his head, anger taking hold of him. "They think they are so powerful they can ride right over us."

"Hugh, what the hell is going on for Christ sake?" Mitchel demanded to know.

"You want to know who runs the moles, Mitchel, you want to know who has just told me the Square is to be *closed* down because they are sensitive to the European situation."

"What? Who?" The American was incredulous, hoping it was a joke.

"Gallant, show him our list, the twelve names."

Gallant cradled the phone between his chin and shoulder as he fished the list out of his breast pocket.

Stationmaster looked across at Grimly, uncertain of the wisdom of this move. "Hugh, we can't be sure. This is an in-house affair."

"Show him, David," Grimly ordered. "The man who called me is at the top, the twelfth man, Mitchel."

Mitchel took the list from Gallant's hands, who dialled another number in his search for Sir Charles. Mitchel couldn't believe it. "Dennis ********? Sir Ian *****? Patrick Smythe, the Rt. Hon. Sydney Furlong, or are we kidding, Hugh? Two in the Cabinet and one with daily access to the PM? Dennis is the one who was hired to clean up, wasn't he?"

"Seven Cambridge men," Grimly pointed out with disgust. "Five red brick, it is a travesty. Even the Secretary for Industry

– no wonder they won't interfere with strikes. This current labour unrest must suit them ideally. It is a mockery of everything we stand for."

"Any labour politicians?" Guss asked, looking at the names.

"It isn't politics, but for what it is worth," Stationmaster explained," Moscow has never been able to trust British Socialists, they go for true blue types everytime. These men, with the exception of Dennis and the two Cabinet Ministers, are all long term senior civil servants, not political at all. Whichever Government is in, they are there."

"Well, what are you gonna do?" Mitchel asked, trying to think what he would do with a list like that in the White House. "Burn down Number Ten during a Cabinet meeting? I mean where can you move? You'll never get this public, you'd be certified insane within hours."

"Sir Charles," Grimly answered, getting up from the table. "The Admiralty is clean. We will move from there, place ourselves under their protection. Sir Charles will lead us in and we will devise a counter attack from there."

"And Poppyseed?" Stationmaster enquired.

"They knew, Steven, though Dennis thinks there are only ten copies of the document, but it is all irrelevant. We have a turncoat."

"Who? For God's sake, is there nothing sacred. Who? There were so few who knew. Not even Hallam."

"Simon Caw," Grimly answered, for how else would Lip-snatchers become the trusted organisation. Traitors recruited traitors. London was no town for an honest man.

"Mitchel, it is my belief that it may not be safe to use our own transportation. Perhaps you would be good enough to lay on something for us? Oh, and when Philip Oosty gets back, perhaps you could get him to us the same way?"

Mitchel nodded, detailing Guss to arrange the details.

"Sir Charles is at Downing Street right now," Gallant interrupted. "What do I say to him? He's coming to the phone."

"Let Mitchel handle it. Mitchel, demand a meeting with Sir Charles as soon as possible, tell him you have important information for him. See how he reacts, then if it's positive, whisk him over to us at the Admiralty; that way he will be over the shock before he meets us. He can flap. Let's hope he hasn't been drinking."

Mitchel took over the phone from Gallant, waiting for Sir Charles to pick up the phone.

Stationmaster, Grimly and Gallant went into conference. "It is possible we might be wrong. It just might be Dennis trying to frighten us," Grimly pointed out.

"No," Gallant countered. "That list of names is more than likely, why else would Dennis make such a final move. He has to close you down, he has no choice. To think he fooled us with his ethics. No wonder Matron spits at the sound of his name."

"It always had to be Cabinet Office," Stationmaster mused," where else all the leaks? The issue is, can we stay alive, or active long enough to turn the tables? We still have no proof."

"We have proof," Grimly said. "Doc Sludgeon has compiled a series of leaks, misrepresentations, misappropriations, cross-checked. We have worked hard. We could make a number of charges stick, Steven. Gallant here has evidence of an almost total betrayal of his Headhunter list, it could only have come from the top. There are no circulated files. We report directly to the top table. Less than 30% of our information goes into print these days. We have electronic thieves as well. It is just a matter of staying in the game."

"The Admiralty will help. We will have allies there," Stationmaster remarked.

"If we get there first," Gallant pointed out. "With the Square closed to us, how will we get our information?"

Grimly frowned. All the proof was in Archives, or on disc. Anything on disc could be retrieved by Simon Caw and wiped. Anything on paper could be forbidden to them in the 'interests of national security.'

"We shall have to act quickly. David, call the Square, see if Oosty has arrived."

Gallant was already on the blue phone tracking him down. "I see . . . and Doc Sludgeon is at St Thomas's you say? Will he be all right?"

Grimly and Stationmaster listened with growing apprehension.

"No I didn't know. I thought VDU terminals were perfectly safe. And Lily Tigre? She's burnt, too."

Grimly darted a look at Mitchel talking to Sir Charles. Things were going very badly, almost orchestrated, though he didn't tend towards such machiavellian thoughts.

"Well, I'm glad they got the fire out before we lost all of Archives. Sussie Sutzman will be heartbroken. Yes I can see that, moving to East Putney will be a lot cheaper than refurbishing the Square, quite understand. Now where is Oosty?"

Grimly walked over to Gallant's side, the whole room listening with horror. The Archives burnt? It was impossible.

"Oosty couldn't have gone to the Ministry. He had no brief to. No, look, Nolan, don't argue. Where is Calon?" It was obvious Gallant was less than amused by all he was hearing. "Oosty would not have gone off with Calon, he had no brief . . . which Ministry? All right, I'll call that office. OK, who is going to guard by the way?" There was no joy in that answer either.

He angrily replaced the phone, turning to the men watching him in the room. "Square's off limits to everyone. MPs will take over door security, it's going into mothballs as of now. I'm ordered back to Wandsworth. Oosty went with Calon to some Ministry meeting in Whitehall, emergency session. If you want to get to the Admiralty, Chief, you'd better get a move on. There's a rumour that all Square personnel will be investigated, the whole lot. They will probably put Nolan to the firing squad."

Grimly turned to Mitchel, feeling tired again. "We'd better go now. We can only hope that one of Simon Caw's computers doesn't replace the Admiralty between the time we leave here and there."

"Sol Guss has a truck waiting for you in the basement, Mr

Grimly," Mitchel told them. "Sir Charles said he would come, says it is under protest, whatever that means."

"It means he has probably arranged for a late lunch at the House, he's a big one for Brown Windsor soup," Grimly answered, not without a modicum of contempt.

"What do we do, Hugh?" Mitchel asked, walking the old man to the door. "GB's headed for Moscow, is that it? Your moles have finally fixed it? What happens next? Grosvenor Square under siege? You think we should lay in preserves?"

"We aren't beaten yet," Stationmaster asserted from behind, a vain attempt at defeat snatched from the jaws of Tinkabelle's victory. "The Navy won't let us down."

As they reached the corridor, a messenger arrived with a cable for Mitchel. He gave Grimly a worried look as he tore it open and, entirely against regulations, took out his electronic pocket code lexicon and decoded the cable in the elevator as they went down. He let escape a low whistle as the message came clear.

British General Officer of Command Berlin rumoured missing/defected. Arrived Milano. Requests asylum for himself and East Berlin common law wife Regina Schmidt. Advise. Daffodil.

Stationmaster snarled. The rot had all started in GOC Berlin. Grimly just smiled in his usual enigmatic way.

"What do you think, Hugh? One of yours, or one of them? Or do we care, just throw him back in the sea?"

"Regina Schmidt is one of Tinkabelle's. The GOC is a dirty old man who should know better. Claim them, perhaps we can turn Regina around. With a child in her she might be more pliable."

"In our darkest hour, Hugh Grimly the optimist," Stationmaster snorted, disgusted.

"The GOC didn't know all this was going to happen," Grimly stated defensively. "Better with the Relatives than with us, Steven. I shall never forget this day of shame. We must fight back."

Mitchel left them to do just that at the ground floor.

"Keep me posted, Hugh. I'm gonna advise Washington of

the situation. They're gonna blow their stacks." Then as an afterthought, holding the elevator doors open, "What do you think the Admiralty can do, Hugh? A blockade of Whitehall? A midnight raid, gunboats trained on the House of Commons?"

"Pressure, resignations, diplomatic force. The Navy's still a force in the land, Mitchel. It's all I've got, unless you are prepared to send us some Marines."

Mitchel smiled. "Yeah and the Seventh Cavalry, you are gonna need it." He let the doors close and began his walk to Communications.

"Dennis the Mole," Grimly was saying, moments later in the back of a Dodge truck. "Dennis has a fundamental flaw."

"Which is?" Stationmaster asked.

"Unelected, complete outsider, no rank, no insider loyalty. He's pushed the PM into power, come in on the tide as it were, but he's not liked. No matter how successful he's been in getting the PM to the top of the pole, he's not liked and he's made enemies."

"There's nothing in his background to suggest Tinkabelle had access to him," Gallant remarked, looking through the smoked glass windows for trouble. The truck bounced out of the Grosvenor Square basement and rounded the Square, seeking the route to the Admiralty.

"He was on Stationmaster's list, Gallant. Dennis does a lot of trade with Jugoslavia and Poland. He has gone a long way to bringing the Soviet electronics industry up to par. He has had many opportunities to meet with Tinkabelle. Masterminding the rise to power of the PM has been a twenty-year job, they knew what they were doing. We haven't been diligent. Not watching Dennis the Mole has been our biggest failure. But he's been watching us."

"Judas, there's always a Judas," Stationmaster declared.

"Gallant, I don't want you at Admiralty House. Don't come in with us. Go back to Wandsworth. Act normally. Headhunters need a man we can trust. Go back before they appoint Rasputin or some such favoured apostle."

"I don't like to leave you, Chief. What are you going to do about tomorrow's injection? The serum's in the fridge, in Stationmaster's outer office."

"I sent it around to Hugh Grimly's town flat, Gallant. Bloater took the package over."

Grimly obviously knew about that for he didn't comment. Instead he looked out of the window and sighed, "Bettina will be happy. She always said Larianov was the better of us."

"You mustn't think of defeat, Hugh. We still have cards to play," Stationmaster insisted.

"Steven's right, Hugh, it's only twelve against the rest."

"It's the crew against the captain and it could be called mutiny, Gallant," Grimly replied, not enjoying the bouncy ride.

"What I don't understand is, why the Second Eleven, if it is twelve men?" Stationmaster complained.

"Probably like the Baker's dozen," Gallant suggested, looking for a cigarette.

"And does it stop at twelve?" Grimly asked morosely, "or is it perhaps the whole of Cambridge we are up against?"

"Now there's a thought," Stationmaster said, clinging on to his seat as the truck braked hard for the lights.

Gallant was staring hard out of the rear window. A black Austin Princess had moved in smartly behind them. Coincidence? It was definitely an official car, three men inside. He turned to check out the front view. His heart began to race. A black Rover had appeared one car ahead.

"Driver?"

"Sir?"

"Forget Spring Gardens, take the next left and head for 33 Belgrave Square SW1. See if you can ditch those Ministry cars fore and aft."

"You pay the fines?" he asked, looking back with a smile.

"You can count on it."

"You got it . . . hold on."

Grimly and Stationmaster did as they were told, as the truck took a violent lurch to the left and accelerated away from the rear car, its V8 316 cube engine easily able to outdistance the British cars. The young American driver slammed on the power breaks and literally made that hunk of metal jump into a narrow side street, screaming away again, burning rubber towards Belgravia.

"Is this necessary?" Grimly asked Gallant, his red head wobbling on his shoulders as the soft suspension tossed them around, worse than Morning Cloud VI.

"It's necessary, believe me, it's necessary," Gallant answered, noticing the Austin had missed that narrow street turn off.

"Belgrave Square is a war school, it's not Admiralty."

"It's safe ground, Stationmaster. I want to leave you on safe ground."

Grimly appreciated the thought, if not the deed. He felt decidedly nauseous.

The truck shot out into the main road and pushed on the power, overtaking everything in sight.

"Shit," the driver drawled happily. "I always wanted to do this." He blasted his horn and laughed, a chilling laugh, not known in the highway code.

Gallant could see they were approaching 70 mph, the Square near enough now for the driver to slow down.

"Er . . . perhaps you could slow down, kid."

But this driver had been too long on a leash. He came upon the Square much too quickly, slamming his brakes on with such force that the rear end immediately began to swing round.

"Hey man, we are going to flip . . ."

All three men, stunned, didn't need to be told, as the truck up ended, hurtling towards the centre. Gracefully it settled down on its side and, with all occupants shouting, fearing the worst, it slid quickly and forcefully along the tarmac and broadsided a brace of parked cars, the thin motortown steel crumpling like paper.

Not one of the men would remember the moment of impact.

*　　*　　*

Simon Caw was aware of a few things. Dennis the Mole, formerly the knife, was in an unassailable position and in charge of Foreign Policy (though still much in the background, operating from a position of 'helpful suggestions'). Sir Charles Edgeware was on extended leave until the next Cabinet reshuffle. The Queen's visit to Rumania was still a vexed issue and Calon had a headache. All blame had been laid at Grimly's feet.

"So Dennis was on Grimly's list, eh? Bloody fool. It's all Sir Charles' fault. If he hadn't panicked, just waited for Stationmaster to come out of Sanctuary, all this wouldn't have happened. I blame Sir Charles entirely. Hugh Grimly was good in his day, but really, Dennis and Sir Ian, Joe and Angus all moles, what did he think he was up to? All that fuss about the Butcher's Boy. You say John Welland was assassinated by the Czechs. Any reason?"

"No plausible ones. Main thing seems to be the Russian girl he was attached to. Her father a VIP, remember. Seems he ordered the assassination, didn't want his daughter compromised."

"Of course, it could be argued," Calon said, "that bringing Grimly in was a pretty effective way of fouling things up. But quite honestly, I thought with his reputation he'd at least flush one or two out into the open."

"His list was quite comprehensive. If I might make a suggestion, Mr Calon, Staunton, in your department. He turned up on Stationmaster's list too, definite problem there." This was almost Dennis' first instruction to Caw. "I want Staunton out."

"But Staunton has been with me years. I trust him with everything."

"Precisely, sir. And I suppose you can account for his numbered Swiss bank account and his frequent visits to Kabul." A fabrication, but Dennis would verify any lie to get Staunton out.

"Kabul? He's never left London in years, a real stick in the mud. You sure you have the right chap? This is what I mean, who is right, Caw? Staunton is 100%."

"They turned up evidence to the contrary. I don't agree with much of his list, but Staunton has to go."

Calon sulked, he hated to loose. "I'll think of something. But the other names. It's laughable, Simon. Might as well accuse the Queen. No, really, this is one book we are firmly closing. The Square will be reorganised and moved to here where you can keep an eye on it. Mitchel has already declared the Relatives are off limits to all British Intelligence personnel. He won't be happy until the whole building is torn down. Well, it's your territory now. Dennis has appropriated a good sum for the transfer. Lipsnatchers was always an ideal candidate for successor. I must congratulate you."

"Pity about the Stationmaster though," Caw remarked. "Collar bone not an easy one to mend at his age."

"Gallant won't be driving his sports car for a long time either. What do we do with him?"

"I've an idea he would like to go to Hong Kong when his legs mend. Lipsnatchers is undergoing radical change there and Gallant is very acceptable in my opinion. He should do all right out there."

"As far away as possible, eh?" Calon said with a wink.

"Mr Grimly will go back to retirement as soon as his back mends. The shock of that accident did wonders for him. His hair is white again, says he isn't going to continue with the drugs."

"Just as well, you can't cheat time, Simon. I didn't get where I am today by cheating time."

"So apart from my Staunton, it is a clean bill of health, eh?" Calon asked.

"Yes," Simon Caw lied, thinking how easy it must have been for Dennis and friends to take power away from men like Calon. Well, he could play their game for now, but all was fair in a lust for power. He was not pigeon-livered, he could bide his time, for the leaders of this little coup were mad and the others not very sound.

Calon twittered on. "Sir Ian was most amused to hear he was on the list. I hear there's several in the Cabinet who are quite put out that they were ignored. Quite a status to have been on Grimly's last purge. He's still well thought of up there."

"Better put him on the Honours List then, he's going to be a bit peeved at his current status."

"Good idea, Simon, jolly good idea. The Lords could do with a teetotaller for once." Calon smiled, he liked the idea very much. It was in the great tradition of rewarding failure with honour and titles.

"Well, I must get back. By the way, our Berlin GOC is in Washington. Yanks seem quite happy to have him for some reason, any clues on that?"

"No sir. I believe Sir Charles is still making a fuss about the Berlin withdrawal."

"Not a problem, Simon, his teeth have been drawn." Calon stood up, heading for the door. "Oh, any word on Hallam?"

"Disappeared about the time Mr Grimly had his accident. Seems his Wendy is in Moscow. There is a committee meeting on him this evening in the FO Green Room. Dennis seems to think Hallam could still be useful, especially now his Wendy has gone over to Moscow."

Calon frowned. "I liked Peter. Couldn't understand his obsession with that girl, but I wouldn't like to see him wasted, we did go to the same school. As far as I can see he hasn't done much harm. I mean, who was the Butcher's Boy? Just an amateur painter."

"A nobody sir," Simon Caw trotted out, already concentrating on the papers set down in front of him.

Calon let himself out and took the elevator down to the front office, ground floor. He wasn't entirely happy. Didn't like the idea of losing Staunton, very trustworthy man in his opinion. But since Caw was in charge of security now, he supposed he had to show some willing, a keeness to get things ship-shape again. A sacrificial lamb, one always had to have a lamb to slaughter.

TEN

Visiting Time

It was one of those brilliantly sunny days again. A high gusting wind playfully attacking young girl's skirts, revealing the secrets of Mary Quant or just plain St Michael underwear, and pinning old men, shuffling along the pavement on their way to get their pensions, to the bus shelter walls. Out of the wind, it was a high 72°F, otherwise a chilling 48°F. Still, it was good to be in London on such a clear, clean air day, with people arriving at work or back home from shopping with a blushing, healthy appearance, normally absent from their lives.

Outside the Charing Cross Hospital, a preferential choice of care by the unfortunate accident victim, it was very windy indeed, and the hordes that pursue the daily ritual of visiting time were having a tough time of it, holding onto hats and coats and skirts and one another. It was with much relief they gained the disinfected corridors of the famed and expensive hospital.

Hugh Grimly was in a general ward. He could have had private, his BUPA account was paid up, but he'd never been one to stomach privilege; besides, whatever they might say, the care was just as good in the public section, perhaps even a mite friendlier. He couldn't bear the thought of being in traction and trapped with a retired District Commissioner on one side, or worse, a retired Major or Judge, drying out, whose sole solution for world salvation was, "Conscription and a return to the dark ages, that will teach 'em."

No, he preferred the company of itinerant salesmen or a ruptured engineer, people closer to the realities of life. In the event, he got himself a corner and a young parson who'd been set upon by kids outside Hammersmith Odeon after a rock concert. In the Parson's view, he felt the Government should, "reintroduce conscription and bring back the dark ages, that'll learn 'em."

Grimly's back had been severely wrenched by the front end of a Mini in the accident. He didn't recall the details, just knew that he'd lost his contact lenses and was bleeding about the mouth. Gallant had been some distance away surrounded by broken glass, gathering quite a crowd. No, he didn't like to think about the accident at all, or what it had cost the nation. No use calling up the Admiralty now, the time had passed. There had been no big changes. The moles had remained almost intact, that was to be expected. Croc had been right: the names were too big, too unbelievable, too entrenched in the very fabric of mainstream society. No–one wanted to believe, they had been hypnotised and, if anything, the failure of Poppyseed and the death of the Butcher's Boy had reinforced them. They had used his and Stationmaster's list to mock them, their age and suspected senility. It was altogether humiliating and doubly horrifying to find his word doubted, villified and a source of amusement in the smart society. They preferred the mole and his smarmy, underhand, yet influential ways, to the tradition and honour of the Square. The prisoners offered release, preferred the comforts of jail and the company of the gaolor.

Hugh Grimly, in pain, in hospital, was a defeated man and if he was quiet and unobtrusive in his corner, reading Kafka's *The Trial* and Camus' *The Plague*, it was only because he was frustrated, angry and betrayed; he felt at a loss. He read these books, not for pleasure, but for clues to his failure. *The Plague* in particular had a meaning for him, only he'd had just one rat die and the disease appeared far from fatal. All but a few seemed to thrive on it. The moles were barely moles anymore, their policies were England's policies, they had surfaced and they now strove for naked power, sealing the gaps with mockery and satire, schoolboy tactics.

With Grimly in this mood, visitors had not found him good company. Only Willy, who'd come with greetings from the Stationmaster (recovering in a private hospital), was patient enough to sit the full half hour and rattle on about the test match in India, blow by blow. Repeating everything Grimly had heard on the radio. But Grimly was grateful for any visitors, especially those who could put up with his moods. And Willy was thoughtful enough to bring grapes (though he invariably ate them all).

Of Bettina, Grimly had heard nothing. She'd been off him of late, his disapproval of her behaviour was noted.

Still, it was visiting time once more and the nurse had bounced his bedclothes around, getting him neat and tidy. He wondered whose turn it was? Croc? He was doing the rounds of all three of them, making quite a profession of it. Or Doc Sludgeon, whose burns in the great Archives fire had proven to be superficial, excepting his neck, where he had to have bandages changed regularly as his skin was weeping.

It turned out to be neither, but a welcome surprise.

"It's a long trek, Hughie," Sussie Sutzman complained gaily, brandishing a simple bouquet of daffodils. "Ninety pence for six, Hughie. It's criminal. Ninety whole pence. It is enough to give me a headache and put me in a hospital bed. How are they treating you? You look like death. Mind you, it's the right hospital for you if you go into your second childhood, Dr Hugh Jolly's in the next ward."

"I'm not about to grow senile, Sussie," Grimly insisted, tetchily.

"I was only joking, they said you were grumpy. Here," she withdrew a bag of fudge from her voluminous handbag. "Home made. I washed my hands first, cross my heart and hope to die."

And suddenly Grimly found himself smiling.

"There, I said I could make you into a smiley boy. Doc Sludge calls me up and says you are impossible. But that's because he only brings you bad news. Today I bring you good news."

"Dennis the Mole has relented and turned himself in to the Beefeaters?" Grimly guessed, half jesting, half wishful thinking.

"No and I refuse to discuss that man Dennis with you, we shall only fight." She saw he was disappointed and relented a little. "There was a party at Chequers. Dennis was there and gave a small pantomime entitled 'Grimly – the Lord High Executioner.' Judging from the reception it got, I'd say we are in for a revival of Gilbert and Sullivan, Heaven forbid." She looked into his sad face again. "Don't sulk, Hughie. You lost, someone has got to lose, you had a good run for your money."

"Sussie, you of all people know that it isn't a game. The man mocks me in public!"

She pursed her lips, sucking on her teeth. She was glad the old man was in hospital, at least he wouldn't be able to hear the worst of it. The odd thing was, there was a warmth to the laughter. Grimly had lost and, whereas before he's always been aloof, distant, superior, he was now a failure, just like the rest of them. He could have joined any club he liked, his popularity had never been higher. She didn't tell him that, nothing could be more calculated to send him into a deeper depression.

"The good news, Sussie?" he asked, enjoying her fudge.

She brightened up again. "Aha, well it's this. Paris is getting cold feet. The Gaullists, the great middle classes, don't like the idea of Moscow getting its finger in the pie after all. Some gaffe at a Paris reception for the Moscow Foreign Affairs deputation. Anyway, there is an upset. Our cocky little President may well find himself out on his ear this coming election. Lot of discontent in the army too. They left NATO to play Napoleon again, they won't be so keen to play second fiddle to Moscow's bully boys."

"No, you're right, that is good news. Source?"

"Hallam. He's practically become Franciscan in his repentance. Working hard over there, trying to change things around. He feels responsible for your fall from grace."

"I'm glad he recognises that."

"He won't last long in Paris though. Dennis will soon have him out of there when he realises what's happening. Peter is very loyal y'know. He'd never play both ends of the candle like Simon Caw."

"Don't even mention his name," Grimly said tersely. "I don't want to know."

Sussie realised that it was a sore point with the Chief. "Besides," she went on, "Hallam is moving to Copenhagen. I don't know why. He wrote to the Stationmaster, told him that he was going to retire there once he'd sold his house in Kensington."

"Copenhagen, that's an odd choice, isn't it?"

"Everyone makes odd choices these days. I've been asked to go to China again. By the FO no less. I thought I'd get the sack, everyone connected with the Square has y'know, including Doc Sludgeon. All got the heave-ho. But I'm useful. They are nervous about China, they need old Sussie for her language capabilities and charm." She laughed. "Have you ever tried to charm a Chinese Government official?"

"No," Grimly answered, reaching out for Sussie's hand, realising she was becoming emotional.

"You can't. When I was young, I used to think I got on terribly well with them. Thought I was the bee's knees, the only really popular Brit in Canton. But they were making fun of me. In fact, I was the only one they were making fun of. I have to admit this to you, Hughie, I don't like them. I never did. They are never grateful. I don't like that in a person. One must be grateful. They nod, bow and scrape, but it is all mockery. It's comical. I'm the China Crystal and I hate the place."

"That's what makes you so objective, so useful. No use in sending out a romantic. You'll always be valuable, Sussie, you're an honest woman and, Heaven knows, that is worth being."

She smiled, her eyes misting up. "How much longer in here?"

"Oh weeks. I'm trying to speed things up, but I don't want

to leave here a cripple. My cottage is all very well, but I'm not going to be able to dig vegetables with my back the way it is for quite a while."

"You need a companion," Sussie declared, pounding the bed.

"Don't suggest Willy. He'll drive me mad in a week. I'm sure he invents half the cricket scores, dreams of fast bowlers in his sleep."

"Sussie laughed. "I know a lady. Lives in Oxford. She's writing a book on the meaning of death."

"And you think I'd make a useful case study?"

"No, silly," Sussie squealed." You might try some of your famous cynicism on her. Make her see things in a new light. I'll get Monica to visit you."

"Not a crazy friend is she, Sussie, one of your radicals?"

"Well, she's not like Bettina. She cooks, Hughie. I have to confess, she made the fudge."

"Ah, then I'm well disposed. It is an excellant fudge."

Sussie smiled, always pleased to get things arranged. "Good. Now I must go. I leave for China on Sunday."

"As soon as that?"

"Urgent, they said."

"Ah – urgent," Grimly repeated slowly, as if running the word through a decoder.

Sussie got up to leave. "I'll speak to Monica tonight."

"Do that. I'll appreciate company whilst I'm recovering. I rather think I'll see less of the old boys now."

"Well goodbye, Hughie, I'll send a postcard from Peking."

"I'll look forward to it."

Abruptly, Sussie bent over him and planted a big soppy kiss on his face. A tear ran down her cheek. "Don't let them bully you, Hughie. Retire with grace. Don't let them joke about you. You didn't fail. We know that. Belive in yourself. It was a conspiracy. You wanted to change the order, you couldn't stop the wheel, Hughie. The snivelling toads wouldn't let you do that. Let them think you're past it. I know you're not."

With that said, she parted from him, picked up her bag and,

without a look back in his direction, she walked out of the hospital ward.

Grimly lay there, his mouth full of fudge, wiping lipstick off his cheek. Not quite so sure what to think really. It was too bad of his back to let him down now. He was powerless to do anything.

He supposed he must have dozed off, but when he awoke with a start, it was still visiting time, near to the end when all the fruit had been eaten and the grape pips get emptied on the bedside table.

Grimly looked to his left sensing a presence and received quite a shock. He had a visitor sitting in his chair.

"Good afternoon, Mr Grimly. May I pour you some orange juice?"

Grimly had forseen this moment, had dreamt of it a thousand times over the years, but never in his dreams had he been the one laying there incapacitated.

Tinkabelle/Larianov smiled at him, a dry, effortless smile, his wrinkled skin pulled back in a grotesque imitation of death. He had aged more than Grimly would have hoped, and still kept his hair, but the thinness of him, he was a living corpse. Chalky, he should have been called Chalky.

"In shock?" Larianov enquired, handing Grimly the orange juice. "Or just speechless. You were good at speeches one time."

"Visiting time is over," Grimly said, sounding unexpectedly harsh.

"Oh come now, Mr Grimly. Don't be angry with me. It is not I who put you in hospital, it is not I who talks about you in the Clubs, stabs you in the back."

Grimly stared at his lifelong adversary and perceived that it was almost so. "My life is steeped in conspiracy, Larianov, your conspiracies. The daggers in my back are perhaps the mark of my failure, a judgement, but they have your name on the hilt."

"I have something for you," Larianov said, reaching into his coat pocket, withdrawing a crumpled piece of paper.

"What is it?" Grimly asked, still without contact lenses.

Larianov unfolded the document and placed it in front of Grimly, handing over the temporary spectacles resting on his bedside table. Grimly put them on and then, knowing his heart was beating at a dangerous rate, he found himself staring at the form ID II, still unsigned. Larianov must have kept it with him since that day in Cairo over twenty-five years ago. Grimly felt a deep sense of abandonment, nostalgia and futility. This was the bond between them.

Larianov brought out his pen and pushed it into Grimly's hand. "You are Achilles, Mr Grimly. Sign it, Achilles."

A doubtful smile spread across Tinkabelle's face, one that Grimly perceived as a smile of coming conquest. It was no major victory, but it was no victory at all unless he capitulated, admitted that Tinkabelle, known as Larianov, was king of the castle.

"It was inevitable, Mr Grimly. We have the resolve, you had a history of weakness. Your country cannot admit it has no Empire, cannot even hang onto the Falkland Islands. Renounce it. Your kingdom is poisoned, for you it is already past."

Grimly stared around the hospital ward. Did it matter so much to Larianov that he signed this form? Defect? He had no intention of doing anything except tending cabbages, until one long, cold winter claimed him and then one or two at the Club would nod when they saw his name in the obituary column of *The Times*. That was his future.

"You are too big now, Larianov. You are a giant. Goliath, look what happened to him."

Larianov only smiled, his teeth all new and poorly fitting, entirely wrong for such a gaunt face. God save us from Soviet workmanship, Grimly thought to himself.

"Goliath was stupid, Mr Grimly. He went to war with a child. We want only peace in the world and we shall leave no stone standing to get it. You don't understand yet. People have been frightened by your own hysterical propaganda. You have been telling them for years that the Russians are barbarians, they will kill everyone, poison the air we breathe. You made a mistake, Mr Achilles. Your fear is our strength. We have grown powerful, sucked energy from your fears. We no longer need to fight. We can knock down the walls and live without fear.

"Our generation, we came out of the rubble of two wars. I believe there will never be another whilst we are strong. In a little while the fruit will ripen in America and they, too, will fall into our arms."

Almost a cock crow, Grimly mused, sensing a familiar headache running for a sensitive nerve.

"And Dennis? How long has he been in your pocket?"

Tinkabelle's eyes lit up momentarily. "A truly curious man, our national hero, a Soviet citizen, devoted husband and hope-less Marxist. I am his guru, is that what you'd call me, a guru?"

"And our Dennis will lead the children out of the darkness to the foot of the mountain to fall at your feet."

Larianov was smiling hugely, enjoying Grimly's eulogy. "It is an occasion this reunion. You are sure you won't have some orange juice?"

This was becoming a tiresome visit for Grimly. He brought the form up to his eyes, merely to re-familiarise himself with it, pleased to see the date was still 1955. He just wanted to inspect a relic from his past, that was all; he wouldn't give Larianov the satisfaction of signing anything as much as the *Morning Star*, a rag due for a new popularity in all probability.

But it was not the form he found himself looking at, but the pen and inscription written upon it: *'To my Prince Larianov with affection — Bettina'*.

There was the twist to the knife, the Achilles' heel. He sank back against the pillow and allowed a long tragic sigh to escape his lips, but saying nothing, nothing at all. His mind disap-peared down some deep shaft, running for cover. He looked at the pen again, punishing himself.

'To my Prince Larianov with affection — Bettina'.

Back in Cairo he'd called her the October woman. He should have paid more attention to what Larianov was saying then and been less concerned with his own problems. Bettina was uncontrollable, and 1955 was a long time ago. It was all so damnably cheap, but now, more than ever, he knew he could never sign. Never in a million years. Russia was as foul, if not more foul. If he was a younger man he'd rededicate himself to the cause, he could only hope men like Gallant didn't loose their nerve.

Larianov shrugged, an empty smile disappearing from his face. He knew Grimly wouldn't sign; it would have been a hollow victory, a disappointment if he had. He had always suspected London would crumble at his feet, but he liked to be sure of his enemies and their resolve. No victory was without an implaccable enemy. He retrieved his pen and tattered form, stood up and slipped away in silence, no expression on his face, no expression at all. Perhaps there was no such thing as victory in a never ending war.

Thirty minutes later, the nurse found Hugh Grimly sitting up in bed staring out across the ward, blank, seeing nothing. There was a wistful look about him, the air of a man with a broken heart.

"Are you all right, Mr Grimly? Can't I get something for you?"

His eyes were moist with self-damning tears, but somehow he summoned the spittle to his dry tongue and the necessary energy to turn his head, and force some pleasant tones into his strange voice.

"Tea, nurse, thank you. I'd love a pot of tea."

BESTSELLERS FROM ARROW

All these books are available from your bookshop or newsagent or you can order them direct. Just tick the titles you want and complete the form below.

THE GRAVE OF TRUTH	Evelyn Anthony	£1.25
BRUACH BLEND	Lillian Beckwith	95p
THE HISTORY MAN	Malcolm Bradbury	£1.25
A LITTLE ZIT ON THE SIDE	Jasper Carrott	£1.00
SOUTHERN CROSS	Terry Coleman	£1.75
DEATH OF A POLITICIAN	Richard Condon	£1.50
HERO	Leslie Deane	£1.75
TRAVELS WITH FORTUNE	Christine Dodwell	£1.50
INSCRUTABLE CHARLIE MUFFIN	Brian Freemantle	£1.25
9th ARROW BOOK OF CROSSWORDS	Frank Henchard	75p
THE LOW CALORIE MENU BOOK	Joyce Hughes	90p
THE PALMISTRY OF LOVE	David Brandon-Jones	£1.50
DEATH DREAMS	William Katz	£1.25
PASSAGE TO MUTINY	Alexander Kent	£1.25
HEARTSOUNDS	Martha Weinman Lear	£1.50
SAVAGE SURRENDER	Natasha Peters	£1.60
STRIKE FROM THE SEA	Douglas Reeman	90p
INCIDENT ON ATH	E. C. Tubb	£1.15
STAND BY YOUR MAN	Tammy Wynette	£1.75
DEATH ON ACCOUNT	Margaret Yorke	£1.00

Postage

Total

ARROW BOOKS, BOOKSERVICE BY POST, PO BOX 29, DOUGLAS, ISLE OF MAN, BRITISH ISLES

Please enclose a cheque or postal order made out to Arrow Books Limited for the amount due including 10p per book for postage and packing for orders within the UK and 12p for overseas orders.

Please print clearly

NAME ....

ADDRESS..

....

Whilst every effort is made to keep prices down and to keep popular books in print, Arrow Books cannot guarantee that prices will be the same as those advertised here or that the books will be available.